Débâcle

Also by Paul Henke

Never a Winner
A Million Tears

Débâcle

Paul Henke

GOOD READ PUBLISHING

First published in 1999 by Good Read Publishing
A Good Read Publishing paperback

10 9 8 7 6 5 4 3 2 1

A CIP catalogue record for this title is available
from the British Library

ISBN 1–902483–01–4

Typeset by Palimpsest Book Production Limited,
Polmont, Stirlingshire
Printed and bound in Great Britain by
Cox & Wyman Ltd, Reading, Berkshire

Good Read Publishing Ltd
Auchleshie House
Kelty Bridge
Callander FK17 8LS

This book is dedicated to my wife, Dorothy

1

P.M. 1 April 1997 – All Fools' Day.

His bleeper went and he rolled over in his sleep with a low groan. By the time the third bleep had sounded, he was wide awake and reaching out to stop the noise. The body lying alongside him sighed softly and, with a distinct American accent, said 'Jeez, it's not time to get up already, is it?'

Hunter smiled and leaned over her. 'No, you can go back to sleep. Unfortunately, I have to go. Duty calls.'

Knowing what he did for a living his companion jerked wide awake. 'What's the problem?'

'No idea. Usually nothing. Just some local plod panicking over something washed up on a beach which he doesn't immediately recognise. It almost never amounts to anything,' he said, reaching for his socks. Remembering where he was and with whom, he dropped the socks and picked up his shirt. He quickly put it on and continued dressing.

'What's a plod?' his companion asked, wide awake, and looking at him with interest.

'A policeman. The local fuzz are told there's an unidentified object on the beach and instead of looking for themselves, they call us straight away. So I'm bleeped because I have the duty. Sod it,' he added under his breath.

'You will be careful, won't you?' she said, worriedly.

'Fear not,' Hunter did his best to sound joyful. 'It's all in a day's work.' He mentally cringed at the banality of his words but could find nothing else to say. He knew, like everyone else operating in the world of bomb disposal, that the most innocuous of calls could easily result in a death – in this case, his. 'Look, if I'm not back by the time you have to leave for your plane,' he leant over her, looked into her eyes and smiled, 'let yourself out and don't lock the doors.'

'I will,' she breathed, softly, kissing him, 'and thanks.'

He gave his lop-sided grin and said, 'Don't thank me. I enjoyed it too.'

'If you're ever in the States . . .'

'I'll look you up. Sorry,' he pushed himself up off the bed, 'I've got to go.'

With a wave of his hand he left the room and went downstairs to the telephone to ring the duty number.

'Hunter,' was all he said.

'Boss. Sorry, boss, to disturb you, like,' said a voice he recognised, the Welsh accent of Leading Seaman Lewis. Although Hunter was a Senior Lieutenant, about to be promoted to Lieutenant Commander, in the close and dangerous world of mine warfare and bomb disposal, his team called him "boss" in private and "sir" only when the occasion demanded.

'Okay, Taff,' said Hunter, 'but I'm warning you, this had better be good.'

Knowing the score, and that the "Old Man" was on a heavy date that weekend, Taff Lewis was very, very sure of his facts and the reason for the call to his boss.

'Boss, I've doubled checked, and it looks like the real thing washed up on the shore at Poole.'

'Poole, in Dorset?' Hunter said, incredulous.

'Em, yes, boss,' said Lewis, nervously.

'Then why can't the Booties deal with it?' Hunter asked, referring to the Royal Marines based at Hamworthy, near Poole.

'I don't know,' came the truthful reply. 'Except that I've been told that they'd had a call out and nobody was available.'

'Okay, I'll look into it later. What you're telling me is that we're needed and there's no way out.'

'Yes, boss. I guess I am,' replied Lewis.

Hunter thought for a moment or two before he said, 'I'll need either the Chief or Samson and one of the others.'

'The Chief hasn't responded, but Leading Seaman Samson has. I've also managed to get hold of Wilson.'

'Okay, that'll do. I'll meet them in half an hour. I take it that whatever it is, is safely ashore?'

'Yes, boss. Em,' Leading Seaman Lewis hesitated, before he said, 'at least, I think so. You know what it's like with the local police. I think . . . em, it's Second World War and German.'

'A mine?'

'Yes, boss. From the description by the police.'

'Taff, if it's a Second World War mine,' said Hunter, with some asperity, 'it's bloody obvious. It's a sodding big, round, black thing with horns.' He didn't add, unless it's an aerial mine set off acoustically.

'Yes, sir, that's exactly what it is,' said Leading Seaman Lewis, with some relief.

'Good, then we know what we need. Tell Wilson he isn't coming but he's to help get the gear prepped and

3

ready. Let's get going sooner, rather than later. Do you know what to do?'

'Yes, boss, no problem,' replied Lewis and rang off.

Hunter put on his mottled camouflage jacket over his white polo-necked sweater, slipped on a pair of black seaman's boots and let himself out of the cottage. Within moments, he was speeding along the country lanes in his old MGB Roadster. It was a cold, clear night, though the weather forecast promised a fine, warm, spring day. He had not yet turned on the heating in the car as it needed time to warm up, but with his mind racing over the myriad of things he needed to think about, he was oblivious to the cold.

He pulled up at the guardhouse and flashed his identity card. The sentry knew him and his car by sight, so cast only a cursory glance at the piece of plastic held in Hunter's hand. 'Morning, sir,' said the Petty Officer, 'what brings you in so early?' As he spoke, the Petty Officer saluted and Hunter returned the gesture automatically.

'We've a job on in Poole,' he replied. He glanced at the clock on the dashboard. 'Is the galley manned yet?'

'The cook was woken up about half an hour ago, sir, so I expect he's got something on the go.'

'Look, do me a favour will you? Ring him, tell him what's happening and ask him to fix a large flask with coffee . . . no, better make that tea,' he suddenly remembered how awful Pusser's coffee was, 'and ask him to make bacon sarnies for three.'

'Aye, aye, sir,' replied the sentry, moving from the car to swing open the single pole barrier.

Hunter put the car into gear and moved slowly around the road barriers which prevented a vehicle from ramming straight through the pole. He put his head out of the window and yelled his thanks to the Petty Officer, before heading for the buildings which housed the tools of his trade.

He parked in the bay marked "Diving Officer" and quickly got out of the car. With the roof up, his six foot two of lank frame did not come out of the small car easily and, as usual whenever he was clambering out, he wondered why he bothered with such a small vehicle. But even as the thought formed, he dismissed it. He knew why. It was his pride and joy and the only thing of any value he owned. Being an officer in the Royal Navy, moving regularly and with tours of duty at sea, he had never bought a house. Until recently, he had always billeted in whatever wardroom he was sent to. The cottage he now rented was part of his efforts to create a private life away from the navy.

The double doors of the large, hangar-like space were open and he could hear cursing coming from inside. He walked in to find Leading Seaman Samson sucking on a scraped knuckle. The cursing temporarily shut off.

'Is everything ready?' Hunter asked, accepting a cup of tea placed in his hands by Lewis. 'Thanks, Taff.'

'Yes, boss. I've checked the bottle pressures, hooked up the steam machine, and made sure all the pipes are there. I've also put the plastic and dets in their stowages. Wilson's just left. We didn't need him anymore so I sent him back to his pit and told him to be here at the usual time.'

'Good. Well done, Taff. Did you remember the shovels?' There were two ways of dealing with old and unwanted explosives. The easiest and quickest was to blow it up, which was their preferred option. If that was not practical they would need to drill holes in the mine casing and fix the steam machine up to the mine. They would then literally pump steam into the mine which would liquefy the explosive and wash it out. As it solidified again, they would need to use the shovels to bag the explosive to get rid of it, usually by burning it at one of the army demolition ranges. It was a long, laborious process which they could do without.

'Yes, boss. I put a couple in the back of the Land Rover.'

Hunter nodded, took a sip of his tea and went to look over the gear himself. Fifteen minutes later the three of them were in the Rover and on their way. Hunter drove over to the galley and said to Leading Seaman Samson, 'Delilah, nip in and see the cook. He should have some sarnies and a flask ready for us.'

Leading Seaman "Delilah" Samson showed gleaming white teeth in his black face and did as he was told.

Once clear of HMS *Dryad* and heading for the M27, Samson broke open the pack of bacon sandwiches and handed them round. Hunter was driving, so Lewis took it upon himself to hold Hunter's sandwich whenever he needed to change gear. Replete, the two leading seamen settled back to try to doze. Hunter concentrated on his driving whilst letting his mind roam to the potential problems ahead.

It took just over an hour to get to Poole where they made straight for the police station. Although there were double yellow lines outside the door, it was barely half past six and since there was very little traffic around, Hunter parked at the front entrance and went in. After introducing himself at the front counter, he was escorted inside to an upstairs office occupied by an overweight, jolly-looking Sergeant.

'This is where you'll find it.' He pointed at an ordnance survey map of the area. 'Right there, at the front in Swanage.'

'Beached?' asked Hunter, puzzled.

The Sergeant chuckled, 'Bless you, no, sir. It's still tied to the back of the fancy boat which dragged it in. Caused a right stir, I can tell you.'

'Say that again. Are you telling me some clown dragged a mine into Swanage?'

'Aye, and you never seen an area clear so fast. We thought it best not to move it, just in case like. And so we moved the people away from the area and shifted a few more out of the houses which we thought to be too close.'

'How did it happen? Was it an accident? Did he get caught up in it somehow?' Knowing mines and small boats, Hunter couldn't see how in the world it could have happened.

The Sergeant shook his head. 'The boat owner said he thought it was his duty to take it out of the sea in case a ship or other boat hit it.'

'Dear God,' said Hunter despairingly, shaking his head at the stupidity of it. 'Didn't he think to stand off, call the coastguard and keep other vessels away? That way, there would have been virtually no danger. Instead of dragging . . .' he trailed off, as the Sergeant shrugged expressively at him. The shrug and look said it all from a man who had spent his adult life dealing with the stupidity of the general public.

Hunter nodded his understanding. 'So where exactly is it now. I mean, is it on a beach, tied to the jetty there, what?'

'We left it tied to the back of the boat like I said,

which is tied to the stone jetty, there.' He stabbed the map again.

'Okay, thanks,' Hunter stood for a few seconds in thought. 'Get onto the lifeboat at Poole and tell them that, if it's possible, I'm going to tow the mine back out to sea off St. Alban's head and blow it up. It will be easier and quicker in the long run. Ask them if they could launch and patrol the area to the east and I'll cover the west. Also, get on to the coastguard and ask them to arrange local warnings over the radio on Channel 16 as a securité message. Could you do that for us?'

'Yes, sir. No sweat. I'd already spoken to the coast-guard, so they're expecting to hear from me.'

Hunter took his leave, went outside and climbed into the Land Rover. As he drove through the streets of Poole, on the A350, he briefed the other two.

'This looks like it,' Samson said, as they neared the front at Swanage, to be met by flashing blue lights and a number of people who turned out to be policemen, outnumbered three to one by the press.

The distinctive blue Land Rover, with the red painted panels, was quickly waved past and allowed down to the jetty where Hunter stopped alongside what was commonly called a floating gin palace. He stood on the jetty, the deck of the boat just a few inches lower than his feet, and looked at the mine bobbing in the water. Somebody had taken the trouble to hang rubber fenders all around the boat and the jetty so that the mine had something soft to rub against. He could see immediately that it was indeed an old, German Second World War mine; a contact V type. The horns made it seem more deadly than it actually was, although it was still a dangerous piece of machinery which needed to be disposed of. He turned to the constable who had followed them down from the barrier. 'Do you have the keys to the boat?' he asked.

'No, sir, we don't, but the owner's just returned and he's probably got them with him.'

'Ask him to come down. If he lends them to me, I'll take this back to sea and blow it up. It won't take me long if I do that.'

The constable walked quickly away, conferred with an individual standing by the cars and returned a few moments later with the man in tow.

'This is Mr. Jessop. He's the owner,' the constable introduced the man.

'Mr. Jessop,' Hunter held out his hand to the short, podgy man standing in front of him. Jessop was about five feet three inches tall, was shaped like a pear with a big round stomach and had a bristling grey moustache which somehow fitted well with his bulbous nose. 'I need to use your boat, I'm afraid,' said Hunter pleasantly. 'I intend to tow the mine back out and blow it up at sea. It'll save a lot of . . .'

Before he could finish, Jessop said in a surprisingly deep, bass voice, 'No chance. You take that thing off the back and let me take my boat back to the marina. I've never heard such nonsense, you borrowing my boat. I've done my bit fetching it in here. I'm damned if I'm going to let you inconvenience me any further. I had to stay at a local hotel last night, at my own expense, too. I can tell you I was not best pleased. No, not pleased at all.'

'Look, Mr. Jessop. The easiest thing to do is to tow the damn mine back to sea where we can dispose of it. That gets life here back to normal as quickly as possible and means the minimum disruption for us, the police

9

and the other services we'd need to involve if we tried anything else.'

'That's your problem,' began Jessop, but before he could continue Hunter interrupted him.

'I think not, Mr. Jessop. I'll make it yours. I can have you booked for endangering the lives of the inhabitants of Swanage by towing that thing in here. Further, there is a risk of serious damage to the buildings around here,' he waved his hand in the air, 'and finally, there's the disruption you've caused. Now, I'm willing to talk to the constabulary nicely and get them to ignore the dozen or so laws you've broken, in exchange for your co-operation to resolve the trouble you've caused.'

'Now look here. I've never heard such rot. I did my duty towing that thing in here away from the sea. I . . .' he spluttered to a halt, as he looked up at Hunter who was shaking his head at him.

'Tell him, Constable,' Hunter hoped the constable would play along with him.

'Yes, sir. Well, it's like this. It is a potential danger to property and life and, em, you could be laying yourself open to charges. But, em, if you help, I'll see what I can do,' he finished lamely.

Jessop looked from one to the other of them. 'Oh, very well,' he said ungraciously, 'here are the blasted keys. I wish I'd never set eyes on that blasted mine.' He held the keys out which dangled from a small polystyrene apple float.

'Thank you,' said Hunter, taking them, careful not to let the sarcasm show. 'I'll be as quick as I can.' He turned to the two leading seamen who had already taken out various boxes and stood them on the jetty. 'Right lads, get the 56lb sinker and load it with the rest of the gear in the stern. I'll start the engines and get her warmed up.'

He stood in front of an impressive array of dials and switches, aware that Jessop was standing watching him, not offering any assistance. A few seconds' perusal told him all he needed to know. He inserted the key to the starboard engine, turned it half way and held it there for a full two minutes. This warmed up the diesel at the ignition point. The starboard engine was isolated from all other electrics on the ship so that there was no danger of the battery being run down so low that the engine could not start. Next, he pressed the starboard starter button. The diesel burst into life with a deep-throated growl and spurt of smoke out of the stern. He now did the same with the port engine and it too burst into life. The engines then settled down to a muted, background throb. Next, he turned on the Decca which gave him their latitude and longitude, the echo sounder and the radio, which immediately started broadcasting a securité message about an imminent explosion, due off St. Alban's head and warning all traffic to keep clear – a bit premature he thought, with a grin.

'All set, Delilah?' He asked the leading seaman who had just put his head through the stern doorway.

'Aye, aye, sir. We're singled up – only a head rope and stern line holding us alongside. The mine seems okay as it is and we thought we'd keep it close until we're away from the wall.'

'I agree.' Hunter opened the window on his left side and yelled up at the constable. 'Let go the stern rope will you and once we're pointing out a bit you can let go the bow.'

The constable did as he was asked and a few moments

later the boat was moving very slowly, stern first, pushing the mine away from the jetty. Once clear, Hunter turned the wheel hard to starboard and put the port engine ahead, the starboard engine astern. The boat turned quickly and smoothly. He centred the wheel, whilst simultaneously moving the starboard engine from astern to ahead and the boat started forward, quickly picking up headway. He kept to a slow speed, but from the speedometer it looked as if she was capable of moving very fast indeed. He resisted the temptation to shove the levers to maximum revs to see how fast she could go.

'Nice boat, boss,' said Lewis, as he and Samson came inside.

It was that. A Fairline 46, three luxury cabins to sleep in, two toilets with showers and a main cabin as big as the sitting room in his cottage. Hunter was on the port side of the living room, sitting at the control consul, holding the wheel. On the starboard side was a well-equipped and well-stocked galley. Samson was busy opening and closing drawers and cupboards seeing what was there.

'Delilah, see if you can make us a cup of tea or coffee, will you?' Hunter suggested. The suggestion was correctly interpreted as an order.

Samson grinned. 'No sweat, boss. All I have to do is plug in the electric kettle!' With that, he began to find the things he needed.

'Taff, go aft and check on the mine and make sure it's riding okay.'

Lewis went out through the glass doors which made up the whole of the aft wall to the cabin and went onto the deck space outside. The deck-well had a comfortable seat running around the stern, with a gateway in the middle. Lewis leant over and looked at the mine following closely behind in their wake. 'No problem, boss,' he called to Hunter.

By this time they were clear of Swanage, past Peveril Point and heading for Durlston Head. Hunter picked up the radio handset and transmitted on Channel 16, the emergency frequency and call-up channel. 'Coastguard this is navy, over.'

'Navy this is Coastguard. Channel One Two please, over.'

Hunter acknowledged the order and turned the dial to Channel 12. 'Coastguard this is navy, over.'

'Navy, this is Coastguard. I take it you've got the mine, over.'

'Affirmative. We're on the boat which dragged it into Swanage, called *The Overdraft*. I'm going to tow the mine out to St. Alban's Head and a mile out to sea. I'll use a sinker to hold the mine in place and strap enough plastic to it, to blow it to smithereens.'

'Concur. The lifeboat is on its way and should be with you very soon. We'll keep broadcasting the securité message but, quite frankly, there's nothing within five miles of you, according to the radar. Those vessels we know about have all been told to stay clear so there shouldn't be any problem. Over.'

'Okay, thanks for that. I'll patrol to the east once I've set the fuse. Over.'

'Roger that. We'll stay on twelve with you and keep this frequency clear. The lifeboat will do the same. Out.'

'Roger, out,' replied Hunter, and he hung up the handset.

A few seconds later he had engaged the autopilot and was sitting in the captain's chair, sipping a cup of coffee. He heard the lifeboat talking to the coastguard and looking aft suddenly saw the orange craft shoot around the point known as The Foreland. With full power she stormed towards them, leaving a wide, clear wake in the flat calm sea. Instead of radioing, the boat continued until it was alongside and Hunter and the coxswain could yell across to each other over a mere twenty feet of water. They agreed the patrol areas, waved at each other and as *The Overdraft* continued on her sedate passage the lifeboat turned sharply to port and continued rapidly to her station.

Thirty minutes later Hunter moved the throttles into neutral and let the boat drift to a halt in the water. Samson and Lewis had been getting the gear ready during the passage and were fully prepared as the boat drifted to a stop.

Hunter looked at the echo sounder and said, 'It's reading thirty-five metres, so cut off forty-five for good measure.'

Lewis took the thin, orange corelene rope and measured off roughly forty-five metres in length. He tied one end to the 56lb concrete sinker they'd brought and coiled the remainder on the deck. In the meantime Samson had been cutting the mine loose from the ropes holding it on the stern until there were only two short lengths left. One he tied off on the guard rail, the other he used to tie a bowline in the end. He then tied the end of the sinker line to the bowline. Satisfied, he confirmed to Hunter, 'Ready, boss.'

'Okay. Lower the sinker over the side and cast off the mine.' This was quickly done so that the mine was bobbing in the water just off the stern, now secured to the seabed and by the line to the hand rail. 'Keep the mine in close while I rig the explosives,' said Hunter to Lewis, who took hold of the rope at the guard rail and pulled it tight. He climbed down onto the platform at the stern and took hold of one of the horns on the mine to steady it.

Quickly, but carefully, he took a sausage of white plastic explosive which Samson and Lewis had kneaded together, and pressed it onto the casing of the mine. He also put one lump, the size of a melon, right on the top. Next, he shoved three holes into the plastic explosive using a pencil and tied the electric timing device to one of the horns. This was connected to the three detonators so all he had to do now was insert the detonators into the plastic. As this would leave the whole apparatus primed and ready to go off, it was the last part of the operation. It was also the most dangerous. In deference to his enduring nightmare of being stranded with a "ticking bomb" but without means of rapid departure Hunter had left the boat engines running before climbing down to the stern platform.

He pushed the detonators home and tamped the PE around them. He turned the clock on the timer to fifteen minutes and climbed back into the boat. Lewis threw away the line he was holding and the boat began to drift slowly away with the tide. Hunter went into the cabin, seated himself at the console, engaged the engines and increased the revs. *The Overdraft* responded immediately and quickly drew away from the mine.

Once he could see the mine floating clear astern, he yelled to the other two, 'Hold tight,' and pushed the throttles all the way over.

The boat sank on her haunches, moved forward with a burst of speed and surge of power and accelerated rapidly, rising to the plane, leaving a wide wake behind her. Hunter turned the wheel a few degrees to starboard and took the boat in a wide arc. The indicator showed she was pushing thirty-five knots, the wind whistling about them. The three of them exchanged rueful and childish grins of pleasure and then Hunter throttled back, let the boat drop down from the plane and watched the speed bleed away rapidly to settle at ten knots. He estimated they were a mile away when he stopped the boat altogether and turned her to face the mine.

Hunter looked at his watch. Ten thirty-five. Not bad progress so far. The usual morning mist was beginning to form on the surface of the sea, causing the mine to drift in and out of sight. Too late, he thought of tying a flag or something to it to make it more visible. He stood up, stretched his limbs and then bent to open one of their boxes of gear. From it, Hunter took out a pair of binoculars and said, 'I'm going up to the fly deck to keep an eye on things. Answer the radio if anybody calls.'

'Who're you expecting, boss? The Duchess of Kent?'

Hunter made no reply. Sometimes naval humour passed him by. In the few minutes it had taken him to get organised and get to the open steering position above the main cabin more mist had begun to appear. This was typical of the south coast in spring; a cold night, followed by a flat calm and clear day usually resulted in a sea mist which would last until the afternoon, by which time the sun would have burnt it off.

The sound of the diesels was a muted, background noise, hardly impinging on his conscience. He was looking at his watch and estimating that they had about two and a half minutes to go when the high pitched call of a young voice carried clearly to him. He looked up startled, unsure from which direction the sound was coming. Quickly he raised his glasses, looked for the mine and began to scan right then left. To look at him no one would have been aware of the frantic thoughts tumbling across his mind.

Now he got the meaning. 'Suzie, close up and we'll tie a piece of rope between us so that we don't lose each other.'

There, got them! The two sea kayaks drifted into his vision for a few seconds before being enveloped once again by the mist. Hunter had rammed the throttles fully home and was turning the wheel even as he yelled at the others. 'Delilah, Taff.' Down below he heard something smash, muffled curses and a great thump as if a body had dropped onto the deck.

A black face appeared over the deck. 'Christ, boss! What the hell's happening?'

'Kids in kayaks. They're about fifty yards from the mine and heading towards it.' By now the boat was up on its plane, the speed indicator showing thirty-eight knots. By a fluke the mine floated clearly in his vision fifty yards to port as he pulled the throttles back, bringing the beautiful craft to a rapid stop. He couldn't see the kayaks but heard a plaintive voice yell in protest: 'Hey, you clown, couldn't you see?' The mist had parted and the two kayaks were five yards away, four frightened and indignant faces looking up at him. It had taken a minute and forty-five seconds from first hearing the voices to get this near. He hoped they had more than the forty five seconds that he estimated was all they had left to get away again.

'Pull them in Taff, as quick as you can,' Hunter yelled at the kids. 'There's a mine about to blow which will blow you all to Kingdom Come. Get aboard, hurry.' Even as he was speaking Hunter was manoeuvring *The Overdraft* alongside the kayaks. Already two of the kids were clambering aboard, a third was grabbing the rail and the fourth . . . the fourth was just sitting there. 'What the hell,' even as Hunter began to speak, the youth was crossing his arms and saying, 'Yeah, and pigs fly. I don't know . . .' the words were hardly out of his mouth when a big, black hand grabbed him by the front of his life jacket and bodily pulled him into the boat, dropping him onto the deck. Hunter missed the protests and squeals from his new passengers as he was already ramming home the throttles, turning the boat to starboard to present a stern aspect to the mine. He glanced at his watch, an old Rolex Oyster Perpetual, and realised that they were now on borrowed time.

Mentally he did the arithmetic. At thirty-eight knots the boat travelled three point eight nautical miles in six minutes. In thirty seconds they had travelled point three . . . even as he was working it out the explosion began.

The electric timer moved the last thousandth of an inch and completed the circuit, fifteen seconds later than estimated. The tiny battery generated enough power to cause an electric current to travel along two short pieces of wire to the detonators taped to the white detonating cord. These ignited the cord and a controlled explosion ran along their lengths in a nano-second. Although they were cut to the same lengths, setting an explosion like this is not an exact science. The explosion running along the detonating cord reached the main detonators hundredths of seconds apart. It made no difference. The detonators exploded, which in turn caused the molecules of the plastic explosive to be thrown apart with a violence that was devastating. Because thé plastic explosive had been shaped like a bar of Toblerone chocolate and the melon-sized lump in the shape of a pyramid, most of the explosive force was directed into the mine. The mine casing blew inwards and such was the violence of the explosion, the old, decayed explosive held in the mine, after nearly seventy years since manufacture, performed the task for which it had been made and blew up.

The blast tore apart the mist, threw a huge gusher of water into the air and scattered small bits of metal in all directions. Luckily none of the casing travelled more than two hundred yards, the water only a few yards further, but the blast spread out from its epicentre carrying all before it. Birds were thrown though the air, some dead, others only stunned. The pressure wave moved out in concentric rings and hit the stern of the boat with sufficient force to throw those who had been standing in the welldeck off their feet. The large plate-glass window doors shattered inwards but luckily none of the glass did any serious damage. The thump of the explosion travelled through the water and hit the hull with a crump that caused the boat to lift her stern about a foot before settling back to flee any further damage. Hunter was shoved hard against the wheel, the breath knocked from him, but he kept his feet.

He looked back to see the water cascading down and everything returning to normal. Already the mist was re-forming, partly obliterating his view. He throttled back and began to turn the boat. 'Are you all okay?' he yelled.

There was a chorus of yesses and more muffled curses, before Lewis put his head over the deck edge. ''Fraid there's a bit of a mess below, sir. But apart from that everybody seems all right.'

'Okay. Tell those kids that if they want to keep an eye out for their kayaks we'll take them back with us if we can find them.' He then left the wheel and darted below to take over back in the main cabin. Once he had control there he lifted the handset and broadcast, 'Lifeboat, this is *The Overdraft*, over.'

'*Overdraft*, this is lifeboat. That was some explosion. Are you all right? We watched you on our radar suddenly move, stop and then go like a bat out of hell.'

'Yeah, sorry if we gave you heart failure but it was nothing compared to what we felt. We had to pick up four kids in kayaks who had strayed into the area, over.'

'Jesus, where the hell did they come from? Over.'

'I don't know yet. I haven't had a chance to question them. Look, we're right in the middle of the blast here and the sea is covered in fish. I can't be bothered to stay and collect it so why don't you come in and lift what you want? Over.'

'Thanks navy that's mighty nice of you. See you again. Roger, out.'

'This is *The Overdraft*. Like our American cousins say, have a nice day. Switching to Channel 16. Out.' Even as he had been speaking, he had manoeuvred the boat alongside the two kayaks which were still intact and tied together.

Samson and Lewis pulled them aboard and put them on the forward deck which was large enough to accommodate a dozen sun bathing bodies should the weather be fine enough. Hunter engaged the gears and headed back to Swanage.

'Boss, you aren't going to believe this,' said Delilah, his feet crunching on the glass scattered across the cabin, a big grin on his face.

'Believe what?' asked Hunter, already distracted with how he was going to get out of any problem which Jessop could throw at him. If he'd read the man correctly Jessop would enjoy causing a stir about the damage.

'The young lady says this is her father's boat and wants to know what we're doing with it.'

Hunter was startled, curious and relieved all at the same time. Startled at the news, curious as to what she and the others were doing out there so early and relieved that in view of what had happened Jessop was hardly going to cause a fuss.

Hunter looked over Leading Seaman Samson's shoulder at the girl standing just behind him. She was looking a little woebegone and white around the gills but seemed to have a lot of spirit still in her.

'Is this true? This is your father's boat?'

She nodded. 'Yes. My name's Lucy Jessop and this is his boat all right.'

Hunter nodded. 'Jessop is the owner's name so I guess she's yours after all. At least if we've saved his daughter I don't suppose he'll make too much fuss about the mess.' He waved his hand airily about the cabin. The double doors had shattered into tiny pieces of glass, just like a car windscreen would, and were scattered all over the place.

She looked pensive for a moment and said, surprisingly, 'I think it would be a good idea to get my mother to meet us. I don't trust Dad.'

Hunter let her comment pass him and asked, 'What were you doing out there anyway?'

Lucy pursed her lips, thought a moment and replied, 'We were on a kayaking trip for our Duke of Edinburgh's Gold Award. This was the only time we could fit it in because we've got "A Levels" coming up.'

'That explains it. But where did you come from?'

One of the others, a boy with sandy hair, a thin face and a gangling body, appeared next to her and said, 'We started yesterday morning. We'd already done twenty miles when we stopped last night and camped on a beach. We left this morning at first light. Hell, we only had about fifteen miles to go and now this. I suppose we'll have to do it all over again.'

The other two were sitting outside and heard him. Both groaned and commented on the unfairness of it. The boy who had been bodily dragged into the boat suddenly stood up.

'I'm sorry I made such a prat of myself. If I was honest I'd admit to having been frightened. When you appeared like that, it scared the life out of me. I wondered what in the world was going on,' he finished lamely, shrugged and looked sheepish.

Hunter smiled encouragingly at them all. 'Don't worry about it. I can understand.'

They were already approaching Swanage, and Hunter turned his attention back to taking the boat alongside the stone jetty. 'Eh, Lucy, what did you mean when you said to get hold of your mother and not to trust your father?'

'Exactly that. I can tell you that he will be furious because of the damage to his precious boat,' she replied with some bitterness. 'He demands rights which, if the truth were known, aren't there. He can be a serious embarrassment sometimes.' She spoke with the candour of youth and experience. Suddenly she smiled. 'Oh look, there's mummy now, standing on the jetty.' Lucy went out on deck and waved excitedly to her mother.

Hunter was concentrating on taking the boat safely

22

alongside but managed to catch a glimpse of an attractive woman he guessed to be in her late thirties.

Lucy was busy telling her mother how they came to be onboard the boat as Hunter stopped alongside the jetty and ropes were thrown up to people awaiting their return.

Lucy scrambled ashore to hug her mother even as her father was jumping onboard. 'What the f . . . What . . . What. What have you done, you bastard!' Jessop was beside himself with rage. His face had turned a mottled red colour and he was moving up and down on his toes, as though trying to make himself taller. His hands hung by his sides, opening and closing as though he was unable to make up his mind about making a fist and taking a swing at Hunter.

'Sorry about the mess,' Hunter began. 'But . . .'

'Sorry! You incompetent fool. I'll have you court martialled for this. You had no right to take my boat in the first place and you return it like this. I'm going to have your guts for garters, I promise you!'

Unknown to either of the men, Lucy and her mother had climbed onboard. 'Daddy, that's unfair. He saved my life and the lives of the others. If he hadn't come back for us . . .'

'Keep out of this,' Jessop almost snarled at his daughter. 'I'll deal with you later. Now, you . . .' he swung back to Hunter but before he could say another word his wife grabbed hold of his arm, above the elbow and shook it.

'Shut up, shut up, shut up. You're a bloody fool Arthur so don't say another word and try not to make a bigger fool of yourself than you have already. Lieutenant, I apologise for this buffoon of a husband of mine, but he over-reacts all the time.'

Jessop was looking at his wife dazedly, never having

been so publicly put down by her before. He quickly recovered and shook her hand off his arm. 'Doreen, I'll speak to you later as well. I won't have my wife speak to me like that in front of other . . .'

Doreen Jessop lost her temper in such a way that would redefine the Jessop's relationship forever. She took hold of his shoulder and pushed and shoved him down the four steps that led to the forward cabins, yelling, 'Get in there and be quiet. These men saved Lucy's life at the risk of their own and you haven't got the good grace to admit it. The whole fiasco was your fault in the first place. I told you not to drag that thing in here but to call the coastguard.' Whatever else she was saying became muffled as she closed the door separating the forward master cabin from the rest of the boat. Only her voice could be heard with an occasional word being understood. After a few minutes there was an interruption by Jessop, quickly followed by the distinct noise of a face being slapped. The door was flung open and Doreen Jessop stalked out and back up the steps to the main saloon. Her colour was high but, Hunter admitted to himself, she looked very, very attractive. She immediately composed herself and stopped in front of him.

Her big, hazel-coloured eyes looked into Nick's dark blue ones and she held out her hand. She was breathing heavily and the white blouse she was wearing under her unbuttoned jacket was straining at the seams. Hunter could not help glancing down at her cleavage, a glance she noted and smiled at. 'If there is anything, anything at all,' she took his hand and held it a few moments longer than necessary, 'that I can do, please do not hesitate to call. You'll find us in the telephone book for Arundel.' She let go his hand but her eyes held his steadily. 'I want to thank you for what you did today. You saved my daughter's life,' Doreen broke eye contact, moved a step and put her arm around Lucy's shoulders, 'and the lives of the others. I cannot thank you enough.'

Hunter nodded and smiled. 'All in a day's work. Lads, get the gear up top and let's get going.'

A few minutes later they bade their farewells. Unknown to either of them, they would meet again, under very different circumstances.

2

Aziz Habib lounged back in the chair and stroked the edge of his nose, a habit he had when thinking. 'Are you sure of your facts?' he asked the small man sitting opposite, who was nervously tugging at the front of his shirt as though trying to pull it from his body.

The man nodded. 'Yes, quite sure. The Mullahs have agreed to pay fifteen million American dollars if you can achieve what you say you will.'

'And my expenses?'

'Those too. Up to a total of a further five million dollars.'

'They have read my report and what I propose and do not disagree with anything?'

'On the contrary, they find it one of the most audacious and clever plans that you have yet devised.' The little man looked into the black eyes of the man he had been sent to meet. Inwardly, he shuddered. Even with the support and blessing of the Council of Mullahs, he was still very uncomfortable in the presence of someone who had committed such violent and terrible acts of terrorism. Habib made Azil Nadir and his Palestinian supporters look like children by comparison. He took

26

no sides, did what he did for money and the pleasure of it, and hid behind the cloak of fundamentalism. He was useful to Iran and Libya, and although he was practically unknown outside a small, select number of people who used his services, there was a great deal of talk doing the rounds of the fundamentalist groups, which spoke of his achievements. With his real identity a closely guarded secret, Habib had used his contacts to spread the word about his exploits, exaggerating the terror and mayhem he had caused. He let his results be fanned by the wind of fanaticism. With the downing of three jet aircraft full of Americans and Europeans on holiday, and the sinking of a ferry full of American servicemen in Jakarta, he had joined the superleague of terrorists. Hence, the fee he was demanding for his next venture.

'Is everything arranged, as I dem . . . asked?' he quickly corrected himself. He knew that every word, every gesture and nuance would be reported back. He had to be careful to demand nothing, only to request. He knew full well how fickle his paymasters were.

This would be his crowning glory. The ultimate act which would enable him to retire with dignity, fame within the world he inhabited, and enough money to last him ten lifetimes. Not only that, it would be the most newsworthy act of terrorism ever carried out and, it had to be remembered, it was the media of the Western world which would carry their message.

'I shall make the necessary travel arrangements,' Habib said, 'for myself and one other. You, in the meantime, arrange for the names I gave you to meet me in Malta in two days time. Do I make myself clear?'

The little man nodded his head quickly. 'Yes, perfectly. I shall make all the necessary arrangements myself.

27

Today!' In his nervousness he had to stop himself from shouting the last word.

'Good. Then I think there is only one more thing to do, before you leave.' He held out his hand.

The little man froze in the act of tugging at his shirt and looked quizzically at Habib, sweat suddenly appearing on his forehead. 'I . . . I . . . don't understand,' he stammered.

'The bank draft, you fool,' said Habib, pleased at the response he was getting from his guest.

'Oh, yes, yes. Here it is.' He picked up and quickly tore open the satchel which had been lying alongside his chair. He dug inside with feverish hands, grasped the paper and leaned forward to pass it to Habib.

Habib took it from him, checked the amount and smiled genially. 'Thank you,' he said, reaching into his jacket pocket for his wallet. He inserted the cheque and replaced the wallet, then stood up to indicate the meeting was at an end. He did not offer his hand or make any other gesture to the little man who also scrambled to his feet.

'Thank you, thank you,' he bobbed his head, like a puppet on a string, and backed to the door. Thankfully, he opened it and stepped backwards into the corridor, closing the door behind him. He heaved a sigh of relief, took out a handkerchief to mop his brow, and hurried away, glad the meeting was over. All he had to do now was report back to the Council of Mullahs, a prospect which did not fill him with joy. He looked heavenwards, 'Surely, there is a better way to live than this?' he asked his God above, but received no answer.

The Holiday Inn at Tehran, where Habib was residing temporarily, was now run by Iranians after they had kicked out the Americans with the downfall of the Shah. It was shabby, not very clean and the service was dreadful. However, it was still the best hotel available in Iran and hence the reason Habib stayed there whenever he was in the country. He had a suite of two bedrooms and a living room, where he was now standing, facing the window, looking out over the city. The door to one of the bedrooms opened and a white European entered the room.

'Did you hear?' Habib asked, without turning.

'Yes, I did. It all seems perfectly satisfactory to me.' There was no smile on his face, no hint of the glee he felt. Derek Fredericks was English, but spoke in a manner which suggested that it was not his native tongue. This was not the case, and was an affectation he had cultivated over the years in an attempt to hide his roots.

Fredericks was stockily built, thick necked with a grey, designer fuzz of a beard. His eyes were like washed grey slate, he filled his well-tailored, light-brown suit with solid muscle and he had the disconcerting habit of holding himself very still. The man was a perverted psychopath, who enjoyed inflicting pain on others. He was also Habib's right-hand man.

'Make the arrangements for us to leave, tonight,' Habib told him. 'We'll fly to Turkey and then to Malta.' He stood pensively looking over the city, stroking the side of his nose, deep in thought. 'Are you sure that the information we have is correct?'

Fredericks stifled the reply that had sprung to his lips, as they had been over the same ground time and time again. 'Quite sure. The information cost us half a million pounds sterling and is absolutely guaranteed.'

'It had better be,' Habib said, ominously.

'Don't worry. I made it clear what would happen if it wasn't.' There had been no threat made to the informant. Instead, Fredericks had enjoyed explaining, in detail, what would happen to the man's wife, son and daughter should the information not be forthcoming and accurate.

'Are you convinced that we have the right people? That they will follow through, no matter what?'

'Aziz, I have personally made sure that they will all follow us, no matter what. They all have an ingrained fanatical hate of the West which will make martyrs of them one day.'

'Soon?'

'Soon. They accept the idea of death in the same way as you and I accept the idea of breathing. They want to die for the cause, they want to fight the great Satan. Fear not,' Fredericks spoke in his pedantic way. 'They will not be found wanting, when the chips are down.'

'Chips? What are you talking about? Chips being down?'

'I mean, Aziz, should things get tough, they won't let us . . . you,' he corrected himself, hastily, 'they won't let you down.'

'Good. What is the state with the weapons?'

'As of yesterday, all weapons were onboard the ship.'

'Everything? Did they give us all that we asked for?'

'Yes, Aziz. We took delivery of six stinger missiles, and enough side arms and machine guns to start a war, and sufficient ammunition to finish one.'

Habib nodded, satisfied. 'And the girl?'

'She will not present a problem.'

'I didn't expect her to,' said Habib dryly. 'The body?'

'It is all taken care of. It will never be found,' said Fredericks, punctiliously.

No mention was made of, nor hinted at, the perversions

they enjoyed together. It was a bond between them which would only be broken by the grave. The mutilated, dead body of the young, pubescent girl would be found in a gutter far enough away not to cause either man any problems.

A short while later they had departed for the airport. They both looked like the West's idea of an Arab, in ankle length Bedouin clothes. They also had on haiks, flowing large cloths draped over their heads and upper bodies. The head scarf was the reason why Arabs were known disrespectfully by the soldiers of the Western world as ragheads.

Tehran airport had been the pride of the Middle East under the Shah. Under the Mullahs it had become another third-world dump in dire need of repairs; dirty, badly run and corrupted to a degree that it took a bribe for a Westerner to get a seat on an aeroplane out of the country. Habib and Fredericks had no such problem. They showed their special passports and went effortlessly through to the international departure lounge. They carried only hand luggage and not much of that. They were both armed but neither set off the alarms at the security check point by the simple expedient of bypassing the normal channels. They carried weapons for their personal protection. Both were high up on the most wanted lists of numerous countries, including America's and Britain's. They had tried hard to keep their identities secret but could not be sure that Western intelligence agencies did not know who they were. They could get into Turkey armed, but they would have to get rid of their guns for the last part of the journey to Malta; they had no way of bypassing immigration and customs of a NATO country, albeit predominantly an Islamic one. There was no love lost between the Turks and the Iranians and at long last the Turkish authorities were helping the West to fight terrorism, wherever it was.

The Iranair flight was uneventful. Both men refused the non-alcoholic drinks and unappetising food offered by surly stewardesses. They had sat on the runway for what seemed like an eternity but had finally taken off to land in Ankara, two thousand kilometres and four and a half hours later. With the change of an hour in time, it was still only just past ten thirty in the evening when they landed. Unobtrusively, they passed through immigration and headed for the Avis sign.

It was a cold, overcast night with a bitter wind blowing from the north. There was a threat of rain in the air which neither of them minded. A mile and a half from the airport they booked into a small hotel which appeared new enough to be still reasonably well furnished.

Habib knocked on Fredericks' door. 'Enter, it's not locked,' came Fredericks' voice. Habib frowned at this lack of routine and went in ready to remonstrate with his colleague. Instead of which, he found Fredericks standing at the window looking out from behind the curtains, studying the car park. The gun Fredericks held was pointed at him for a few seconds until he was satisfied that it was Habib and he alone who had entered.

'What's the matter?' Habib asked, frowning.

'Nothing. I was just checking. I had a feeling we were being watched but I think I was wrong.'

'After the care we took I don't believe anybody could have followed without us knowing about it,' he retorted, anger in his voice.

Fredericks shrugged. 'As you say. It was just a feeling;

little things that didn't add up but I guess you're right. It's my paranoia working overtime.'

Unknown to either man, they'd been "clocked". A young female operative working for Turkish State Security had been at the airport looking out for possible Kurdish dissidents. In the crowd she spotted them when they had arrived but not recognising either of them had dismissed them from her thoughts. However, when they had left the Avis counter to walk to the car lot, Fredericks had accidentally brushed against her as she had been hurrying to another door, trying to get a further glimpse of someone she thought she did recognise. Alim may have been young and inexperienced but she was sure that what she had felt under the Arab's caftan was a gun and holster. Startled, she had pulled away and looked at the two men's retreating backs. Was she right? Surely, it was ridiculous to think that anyone could come through from an international flight carrying a gun. On the other hand, it was from Tehran. She decided to play safe and went to find her superior at the airport, Lieutenant Zim Albatha. Luckily, he was an easy man to spot – six feet six inches, weighing over 220 pounds, with a large handlebar moustache; he was the last person one expected to find surreptitiously staking out an airport. However, after fifteen years of service, Albatha was good at his job, very good.

'Zim,' Alim looked up at him from her five feet and four inches, grasping his arm.

'Alim, what is it?' Albatha had a surprisingly soft voice. He looked down, concerned, at his pretty, dark-eyed and brown-complexioned companion.

'Those two men, the Arabs,' she nodded in the direction of Habib and Fredericks, 'I'm sure one of them has a gun.'

Albatha started walking after the men, Alim almost trotting to keep up with him. 'Okay, let me try and get a look at them. Put your hand through my arm and look up at me and smile. Don't look at them. Let's try and get a better look before we do anything that might alert them or cause us any mistaken embarrassment.'

They followed the two men outside and across the road to the rent-a-car parking lot. Albatha did not once appear to be looking at either of them but from the corner of his eye was building up a mental picture. Albatha had spent years training himself in observation techniques. Mentally, he described each of them to himself and as he did so he was able to discard them from his vast memory bank of known and suspected terrorists. Even as the two men were getting into their car he had them. Habib and Fredericks. It was true that no Western agency knew them by sight. However, thanks to Zim Albatha the West did have detailed descriptions of them. There was no indication of the tremendous surge of excitement that had coursed through his veins when he "clocked" them. Mentally, he ticked off the outrages he knew they had been responsible for even as he nodded to Alim to get in to the car.

'We follow them,' he said, 'but very, very carefully.'

'Why Zim, who are they?' Her own excitement showed through, although she tried hard to act as nonchalantly as Albatha.

He didn't reply for a few seconds, as he concentrated on following the other car, whilst keeping as far back as possible. So far he did not think they'd been spotted. The traffic was heavy, slow moving and dangerous. Dangerous because the Islamic Turks thought that if they had an accident there was nothing they could do about it as it was the will of Allah. Safe driving was a contradiction in terms in Turkey. 'I can't be sure but I think they are two terrorists named Habib and Fredericks. If I hadn't seen them together then I don't think I would have recognised them. However, as a duo they're unmistakable.'

'Who are they? I mean, not their names but what have they done?'

'They are seriously bad,' said Albatha. 'They will blow an aeroplane out of the sky to get at one person. In fact, we are quite sure they have done exactly that. Remember the Sabena flight 101? We are quite sure they were responsible and that they did it to get one man, a dissident working against Saddam Hussein.'

Alim gasped. 'That's terrible. I remember the incident well. It was seven years ago and I had just joined after my initial training course. All those deaths! Wasn't it something like one hundred and twenty men, women and children?'

'Eight years and one hundred and twenty-seven, excluding a crew of seven,' he replied grimly, his hands clenched tightly around the wheel, his knuckles gleaming white. 'A total of one hundred and thirty-four . . . including my sister.'

'I . . . I'm sorry, Zim. I had no idea.'

'There's no reason why you should have. I spent two years putting together the information about those two bastards, trying to get enough on them to extradite them to stand trial. It was no use of course.' He forced himself to relax. Sheer will power was holding him back from charging after them and ramming them off the road. He knew he had to be careful, one false move and they would be on to him. He didn't want to lose them now. 'We found sufficient evidence to link those two with the bombing of the plane and I tracked them down to Iraq. Unfortunately, the regime there backed up their stories that they had been in Iraq throughout the period and couldn't possibly have had anything to do with the downing of 101. All lies of course, but nobody in the West was prepared to go as far as to call Saddam a liar. So it all went cold and nothing further happened. All the intelligence agencies world wide who are trying to stamp out terrorism are on the alert to arrest them but so far nobody has reported a sighting. Until now.'

'What do you propose? Are you planning to shoot them?'

He smiled mirthlessly. 'My heart tells me to shoot them whilst my head tells me to arrest them. If we arrest them and put them on trial, then a conviction will be very damaging to more than a dozen regimes around the world. We can milk the propaganda for all it's worth, maybe point a few fingers of accusation at states which have used their services.' He shrugged. 'There's a lot of information held in their heads which would also be worth having.' Suddenly he smiled. 'Afterwards, I'm sure an accident could befall them even if we didn't have them executed.'

'What are you proposing to do?' Alim was reaching for her gun as she spoke, checking to see that it was ready to fire immediately.

'Good girl. I like to see someone who's ready for the worst. If they are who I think they are, then they will not be taking any chances. I'm surprised they're here.' He thought for a few seconds. 'No, I'm not. Of course, they've come in from Iran and are on their way somewhere else. Do you know under what names they travelled? No? It doesn't really matter. They will be trying to leave under different names with different passports. Those two are renowned for their ability to act ruthlessly and to vanish quickly. Only this time they made a mistake. They couldn't have known Zim Albatha would be at the airport.'

'What are we going to do?' Alim repeated herself.

'Follow them. Find out where they hole up and send for back up – a full-scale search and arrest squad, armed to the teeth. Let me tell you about those two. Habib is the master, Fredericks his aide. Habib does the planning and thinking and Fredericks most of the dirty work. I say most, because Habib likes doing some of it himself. I managed to get enough information on those two to convince me of their involvement with at least a dozen atrocities in the last four or five years. They do not do it for ideology but for money. I estimate that Habib controls a fortune in excess of twenty million pounds sterling which is thirty million dollars American. I had also heard that they had retired, so what brings them out of hiding at this time?'

'Perhaps they have retired and are taking a holiday,' Alim said, half jokingly.

Albatha took her reply at face value. 'No, I don't think so. They're up to something, I can feel it in my water. If we can stop them, then all well and good. If we can't, then Allah alone knows what they're planning. But whatever it is, it will be very nasty. Very nasty indeed.'

'Zim, I can't see them. They aren't there,' Alim looked about her wildly. Along the brightly lit road the other car had been easy to follow. In keeping with the high standards set and demanded of Avis world wide, the gleaming white VW Polo had stuck out like a sore thumb

37

in a country where car washing was unheard of. Now, it was no longer ahead of them.

'Relax. It turned off into that hotel we passed. I'm going to turn and go back to see if their car is still there. If it is, I'll go in and question the receptionist and find out if they've checked in. You stay in the car and keep your head down. Okay?'

'Shouldn't I follow you, just in case?' asked Alim nervously.

'No! Stay well away! I told you, these are very dangerous men. They have not lived as long as they have by carelessness or stupidity. I expect them to be watching.'

'Why is it that nobody's got them before now, if they're wanted as much as you say they are?'

'I don't know. I do know that agencies all over the world have got very close to them but always, at the last minute, they evade any trap that's been set. The Belgians came closest about a year ago. A paramilitary squad were literally surrounding the building the two of them were in when they suddenly ran out, shot four bystanders including a kid and got away in the confusion.' He thought for a few seconds. 'It's as if they had been warned but if that's so, nobody has been able to find out how. Rumour has it that Habib has a world-wide network of paid informants.'

'Perhaps there's another explanation,' said Alim brightly.

Albatha had turned the car and was driving back along the road. The VW could be seen gleaming in the car park, turned and ready for a quick getaway, if it should prove necessary. He stopped further along the road in a lay-by and said, 'Stay here. I'm going to speak to the receptionist and see if they are in the hotel. If they are I'll stay there and phone for back up. Do not, under any circumstances, come after me.'

'Zim, that's not fair. You know I'm a good shot. I should be your back-up.'

'Alim, have you ever shot anybody?'

'Zim, you know I haven't,' she spoke quietly, fingering her gun.

'I have. And what I'm telling you now was told to me, yet I still did it.'

'Did what?'

'Hesitated. I suddenly thought about what I was doing. I'd been told and told again. It was screamed at me by my instructors, it was drummed into me by my lieutenant. Don't think about it. Just do it. Don't give them a chance because they won't give you one. Yet, when the time came, I hesitated. I could see the bullet impacting, the blood and gore. The enquiry! What about the enquiry? Would I be exonerated for the killing? What if he survived and accused me of attempted murder? I'm telling you, it isn't natural to kill somebody, unless you're a psychopath, or you're really trained for it. We aren't. So, stay away.'

'What happened to you the first time?'

Albatha half laughed, half snorted. 'I did it all wrong. I froze. I yelled stop! The other man didn't even think before he started shooting.'

'He obviously missed, otherwise you wouldn't be here,' said Alim.

Albatha, shook his head ruefully and suddenly pulled up his shirt. In the light from the street Alim could see, against the deep tan of Albatha's skin, white puckered skin. 'No, he didn't. I took three bullets in my body before I shot him in the head. And all because I hesitated. I haven't hesitated since.' He tucked his shirt back into the waist band of his trousers. 'You'll hesitate, and then you'll be dead.'

'No, I won't. I'll be ready. Especially now. Especially now you've told me.'

Albatha shook his head. 'Please, do as I say. I know what I'm talking about. Stay hidden and watch.' With that, he got out of the car and walked in the shadows to the hotel entrance.

Alim watched his big bulk enter through the doorway.

Inside the hotel Albatha went up to reception. It was a small counter behind which sat a fat and bored woman, reading a cheap romantic novel. He stood in front of the counter but she did not bother to look up. After a few seconds, because he was in that sort of a mood, he leaned forward and said, 'If you don't speak to me I'll stuff that book where it'll hurt the most.' As soon as he said it he was sorry, because it was out of character for him. But, with all that had happened and could happen, he was completely on edge.

'Oh, sorry, sir,' she looked up, pretending she had just noticed him. She was startled, nobody spoke to her like that. Except maybe the police, she was thinking.

'The two men who came in just now. I want to know which room they took and what they said.'

'I'm sorry, sir. It's the policy of the hotel not to divulge any information . . .' She stopped talking when she saw the warrant card shoved under her nose. 'Two rooms, 204 and 206, second floor, next door to each other.'

'That's better. Have they made any phone calls since they got here?'

'No,' the reply was truculent, as if her original answer had been too co-operative.

He picked up the telephone lying on the counter and dialled. After a few moments it was answered and he said, 'Albatha. Code blue. Hotel Aeroport on Kanari Street.

Come very quietly.' He paused to listen. 'Look, I don't want to say,' he hissed. 'I don't give a dog's turd what the captain said. All right, all right, all right. Shut up. I think it's Habib and Fredericks. Yes, I know what I said. Which is why I said code blue. Right. Come quietly.' He put the receiver down.

'Is there trouble?' the woman asked, nervously.

He shrugged. 'There could be. Yes, I think there could be.'

She didn't wait. She grabbed her handbag and bolted for the door. Zim Albatha cursed and grabbed her by the shoulder. 'Stay here. You'll have to be here until my men arrive,' he said.

She shrugged his arm off him. 'I'm not waiting,' she panted, her eyes bulging, an overactive imagination already adding two and two to make six. She didn't want to be around when the other lot got there. She didn't trust the flics anymore than she would a serial rapist in a nunnery.

'You have to stay,' Albatha hissed at her. 'If you don't I'll arrest you for obstruction of a police officer in the execution of his duty.'

She glared at him. She was a big woman, fat with a round face. 'I don't care,' she spat out at him. 'There's nothing you can do to me. I know my rights. I'm not staying and that's final.'

'If you don't stay behind that counter,' Albatha waved his hand in its direction, 'and act normally, I will arrest you. Believe me. I will search you in the presence of another officer and find a little cannabis on you. I will then hold you in Ravina Prison for a week before I take you before a magistrate. Do I make myself clear?'

'Bastard,' she said with venom, but her shoulders

sagged and the fight went out of her. She knew about Ravina. Who didn't? If the stories told were only half true, she shuddered. In Turkey, being in prison was like an intimation of what hell would be like. Ravina was a notorious women's prison where beatings were a punishment for the smallest infraction of the rules. However, it was said that gang raping took place regularly, women on women, the filthy cows, and that drugs were rife. If you didn't go in a drug addict, you came out one. Even a week would be too long. She walked back behind her desk as the phone rang. Nervously she picked up the receiver.

'Front desk,' it came out a croak. She cleared her throat and tried again. 'Front desk.' She listened a moment before replying. 'I'm sorry, sir, we have none.' Although she was a Turkish peasant who had never been out of the country she spoke recognisable English, albeit with a strong accent. Satellite television and CCN were helping to spread the word – in English with an American accent. She was sweating, dark patches spreading under her armpits, the faint hairs on her upper lip glistening. 'The bar is closed for the night. I'm sorry . . . I . . . I don't have a key. No, sir. Only the manager.' She hung up after the caller slammed his phone down in a temper. 'It was them,' she said.

'Stupid cow,' Fredericks said, angrily. 'All I wanted was a beer and she said the bar was closed and she couldn't get . . .' he stopped mid sentence as the muted signal came clearly from the wristwatch each man wore.

Zim Albatha seriously underestimated the wealth controlled by Habib and by extension, Fredericks. With worldwide interests exceeding a hundred million dollars, they could easily afford a huge network of spies, some in important places. By hiding behind dummy corporations, false names and using go-betweens, they had acquired property in a dozen different countries from Scotland to Australia to Turkey. In each of the countries the properties had similar characteristics. Remote, well fenced in, easily guarded. Most importantly, not only did they have their network of spies but they had also penetrated the security forces in all the countries where they had their bolt holes. Habib had painstakingly built up his informants, carefully finding and selecting men – and one woman – who could be relied upon to send the message they had just received. All that was required of them was for their informant to ring a certain number, different in each country, and let the number ring once, before hanging up. That was sufficient to send a signal to a communications satellite. In turn the signal was sent to each of them, wherever they were in the world. So far, it had saved them on no fewer than five previous occasions. This looked like being the sixth, or was it the last? each man couldn't help thinking. If they survived and got away, their contact in Turkey would receive half a million American dollars in a Swiss bank account within the week. Habib considered it money well spent. It also gave him more control over the men and the women he used. The terrorists had access to satellite warning signals whilst the Turkish security forces didn't even have mobile phones.

Neither man spoke except for a brief curse from Fredericks. There would be plenty of time to wonder what had gone wrong once they got away. The tone had barely sounded before they were diving for their bags, slinging them over their shoulders and switching off the light in the room. Fredericks was berating himself, he had known something was wrong. He had sensed it all along.

They both carried Heckler and Koch 9mm pistols with a hundred rounds of ammunition each. Designed at the height of the cold war by an East German company the gun had become the favourite tool of terrorists and so-called freedom fighters internationally.

Until now terrorists in every country had used modern equipment and technology, including the internet to exchange information. The security forces fighting them had never been able to keep up because governments were not prepared to pay for the resources needed. So bit by bit, terrorism was winning. Not only by accumulating vast resources but by corrupting officials all over the world. They were beginning to undermine governments and hence increase their evil. Vast drug empires were spawning undreamed of wealth. In turn, this wealth was being channelled to groups of dissidents and malcontents world wide. Money, greed, the lust for power, a desire for change, all of these things helped to create the modern terrorist. But behind the label also lurked the psychopath, the twisted and warped personality who would have been long caught and in prison if he had not had a mentor to keep him in check and allow him off his leash only when he was needed; someone as warped as Fredericks.

In spite of the danger they were in, Fredericks hoped for the chance to kill somebody.

With the gun in his left hand he darted to the curtains. The threat of rain had become a reality and a heavy downpour was reducing visibility to a matter of ten metres or so. He saw nothing. He shook his head at Habib who had already opened the door to glance up and down the corridor. Holding their guns at the ready both men slipped into the corridor and crept along the wall towards the emergency exit. They did not try to

conceal their weapons. If anyone got in their way they
would shoot them. Fifty paces along they came to the
stairwell and Fredericks silently dropped to ground level
to look around the corner. Nothing. He signalled Habib
and both continued carefully but quickly down the stairs.
They found themselves at the emergency exit which was
illegally chained. Habib quickly reached into his holdall
and removed a small, hydraulic bolt cutter. It was less
than six centimetres long and two wide. He put the cutting
edge around one of the links and turned a small handle at
the base as quickly as he could. There was no pressure
required and the hydraulic pump caused the cutting edges
to close together as though they were passing through
spaghetti, not steel. He unthreaded the chain from around
the door and put it on the floor.

'Ready?'

Fredericks replied. 'Yes, let's go. Before they start.'
They had no plan. Long ago they had learnt that a plan
was useless because they could have no idea what they
would be up against. Speed and ruthlessness was all that
they had going for them. To date, it was all that they had
needed.

Habib shoved the crossbar and charged out of the hotel,
Fredericks right behind him. Neither man made for the
car, as by now it could be under surveillance. Instead, they
sprinted for the back, zig-zagging as they ran, crouched,
ready to shoot, more deadly than two angry mambas.

As soon as the doors had been flung open an alarm
bell had sounded at reception. Albatha had been talking
to the woman, asking her about the hotel layout, where
the doors were, could they be opened.

'What the . . . What's that?' he asked stupidly, knowing the answer already.

She glanced at a panel behind her where a red light was flashing.

'Come on, quickly. Which door is that?' Even as he was asking he was grabbing his gun.

'Side door. Around to the left,' with that she dropped to the floor and tried to squeeze herself under the counter. In any other circumstance Zim Albatha would have found it hilariously funny. As it was, he didn't see her antics as he was already charging out of the door.

For a big man he moved surprisingly fast. Although his gun was at the ready the other two had a distinct advantage. Whereas they could and would shoot anything that moved, he needed to be sure of his target before he could fire.

The rain was even heavier now. In the car park, as he dodged between the cars, rushing for the side entrance, he saw and heard nothing. At any moment he expected one of them to appear. His shoulder blades crawled with the anticipation of a bullet. Nothing. At the corner of the building he paused to look round, saw nobody and began to move quickly towards the bushes that separated the road from the grounds of the hotel. Even as he reached them he heard the shots, and, thinking of Alim, ran headlong onto the road.

She had left the car and in spite of the rain had settled behind a stunted tree next to the road. Above the noise of the traffic she had heard nothing, but in the glare of the lights had seen both men run out from the bushes directly towards her. She could see their bags and the guns they held. She didn't give it a second thought but started firing. Three shots in quick succession sent both men sprawling to the ground and rolling for cover. Neither bothered to return fire as they hadn't seen where the shots had come from. Instead, they began running back the way they'd come.

In the headlights of an oncoming car they saw the big man running into view, a gun in his hand.

The traffic was not as heavy as earlier, as the flight from Tehran had been the last for the evening. Even so, there were still cars and lorries moving in both directions. Albatha looked at where he had left Alim sitting in the car, but could not see her. He saw the two men thirty metres away running towards him but had wasted time looking for Alim. The first bullet hit him in the right shoulder and spun him round, which saved his life. The second hit him in the left with a blow which knocked him off his feet.

He lay still, unable to grasp what had happened. He heard them running past and then the sounding of a horn and shriek of tyres. He recognised the cough of a silenced gun and a car engine being revved, fading in the distance.

The next moment Alim was bending over him. 'Zim, Zim, are you all right?'

He nodded. He was an immensely strong man. Even so it was still lucky for him that in order to reduce the noise from their guns, Habib and Fredericks used shells which were doctored to have a lighter than usual load. At close quarters they were still formidable weapons and if he had been hit in a vital spot he would have been killed. As it was the bullets had left him unable to use his arms, but he sat himself up and got to his knees. He stayed there for a few seconds, gathering his strength, his head hung down. Alim thought he was more seriously injured than he really was, as the rain was mixing with the blood and saturating his clothes, spreading down both arms and across his chest. She could not see that he had his eyes closed, berating himself.

She knelt by his side and said, 'Stay still. I'll send for an ambulance.'

He looked at her. 'Thank Allah you're not hurt. I thought . . .'

She smiled, tears glistening in her eyes for the pain he was in. 'I did as you told me. I fired straight away.'

He forced a smile. He was not yet in pain, although he could feel it starting. With a gunshot wound the shock is so great initially that the nerves are overloaded and are unable to carry the message of pain to the brain. As the shock wears off the pain starts, though he would carry it stoically.

'Don't bother with an ambulance. We'll wait for the others to get here. They can radio for an ambulance. What happened?'

'I saw them running and I fired at them. They turned to run away and then I saw you. I didn't fire for fear of hitting you. I didn't hear anything but I saw you fall over. I ran here and saw them stop a car. I . . . I think they killed the driver. They got away heading into the city.' She stopped speaking as cars drew up around them, disgorging armed men. They had a lot of explaining to do. What, thought Albatha, had gone wrong?

3

About the only place in the United Kingdom that was manned by government employees and worked normal hours on a weekend was GCHQ at Cheltenham. It was the listening post of the UK, eavesdropping on conversations throughout the country and receiving satellite information from all over the world. Computers listened in to millions of voices on mobile and land-based telephones and, if certain words were used, those conversations were brought to the attention of people whose job it was to assess what was being said. For years GCHQ's reason for existence had been to listen in to signal traffic between the USSR and its military facilities world wide. This had meant the monitoring of traffic to their nuclear submarines, orders to their ships at sea and routine instructions to land-based establishments whether army, air force or navy. As the direct threat from the USSR had declined and with the cold war effectively at an end, more and more personnel and equipment at Cheltenham were being turned towards fighting terrorism. To help them in their fight, the computers had been programmed to listen for words like drugs, explosives, blackmail, extortion, murder, assassination, terror or terrorist.

In the war against terrorism there were whole agencies of people investigating money laundering. The listening deviccs were tuned to key words like bank, cash, money, millions, dollars, yen and other currencies. Not surprisingly, with such everyday words in constant use the computers had extremely sophisticated search algorithms. Once the "innocent" conversations were eliminated, a second recording device replayed the potentially suspect conversations to teams of human operators. The whole sequence was taking place continuously, completed in seconds, until the recording was stored and transferred to the operators. If they were lucky the listeners worked only six hours behind the recording. If they were unlucky, due to heavy traffic, they could be as much as thirty-six hours behind. Massive effort was being put into the development of the software to reduce still further the requirement for a human listener and although there had been great strides forward there was still too much for the humans to do with the resources of manpower available. Not yet being sold commercially, the computers at GCHQ could take virtually any language in the world and translate it into English. This was already saving a vast amount of time because previously the translators and the listeners often were not the same people. It had taken years and tens of millions of pounds to develop the software to an acceptable standard whereby the speech and translation were correct to 99.1% accuracy. The final 0.9% was deemed impossible to resolve within a reasonable cost frame.

In space, satellites were being used to photograph the world in amazing detail, the boast in some quarters being that it was possible to read a newspaper held in the target's hands. Geostationary or Geosynchronous satellites orbited the earth in a fixed position relative to the equator, relaying aural and ocular information constantly. Other satellites could be sent into a different orbit by the simple expedient of programming in to the controlling computer the new latitude and longitude to search. The only problem was the change in orbital pattern which was relatively slight and so there had to be a satellite in the vicinity of a specific target in the first place. The joke amongst astronauts was that there was so much rubbish flying around space that soon it would be as busy as Interstate 95 in America or the M25 in England. GCHQ could identify with the M25 comparison.

Over thirty years' of rubbish, obsolete and useless, was orbiting the earth. It neither rusted away nor left orbit unless, as sometimes happened, a satellite gradually worked its way into a decaying orbit and eventually burnt itself up as it hit the earth's atmosphere. As that was all too rare an event and as the nations of the world were launching new craft at a rate of at least one a month, space was getting crowded. TV stations were proliferating around the globe and nearly all the new ones were by way of satellite transmission. There was an advantage to the authorities every time a commercial enterprise sent something into space. A part of the spacecraft or the satellite was used by the different governments to their own ends; usually aimed at anti-terrorism for their own protection only. However, for the first time there was real co-operation between governments and a sharing of all information, not just the selected edited versions of previous years.

One of the satellites was on an orbital track which took it over the Middle East. Originally the task of WS27, a designation meaning weather station number twenty seven, was to track the weather. Everything from cloud patterns, wind strengths and direction to the formation of storms. It was all fed back to earth. Because the satellite could read temperatures at specific spots on the earth to an accuracy of 0.1 degrees centigrade, another use had been found for WS27 and some of her sisters. It could tell if certain areas of the world were populated by comparing the temperature of the ground with that of any bodies in the area. For instance, there were twenty-three training camps currently in use around the world where the core subject was terrorism. Six of these were in the Middle East: two in Iran, two in Iraq, one in Syria and one in Yemen.

After years of monitoring the camps, certain information had become evident. They were normally in use for ten to twelve weeks at a time either as basic training camps or for more specialised work, particularly when they had a specific target. It was found that whenever a camp emptied, someone somewhere in the world found themselves on the receiving end of terrorism. In the UK, there were different alert states, depending upon the terrorist threat, called bikini alerts. Bikini green was the lowest with no expected terrorism activity in the foreseeable future. By 1996 it had been many years since bikini green was in force. Bikini amber, red and black followed. The first was the normal state. It said, "be alert something is in the offing but we don't know where, how, what, or who." Bikini red, an all too regular alert state said, "something's up, but as yet we don't know what, but there's danger in the air." Extra vigilance was needed everywhere, airports were warned, as were all military and government places in the UK. Bikini black was issued when a strike by terrorists was imminent.

Bikini black did not say where, how, what or who. Just that it was.

From the satellite readings she had received, Sarah Fleeting knew that the camp near Khvor in Iran had been vacated. She double-checked her readings, made a note and began to put together everything she had on Khvor.

Sarah was a divorcee. She had married at the age of twenty-three after graduating from Oxford with a double first in Far Eastern politics and with a special knowledge of the Chinese. She could speak passable Mandarin and could identify at least a dozen other dialects used in China. By the logic of the civil service she was ideally suited to work on the Middle Eastern station! After twenty-two years of marriage, no children and more abuse than she cared to remember, she had walked out. That was two years earlier. Now forty-seven, she was wedded to her job. Which was just as well, because although she had been blessed with a brilliant mind she knew that men did not find her particularly alluring. She had a figure best described as dumpy, hair that hung straight to her shoulders and was best described as lank, and wore old-fashioned horn-rimmed glasses which made her look much older than she was. She had a fair complexion and steady, hazel eyes, which saw the humour in most things. She also had a kind heart. By the time she had realised that she did not have to suffer the abuse she received from her high-flying, civil-servant husband, she had built a barrier between herself and other people, especially men. She had no friends outside of her work, but many acquaintances within it. As she actually liked people and their company she spent an inordinate amount of time at GCHQ. She stood in for other members of her team whenever they asked, sometimes volunteering even when they did not.

At her level of seniority she normally would not have been monitoring a satellite pass but evaluating the results. Today she was doing both.

After she finished, she sat at her desk for a few moments, her hands automatically reaching for her hand-bag and a packet of cigarettes, whilst she thought about her findings. Even as she was groping inside her bag she said "damn" to herself and withdrew her hands remembering that it was now (she looked at the bank of clocks along the far wall) six days, five hours and a few minutes since she had stopped smoking. She had been aghast at her latest medical check-up the previous week to find she had progressed to over forty cigarettes a day. Something she had not thought about until she was asked. She had disdained the use of anti-smoking patches, preferring to use her will power. She found her craving for the weed came and went depending upon what she was doing. She was fascinated by the analysis she was making of her own nicotine dependency. Sarah had quickly realised that most of the time she did not want a cigarette but that she had derived pleasure from handling the box, taking one out, using her gold Dunhill lighter. There had been no real craving. Then it would hit her. She craved a cigarette like the nicotine addict she was and had to stop herself from lighting up. The craving would pass after a short while and she could stop thinking about it. Immersing herself in her work sometimes helped but now, right now, she really did want a cigarette, badly.

She opened the file again and read it through, to make sure it was all there. Like all the operational files this one was classified secret, not just because of its contents but because it could also give away how the information was gathered. It was her job to write the conclusion. She did not like what she saw.

She drummed her fingers on the desk, aware with a part of her mind that she kept looking for the comfort of a cigarette, almost like a baby which wants its dummy or, more appropriately known by her American friends, its comforter, because that's what it was, a comfort in times of unhappiness or stress. Right now, it was stress she wanted to relieve. To do so she stood up and paced her small office, thinking out her conclusions, unaware of her surroundings and the knowing looks being thrown at her from her colleagues on the other side of the glass partition.

Sarah occupied a corner room which contained a desk and swivel chair, three filing cabinets, two other straight-backed chairs for visitors and a coffee table stuck in a corner. Two of the corner walls were brick and had no windows. The other two projected into a large room and were made of partitioning to waist height and glass above. With the door closed, the room was sound proof. Right now it was open and if she had bothered to look Sarah would have been able to see over the heads of every occupant there, as her room was raised two feet higher than the rest. Strictly speaking, it was not just her room. Even at her level of seniority, she shared the room with the night supervisor who was also her deputy. In order to work a little privacy into the system, Sarah had the drawers in the right side of the desk, her deputy had the left.

The main room looked like Hollywood's idea of a space mission control centre, which in some respects it was. There were banks of computer screens, all manned. A huge screen completely filled one wall showing the world like the open pages of an atlas. Lines moved slowly across the screen showing the paths of satellites – blue lines for those controlled by the UK and red for those over which they had no control but had access to the information transmitted. The same picture was also on the screens of the twenty-four manned consuls as analysts monitored world-wide activity. Each one could take a part of the picture and home in on an area of the world in which he or she was working. On her desk, Sarah had an enlarged picture of the Middle East. It was being recorded automatically and so there was no need for her to sit and watch the screen. She already knew what was going on, up to a point. That was the frustrating thing, the point at which her knowledge ended. If she knew more, it was possible she could prevent a new disaster occurring. She sighed. That was always the problem; the point at which her analysis ended and sheer conjecture began.

She thought about the cluster of buildings, eleven kilometres from Khvor and hence named after the local town. To get to Khvor was not easy. From Tehran it was five hundred kilometres to the south east along some of the worst roads imaginable. Situated eight hundred metres above sea level, it was surrounded to the north, south and west by mountains reaching four thousand metres high. It was a bleak and desolate place, hot in the summer, freezing in the winter, particularly at night. It had been in use for at least twenty years or more, originally as a training camp for the Shah of Iran's elite personal guard. There were ten huts, nine of which could sleep ten people. These formed three sides of a quadrangle, three huts down each side. The fourth, larger hut, was for the instructors and managers of the camp. It was usually unoccupied unless being used for a specific purpose. If it had been occupied this time for ten or more weeks then Sarah would have known that a new batch of terrorists were being trained and sent out upon an unsuspecting world. Because the first sign of activity had been barely three weeks earlier and the camp was already deserted, then, from the historic pattern of things, she knew that whoever had been occupying the place had been training for a specific target. WS27 was a clever beast. It had cruised serenely through space, recording all the information asked of it. Then, when it discovered the difference of temperature between the normal, unoccupied buildings out in the desert and the body heat thrown out by humans in situ, it sent an alert to the computers which immediately alerted the listeners. They were called "the listeners" in a hangover from the old days when that was all they could do – listen in on radio transmissions. Once the satellite had alerted the listeners they had sent the requisite radio signals to change its orbit slightly, so that WS27 passed directly over the camp. The probing equipment carried in the satellite was now focused onto the camp, so that better information could be gleaned. Every time it passed over, Sarah had been able to count individual bodies by the heat they radiated and been able to work out their movements and guess what they were up to. During the period she identified seven night exercises and the firing of at least three hand-held missiles. From the data she thought they were Stingers, anti-helicopter and anti-aircraft, once only missiles, favoured by military forces the world over and by terrorist groups in particular. Shoot, forget and throw the launcher away. The missile homed in on the target by itself, without any further guidance. In the case of a jet aircraft it went for the exhaust from the engines; in the case of a helicopter it went for the heat radiated from the engine. It was virtually impossible to dodge but it could be confused by counter measures. Altogether a very nasty and dangerous bit of hardware and used by terrorist groups only when the target was out of the ordinary. Usually, terrorists stuck to simple, old-fashioned bombs that could be hidden on a person or in a suit case. Like Lockerbie.

Sarah had known that on two occasions the camp had been visited by two men who arrived by helicopter but had only stayed for a few hours at most. The previous Saturday someone had arrived by helicopter. In the middle of the night, Iranian time four o'clock, or one o'clock GMT, the camp had quickly been abandoned. The latest set of readings from WS27 showed that nobody was left behind.

By cross-referencing activity at the camp and a short while later a terrorist incident somewhere in the world Sarah had, a few years earlier, come to certain conclusions which were confirmed by later events. She was as certain as she could be that within a week, and at the outside a month, something would happen. It could be a bombing, an assassination, although that was rare, or a hijacking. To date, it had always been an incident in the Western world; although there was always a first time for everything, she thought. It could involve one suicide bomber, the other occupants doing further training for other jobs; or perhaps the other occupants were there to encourage the poor, deluded bomber who was going to meet his God. Or perhaps it was a job which needed the whole team. Ten to fifteen people was a very big team by terrorist standards. So what could be that big to need so many, unless it was an attack like the one at the Munich Olympics? Christ, the World Cup in France! Okay, the time scale was not right because they were not due to start until July but it was a big enough target to warrant a lot of resources. And from the Arab point of view what could be better than an attack on Europe? Perhaps against the American football team? The more she thought about it the more sure she became that she was on the right track.

It was the only error she made in her analysis.

Her superior was a Permanent Secretary with enough clout to get through to Downing Street if he needed to. In this case he didn't need to go that far up the chain of command. What he did was to go much further in metaphysical distance and call a contact of his at the CIA in Langley.

'Jim Baker,' came the southern drawl over the phone.

'Jim, it's Clive Paterson.'

'Clive! Hi, buddy! How's it going in little old England?'

Paterson and Baker had met briefly when Baker had been serving in the American Embassy in the late eighties. He had visited GCHQ and struck up a tentative friendship with Paterson. It had blossomed sufficiently for the two men to meet occasionally for a drink whenever they visited the other's turf and the previous year for Paterson and his family to visit Baker and his family for a few days before going on to Disneyland in Florida. Baker liked to hide one of the best analytical brains in Langley behind southern states buffoonery. The act fooled those who did not matter and did not fool those who did.

Paterson smiled. After exchanging pleasantries and asking after each other's families Paterson got to the point. 'Jim, what have you got on Khvor?'

Baker thought for a few seconds before he replied. 'Not a lot. It had been in use and now it's not.'

'You remember Sarah Fleeting when you were here

last? I introduced her to you when you came to talk about the bomb at your base in Saudi last year.'

'Sure, I remember,' the drawl had gone as his mind started to race. 'I was sure impressed by some of the conclusions she had reached. Her analysis helped us a lot to track down the bastards who did it.' The fact was Sarah had come to the same conclusions as Baker but from a different angle. However, jointly they had been able to help the CIA track down the men responsible for the bombing of a US base which had resulted in the deaths of twenty-three servicemen. The four men, a cell belonging to an organisation dedicated to the overthrow of the Saudi ruling family, had been beheaded on Christmas Day 1995. One thing about Saudi Arabia was that justice was swift and merciless; no keeping prisoners on death row for years.

'Well, Sarah has been monitoring Khvor closely over the years and has come to conclusions which for the past five years have proven to be right.'

'Carry on, I'm listening,' came the laconic reply.

'Well, she thinks that there's going to be a terrorist attack soon and that the obvious target will be France, the World Cup, in a few months.'

After a few seconds for thought Baker said, 'That's what my boys tell me but I don't get it. It doesn't fit the pattern of a maximum thirty days between abandoning the camp and something going down.'

Paterson smiled. You lived in your own little ivory tower and thought you were the only people working on the problem and coming to the right conclusions when all the time other governments with first class analysts were doing the same. Why the hell didn't they work more closely together and share what they knew?

'Yes, that's what Sarah said as well. But with a force as big as this one what else could it be?'

'I don't know. I'm thinking about it. I've got one of my people looking at all major events programmed for the next few months to see if we can come up with a better target.'

'What, from their point of view, can be better or bigger than the World Cup if the American team's targeted?'

'I take your point, Clive, and I don't disagree, but I heard something mighty interesting in the bar downstairs the other day.' Langley not only had its own fitness club but also a superb bar and restaurant.

Paterson's curiosity was piqued and he asked, 'What was that?'

'Well, it seems like our Secretary of State sent for a few of the Ambassadors from a few of the, shall we say, less friendly countries and gave them a warning.'

'Oh? What sort of warning?'

'It seems that he told them in no uncertain terms that we would be seriously pissed off with them if they tried anything in France. Good old Uncle Sam would be down on them like a ton of bricks and damn the consequences. It seems that they didn't like the undiplomatic way in which the message was given but, boy, they sure understood it.'

Paterson smiled. 'That's a turn up for the books. Any idea what was specifically threatened?'

'I can't be sure because it's speculation. But . . .' Baker hesitated, although they were friends, how much could he tell him? What the hell, he was only repeating a rumour after all. 'It seems that Mr. Secretary told them that if any country did anything during the World Cup then the leaders and top brass of the country or

61

countries involved would be assassinated – and that was a promise.'

'How could that be done? Congress would never stand for it. If you tried to do something like that in secret then all that would happen is it would appear on CNN forty-eight hours later instead of twenty-four!'

'That's more or less what I said.'

'So?'

'So. It appears that the President is prepared to go out on a limb and use his executive powers under the Clear and Present Danger Order for the people of America. He sees it, and I suppose rightly, as his duty to protect the citizens of the USA and he would put this in that category.

'Would he get away with it?'

'I don't know. Probably. The people here are getting mightily sick of the way we're treated by the likes of Iran and Iraq. A powerful response would be very popular. And let's face it, provided all went well, the President has little to lose and a lot to gain.'

'That's a big proviso. Remember Carter and the fiasco over the hostages in Iran?'

Paterson was referring to an operation in the early '80s when Iranians had stormed the Embassy in Tehran and taken the staff and their families hostage. Over two hundred people had been kept in poor conditions for weeks. A rescue attempt had failed disastrously, which had seriously dented the esteem and self respect of Americans.

'A lot was learnt from that mess. And anyway, it's nineteen ninety-eight and now, let me tell you, we really do have the ability to perform. All that's been lacking for the last fifteen years is the will.'

Paterson knew that to be the truth. The men and equipment were ready and available. Only the will to fight back at the terrorist supporting regimes was lacking and had been for too long.

'My God,' said Baker. 'What about the summit in two days time?'

He was referring to a meeting which was due to take place in France. At the invitation of President Clinton the heads of governments of the Western allies, along with their ministers of defence, were meeting to discuss a way of combating terrorism on a world-wide scale. It had been hailed by the media as a breakthrough in the fight which involved all free men and women, the world over.

'Too soon,' Paterson replied. He scribbled the words "summit" on a piece of paper and "2 days" after it and showed it to Sarah. She nodded agreement and mouthed, 'too soon', as well. 'Sarah agrees with me. The protection measures in place for the meeting are too good. The French have been fully co-operative for the first time since the Second World War and anyway, they are no slouches when it comes to this sort of work.'

'True enough. Well, I'll see what else I can find that will look like a suitable target. Unless, of course . . .' Baker paused.

'Unless, of course, what?'

'Unless of course, they go for that meeting in a fortnight's time, in Wales.'

Paterson thought a moment. 'It's a possibility, but what the hell have they got to gain by attacking a bunch of finance ministers discussing third world poverty?'

'Who said they had anything to gain? Whenever has anything been gained, no matter what they've done? We both know we aren't dealing with rational people.'

63

Paterson nodded in agreement. 'Look, I'll be passing everything on, obviously. After all, we're only the analysts. Wales is a target, no matter how unlikely. I don't really see it but we can't be too careful. Anything else you can think of?'

'Not at the moment. There's the usual, of course. But we're as ready as we can be. The bikini states will be raised fairly soon I expect and then all we can do is sit and wait.'

Sitting and waiting summed up their whole existence. Analysis, followed by forecasting which was really educated guessing, and sitting and waiting for something to happen; followed by clearing up the mess. Even desk bound senior managers like Paterson and Baker fretted at their lack of control in preventing terrorism. The procedures of the courts hamstrung the Western world into virtual total paralysis.

'You're right. There's nothing else we can do at present. Give Sarah my best and tell her the minute she thinks of any more possibilities to let me know about it.'

They said their goodbyes and hung up.

Paterson said to Sarah, 'You heard most of that. Is Wales an option do you think?'

'You know as well as I do that anything's possible with these people. I still think the World Cup is a likely target no matter what Jim told us.'

'Do you think it's true – the rumour about Clinton warning the Ambassadors?'

'Curiously enough, I do. I think that Clinton has a feel for reading the American people and responding accordingly. He's a second-term president who wants his VP to win next time; and he thinks he can win it for them, in spite of his problems with Monica. The Americans, as well as the rest of us, are fed up by the way Iran and Iraq and a few others behave. So yes, I could see him doing that. But,' she paused, thinking, 'but, it could backfire and the response of the Mullahs and Saddam is to hit and hit hard. It will be interesting to see if either country sends any teams to France,' Sarah added as an afterthought.

There was a knock on the door and a messenger put his head in. 'Sorry to trouble you, but I thought you ought to look at this. It's a signal from Turkey. Seems their boys have been having some trouble over there.' He handed the sheet of paper to Paterson and with a cheery nod left them alone. Paterson quickly scanned the signal and handed it to Sarah, wordlessly.

Sarah read it and put the paper on the desk between them. They both stared at it as though it was going to bite one of them. 'Habib,' was all she said after a few moments silence.

'Yes, our old friend. Or rather,' Paterson said, hastily. 'Your old friend.' He was referring to the private file that Sarah had been keeping on Habib for years. Paterson had found her adding to it some time ago and asked her what she was doing. She had explained her theory about Habib. His involvement with so many of the attacks which had taken place in the past and his motivation. Money. Paterson had read the file and was of the opinion that although there was a lot of merit in it, it was all supposition and circumstantial. Nothing for a court to use. To which Sarah had replied, somewhat enigmatically at the time, that it was not for the use of a court.

'The coincidence is too much,' she said. 'Habib is on the move. The camp is empty; the World Cup in a few months time. Something is going to happen and it will be very, very big.'

Her words were prophetic, only neither of them realised how big.

4

P.M. 22 April 1998. HMS Dryad, *Hampshire, England.*

It was the start of the weekend, and a mess dinner was due to begin in two and a half hours time, at 20.00. Hunter had just finished a load of paperwork and stood up to stretch his aching limbs. He hated sitting still for too long. He was now a Lieutenant Commander having received his half stripe just two days earlier. He locked away the papers, checked the safe was fastened securely and let himself out of his office. Since the encounter with Jessop and the mine he had been busy at HMS *Dryad*. His thoughts wandered to Doreen Jessop and then he dismissed her from his mind and instead, thought about his future. He had been at the job for a year with another year to go. At the end of his tour he could expect to be sent as the First Lieutenant of a frigate – all in all, not a bad prospect but not one he found particularly exciting. Except for this new thing.

He left the building and walked the half mile to the wardroom. He was staying "on board" for the weekend – all shore bases in the Royal Navy are spoken of as if they were ships, hence the term "a stone frigate". Normally he would have been in the cottage but this weekend not only was there the dinner to attend, but he was also duty Lieutenant Commander. This meant that he was responsible to the Captain for the running of the whole establishment out of normal working hours and over the weekend. In effect, after hundreds of years of practice, the navy ran the place like clockwork and only needed a prod now and again when somebody slipped up. There were seldom slip-ups and with the dinner that evening attended by the First Sea Lord and sundry other senior officers from the different services, there was even less likelihood of any occurring.

He walked past the hall porter and went to look at the plan of the evening's seating arrangements which was pinned to the notice board by the door. He was relieved to see he was surrounded by friends which would help a pleasant evening pass even more pleasantly. He walked along the corridor to the cabin with a sign on it which said DUTY LIEUTENANT COMMANDER and let himself in. As with all Royal Naval shore establishments the public rooms bordered on the spectacular, with their paintings, photographs and decor, whilst the private cabins were something else. Small, poky and uninspiring, they left a lot to be desired. There was just sufficient room for a bunk with drawers underneath, a desk by the window, a wardrobe and a wash hand basin next to it.

He stripped off his uniform and hung it away, and changed into shorts, a tee-shirt and running shoes. He looked out of the window to remind himself of the weather, thought about it and slipped on a track suit top. Although the day had been unusually mild, there was now a distinct chill in the air. He left the cabin and went back to the main entrance.

'Chief,' he said to the hall porter, 'I'm going up

to the playing fields for a run. Be about forty minutes.'

'Right you are, sir,' replied ex-Chief Petty Officer Blakely. 'If anyone comes looking for you I'll send them up. The Commander was prowling about a while ago, checking on things for this evening. He seemed happy with everything . . . so far,' he added.

Hunter smiled. The dinner had been planned to the "nth" degree by a man who liked planning to the "nth" degree – the Commander. It always surprised those who had served with and who were now serving with Commander Ronald Huggins, that he had been promoted as far as Commander. Perhaps it was his inordinate capacity to pay attention to detail which had earned him his promotion. Whatever it was, it was not his leadership and people skills. Other officers were beginning to arrive and, nodding to one or two, Hunter walked smartly out through the swing doors.

He broke into a jog and headed for the playing fields about three quarters of a mile away. After the day he'd had he felt the need to work up a good sweat and to get the endorphins flowing through his body. As he reached the running track which ran around the perimeter of the rugby and soccer fields, he opened up his stride and picked up the pace. He was no longer jogging but into a serious run. His pace was a mile in five minutes and he could keep it up long enough to have been a serious contender for a medal in the marathon at the Olympic games. As he ran his mind wandered over the past fortnight. It may have been a Chinese curse to live in interesting times, but for him, it was the spice of life.

The previous week he had been sent on a three-day seminar held at HMS *Mercury*, the communications headquarters of the Royal Navy. There, he had been introduced to Colonel Robert Macnair, an anti-terrorist specialist who had done three tours in the Special Air Service (SAS) during his career. This in itself said a lot for the man, as normally only the troops and NCOs were full time in the SAS. The officers were drafted in if they were deemed good enough for a tour of duty with what was, without doubt, one of the toughest and most resourceful regiments ever to have existed in any army in the world. Macnair was now working with other NATO officers, including the Americans, to find a way to combat what was seen as the greatest scourge of the last years of the twentieth century – terrorism. His ideas were so far only that – just ideas. However, Macnair now had the full backing of his senior officers and, more importantly, their political masters, to create a force with all the resources necessary to combat terrorism world wide. He was now beginning to put into being an organisation, European based, which would be in the forefront of the fight.

Needless to say, with their elite Delta Force already available, the Americans had argued that they should create and control the new organisation, using Delta Force as the core. However, with the whole of their allies ranged against them, the Americans were forced to accept a European led, controlled and stationed operation. Colonel Macnair was about to be promoted to Lieutenant General and given the command. His number two would be an American named Colonel Hiram B. Walsh, presently a senior officer with Delta Force. The remainder of the staff would be highly qualified, carefully selected officers from America and other European armed services. Furthermore, for the first time ever, the invitation had gone out to Russia, who had accepted the offer to help fight world-wide terrorism.

Hunter remembered the first briefing he had attended and the opening words of General Macnair. 'If we are to fight terrorism, protect our people and punish the perpetrators then we need the best we have available. All of you here today have been chosen because, according to your records, you are the best. You will form the nucleus of the organisation which will operate solely in the anti-terrorist role. At present we have no base, no headquarters, no equipment, few men, no . . . no nothing,' he'd smiled as his audience of thirty-three people chuckled with him. He'd given them a few moments to think about what he'd said and to look around the room at each other, as they began to be more aware of who they each were and what they represented.

Hunter was intrigued as well as interested. He had been at the Falklands as a Sub Lieutenant on board HMS *Antrim*, a guided-missile destroyer, now in moth balls, as the governmental cutbacks continued to bite. He had enjoyed his time on *Antrim*, a County Class destroyer designed to protect aircraft carriers. She had sustained a direct hit with a bomb on her helicopter flight deck from an Argentinean aircraft. Luckily, the bomb had failed to explode. The flight deck officer, who was also the ship's supply commander when the ship was not at action stations, had cleared the flight deck and bravely manhandled the bomb over the side. Hunter had helped him. It was after that, that Hunter decided to become a bomb and mine disposal specialist. At least then, should the same happen again, he'd have a better idea of what he was doing.

The course he took to qualify lasted nearly a year

and was deemed to be the most physically tough in the RN. Of the five original lieutenants who had started only three survived to the end. Since qualifying, Hunter had blown up or rendered harmless, more than two dozen mines and bombs. Of the other two who had qualified with him, one had resigned and taken up a job in the offshore diving industry and the other had gone back to general service, relinquishing his specialisation pay – thirty pounds a day danger money. In the meantime, Hunter had gone on to work for two years with the Royal Engineers, the real experts in IEDs. Impromptu explosive devices was the term used to describe a terrorist's home-made bomb. Hunter had become one of the best in the field when it came to IEDs. Because of this, coupled with his underwater experience, he was at the anti-terrorist meeting, chaired by Macnair.

'I was going to suggest that if there are any questions, you ask as we go along. However, as I will probably cover most of them during the course of the morning, why don't you write them down and ask me anything you like at the end?' There were a number of nods of agreement to Macnair's question and most of the occupants of the room began to write.

During his briefing Macnair covered everything from establishing a base at Plymouth in the Naval docks, where there was a vast array of buildings and offices empty and available, to the need for liaison work with all the armed forces of friendly nations, to the vast computer network and data bank he was intending to create.

'Of all the different things needing to be done I consider the data bank to be the most important. Indeed, I have already agreed budgets and started work putting together a team of operatives to get that side of things up and

running as quickly as possible. Already, we have begun
to download information from systems across the world
on potential and actual terrorists. We've been building
up a profile on their *modus operandi* and trying, most
importantly, to get to the bottom of their ways and
means of funding their activities. I have managed to
head hunt a very talented lady from an international
software company to head up the department and she has
already come up with an array of ideas and suggestions
which will enable us to create the most comprehensive
data base in the world. Her name is Isobel Sweeney and
you'll meet her later this afternoon.'

While Macnair had been talking Hunter had written a
few headings down which he would want to cover, the
first of which was financing, underlined three times. In
this day and age of cut-backs and options for change and
rationalisation and all the other political names meaning
less money, less hardware and less people, where was
the funding coming from?

'I am aware that there must be at least,' Macnair paused
and allowed himself a smile, 'thirty-three cynics amongst
you.' His audience chuckled. 'So let me talk briefly about
funding this venture.' Hunter was aware of the raising of
heads and the quickening of interest and realised that he
had not been alone in thinking that financing was an
important issue. 'When I was asked a year ago to examine
this whole subject and to make my recommendations, I
did so on the basis of a number of conditions. The first
was that if I did come up with what we needed would
it be implemented or would it be a venture in futility,
as is so often the case? On that point I was assured that
whatever I suggested would be treated with the utmost
seriousness and due regard given etc., etc. I needn't spell

it out. What I was being told was it may or may not see the light of day.

'I completed my report six months ago and, as we say in the army, as quick as a flash, nothing happened.' Again, there were wry chuckles as each officer identified with the joke. 'Then, everything changed. With the bombings in America and the twenty-five point plan agreed ten days ago in France to combat terrorism, my report saw the light of day again.' There were nods from around the room. Everyone there had seen the recommendations from the summit meeting of Western leaders, which were fine on the rhetoric but sadly lacking in detail. A politician's charter to do nothing was one description of the result of the summit. 'What was not said, and will not be made public just yet, is the real work which we, this new organisation, will carry out in the fight against terrorism. Thanks to President Clinton and our Secretary of State for Defence – who convinced our PM it was a good political idea,' there were grins in the audience, 'we have actually managed to agree with our partners in NATO that something needs to be done. That something is to fight terrorists with their own weapons.' There was a stirring of bodies. A frisson of excitement circulated the room. At long last, they were all thinking.

'Funding will be reasonable,' a few groaned, 'but, and it's a big but, all the original costing and planning submitted by me will be met.' Macnair gave a wide, toothy grin. 'Please, believe me when I say that I did not stint in my original proposals. I think that if you come onboard, none of you will be disappointed with the outcome.' He paused to allow his words to sink in.

'You are all aware, as you look about you, that we have quite a representation from different countries within the EU and one representative from our, em, American cousins. With the singular exception of the Swedes, every Western European country has agreed to work with us and, of course, the Americans. The Swedes are not being ruled out at this stage but suffice to say that they will not be with us this year. Before I go any further, I appreciate that this is the first time you have heard anything about this and I think I have said enough to whet your appetites. Is there anyone here who does not wish to continue with this briefing with a view to becoming an integral part of this organisation? Please indicate now and I will ask you kindly to leave.' As Macnair had half growled his last comments a few of them wondered how kindly that would be. All heads scanned the room but nobody moved a muscle. 'Good,' he continued, highly satisfied. Then a hand was raised.

'Yes, Otto?' asked the General, with a raising of the eyebrows.

Otto von Gehrig was wearing the uniform of the German army, his tabs showing the rank of Captain. His bull-necked, thick-set body looked as tough as an oak tree, his voice sounding like the rasp of a file on metal. 'Sir, have you agreed secondment arrangements, terms of service and so on?' he asked reasonably, in perfect, unaccented English.

'Yes, I have. It will be a two-year posting, if you want it. The fact that none of you have raised a hand to leave suggests that you wish to join me in this, em, enterprise, shall we say? However, I shall be asking you at the end of the next few days, to take a week to think about it, before making a final decision. I needn't remind you all that you are subject to your own national equivalents of our Official Secrets Act and so anything you learn here will not be talked about with anyone outside these four walls. This also means that you will be unable to seek advice from anyone, but will have to make up your own minds. Which, incidentally, looking at your files, I can't see as a problem.' There were more chuckles. Macnair knew the calibre of the men he was addressing. All of them were extremely tough – physically and mentally – and all had complementary skills which, he hoped, would form the nucleus of his force. The most junior man there was an SAS sergeant, the most senior an REME Major who was one of the world's foremost experts on terrorist bombs. The remainder were lieutenant commanders and lieutenants from various navies, captains and lieutenants from European armies and senior enlisted men from all of the services. There were three pilots – a Royal Naval Lieutenant Commander, an RAF Lieutenant and a French Air Force Captain. From the hundreds of confidential files he had trawled through to find the audience he was now addressing, these three were considered to be the best helicopter pilots in Europe. It was an accolade he did not intend sharing with them. In Macnair's opinion, pilots already had inflated enough egos.

'Sir,' Hunter held up his hand. 'I know you said to wait to the end before asking any questions but do you seriously expect to keep us secret from the newspapers and the general public?'

'No,' came the blunt reply. 'My intention is to get the whole thing up and running before anyone takes a close interest in us. If we are lucky we will have a month or so before anybody starts asking too many of the right questions. By that time we will be a *fait accompli* and, I think, once we are known, we'll have the backing of the public.' There were further nods from around the room.

Another hand went up and a French accented voice asked, 'Sir, you said that we will be fighting the terrorists with their own weapons. Will that mean,' the speaker gave a Gallic shrug, raising the palms of his hands a few inches, 'shooting before we ask questions?'

'Henri, thank you for that but I'll come to it later. Look, I know you are all burning with questions which I promise you I'll answer but just leave it for now and let me continue. I think you'll appreciate why when I've finished.'

They did. Macnair spoke all morning, he never once referred to any notes as he occasionally moved from one side of the room to the other, using an overhead projector and a flip chart to make his points.

The three days that followed left them with their questions answered, a real excitement in the air and a feeling that at long last something was going to be done against the unseen enemy.

They were targeted at state terrorism.

Hunter's thoughts had taken him for nearly sixty minutes around the running track and he slowed down. He was sweating heavily in spite of the drop in temperature since the sun had set, and he made his way back to his cabin. He had never had any doubts but, replaying the time with Macnair in his head, he was convinced that he wanted to be a part of whatever the General organised. The scope of their charter was such that it inspired them all to think that, at long last, governments world wide were ready to fight the terrorists with both hands, not, as was more common, with both hands and a leg, as one wag during their briefing had put it, tied behind their backs.

After cooling down and enjoying a cup of tea in his cabin, Hunter went to the bathroom for a shower and shave before returning to his cabin. As he stood in front of the mirror tying his bow tie, he gave an ironic smile. The Commander would not be best pleased to learn that he would be leaving soon for his new post. In Naval jargon it was termed a pier head jump, that is, an unexpected posting at short notice. Ah well, there was another useful saying: if the Commander couldn't take a joke, he shouldn't have joined.

Already there were forces massing which were about to plunge them into a maelstrom of terror and extortion which would put their fledgling organisation on the map once and for all. Luckily, as he slipped on his doeskin mess jacket, he was completely unaware of what was about to strike at the heart of the Western, civilised world.

Hunter walked down to the bar where most of the revellers had already gathered. As was the custom there were white-jacketed stewards holding trays of dry sherry, gin and tonics, and horses necks (brandy with dry ginger ale) and for those who preferred a beer, the bar staff were ready to pull pints. Hunter picked a dry sherry off one of the trays and went to find a friendly face with whom to talk.

At precisely 20.00 the gong sounded and the Chief Steward intoned, in a sepulchral voice, 'Ladies and Gentlemen, dinner is served.'

'You know, Jeff,' Hunter said to the man standing next to him, 'you'd think we were about to be fed by the Borgias the way the Chief announces dinner.'

Jeff Hughes smiled. 'Worse, you'd swear he knew that a double helping of arsenic was planned with the pudding.'

'Jeff, you're seriously a peasant. Pudding my great

aunt. It's an iced gateau with a large amount of Drambuie laced through it,' retorted Hunter. And with that they followed an Admiral, half a dozen Captains Royal Navy and an assortment of guests into the dining room.

Having found their seats they sat amidst the hubbub of chairs being pulled back, introductions being made to their neighbours and the tinkling of cutlery as they picked up and shook out their starched, white table napkins. Jeff Hughes sat on Hunter's left while the chair on his right was taken by a Lieutenant Commander named Charles Arkwright, an instructor in navigation. Hunter knew Arkwright well, and though he had been passed over for promotion, he was one of the most pleasant people with whom to spend an evening.

As always, with over two hundred sitting down to dinner, it was an impressive sight that met the eye. The room was dark panelled, the walls dimly lit and covered in an impressive array of paintings of old ships of the Royal Navy. The candelabras on the table sent flickering lights across the faces and uniforms of those gathered, reflecting in the array of miniature medals on the uniforms of men and women who had served their country well. Because of the Falklands War, the Iraqi War, Bosnia and, of course, the continuing unrest in Northern Ireland, once again the armed forces could boast of meaningful active service on behalf of their country, their medals a sign of their nation's gratitude.

There were at least forty ladies present, all serving officers, many of whom also wore medals they had earned in the same combat zones as their male colleagues. Even so, there was little to detract from their femininity as they bent their heads to speak to the people next to them. The Commander picked up his gavel and struck it once. Instantly a hush fell on the tables. 'Chaplain, if you please.'

Remaining seated, the Chaplain said, 'For what we are about to receive, thank God. Amen.' There was a chorus of "amens" and the babble picked up once again. The dinner itself started with fish soup, followed by a piece of fillet steak and all the trimmings and the pudding as Jeff Hughes had so inelegantly put it. A superb Stilton followed and then the port.

The Commander rapped his gavel again for quiet and said 'Ladies and Gentlemen, the Queen.' The naval officers remained seated as tradition demanded whilst the remainder stood and lifted their glasses. 'The Queen, God bless her,' was the reply. Again the gavel rapped. 'Those who must, may,' said the Commander, referring to the fact that those who needed to, could smoke. The stewards made the rounds once more, offering cigars and taking the mess numbers of those who accepted; the price would be added to their mess bills at the end of the month.

There followed speeches: first of all by the Admiral, and then by the commanding officer of HMS *Eagle*, which had just returned from a deployment to the Mediterranean Sea. The first was really a policy speech about the way forward for the armed forces and the second was a highly entertaining hotch potch of statements about serving officers known to many there, which in any other setting would have been libellous. However, it was all taken in good spirits, the port was passed often enough, and, all in all, a good time was had. Afterwards they adjourned to the bar, to continue their conversations and to wash away the taste of the port with a fine whisky or two.

Jeff Hughes had moved on to talk to another group and left Hunter alone leaning on the bar. A voice at his elbow brought him from his reverie. 'Nick, why so pensive?'

He turned to smile down at the beautiful, blonde Lieutenant Commander Jacqueline Turner, Royal Navy, a dentist by profession. 'Hullo Jacqui, just thinking about one or two things, that's all,' he replied.

'Huh, knowing you, it will be nothing above the navel.'

'*Moi*? Me?' Hunter said, surprise in his voice, his hand to his heart and laughter in his eyes.

'Yes, you,' she retorted. 'I heard about you and that visiting officer from the American Navy.' Jacqui was referring to Lieutenant jg (junior grade) Molly Saunders who had spent a month on secondment at HMS *Dryad* and whom Hunter had last seen in his bed before he had left for Swanage.

'I trust you heard nothing good,' said Hunter, smiling broadly in memory.

'Actually,' she replied with honesty, 'nothing bad. She seems to have enjoyed her stay immensely. I'll have an orange juice,' she broke off to say to the bar steward, who was hovering on the other side of the counter.

'Ah, well, leave them smiling, I always say.' He took a sip of his whisky and soda and debated with himself whether or not to make a pass.

'Don't even think about it,' she said mischievously, laughter in her voice, startling him.

'Don't even think about what?' he asked innocently.

'Oh, Nick, you can't fool me. You were just wondering whether or not to try and pull me. Well, for your information, you can't.'

He thought about denying it but then shrugged and

said, sheepishly. 'You can't blame a man for thinking about it.'

She looked coyly at him before replying. 'Another time, another place . . . more importantly, another uniform . . . and who knows?' She let the tantalising thought hang between them and turned to leave. Suddenly she turned back again and said, 'By the way, what's this I hear you're in for a pier head jump?'

This time he was really startled and looked at her aghast. 'What in hell do you know about it?'

'Sorry, Nick. Have I put my big foot in it? I didn't mean to. I heard someone say just now that they thought they'd heard you were going elsewhere. Very suddenly too, from what I understand.'

Hunter's mind went into overdrive. He had certainly not mentioned it to anybody, so how did this scuttlebutt happen to have started? It was practically impossible to keep anything quiet in the service but at least he thought with the secrecy surrounding this new project his departure would not be noted until the day he left. Suddenly he doubted that Macnair would have as much time as he thought to get the organisation up and running before their existence was public knowledge. He smiled at her. 'If I am going, will that make a difference?'

'To what?'

'Why, to us, of course,' he leaned closer to her. 'Same uniform, different places,' he said softly. 'We'll be ships that will have passed in the night.'

She looked pensively at him for a moment. 'We'll have to see,' she said, a small smile playing about her lips. Again she turned to leave and looked back at him, over her shoulder. 'Well done. You got out of answering me very neatly.' She let him know that she had understood what he had been up to and, at the same time, didn't try to pursue the subject, as he obviously did not want to reply.

Shortly afterwards he had finished his drink, said goodnight to those who remained and wandered back to his cabin.

A week later all hell broke loose.

5

A.M. 23 April 1998. Onboard MV Nymph, *off Sardinia.*

The boat was 140 feet long from bow to stern and drew nine feet eight inches along the length of her keel. She was twenty-three feet wide at her midships and weighed 220 tonnes. She had been built in 1972 for an Australian brewing tycoon who went bankrupt in the middle of the eighties. She had since changed hands a few times until she had ended up in a yard in Malta, destined for scrap. In 1992 Aziz Habib had found her and recognised her potential. He bought her for scrap for twenty thousand Maltese pounds and spent a small fortune refitting her back to her former glory. There were numerous alterations to the original design which Habib found particularly useful, such as the moon pool which allowed him to launch a submersible or divers out of the bottom of the hull without anyone knowing. By the time he had finished her reconstruction she was worth in excess of two million pounds sterling and had cost less than seven hundred thousand pounds to refit.

Habib was sitting on the bridge, his feet on the consul in front of him, surveying the sea ahead, highly satisfied with himself. There was no one else with him and he was enjoying the peacefulness of a calm, blue sea and sky and a horizon empty of other vessels. He was surrounded by the latest in technological aids to seafarers. The geopositioning satellite system told him where he was to within five feet of his latitude and longitude, his communications systems allowed him to converse with anyone he wished, world wide, and his radar could spot a rowing boat at five miles. The engines beneath his feet, or more accurately, two decks down, were capable of pushing the boat along at over thirty knots and her stabilisers helped to dampen the effects of rough weather. Yes, he was well satisfied.

The bridge door opened, letting in some warm air to the cool of the air conditioned bridge. He turned around. 'Ah, my friend,' he smiled at Fredericks, 'I see you have brought us some coffee. Thank you.' He took the proffered cup and gratefully took a sip. 'Excellent. Thick, hot and sweet, just as I like it.' The Turkish coffee was quickly finished and the small cup placed on the chart table at his elbow. 'It was a close thing,' he said softly.

Fredericks grunted agreement. They had not discussed the events which had followed their escape in Turkey. After they had shot Zim Albatha they had killed the driver of a passing car and taken it for their own use. The Turkish authorities had been slow in chasing them which had given them time to change cars, this time without killing anybody, and escape into the port at Bandirma. They had stayed in the car, around the dock area, until first light when they had abandoned the car and taken the ferry to Istanbul, a four and a half hour crossing. By eleven o'clock they were safely holed up in a small hotel at Eyup, a suburb of the city. Using one of their numerous identities they hired a private plane to fly them to Sofia in Bulgaria. From there it had been simplicity itself to fly to Athens and then on to Malta. Twenty-four hours after shooting Albatha they were safely in Habib's villa, on the outskirts of Rabat.

After completing their preparations, they had joined the remainder of their men on board the *Nymph* and departed for Cagliari in the south of Sardinia.

'For the first time I feel as though I can really relax,' said Habib. 'I must be getting too old for this game.'

Fredericks grinned mirthlessly, showing his tobacco-stained teeth. He never smoked, but used chewing tobacco, endlessly. 'You? Too old? Never. We weren't even pushed this time. Think of the other difficult times we've had. Christ, remember when Saddam took it into his head that we were going for him!'

Habib shuddered at the thought. It had taken all his negotiating skills to get out of that one. And what was worse, he had been forced to carry out a job just to show good faith. Bastard!

'No,' continued Fredericks, 'this time it was easy. We didn't even need to use any real fire power, thanks to our contacts. It shows what friends in really high places can do for us.'

Habib nodded. 'True, my friend. However, it cannot go on forever. I think that this will be our last job. We can live where we want, be as comfortable as we want, and stop looking over our shoulders all the time. It is time to stop.'

Fredericks shrugged. 'Whatever you say. This will be the crowning act and put you at the very top. They will talk of your name with deepest respect for many years to come in the bazaars and market places of the world. No longer will that cur known as the Jackal be thought of as the greatest terrorist of the twentieth century, but Aziz Habib. With one blow you will . . .'

Habib waved his hand in self mockery, a thin smile on his lips. 'Spare my blushes, please. We'll have ten million pounds sterling in the bank and that is what matters.'

Fredericks also smiled. Hiding behind their anti-Western posture were their true colours. They only did it for the money. 'By the way, Aziz, I've telegraphed the money to our Turkish friend's Swiss account.'

'Good. I'll make sure that the bill is added to our expense account for this operation. I am sure the Mullahs won't like it but,' he shrugged, then added, 'tough.'

Fredericks picked up a pair of binoculars and idly scanned the horizon.

'How are the men settling in?' asked Habib. Not that he cared particularly for their welfare.

'Fine. This is one of the best teams we've had given to us. Not only are they tough but fanatically dedicated.'

'Excellent, excellent,' Habib rubbed the palms of his hands together. 'Fanatics are ideal for our purpose.'

'Without doubt they are all prepared to die for the cause,' Fredericks said, cynically.

'As long as they know what is required of them, I don't care. Is everything stowed away in the submersible? When we get Customs and Excise here I want them to find a spotlessly clean ship.'

'Have no fears, it's all taken care of. I suggest we anchor off Falmouth like last time. We can call them up and get them to come and search us before we head north.'

Habib nodded. 'All well and good, but I think we can expect trouble from Scottish Customs also. They seem to be even more paranoid about drugs than the English.'

'I agree. Why don't we go into Greenock on the Clyde and have a second inspection? That way, we'll be seen to be as clean as a whistle. If anything goes wrong later, we can call on both lots of customs officers to vouch for the fact that we'd been searched and nothing found.'

Habib stood up and walked the width of the bridge. It was spacious enough to hold a dozen people, with seats either side and a chart table in between. There were doors on both sides of the bridge giving access to small platforms which overlooked the deck running around the ship. After a few moments of thought he said, 'What is happening with the women?'

Fredericks shrugged. 'They are doing their jobs. We could probably have used a few more but these four seem to be managing. At least they appear to enjoy their work.'

'There's been no trouble with the men?'

'No. They seem to enjoy sharing. Four women amongst twelve seems to me to be overdoing it but then, they're animals. I shouldn't go in the main salon if I were you, it's not a pretty sight.'

'I don't intend to. Did you tell them that they would be leaving in Gibraltar?' Habib was referring to the four women. In Malta they had picked up four, fair-haired prostitutes working in Sliema. The arrangement was that they would be taken to Gibraltar on a cruise but would have to work their passage with the twelve men in the crew. They were to be paid a thousand Maltese pounds for the work plus their airfare home. The women had jumped at the chance. For them it would be easy money. A pleasant cruise, work they enjoyed, all the food and drink they wanted and payment which normally took them a month to earn, if they were lucky. Luckily for their peace of mind, they did not know that they would never use the air tickets.

'I take it that we are still on time?'

Habib swung round to glare at Fredericks, his thoughts interrupted. 'Of course. What do you take me for? A fool?'

'Sorry. I . . . I didn't mean anything. It's just, well, you look worried. That's all.'

Habib forced himself to relax. 'Not worried exactly. Just going over everything we need to do. Timing is all important. If we hit really bad weather in the Bay of Biscay all our plans could be destroyed. We need to be at a certain place at a certain time. We need the helicopter to pass us at the right time and we need . . . Allah with us,' he said, finally.

'Aziz, stop worrying so much. We have paid, threatened and promised those we needed to. We are as ready as we can be. We know precisely when, how and who will be travelling to Balmoral. It's perfect. We can't fail.'

Habib smiled, slouching off his pessimism. 'True, my friend, true. I think that you are right.' He walked over to the satnav station and pressed a few buttons. Immediately, the read out showed him that they had sixteen nautical miles to go to Cagliari and then 910 miles to Gibraltar. Once through the Straits then it was, he pressed a few more buttons, exactly 1492 miles to Falmouth. At sixteen knots they would get there in four days, which would take them to the morning of Thursday 27 April – plenty of time.

'Tell the men we'll be arriving at Sardinia in an hour. I want the women out of sight, along with those who aren't acting as crew.' He paused. 'No, wait. Better still, have the women in evidence. Get them dressed in bikinis and lying around the aft deck. Yes, that's what we'll do. When the Italian Customs come on board take them for a drink where the women are, before showing them around. Have the papers ready in your hands, with the log.' Habib smiled again. 'Better still, have the women topless. That'll keep customs busy.' He gave Fredericks a few more instructions and told him to get on with it.

If he was in any way resentful of the way he was spoken to, Fredericks did not show it as he left the bridge. He slid on his hands down the banisters either side of the steps leading down below. There was a short passageway which had two doors on the port side which opened into two well furnished staterooms, both en-suite, and a door on the starboard side which led to the main salon. He went into the salon.

The sight before his eyes brought a sardonic grin to his lips. Four men were busy with two of the women, whilst the other two were leaning against the mahogany bar, watching.

'Where's the others?' he asked. He couldn't help it, but the petite natural blonde leaning on the bar was affecting him.

One of the men said, 'They'd had enough and went to get some sleep.' He put his hand on the dyed blonde head in front of him.

'Don't be much longer,' said Fredericks. 'I want this place cleaned up and immaculate in twenty minutes. We're arriving in Cagliari within an hour. I want everything to look reasonably respectable.' The smell of hashish, cheap perfume and drink was overpowering, as was the reek of sweating, naked bodies. He knew that none of the men would drink alcohol but would smoke cannabis until they were cross-eyed. In his opinion, they were a seriously screwed-up people – but useful, very useful, for his and Habib's purposes. He looked into the mirror again and saw the blonde looking at him. Suddenly, she opened her mouth and ran her tongue around her lips, her meaning unmistakable. Fredericks turned away, hiding his reaction. He'd have her later, in private.

He went back out and further along the passageway to another set of similar stairs. Again, he slid on his hands down the banisters to the lower deck and hammered on one of the doors. It opened quickly, and he found himself staring down the barrel of an Uzi machine gun. 'Take it easy. I just came to tell you that we'll be docking in,' he looked at his watch, 'less that forty-five minutes and to get ready. We'll fuel, water and get the hell out of there. Okay?'

The surly head behind the gun nodded. He was a youngster, nineteen years old, no facial hair, brown eyed and with thick black hair. He was skinny to the point of emaciation but with knotty muscles. He had killed his first Jew when he was thirteen, on the West Bank of Gaza. Since then he had killed another five times, not always Jews.

'Good. And get rid of that thing. We don't want anything found if their Customs do search us.'

Fredericks went up on deck. The Italian Customs and Excise Officers were a lazy lot. Furthermore, they intended staying in port for an hour at the most and nobody would be going ashore. Knowing the Customs men as he did, he knew that they would be content to look at the ship's papers, have a drink and at most, take a cursory look around the ship.

Some of the other members of the crew were already getting fenders and ropes ready and tidying away some of the odd bits of gear lying around the deck. In spite of who they were and what they were intending, Fredericks ran a tight ship to which nobody objected. More to the point, he ran the ship the way Habib liked it. Fredericks went back up to the bridge and watched as Habib tuned the dial on the autopilot to turn the heading from 300 degrees to 350.

'I've spoken to the port authorities. They were expecting us and they said that there's already a fresh water bowser and diesel tanker waiting. Customs will join once we get alongside.'

'Good. I've got them cleaning up the place and hiding away the guns. I also checked the lower hatch. It's well sealed. All the clips are firmly shut. If they really want to go down there, they'll have a hell of a job.'

Habib looked sharply at Fredericks. 'If they go down there it will also be their last job,' he said curtly.

Fredericks nodded and picked up the binoculars. The port of Cagliari leapt closer as he focused on the entrance. The noise of a large passenger jet overhead instinctively caused him to look up. He saw that it was a British Airways Boeing 757, heading in to land at the airport.

Forty minutes later they were tied up alongside the jetty, very close to the harbour entrance. Fuel and water were to be taken on board, all tanks to be filled to overflowing.

'Here come the Customs men,' Fredericks said as a small, green car drew up alongside the brow. Two men got out, one middle aged and fat, the other young, keen and new.

'Shit,' said Fredericks, watching them come up the brow. He grabbed the log and registration documents and went out on the bridge wing to greet them. 'Ahoy, there,' he called down, his cheerfulness hiding his annoyance.

There was going to be trouble with the youngster. He
pointed aft. 'Go down to the deck there and I'll get you
a drink while you go over these,' he waved the two books
he held in his hand. The fat man waved a greeting and
did as he was bid, whilst the other hesitated and turned
towards the steps up to the bridge. The older man spat
something at him in staccato, heavily dialectal Italian and
the younger officer followed, reluctantly.

Fredericks fell into step as they approached the aft
deck. As he turned the corner he had to fight to prevent
himself from grinning. The two Customs Officers had
stopped in astonishment, mouths opened, eyes popping
out of their heads. The four women were draped artisti-
cally around. The one known as Mary, the petite blonde,
had a glass in her hand and a cigarette in her mouth.
She was lying on a mattress, her head propped up on
pillows, completely naked. Samantha was kneeling over
her, rubbing cream into her thighs. She was wearing a
bikini bottom which hid nothing, her large pendulous
breasts swinging free. She stopped what she was doing,
looked at the three men and smiled. 'We have visitors,
girls,' she said, as though the arrival of the customs
officers was totally unexpected. The other two were lying
on their backs, wearing only bikini bottoms, which were
little more than pieces of string with a four centimetre
triangle of cotton, covering their pubic hairs. With small
squeals, they acted surprised and sat up. Sandra reached
for her sun glasses and put her hand across her breasts
whilst the girl known as Madonna arched her back at the
men, her breasts thrust provocatively at them. Mary did
nothing, just lay there, watching the men.

'Take a seat,' said Fredericks, indicating three deck
chairs around a small table. 'I'll arrange drinks. What

93

would you like? A beer? Wine? Something stronger?' He was amused to watch the antics of the Customs Officers as they groped for chairs, unable to take their eyes off the women, not sure where to look.

Samantha stood up and walked towards them. There was a towel lying at the feet of the older Customs man and she bent over, in front of him, to pick it up. She had large, well-shaped breasts with big brown nipples that hung for a couple of seconds only centimetres from his hand resting on the arm of the chair. He was mesmerised, unable to look away. She smiled into his eyes. ''Scuse me, I need to wipe off the cream before I get you a drink.'

The Customs Officer nodded. 'A beer,' he tried to say, but it came out as a croak. He cleared his throat and said it again. She looked at the younger man who shook his head.

'Nothing, thank you.' He shifted awkwardly in the chair, his arm across his lap, unsuccessfully trying to hide his reaction to the women.

As Fredericks had thought, this one could be trouble.

Finally, the older man looked at Fredericks. 'I would like to see your papers, please.' His English was heavily accented.

Fredericks immediately smiled and handed them over. 'Here's the log book and registration documents. You know we've only come from Malta, don't you? On our way to England. Scotland, actually,' he added hastily.

'Yes, the coastguard were at pains to tell us of your movements,' he spoke slowly, ponderously. While he spoke he was quickly scrutinising the log and registration certificate. He handed them back. 'Thank you. They appear to be in order.'

The younger man spoke up. 'I wish to look around the vessel, please. Now.'

Fredericks nodded, somehow managing to smile. 'Certainly. Why don't you follow Madonna. She can show you around.'

The Customs Officer gulped. He looked at her near naked body and prayed for deliverance. He remembered his wife and new born baby and tried to keep his mind off the luscious body in front of him. He nodded.

'On second thoughts, perhaps it would be better if I showed you around. Madonna is not that knowledgeable about the ship as she only joined in Malta.' Fredericks stood up smiled at the younger man and waved his hand towards the front of the ship. 'Let's start at the bows, shall we?'

Within fifteen minutes they were finished with the upper deck, the bridge and the main staterooms and salon. There was nothing to find. They looked in the crews cabins and worked their way to the lowest deck. Still nothing.

'What's down there?'

Fredericks shrugged. 'The bilges.'

They were standing on the lowest deck, in front of the engine room. The hatch they stood at was held down by a dozen butterfly clips which looked as if they were painted in position. The Customs Officer leant over and tried to undo one of the clips.

'It's seized solid. The bilges are down there but we haven't been into them for a hell of a long time,' said Fredericks

The Customs Officer grabbed the butterfly nut with both hands and tried to turn it, using all his strength.

Nothing happened. 'How do you get to the bilges?' he gasped, the sweat pouring from his face.

'We don't. To my knowledge we have never seen in there.'

'These are the bilges, for God's sake. You have to look inside. For maintenance of the pumps and so on.'

Fredericks shrugged. 'I don't know about that. I'm sure that if you ask one of the crew they can tell you about it. Why don't we do that?'

The Customs Officer was furious. He glared at the other man, unaware of how close he was to death . . . his own.

'Look,' said Fredericks, 'you can see the butterfly nuts are solid. Get down and examine them. You can see the paint is solid right around the nut and flange.' The Customs Officer peered closely at the hatch covering and securing arrangements. He did not notice the hairline crack in the paint around the base of the hatch. As the Customs Officer began to carefully look all round the hatch, Fredericks realised that at the back of the hatch combing he would be able to see the join. The join which showed that the whole hatch and combing lifted away, giving greater access to the deck beneath. Fredericks shifted his stance ready to drop onto the other man's back and break his neck. At that moment Madonna came into the corridor, breathless, bosom heaving. The Customs Officer looked up, his eyes fixed on her breasts, his reaction immediate.

'I . . . I was sent to see if you needed anything,' she spoke with a slight lisp, feet apart, her left hand near her crotch, her right hand cupping her right breast, squeezing her nipple. Neither man knew it but Habib had sent her as a precaution, to distract the customs man – in any way necessary – had been his instructions.

The young Customs Officer scrambled to his feet, all thoughts of any more searching forgotten for the moment. Fredericks looked at him and made his decision. 'Madonna, please show this officer the aft state room while I go back to the bridge and see how the fuelling is progressing.' He didn't wait for a response from either of them but walked quickly away. As he went up the forward stairwell he looked back to see the girl put her hand on his crotch.

On the bridge Habib was alone and pacing restlessly back and forth. 'How's it going with the Customs inspection?'

Fredericks grinned. 'I thought we were in for trouble but the girl Madonna came down, just in time. I think he missed the hatch opening.'

'Good. Where is he now?'

'Presumably getting balled down aft,' Fredericks replied, dryly.

In fact, there Fredericks had it wrong. Neither the Customs Officer nor Madonna had moved from where Fredericks had left them. Madonna was on her knees in front of the man who had his trousers down round his ankles. No more of the ship was searched.

Ten minutes later the Customs Officers waved their goodbyes. Fuelling and watering were completed and bills paid in cash. An hour and five minutes after entering the harbour the ship was on her way again.

Once clear of the port and main shipping lanes Habib put the controls to automatic and checked their position. The Straits of Gibraltar were precisely 910 nautical miles away, on a heading of 255 degrees true. After a few minutes of contemplation he increased the speed to twenty-two knots. 'I'll just give us a little more time, in case of bad weather in the Bay.'

'You haven't changed your mind about the women, have you?' asked Fredericks.

Habib looked at him is surprise. 'Of course not. I never change my mind,' he said angrily, 'you know that. We'll get rid of them tomorrow night.'

Fredericks nodded his head with relish. It would be all the better for waiting and thinking about it.

The MV *Nymph* sped effortlessly and serenely through the calm, blue Mediterranean. They saw numerous other ships, yachts and large private cruisers but nothing passed within a mile of them. Apart from two crew members, one on duty as lookout and the other monitoring the controls down in the engine room, the ship appeared deserted, the others having gone for an afternoon's siesta.

Fredericks and Habib left a lookout on the bridge and went below to the lower hatch cover. Instead of trying to open the painted butterfly nuts Fredericks pressed a button hidden in a corner of the overhead bulkhead. Silently the hatch came up a few millimetres and slid open, leaving a gap a metre wide, by a metre and a half long.

They climbed down the ladder, Fredericks, going first, switched on the lights as he did so. They entered a large, gleaming, white painted area, cluttered with equipment and machinery. The space covered over a quarter of the length of the ship, amidships, and was five metres wide. Down here, they could hear the noise of the sea rushing against the hull, the engines pushing out nearly two thirds of their power, as they sped towards the history books of terrorism.

The central section had a moon pool which, when opened, would be four metres long by three wide. The moon pool hatchway was half a metre proud of the deck and had a dozen well-greased butterfly nuts holding the covering hatch in place. At the speed they were travelling, sea water sometimes forced its way inside. A glance showed them that everything was watertight. When unlocked the hatch was pushed open on hinges running down its port side. Two ratcheted handles at either end lifted the heavy metal cover, holding it vertical when fully opened. On the starboard side of the moon pool rested a two-man submersible, ready for launching. Many of the weapons, explosives and missiles they were going to be using, were stowed in the forward and aft compartments of the sub. The black hull gleamed in the overhead light, looking dangerous and evil. An umbilical cord ran from a wall socket into the side, keeping the batteries fully charged.

Both men knew what they needed to do without talking about it. Fredericks checked the levels of air in the bottles housed along the starboard side of the sub's hull and made sure that the demand valves were fully operational. Habib checked the power and the array of equipment in the sub's cockpit. When in use one man sat in the front, another behind. When launched, the one in front drove the sub like a pilot flying an aircraft, whilst the other monitored the radio and did the navigation.

The depth to which they submerged governed how long their air would last. They knew that at twenty metres they could stay underwater for nearly five hours. However, they then encountered decompression problems. Both men had been well trained in the problem facing all divers, which was one of nitrogen dissolving in the bloodstream. When a diver returned to the surface the nitrogen bubbles increased in size and did not dissolve out of the bloodstream quickly enough. Instead, nitrogen molecules got caught in the restricted blood passages of the joints. As the depth of water decreased the bubbles increased in size and the nitrogen began to press on the nerve ends at the joints. The result, if not treated properly or if enough time wasn't allowed for decompression, was excruciating pain and probable paralysis or death.

The highly efficient electric motor was capable of propelling the sub at speeds up to six knots though four knots gave maximum range with the batteries lasting up to six hours.

After checking the submersible and its equipment Habib started the engine. The high-pitched hum filled the space like a swarm of mad bees. Habib lent into the cockpit and engaged the forward gear lever. Immediately, the hum changed and settled into a buzz as the two contra-rotating propellers chewed the air. Connected to one shaft the propeller design drove the sub forward without any pull to the side, giving a highly sensitive control system, which was particularly important when returning to the moon pool. Satisfied, he switched off the engine and turned to the aft compartment of the sub. Undoing the bolts using a specially designed spanner he checked the contents whilst Fredericks did the same in the front. Amazingly, the sub could carry half a tonne of goods. Normally, this was fifty percent ballast and fifty percent other items, but for this trip the sub was packed with their weaponry. The submersible had been designed to smuggle drugs by a Colombian who saw the Middle East as a potentially huge market. The Colombian had reasoned that nations which did not allow alcohol and were filthy rich in oil needed something to help them enjoy life and pass the time. His first shipment of cocaine had been his last and he had been beheaded for his trouble. The Mullahs had got their hands on the sub and eventually Habib had acquired it for his operations. It was now used to hide a different sort of contraband particularly when there was a likelihood of being searched by Customs and Excise. At Cagliari neither man had expected such a thorough search as the one carried out by the younger customs officer. In England they did expect it.

They finished checking the small, one-man decompression chamber and their own diving bottles and equipment. They did not check the gear belonging to the other members of their team, as that was each individual's personal responsibility.

Less than an hour after entering the compartment their tasks were complete. They left, carefully relocking the hatch behind them.

'Every man knows that once we near England their personal arms are to be thrown overboard?'

'Yes, Habib. Once we get near enough, we'll throw away anything that can be in the slightest bit incriminating. They don't like it but I explained that when dealing with the British the last thing we need are any weapons, anywhere.'

'Until we start.'

Fredericks nodded, grinning in anticipation.

During the night either Habib or Fredericks spent time on the bridge. Another member of the crew took responsibility for the ship's safe passage but one of them was available to make decisions should it be required. Now that they were operational they worked with complete professionalism, an important reason why they had never been caught. Intelligence and ability were not the prerogatives of government security services as Habib and Fredericks had shown on numerous occasions in the past.

Dawn passed peacefully and beautifully in the clear spring air.

During the night there had been a repeat of the earlier orgy but neither of the two had taken part. They wanted a private show, later that night.

By 22.00 that evening, they were 250 nautical miles from Gibraltar and had made very good time. Nothing had interrupted their passage. The four women had bathed and changed and now joined Habib and Fredericks on the bridge. No other members of the crew were present. They had been told to stay away, no matter what they heard.

At the back of the bridge was a small cabin with a bunk for the captain to sleep in, in case he was needed urgently when at sea. Habib took Madonna and Samantha by their hands and led them into the room, closing the door. Fredericks scowled. Habib had taken the two he had wanted.

Fredericks sat in the chair and beckoned to the petite woman who was standing quietly nearest the door. 'Come here and take your clothes off.'

She did as he said, slowly peeling her blouse off her shoulders, stepping out of her skirt. She wore no underclothes. The other woman did the same, exposing large breasts with surprisingly small, pink nipples.

Fredericks changed places with the one known as Sandra. He sat her in the chair, smiled and winked at her and tied her wrists to the arms of the chair, making a game of it. The other woman, Mary, had been taking his clothes off him, until he was as naked as they. He pushed her against the chart table and without preamble, rammed into her. As he did so he put his arms around her neck and began to squeeze. At first she thought it was part of a game but as his grip tightened she began to struggle. The more she struggled the more he liked it.

Sandra was also beginning to struggle against her bonds, fearful, not liking what she saw.

'Stop . . . don't,' she begged, speaking for Mary who was beginning to resist less and less. Fredericks stared into Mary's eyes as her body went limp and a few seconds later he ejaculated.

'You . . . you've killed her,' she said in horror. Just then came a piercing scream from the other cabin. Frantically, she struggled harder, desperate to get free. When Fredericks turned to her she saw the sadistic look on his face, the pleasure he was having. Suddenly she began to whimper, begging him to let her go. There was an anguished cry from the cabin and a sound she could not, did not, identify. She did not know it then but her friend Mary had been the lucky one. Sandra's horrors were about to begin.

An hour later Habib and Fredericks carried the bodies of the four women down to the stern. They tied weights around the feet and unhurriedly they threw the bodies overboard, each one vanishing below the surface of the sea with hardly a splash. Neither man spoke. They got their own buckets of warm water and cleaned the mess up in the cabin and on the bridge. Then Habib climbed onto the bunk in the cabin and quickly went to sleep.

Fredericks, by contrast, went out on the bridge wing and breathed in the night air, highly satisfied, fully charged. It was always the same, he thought. He could have climbed mountains, he felt so . . . so alive, whilst

Habib needed an hour at least, preferably two, to recharge his energy. Fredericks knew that Habib would be hyperactive the next day as a result of what they had done – an ideal time to have a training session with their team. To go over again what was required of each of them. To make certain that no one would fail at their allotted tasks.

At dawn on another cloudless, sunny day, Fredericks could see the top of Gibraltar pushing up over the horizon. He was now down off the adrenaline high he had been on and felt weary, tired to the soul – that was, if he had one. Habib came through, clapped his friend on the shoulder and told him to get some rest. Habib bounced as though he had surplus energy coursing through his veins, unable to sit quietly. The previous night's activity had awoken something in him which he didn't understand, only that he needed it from time to time.

Once Fredericks had gone below, Habib checked their position, speed and estimated time of arrival off the English coast. Should they go to Falmouth or on to Milford Haven? He looked at his charts once more. It didn't really matter one way or the other. He would not decide until they had at least passed Brest and the Ile d'Ouessant. It would depend on how much time they had and whether they needed to hurry to get to their rendezvous position.

Unfortunately for his plans, the Bay of Biscay lived up to its fearsome reputation for bad weather.

Gibraltar was fading astern when the weather closed in. The wind slowly picked up until a gale was coming out of the west. The Beaufort scale showed a ten on the anemometer, the waves were wild and white capped and the swell caused an uneasy roll to the ship, in spite of the stabilisers. All the crew, with the exception of Habib and Fredericks, took to their bunks, ill.

Both men were on the bridge, each in a chair, with their feet on the consul in front of them, bracing themselves against the pitching and rolling of the vessel. A wave crashed over the fo'c'sle and deluged the reinforced glass front of the bridge. Like a thoroughbred, the ship raised herself from the sea, the water cascading off the foredeck, as she continued speeding north.

'Shouldn't we slow down?'

Habib nodded slowly in reply. 'Yes, I think so.' He leant forward and moved the controls backwards a few degrees. After a few moments the ship responded and the pitching and tossing subsided a little. 'Are any of those useless turds on their feet?'

'No. All of them are in their pits.' Fredericks grinned and said, 'Which is exactly what we expected. Tough talking and tough fighting when it's all going their way, but no real balls.'

'True. They are unable to raise themselves above their discomfort. No willpower, or, as you say, no balls.' He lifted a pair of binoculars and scanned the horizon, seeing very little except the heavy rain and wild seas. 'I think I'd better try and rest. You stay here on watch while I go and lie on the bunk.'

Fredericks nodded aware that Habib was very close to being ill from the look on his face and the greenish tinge he had around the gills. Fredericks was never effected by sea sickness no matter how rough it became.

The storm lasted six hours before it began to abate but even then there was still a great deal of unpleas-ant motion to the ship. After checking their speed and distance to go Habib decided that it would be better to go to Milford Haven on the Welsh coast, rather than into Falmouth. It would save them nearly six hours of steaming time.

6

Whilst Habib and Fredericks battled across the Bay of Biscay Nick Hunter was packing his kit. He had received his pier head jump papers and was ordered to Plymouth as soon as possible. Because the navy had limited resources and stretched manpower, it upset a great deal of the Ministry of Defence's plans to despatch personnel unexpectedly, as the vacated post needed to be filled. There was a domino effect of personnel shifting from job to job as the dictates of rank, seniority, experience, promotion prospects, suitability, family life and so on were taken into account. In order for Macnair to appoint the people he wanted, the appointers, the officers who handed out the jobs, of the army, navy, marines and air force, held a week of continuous meetings and, unusually, gave complete co-operation, to achieve the required results. Even then it had taken the intervention of the Prime Minister who had sent for his most senior officers and told them to expedite matters.

Hunter handed over the team and his job to a lieutenant (sd), special duties, which meant his relief was ex-lower deck, an ex-petty officer in fact, and had been in the RN for twenty-five years. There was nothing Hunter needed to explain to his relief who had held similar appointments in the past. All that was required was for the permanent loan record to be completed. This is the biggest bane in the lives of all serving officers in all the services. Every item of equipment which Hunter had or used was accounted for. Annually and when leaving an appointment all the gear he and his team used was checked, serial numbers compared to the records and ticked off. It was always a huge relief when the mustering was done and the records signed. Having been aware that he would be leaving sooner rather than later Hunter had taken the precaution of getting everything ready so that when the time came, they were able to finish the task quickly. It was with a sense of relief that Hunter finally signed over the permanent loan record.

He made his goodbyes and by the middle of the afternoon was on the road, speeding towards Plymouth. He enjoyed the feel of the car, the noise it made, the deep-throated roar of the engine combined with the wind whistling against the soft top. The sky was overcast with big, black billowing clouds. He knew them to be nimbo-stratus, a sign that rain was imminent. The trees were bending in the wind and it was obvious, even without his training in meteorology, that a storm was brewing. His Scottish roots left him steeped in the folklore of the sea and the weather. His father had been a fishing skipper until the last quota cuts. Now, his father enjoyed telling sea tales and tending his roses in his house in Balfron, far enough from the sea that he didn't have to look at it every day. Hunter smiled; more specifically he had been Chairman of the Board of a company which owned, at its peak, a hundred trawlers and seines. Hunter had spent his school holidays aboard one or the other. The men liked taking him with them, they considered him their lucky mascot. As always, being a seaman, Hunter thought pityingly of the poor sods at sea on a day like this.

He was hardly past Eastleigh, the airport at Southampton, when the rain started. It poured down from the very start, the wind whipping it across the road in front of him. It was suddenly prematurely dark and he switched on the headlights, somehow content, his warm cocoon of metal giving a false sense of security. He let his mind wander to his new job and at the same time he thought about his abilities, knowledge and what he would be able to bring to the new set-up.

Without any false modesty, he was aware that he was very good at disposing of impromptu explosive devices and that, somehow, he had gained a reputation as an expert with plastic explosives. He knew that he had a "feel" for what he did; an instinct which he had been told he was born with, rather than acquired. He was also something of an expert with fire arms, having represented the Royal Navy on three occasions at Bisley. One of these had been an inter-service competition which not only involved the usual shooting up of fixed targets but also the shooting of moving silhouettes in different situations. He had enjoyed that immensely, pleased to come second in a field of over fifty. He had completed a parachuting course and had enjoyed it so much that on some weekends he could be found sky diving over the Surrey countryside. He grinned to himself. On top of that, he was a first dan, black belt in Shotokan karate, a Japanese version of the art; though the truth was karate helped his general fitness and co-ordination. His killing skills had been learnt when he was seconded to the American SEALS for two years. He also had his private pilot's licence with nearly a hundred hours logged. Maybe there was a lot he could bring to the party after all.

Due to the rotten weather, he took his time and didn't get to Plymouth until nearly 20.00. He pulled up at the gates to the dockyard and wound down his window. An armed sentry came forward and bent his head towards the car. Hunter noticed the second sentry standing to one side, holding a rifle which was, more or less, pointed in his direction. Somebody had been sharpening them up and, with a smile, he thought that he didn't need too many guesses as to who. He took out his identity card and showed it. Instead of the usual cursory glance, the sentry took the card without a word and went back to the guard house. Hunter could see in the room a petty officer to whom the card was handed. The PO consulted a list on a clip board, nodded and handed the card back to the sentry. There was a marked difference in attitude when he returned to Hunter.

The sentry threw him a salute and said, 'Sorry, sir. We can't be too careful. You're expected. Do you know the way?'

Hunter returned the salute and replied, 'Afraid not. I haven't been here for donkey's years.'

He was given the directions, the gate was opened and he drove through. Plymouth dockyard is one of the oldest naval yards in the world. Some of its buildings were hundreds of years old and most of them were listed for preservation. This meant that there was no chance of modernising the area or making it more useful for the twenty-first century. Like most naval officers Hunter was a reactionary about some things and he liked the feel of the old place, the aura of tradition and greatness, which had really passed by decades earlier.

He pulled up at the doorway to which he had been directed and parked his car. He noticed quite a number of other vehicles were there, some with foreign number plates. By now it had stopped raining, although it was still a dark, overcast and blustery night. He climbed from the car and closed the door, careful to lock it. He left his kit where it was, as he was unsure where he would be staying. He assumed arrangements had been made for him to book into the wardroom at HMS *Drake*. However, his joining instructions had ordered him to report to where he now found himself. Like all people who served in the military, the one thing he could be sure of was that somebody would have made the necessary arrangements.

He walked into a well-lit room which had been turned into a reception area by the simple expedient of putting a desk and chair just inside the door. Room dividers blocked off the rest of the room but he could hear a hubbub of voices behind. A sergeant with parachute wings on his sleeve sat at the desk, a hand gun of a type Hunter had never seen before lay on the desk within easy reach alongside a clipboard with names, some ticked.

'Yes? Can I help?' The man looked professional, in his late twenties, with a toughness about him that only came from years of training.

'My name's Hunter, Lieutenant Commander. I hope I'm expected?'

A warm smile replaced the scowl, the sergeant stood and offered his hand. 'Glad to have you with us, sir. My name's David Hughes.' There was an unmistakable Welsh lilt to the voice.

'Pleased to meet you, Sergeant. What's the drill?'

'Go on in, sir. The Colonel's waiting for you, to show you around.'

111

'Thanks. Any idea where I'll be kipping tonight?'

'The wardroom. Cabins have been booked for everybody, either there or in the chiefs' block.'

'How many are you expecting?' Hunter was curious.

'Tonight there's thirty-four coming and another twenty-six tomorrow.'

Hunter nodded his thanks and went around the dividers into the main room. There were a couple of dozen people busily sorting themselves out, unpacking crates, arranging desks. The room was massive, capable of holding at least a couple of hundred people with a desk and chair each. Hunter wasn't in uniform but dressed neatly in slacks, blazer and wearing a tie. Nobody took any notice of him as he scanned the room looking for the Colonel. He heard him before he saw him, over in a corner, talking to two other men and a woman.

'I want, no, need this data down-loaded as quickly as possible. So please, no more delays.'

Hunter walked over and waited patiently for the Colonel to finish his remarks. He appeared to have done so for he suddenly looked up and noticed him.

'Ah, Nick, welcome,' he held out his hand and shook Hunter's with evident warmth and pleasure. 'Glad you made it and glad you made the decision you have.'

Hunter grinned. 'Couldn't refuse Colonel . . . no . . . sorry, sir,' he noticed the epaulettes. 'General.'

Macnair grinned. 'Can't get used to it myself, yet. Let me introduce you. This is Isobel Sweeney. She's in charge of our information technology.' They shook hands.

Hunter smiled at the plain, serious face in front of him. She was about five feet six inches tall, a nice figure, neither fat nor thin, with fair hair, almost blonde. Then she smiled and her whole persona was transformed. She was suddenly very attractive without being obvious.

'Pleased to meet you, Lieutenant Commander,' she said.

'Call me Nick. Pleased to meet you, too.'

She nodded. 'Nick, this is Leo and Gareth. They're my team.'

Hunter shook hands with the two men who were in sharp contrast to the others in the room. Hunter had noticed how tough and alert the men were who were busy sorting out the room. These two though were obviously not military types. Dressed in jeans and sweaters, Leo was short, fat and wore glasses whilst Gareth was tall, skinny and weedy looking. Hunter felt that if he blew in Gareth's direction Gareth would fall over.

'Okay, General,' said Isobel, 'we'll get going. Most of what you wanted has been done, it's now a question of networking the other consoles.' She looked at her watch. 'Do you mind if we finish tomorrow? It's nearly nine and we've been at it since six-thirty this morning.'

'Of course not. You go ahead. I'll see you in the wardroom shortly. I think it's time we wrapped things up here anyway.'

He turned back to Hunter. 'Have you signed in yet?'

'No, sir. I didn't know what the arrangements were. My instructions were to come straight here.'

'Right. Basically, we're all on the base. If you're asked, then say you're on a course connected with inter-service and European co-operation. That should hold things for a while until we become better established. By which time, it'll be too late.'

'Too late for what?'

'Too late to stop us, that's for what. Look, I may

as well tell you that we aren't exactly flavour of the month. Different agencies in different countries tried to stop us being formed. Senior officers have split down the middle as to whether we're useful or not. We need time to prove we are. Frankly, if it hadn't been for President Clinton and the SecDef, Stuart Roberts, I don't think we'd have succeeded. Clinton pushed this whole thing through. He wants an international response to terrorism with members of NATO as the centre core. If it works as we anticipate then he will push for an autonomous anti-terrorist group to work under the United Nations – more specifically, under the control of the security council at the UN. Hell, Nick! You know what it's been like. If it wasn't for the Americans nothing would get done, ever. By forcing this whole set up onto the West, Clinton is making it impossible for the other leaders to keep ducking and diving their responsibilities. He's also trying to take some of the flak away from America by spreading it about more,' he smiled. 'That's the real reason I'm in charge and not a bloody Yank. We'll take more of the stick from the Middle and Far East in the future. Less heat on the Great Satan,' Macnair was referring to the disparaging name the Arab world had for the United States of America.

Hunter nodded. 'It makes sense. Em, how much pressure is there to stop us before we get started, sir?'

Macnair turned grim. 'Let me take care of that. You do your job and I'll keep any interference away from you all. Let me say that there are a hell of a lot of people out there hoping we'll fail.'

'Why the hell should they want that?'

'Vested interests, Nick. Vested interests,' he said enigmatically. 'Come on, let me introduce you to the others before we go over to the wardroom. This, by the way, is the operations room.'

The next morning Hunter was up early, had breakfast and was back in the operations room by seven o'clock. He wasn't the first there by any means. Isobel and her team were already at their desks, computers switched on, working their keyboards rapidly. Other men, now in uniform, were scattered about the room, continuing to sort desks and chairs for themselves. Macnair was in the middle, talking earnestly to an army major. Hunter walked over, still unsure what he was supposed to be doing.

'Morning, sir,' he saluted.

Out of courtesy Macnair returned the salute and surprised Hunter by saying, 'Don't salute again, Nick. I don't want any bullshit around here, only professionalism.'

'Right, sir. Huh, what do you want me to do? I mean, this is all new to me. Any other job and I know exactly what I would be doing, but this,' he waved his hand, 'is different to anything I've done before.'

Macnair stared at him for a few seconds, disconcerting him. 'It's all new to all of us, as well. I picked you because I thought you had the initiative necessary for the job. Don't prove me wrong. Get yourself a desk. Get yourself a coffee and be ready for a briefing in fifteen minutes time. Oh, and by the way. This is Jim Carter. He's in charge of logistics. If you want anything, ask him.' He hurried away, leaving Hunter with the major.

Jim Carter was about fifty, balding and with a slight stoop. He stood five feet five tall and weighed less than nine stones. Hunter was to learn that the major could run the marathon in record time and taught karate at black belt level. He was also one of the most astute operators

115

there was when it came to acquiring equipment for the new outfit. He was a rare officer indeed; one who had voluntccred for the catering corps and enjoyed it.

'Take no notice of Malcolm, his bark's a lot worse than his bite, believe me. He's been barking at me for the last fortnight. Have we got this? Get that! Find the other, and so on,' he smiled. 'As soon as he's yelled, he's forgotten about it, so don't take it personally. He's under a lot of strain to make this work but once we're operational, he'll be as cool as a cucumber.'

'I don't doubt it for a moment. I feel a complete prat for asking.'

'If it's any consolation you aren't the only one. We're all a bit like fish out of water right now. We need to become a cohesive team, working together and that will take a hell of a lot of doing and a lot of leadership . . . from all of us.'

Hunter nodded. 'Which desk . . . ? No, forget it. I'll sort something out.' With that he left the major and walked over to an empty desk. He quickly found that all the desks which were already in tidy rows belonged to someone. He found a French officer who had been with the elite *Commandos de Recherche et d'Action en Profondeur* before being seconded to Macnair's outfit, who was trying to put a humorous face on the fact that the acronym for his old regiment was CRAP, much to the amusement of the others. Hunter was impressed, having worked with them a couple of years earlier. Hunter knew that the regiment consisted of two CRAPs, one working for the headquarters company (CCS) and the other for the Reconnaissance and Support Company (CEA). The regiment was tasked with deep penetration operations including intelligence and direct action. The Frenchman's

parachuting skills included HALO – high altitude low
opening from 6,000 metres, and HAHO – high altitude
high opening from five miles up. He was skilled in attack
swimming underwater using a pure oxygen rebreathing
diving set and was used to debarking from a submarine at
depths of twenty-five metres. Pierre Flambert was a very
tough, good looking and humorous lieutenant who took
nothing seriously, particularly himself. Between them, he
and Hunter got themselves a couple of desks and chairs, a
cup of coffee and spent a few minutes exchanging experi-
ences and information about their relative specialisations.
Their backgrounds and training were very similar with the
exception that Flambert was land orientated and Hunter
was a seaman.

What Hunter noticed and found interesting was that
not a single military man smoked, whilst the two male
civilian computer operators did so almost incessantly.

'Pay attention!' Macnair stood at the front of the
room. Silence descended as each group in turn realised
he wanted them to listen. 'I will apologise only this once.
I'm sorry I brought together one of the finest group of
professionals to have you move furniture.' There were
many grins and shrugs. 'It won't happen again. We will
be recruiting back-up staff but that'll take more time. I
want good people from all over Europe and the States
who have at least the ability to speak one language other
than their native tongue. For the non-Americans and non-
English amongst you that will be easy.' More smiles.
'For the rest of us it'll be a hell of a lot more difficult,'
Macnair smiled. 'Most British think, "I love you," in
another language, is about all they need. Well, not here.
Okay, I appreciate that this is the beginning of something
different. I believe that we'll have our work cut out for

us in all areas of operation, all over the world. That's the strategic plan. A global, inter-governmental organisation which will stop terrorists wherever they operate. We already have most of Europe represented here, as well as a Latvian and a Russian.' He nodded his head in the direction of where the two men sat. 'This is a first which is of historic importance. If we can get the momentum on this moving, and moving fast, then we could prevent any political interference, should it arise in the future, as we tackle some of the issues. One thing has already happened which, frankly, is good news. We are staying here only temporarily – maximum a month. We'll use the time to bed down and get to grips with the vast volume of tasks we have before us. We'll then shift the whole operation to HMS *Cochrane* in Rosyth. Any of you know it?' There were a few nods, including Hunter's.

'Why, sir?' asked someone.

'*Cochrane* is empty. It's a huge base, with excellent transport facilities including a helicopter pad. It's completely self contained and there will be no sharing with other personnel from other services. It will mean that we can be as relaxed about matters as they are at Hereford.' That made sense. The SAS kept itself to itself and after an operation could take it easy with their own kind, without worrying whether or not something was said out of turn. 'We will be right on the sea and will have our own equipment, men and all that we need to run the show. Barry Buddon range is only an hour away for explosives practice and we will have access to the army's firing ranges. International travel will be from Edinburgh Airport. Any questions?'

'Why wasn't this thought of sooner?' asked Hunter.

Macnair scowled and then shrugged. 'It just wasn't,' he

said with honesty. Then he corrected himself. 'Actually, that's not quite true. It was brought up some time ago but for some reason quickly discounted. This place was also one for consideration and in view of the time scale, i.e., they want it like yesterday, it was chosen. Jim Carter and I went up a few weeks ago to look *Cochrane* over. We already had this place if we needed it. Jim put forward a compelling argument as to why Scotland would be more suitable and we got word this morning that we were to get it. I can tell you a lot of the problem was budgetary arguments between the different governments. Anyway, enough of that. Jim has been working non-stop on pulling in the gear we need. Today, you will all start writing lists of what you want. I have already arranged for much of the specialist equipment you all know and love to be brought in. I can tell you much of it's on its way. There are some things I know you are aware of. Ask, show me we need it and it'll be given. We are about to enter a whole new cricket game, or as our American friends put it, a whole new ball park. We are going to apply our resources, knowledge and men to fight what is called the scourge of the twentieth century, terrorism. No handcuffs this time. No repeat of Gibraltar, the Iranian embassy affair or anything else like it. For the first time we shall not be playing by our rules, we'll play by theirs.' There were nods around the room. This was what they'd joined up for in the first place.

'Do you know,' Macnair went on, 'that for years we have been telling the politicians in Britain that the IRA are not as afraid of the British forces and that includes the SAS and Paras, as they are of the loyalist paramilitaries? And why? Because we play by the rules and they play dirty. I have argued in meeting after meeting that there's no point us playing cricket if the opposition is playing rugby. Today, that all stops.' Macnair liked the reaction he was getting from the men sitting in front of him. 'Okay, that's enough from me. I'm going to hand you over to Isobel who has a few things to tell you about the computer system and how you can get things rolling.'

Macnair walked from the room as Isobel Sweeney pulled over a flip chart and pointed at the first page. 'I need you all to have a good working knowledge of the system and what we can do. Already we have down-loaded into our systems information from all over the world on known and suspected terrorist groups. The co-operation we are receiving is phenomenal. Our job will be to collate that information and make it, shall we say, user friendly. In the meantime, I want you to sit at your consuls and start writing in the lists of equipment you think you want. We shall again do the collating as you will obviously be choosing many identical items. We shall, simultaneously, be deleting those things we have already ordered and can be expecting to arrive later today and onwards into the foreseeable future. This is the way that you'll access the data base and here are some of the code words you'll be needing.' Her briefing took a further two hours, by which time every person there felt brain dead. Knowledge to a certain level was all very well, but they felt that they were not computer experts and that they did not really want to know so much. Just enough to know what they could and should ask for. Luckily, Isobel realised it and cut her lecture short. Her audience, meanwhile, thought she had finished.

Hunter sat at his computer terminal and started writing, as did the others. It didn't matter what language was typed in, it all went to the master file in English.

There, the cross-checking of each item was done, and those things ordered more than once, deleted. Now the real wonder of the computer system came into being. After identifying the item, the nationality and which service it was used in, the computer gave the item its correct designated code number to order it from stores. Automatically, using secure fibre optic lines, the orders were passed to each depot wherever it was in Europe, where the item was stored. On receipt, acting on the priority coding attached, the depots began to collect the equipment, ready for despatch. It was the most incredible logistical operation ever conceived, as it called on so many nationalities and so many different systems to work. It did not compare in size to Operation Overlord, the Allies' invasion of mainland Europe, but its speed and ease was awesome. It had taken Jim Carter six months to arrange it and Isobel and her team, on private contract at the time, three months to write and implement the software.

Carter looked at the data going through the master file and smiled at Isobel. 'Well, it seems to be working from this end.'

Isobel looked over her shoulder from where she sat at the screen and said, 'As long as we get plastic explosives and not oranges.'

'Don't say that please, Isobel. Don't say that. You're tempting fate.'

'There are bound to be some hiccups but we've had so much help from so many willing people. It's been very surprising. One thing puzzles me, though. You're keeping this secret for a while longer, until we're up and running. So how did you prevent this from getting out? After all, there must have been someone with half a brain out there wondering what this was all about, giving us their on-line time, their codes, everything.'

Carter shook his head. 'Actually, it wasn't that difficult. We can see the net result here, as we have the overall picture. Each individual supply depot had no idea of the big picture. The level of authorisation to get this going was as high as you can get so we were able to keep the lid on it for a bit longer. Mind you, once the equipment starts arriving God alone knows what'll happen.' He thought for a moment. 'No, that's not true. This is a very big naval base. It won't be that untoward. I think we'll keep things under wraps until we're ready to announce to the world what we're up to.'

By Thursday afternoon they were finished. Next, they were instructed to think about other personnel with whom they had served and make recommendations for their recruitment. Those recommended would have their service files pulled immediately and scrutinised. Each person making the recommendation would also be responsible for reading the file and deciding whether the candidate had the qualifications they wanted. There was a vast amount of work to be done and none of them left their desks until after midnight.

Macnair worked alongside them, content that he had found the nucleus of his operation. The room was filled with dedicated, focused professionals. He was satisfied.

The next morning, without prompting, from shortly after 06.00, the roads around the base were busy with running figures, working up a sweat, doing their katas – the stylised movements – for the different disciplines of unarmed combat they used. Some of them worked out together, others alone. Not one of them had needed telling. It was all very well to do the desk work but their real jobs were operational. Fitness, toughness and ruthlessness were their stock in trade – and none of them ever forgot it.

More personnel began to arrive along with lorry loads of equipment. Introductions had to be made, orders given, equipment unloaded and stored. It was a mammoth task which should take months to complete. They had just over thirty-six hours.

In Iran, the sell orders went out. In spite of their adherence to a way of life which was medieval in thought and action the Ayatollahs acknowledged, indeed embraced, some aspects of modern life. Computers and finance were some of those aspects. In order to survive, Iran owned hard currency holdings and investments across the world. They amounted to billions of dollars' worth, all carefully hidden behind dummy corporations and businesses in a world-wide network. It allowed Iran to buy goods and services without the Western world being fully aware of what they were up to. An order to sell short on their vast holdings was given and electronically implemented. Brokers and moneymen were about to earn huge commissions for doing something which did not make sense to most of them.

Within three hours the Iranians had made deals worth twenty-five billion dollars. The currencies they had sold short included the American dollar, the British pound, the Deutschmark, the ECU and the Yen. Holdings in major companies from IBM, General Motors, BP and McDonalds to shares in the international banks were traded as options. This levered up their dealings by fifteen fold and, provided the shares dropped in value by as little as three percent, would mean profits across their holdings in the region of five billion dollars.

There were isolated pockets of brokers and moneymen across the world who wondered what was going on. Most of them didn't give it a second thought and merely obeyed their instructions. Those who did the wondering came to the conclusion that the people who gave the orders had taken leave of their senses . . . or else knew something which no one else knew.

7

A.M. 2 May 1998. Cardiff, Wales.

'Is everything ready?'

'Yes, sir. The delegates started arriving just after nine. They'll be going into the auditorium on time.'

'Thank you,' replied his Royal Highness, the Prince of Wales. As usual when nervous, he was twisting the signet ring he wore on the little finger of his left hand. 'I see there are plenty of signs up telling people to leave their mobile phones at the coat check-ins. A good thing, too. The last thing I want happening is a phone to ring in the middle of my speech.'

Or a bomb to go off, thought his bodyguard, a Chief Inspector from Special Branch. That was why entrance to the auditorium was through a metal detector of the type used at airports. All night, men with specially trained sniffer dogs had been searching the building for IEDs – impromptu explosive devices – of the type favoured by terrorists.

The Prince smiled knowingly. 'I don't want a bomb going off, either. Talking of phones, Chief Inspector, what have you done about the passengers?'

'All mobile phones have been placed in their luggage and will go with you, sir. We removed the batteries in

125

every case, just to be on the safe side.'

'Good. We don't want another incident like the last time.'

The Prince of Wales was referring to a few years earlier. A helicopter carrying over twenty-five anti-terrorist and security specialists had been flying from Stormont Castle near Belfast to a meeting in Inverness, Scotland. It had crashed in the Highlands killing all the passengers and crew. At first, a terrorist operation, probably IRA, had been feared as the cause. The likelihood was, it was later discovered, that the helicopter had crashed because of the unauthorised use of a mobile phone onboard. Since then paranoia ruled when it came to the carrying of mobile phones on military aircraft and particularly helicopters.

Like all good public speakers, The Prince of Wales worried before he started. Once on the podium, however, he would settle neatly into his speech. Today was an important event for him. He needed the approbation of the press and his subjects. Following the death of his ex-wife, who had been almost beatified in death, he knew that he had a great many bridges to build between himself and the public. He intended to try damned hard to help his country as it approached the twenty-first century and he could make a difference. He could talk about the major issues which were affecting the whole world. A political speech would be constitutionally taboo, of course, but he could be reasonably controversial and he could have some influence because whatever he said today would be reported world wide. Poverty might be an uncomfortable subject for many to contemplate, but HRH believed that if it was not tackled on a global scale then unrest would follow. Did it matter if you died from starvation or a bullet? Either way you were dead.

His security detail were as watchful as ever, eyes roaming, hands never far from their waists. Unlike the American Secret Service who were trained to stop a bullet if needed, the British intended to stop the assassin. Their duty had certain bounds and giving up their lives was outside them. Hence their extra vigilance.

'Are the arrangements complete for this evening?'

'Yes, sir,' replied the inspector in charge of the detail. 'We'll be taken by car to Rhoose Airport and then by Crabair.' Crabair was the derogatory term applied to the Royal Air Force by those who used their services regularly. 'The other delegates will follow after the Secretary General concludes her speech. They have a Sikorsky laid on.'

HRH nodded absently. He already knew the details, but his nervousness made him want to talk. He smiled to himself, prattle was a better description. He needed to claw his way back from an abyss if he was to become king and he was aware of it. His ex-wife had courted the public on an international scale he had never achieved. Her gold medal for services to humanity or whatever the hell she had been given in Italy was another indication of how she had been winning the propaganda war. His thoughts plunged him into gloom as they always did. 'Damn it all to hell!'

He heard the introductions being made and his name mentioned. He listened to the description of his achievements in the field of conservation, his dedication to organic farming, his desire to reduce and eventually obliterate the use of artificial fertilisers on the farms of the Western world. The hand clapping started and he walked onto the stage in front of an audience of over five thousand people from all over the world.

He stood for a few moments collecting his thoughts and arranging his papers. He had practised what he was about to say so often that he did not need the notes. However, he was also too well aware of the danger of going off track and saying something unscripted. Controversy was not on the agenda for the day – apart that was, from what he planned to say. Now he was looking out past the lights, glimpsing the sea of faces before him; he relaxed, took a deep breath and began.

'We are sitting on a time bomb. Unless the Western world recognises the inequality of life as we know it then I fear that life itself, as we know it, will end. The internet and other information technology systems mean that people on a world-wide basis are beginning to understand how different our lives are from their own. How can a father or, for that matter, a mother, sit in a third world country and watch his or her children starve? I am sure that there is nobody in this audience who would. So ask yourselves, why should they? Let me make a prediction. They won't. At some point in time they will say – stop! Give us our share. And if you don't give it, we'll take it.' His audience recognised the justness of his words and many shifted uncomfortably in their seats. The Prince of Wales paused and then continued. 'In Europe we presently subsidise our farmers, set aside twenty percent of the land and pay them not to grow food. It is the economics of the mad house. People are starving to death and we are paying farmers to grow food we don't want, paying prices which are subsidised by the European taxpayers and then having to destroy the food mountains we have created.' Another pause. He looked up and saw the heads nodding. They all knew, were aware that the system was an abomination and yet seemed incapable of rectifying it. He raised his hand and brought it down softly onto the podium for emphasis. 'We cannot allow this state of affairs to continue. The lunatics are running the asylum.' This raised a laugh from the audience. The lunatics were running the asylum and yet nobody seemed capable of retaking it.

'Many of the third world countries now have the technology to retaliate. These countries have nothing to lose. We try to prevent nuclear proliferation and have done for many years. The measures being taken are failing . . . and we know this, because other countries have now joined the so-called nuclear club. If your child is starving would you use every means in your power . . .' he went on. His audience were appalled by his words and captivated by the speech. He was right, they knew he was right and yet what could they do about it?

'Let me talk for a few moments about the damage we are doing with our intensive farming methods – damage to the land and to the people.' Again, as he spoke, there were nods across the vast hall. He was striking the right chords, getting the correct responses.

'If we are serious about solving the problems, then we have to do something. Soon.' He paused. 'We must find the political will to act in a way which makes sense. Is there anyone else in this hall who finds it as ludicrous as I do that we, in Europe, subsidise tobacco growing which kills hundreds of thousands of people every year? Yet we penalise the beef industry to the point of bankruptcy on the off chance that there is a danger of BSE. Then we pay to destroy the cattle which, if sent to the starving nations could solve one of the greatest famine problems in memory to hit the third world.' There were nods and now a lot of shakes. This was seriously controversial.

Tough. It was time it was said. He paused for a few moments as he scanned his audience.

There was more, a lot more. He spoke fluently and decisively for an hour and five minutes. At the end he was gratified to receive a standing ovation which went on for nearly fourteen minutes. He smiled, tried not to look gloating and smug, and mostly succeeded. This is where it really matters, he thought.

After he left the stage, the Prince of Wales walked down into the hall and took his seat in the front row. There were another three hours of speeches from the Secretary of the United Nations, the Vice-President of America, the President of Save the Children and a leading Swiss official from the Red Cross. The speeches interlocked. The theme was world poverty, farming and third world debt. All the institutions were creaking under pressure, America still had not paid its bill at the UN and there was fresh trouble brewing even as they spoke. Unrest could so easily spill over to open warfare. Was it right that a child in the Western world would consume one thousand times as much of the world's resources as somebody born in Africa, or South America, or . . . his mind went through the litany of countries and their problems.

By five o'clock the conference started to wind up. A lot had been said. Pledges had been made. Something would be done. Amongst the hundreds attending there were those who fought to keep the anguish from their faces and the despair from their thoughts – not more platitudes. This time something had to be done and they would see to it. The meeting scheduled to take place in Balmoral the next day would be the start. Thirty-one of the delegates in the room were to be ferried by helicopter to Scotland that evening, ostensibly for a banquet and dance, hosted by His Royal Highness, the Prince of Wales. The real reason for the gathering was to hold the meeting. This time something would get done. Pledges of money had poured in from across the world. Individual wealthy men, women and heads of states were prepared, at last, to act. The figurehead for a world-wide movement for the eradication of poverty was to be the heir to the British throne. Plans were already being made which would make governments sit up and take notice. Band Aid had been a huge international success. This was to be Band Aid times a thousand. It was time to eradicate poverty as the world approached the end of the century.

The Prince of Wales shook hands with many people, circulated for an hour and just after six o'clock made his departure. He was thoughtful as the car sped out of the city on the A48, not really taking in the Welsh scenery. Quickly they reached Ely at the edge of Cardiff and passed into the countryside. Soon after that they arrived at Rhoose Airport and drove straight to the waiting aircraft. He was flying to Scotland courtesy of the RAF with a flight time to Aberdeen of an hour and fifty minutes. There he would transfer to a helicopter for a twenty minute hop to Balmoral Castle. As the host for the evening he had a lot to do before his guests arrived. They would be travelling a short time behind him but by helicopter all the way. Because of the necessity to get cars and people organised he was going ahead with all the luggage so that everything would be ready and waiting when the VIPs arrived. He smiled to himself. There was an irony – not lost on him – to be holding a conference on world poverty followed later by a banquet fit for kings. And there was a further irony that as a future king he was travelling with the baggage! Not that it mattered.

This time something would be done. By God, he would see to that.

The special branch detective spoke into his lapel. 'They're on the move. That's the last leaving now.' He received acknowledgement and followed the Vice-President and his secret service contingent outside. The thirty-five dignitaries had begun leaving half an hour previously but the Veep, as he was known by his minders, had needed to spend a few minutes with the Prime Minister of Israel. The latter would not be going north but back to his embassy in London, whilst his deputy would be attending Balmoral. Those who were heading for the airport and the helicopter read like a sub section of Who's Who International. The detective was glad that he did not have responsibility for ferrying them to Scotland. Hell, had no one heard of actuarial principles? If the helicopter crashed there would be reverberations across the stock markets of the world, oil prices would be shot to hell . . . which way he wondered? Up or down? He could not work it out.

He climbed into the car behind the limousine and sat nervously eyeing the crowds. Although the day had been mild for the time of year, with spring definitely in the air, a wind had blown up and there was a hint of rain. Clouds were gathering and the temperature was dropping. It was growing dark as the cars sped through Cardiff and followed the same route as the Prince of Wales had taken an hour earlier. All along the route people stopped to stare and some to wave. The cars carried the flags of their nations and people enjoyed pointing them out to the children. The Welsh kept their good humour in spite of the disruption to their daily lives caused by the chaos visited upon them by the simple fact of holding the meeting in their capital city. Even so, they would be glad to see the back of them all, he was sure.

The Vice-President's car drew up at the steps of the helicopter and he quickly climbed out and was hustled aboard. His wife, along with the wives of the others, had been taken to Balmoral that morning. They had neither wanted to be, nor were they, invited to the conference itself. Ben Bradley was an unusual animal in the herd of American politicians. He was honest, conscientious and hard working. Although he was aware that the game was politics, he was also determined to make a difference. Today, he felt, was the start. He had come to his present position more by accident than design.

At the age of forty-four, Bradley had been a Colonel in the Gulf War. There he had distinguished himself with Delta Force. The fitness and toughness he had then still showed in the way he moved and held himself. As he strapped himself into his seat he could not help wondering about the events which had brought him so quickly to this point. One thing was for sure, it was a damned sight harder being a politician than it was being a soldier. He grinned. Hell. Those had been good days. Delta had not only been a personal pinnacle of achievement but a capping of his military career. It was hard to get back into the main stream of military life from the special forces. Having resigned his commission to take over the family construction business, he had found himself being offered the post of senator of his state within a year. Four years later, due to the untimely death of the then vice-president, he found himself in the job running with a popular second-term president. He was the preferred choice by the Democratic Party to run for president, and, importantly, he had the wholehearted support of the present incumbent. There was a serious danger, as his wife often put it, that he could become President of the United States of America. All he needed to do was keep his hands clean, follow the party line and slowly but surely build up his public profile. He looked at his hands even as the thoughts passed through his mind. They were clean enough. He'd never done a dishonest act to the best of his knowledge and goddamn it if he wasn't a certified hero after the Gulf turkey shoot.

He felt the helicopter lift as smoothly as an express elevator and a collective sigh of relief went around the cabin. Even cynical and hardened travellers like those onboard wondered about events during take offs and landings. Unlike other, ordinary helicopters, this one had been specially modified to carry thirty-five passengers in comfort and reasonable peace and quiet, thanks to the latest technology in noise reduction.

Bradley turned to his neighbour, the elderly but spry Chairman of the World Bank. 'Nice to see you again, Matthew,' he said with a grin.

Goodall smiled back. 'You too, Ben. What did you think of today?'

'A lot of sense was spoken. But,' he shrugged his shoulders, 'and it's a big but, will anything be done?'

'I hate to say it, but that is the sixty-four thousand dollar question. I agreed wholeheartedly with the Prince's analysis. Maybe he can do something. I hope so, and not for my sake, but for the sake of my grandchildren. You know, I took this job hoping I could make a difference and here I am five years later covering the same ground as I was then.' He shook his head sadly. 'There have been so many missed opportunities in the past that this time I think we're . . . what's that saying? We're drinking at the "Last Chance" saloon.'

'I wouldn't go that far, but I agree time is running out. The trouble is, can we convince the people of the necessity to change?'

As he spoke a figure leaned across from the other side of the aisle. 'We have to convince them,' said the Prime Minister of France, Jacques Beloit. 'We need a complete change of attitude, world wide, if we are to prevent anarchy, starvation and mass mobilisation by destitute people which will make the present refugee problem seem like a wayward picnic outing.'

Sitting next to him was the Vice-Chancellor of Germany, Herbert Conrad. He leaned across for his say. Pretty soon there was debate throughout the aircraft, but no real argument. The twenty-eight men and two women from around the world were in accord. The only people not to say anything were the two special branch officers sitting next to the door. They were not paid to voice an opinion, no matter what they thought.

A stewardess came round the cabin offering drinks and snacks which were, on the whole, declined. Then the captain of the aircraft made his announcement, welcoming them all onboard. 'We shall be travelling under radar surveillance all the way. This means that we shall travel to just overhead the Isle of Man and then onwards past the Mull of Kintyre. From there we shall pass over Fort William and then straight across country to Balmoral. As a route it's a little bit roundabout but we shall stay under military air traffic control which is deemed, em, shall we say, more suitable. The weather is fine with a light covering of cloud at ten thousand feet. We're flying above the clouds and so don't expect any problems. We shall be dropping down, after the Isle of Man, to transit the West of Scotland, again because of air traffic problems but that won't be for long. Enjoy your flight and if there's anything we or the cabin staff can do for you, please don't hesitate to ask.' The pilot thumbed off the microphone and said out of the side of his mouth, 'Not that they would hesitate.'

His co-pilot, Flight Lieutenant Donald Spencer grinned at him. 'Not getting cynical in our old age are we, Sweeney?' he asked.

The pilot, Fred Todd, nicknamed Sweeney, after the infamous Victorian murderer, grinned back. 'Probably. That lot back there,' he jerked a thumb over his shoulder, 'control, influence or own over ninety percent of the earth's wealth. Christ, man, if you think about it, it's awesome. I tried to argue that we should have other aircraft, other routes just to reduce the . . . what shall I call it? The chaos which would result if we crashed and all of them were killed.'

'What do you mean them? Think about us. I'm too young to die,' Spencer rolled his eyes in mock terror. At twenty-eight he was considered a man with a future in the Royal Air Force. Recently engaged he was contemplating marriage in November to a fellow officer, a doctor whom he had known for more than five years.

As a Flight Commander, Todd was in reality too senior to be ferrying a passenger-carrying helicopter. However, he was one of the best and most experienced pilots in the RAF, which meant the world. So he got the job. He sighed and called Rhoose Airport. After exchanging pleasantries and ensuring they had him clearly marked on their radar scopes he checked his transponder and switched to a listening watch on his radio. It was all quiet, the night held no terrors, and the helicopter was purring along at 210 knots. There was a slight tail wind which gave them a speed over the ground closer to 225 knots, the heading was a steady, autopiloted 350 degrees, and there was nothing visible except the early evening stars and the last light of the sun, as it vanished below their horizon. Both pilots settled down to an anticipated uneventful and enjoyable journey.

A few minutes later the door behind them opened and the head of Jane Felton appeared. 'Can I get you anything, gentlemen?'

'Coffee, please,' said Todd. 'Milk, no sugar.'

'Same again, and a biscuit or two if you have any,' said Spencer.

'Coming up. I won't be a moment,' she withdrew to the galley and began pouring the coffees. She was a sergeant, very pretty, with blonde hair and a good figure. She was known for her unfailing cheerfulness and her ability to get on with anybody she wished. If she had been working for British Airways she would already have been a Chief Purser. As it was, she loved the RAF and all it entailed. Her husband was a flight mechanic who adored her and whom she adored back. Their one sadness in life had been Jane's inability to bear children due to ovarian cysts. However, they had been told that with treatments available nowadays, there was hope that the problem could be overcome. They were both due to see the doctor the following week.

She put the cups on a small tray and loaded it with a dozen chocolate biscuits. She returned to the cockpit, knocked on the door and entered. 'Here you are, gentlemen.' She handed them each a cup and then paused to look out through the forward window.

'Where are we?'

'That's the tip of Anglesey and those lights ahead, see them through the break in the cloud? That's the Isle of Man,' replied Todd. He checked his instruments and continued, 'We're on track, on time and at the right height. All, as the town criers used to say, is well.'

Jane paused for a few more moments, enjoying the sights ahead and the rhythm of the helicopter's movements. 'I'd better go, duty calls. Somebody probably needs something.'

'How's it going back there?'

'Fine. They are all talking about today's events. I have to say it's fascinating listening to some of the comments. This is really insider stuff.'

'Don't forget you've signed the Official Secrets Act,' said Todd over his shoulder. 'It's why they're flying with us. They can talk about today without any worries.'

Jane nodded. 'I know. Mum's the word. I won't tell a soul. Except my husband, oh, and my mother. And of course Aunt Sadie. Oh, and I mustn't forget my neighbour.' She stopped and smiled mischievously at the look of horror on the faces of the two pilots as they stared back at her. 'Only kidding chaps, only kidding,' Jane said, with a laugh.

She went back into the main cabin and walked slowly down the aisle, checking to see if there was anything she could do for her passengers. She dispensed a smile here, a nod there and a drink where it was wanted. She noticed that on the whole they were an abstemious lot, which came as a surprise to her.

'Excuse me, miss. Sorry, I mean, sergeant.' Jane recognised the Secretary General of the United Nations, an

austere woman, with iron grey hair who never seemed to
smile. Canadian by birth, she had only just been appointed
to the position. After the disaster of the last incumbent she
had been a surprise candidate following nearly a year of
wrangling amongst the leaders of the world. Contrary to
expectation, she was proving to be a caring and thoughtful
individual, who was not prepared to compromise on the
big issues. She was also proving to be a driving force in
the initiative now beginning to appear from that day's
conference. 'May I have a cup of tea, please? No milk
or sugar.'

'Certainly, ma'am. You, sir, can I get you anything?'
Jane looked at the man sitting next to the Secretary
General whom she knew to be the special assistant to
Nelson Mandela of South Africa.

'Yes, please, that will be very kind. Actually, I'll have a
large scotch on the rocks with a touch of soda.' His brown
eyes twinkled merrily in his black face. He was a jovial
sort of person, as thin as a stick insect in spite of the fact
that he ate and drank enough to feed a regiment.

As she moved back down the cabin she heard him say
'Madam Secretary, we need to follow today's proposals
as a matter of urgency . . .' Jane tuned out her mind to
the rest of what he was saying and concentrated on her
job. This was, without doubt, the most interesting journey
she had ever undertaken.

In the galley she quickly prepared the drinks required
and casually looked out of the porthole. The cloud was
thinning and she could see lights way over to starboard.
She guessed that they were now nearing Scotland and that
she was looking at the area known as Galloway.

Meantime, in the cockpit, the pilot was on the radio.
'Roger your last. Switching to Machrihanish control now.

Thank you for your company. Out. Machrihanish control this is Golf Bravo November Lima Foxtrot, over.'

'Golf Bravo November Lima Foxtrot this is Machrihanish control. We have you loud and clear. Maintain your current heading and height until further notice, over.'

'This is Lima Foxtrot, wilco your last.' Now that contact had been made and identification confirmed the controller and the pilot reduced the call sign to the last two letters to save time. Wilco was verbal shorthand for will comply.

'We'll be over Campbeltown in twenty minutes,' said Spencer. 'Spot on time.'

'Good. The weather is clearing and we seem to have the promise of an easy flight ahead of us. Let's just keep it that way. I don't want anything untoward to happen. So, maximum alertness. Let's get this over and done with.'

'Roger that, skipper. I've checked the sat nav and way points on the computer. We should be south of Mull on time, when we change course to a heading of 048 degrees true. That's a straight run to Balmoral. ETA still 21.00.'

'Good. You have control. I'm going back to do some PR.'

'I have control,' Spencer replied, thereby taking official command of the helicopter.

Onboard the ship, Habib and his men were at maximum alertness. It all depended on the next hour or so. They had stopped off at Haverfordwest finally, to pass through Customs. This time they did not hope for the slap-dash ways of the Italian Customs. They knew that whatever they were, the British were practically incorruptible, could not be distracted and worst of all, had a pathological distrust of foreigners. Once they were off the Welsh coast, Habib had filled the submersible with all the weapons and explosives held onboard and launched the sub under the control of Fredericks. They had called at Haverfordwest to replenish their fuel, water and fresh provisions. It also ensured that they had passed through Customs Control and, hopefully, would not have an unexpected visit later on.

The ship had been thoroughly and carefully searched. If they had not taken the precautions they had, there was no doubt that the weapons would have been found. As it was the Welsh Customs officers gave them a clean bill of health and wished them bon voyage. Habib made it clear to the customs officers and to the coastguard that they were heading for Scotland and would probably be stopping next at Fort William. He confirmed that they would not need a further inspection by Scottish Customs.

Five hours after arriving in Haverfordwest they were leaving again. An hour later they had recovered the submersible through the moon pool with nobody outwith their crew any the wiser. From their point of view it had been a text book operation.

Now they were two miles west of Gigha Island, off the coast of the Mull of Kintyre, made famous by the rock group "Wings" in the mid seventies.

'We are on track and on time,' said Habib. 'If we stay at twelve knots we should be in the right area at exactly the time we calculated. Is everything ready?'

'Yes, Aziz. The tender has been checked out and the engine run up. All the gear is already stowed safely onboard and both men properly briefed.'

'Good.' Unfortunately for those around him, Habib couldn't leave it at that and continued to cross examine Fredericks about the remainder of the arrangements. Having worked with him for so long it came as no surprise. Resignedly, Fredericks gave the replies Habib wanted to hear.

Habib paced the deck as he spoke, becoming hyped up now that the time for action was closer. After a while he stopped and placed a hand on Fredericks' shoulder. 'We haven't forgotten anything, my friend?'

Fredericks shook his head. 'No, nothing,' he said, with certainty.

'This will be a great day for Allah,' Habib was speaking for the benefit of the three other crewmen who were also on the bridge, although he addressed his remarks to his friend. 'Yes, indeed. A great day. We shall, in one action, give a devastating blow to the west. Our reward will surely be wonderful when we meet Allah in heaven.' He did not know whether they believed his claptrap or not. What was important was to maintain the illusion of working for the Moslem cause and the good of Allah. They all knew what they had to do and, Habib was sure, would die to achieve it. However, a little bit of reinforcement propaganda never hurt anyone.

The last few hours were proving hell on their nerves but they kept them under control. Some of them went below to get their prayer mats and have a few last words with their God, whilst others kept themselves busy checking and rechecking the equipment. They all knew that if they pulled off tonight's operation they would be honoured above all men when they returned to Iran.

The ship passed through the Sound of Islay. Habib watched the lights of the Colonsay to Oban ferry move from left to right three miles ahead of them before he increased speed to nearly thirty knots and changed their heading to 035 degrees.

He took the way off the ship and hove to, four miles south of Mull and five cables west of the tiny island of Gravellachs. The ship's tender was launched quickly. Habib watched as the outboard engine was started and the boat veered away, heading for the other side of the island. The claw of the pincer was in place.

He went back onto the bridge and gave orders to head slowly west. Because it was a Saturday night, there was not a single vessel showing anywhere on the radar screen. He hoped it would stay that way.

Fredericks worked the radar and changed the height settings for detection. Seabourne radar is normally good for heights below 5,000 feet. After all, what ship is interested in anything that far above sea level? The Japanese radar installed less than six months ago had settings which went up in bands to 60,000 feet. After fiddling with the gain control and brightness, Habib got a perfect picture in the 10,000 to 15,000 feet range. Originally, a radar screen showed an all round picture as the transceiver rotated. Now, there was no rotation but a 360 degrees pulse. This enabled the point source, that is, the radar position, to be moved around the screen giving a far bigger picture of one segment. So it was that Habib moved the cursor to put the ship, as the source, into the north west corner and looked south east, the direction from which he was expecting the helicopter.

Twenty minutes after launching the tender, the radar picked up a fast moving object and automatically made an identification. The fact that it was at 12,000 feet, heading 350 degrees at 210 knots made identification easy. A warning, low-toned buzz, told Habib that possible detection had been made. He spent a few minutes watching the screen, reading the contact data which appeared on the screen near the orange blip. The information stayed steady and accurate. It was exactly as he had been told. The radar showed him that the helicopter would pass half a mile to the east, at 12,000 feet, in exactly eleven minutes.

'Tell them to get ready. Four missiles at thirty second intervals. I will tell you when to fire. Helmsman,' Habib never bothered to learn the names of the men he was leading as usually they did not live long enough for it to matter. Inevitably, because they had been on the ship and in close proximity to each other, he had picked up some of their names, but it was not as part of his leadership technique. If anyone disobeyed an order once an operation had started, he instilled discipline by the simple expedient of shooting the miscreant. It had only happened once and that had been a very long time ago. Since then, the fanatics he worked with obeyed orders without question or hesitation. 'Head 090 degrees at slow speed.'

The helmsman moved the dial on the automatic control and pushed a button which took the speed readout up to two knots. The blades on the screws moved a few degrees and the ship picked up speed and turned to a heading of 090 degrees. It was only when leaving or going alongside that the wheel was used. The computer-controlled steering gear could do the job far better than an individual. Habib needed the helmsman to carry out his orders, leaving him free to control the action and to ensure that the firing took place at exactly the right time.

He had estimated that four missiles in the air over two

minutes would give the pilots enough to think about. He had also estimated that three would not reach their destination but that the fourth would. Even if one of the first missiles got through he still had time to self destruct any others still in the air. Then, if the pilot had the luck of the devil on his side and all four missed he still had the tender. That was why his plan was to drive the helicopter to the east, to the obvious, nearest hiding place, behind the island.

Habib was using his binoculars, trying to pick up the flashing lights of the aircraft through the thinning cloud. He had one or two glimpses and then it was in clear view, the clouds virtually cleared away, leaving a moonless, clear night. Allah be praised, he said to himself. Thank you for your help, this great night.

He watched the radar screen and the contact readout, telling him distance and time to the helicopter. 'Standby.'

Fredericks was standing on the starboard bridge wing and yelled to the four men who were nervously standing near the bows of the ship. 'Standby. Off safety catches.'

Each of the men flicked the safety catch to off and lifted the missile launcher to his shoulder.

'Fire one,' said Habib. The order was yelled by Fredericks and the first missile launched. It was at maximum range but now Habib ordered the helmsman to turn the ship directly towards the contact and increase to maximum speed. The ship quickly picked up speed, chasing the missile. 'Fire two.' They were now travelling at eight knots, the helicopter still on her original heading and speed. Suddenly, the radar readout changed as the helicopter started to lose height, turn to starboard and pick up speed. By now the helicopter was well within range of all the missiles. 'Fire three.' Habib watched the target like a cat playing with a mouse. He was sure the fourth missile would hit home. 'Fire four.' He fired too soon, only tcn seconds after the previous missile launch. It was a serious mistake.

8

P.M. 2 May 1998. Scotland.

Todd first went to the toilet, washed his hands and face and then continued into the galley. There, he helped himself to a drink of orange juice and a handful of peanuts. Next, he pulled back the curtain and went into the main cabin. In all his life he had never seen so many seriously important people in one aircraft. The phrase actuarial madness passed through his mind. He was still twenty minutes away from realising how great that madness really was.

As he wandered through the cabin, he exchanged pleasantries with the dignitaries he passed. Many of them thanked him for a smooth flight and most asked where they were and how much longer to go. He recognised many faces including John Williams the Deputy Prime Minister of the UK and Felicity Cornwall, the Minister for Agriculture. He couldn't help noticing that for a woman of forty-five she was extremely well preserved and in the vernacular of the RAF, high in the brackets for bed-worthiness. He wondered, with a smirk, whether lusting for a Cabinet Minister would be classed as treason. Probably not, he thought to himself.

At the back of the cabin, near the tail end, he came up

to Jane Felton and her assistant Billy Jones. Jones was a corporal, had just put in his papers to buy himself out of the service and was looking forward to applying for a job as a flight attendant with an airline. Being gay, he had discovered that life in the services was virtually untenable.

'Evening, sir,' Jones said, smiling. 'Unusual flight with this lot, isn't it?'

'It is that, Jones. Is everything okay?' Although he suspected Jones' sexual proclivity, Todd was indifferent to it. He was one of those rare people who had absolutely no prejudice whatsoever and only cared whether his crew did their job properly. That being said, he could sympathise with Jones and wished him good luck in civvie street. The tolerance and understanding he showed was, unfortunately, not common throughout the services. Because of that good, loyal and fundamentally decent people were driven out, back to civilian life. It was, without doubt, an unjust society.

He walked back down the aisle and into the cockpit. As he strapped himself in to the left hand seat he said, 'Everything okay?'

'Yes, sir. No problems. We've just passed over Jura and that's Mull ahead. You can just see the lights of the houses and . . .'

At that point all hell broke loose. The computer started flashing a warning that a missile was locked on, the emergency tone, warning of the same thing, started and both pilots suffered a sphincter contraction at the same time. Todd didn't even stop to think. He took the controls, flicked off the autopilot, and immediately sent out the counter measures he had available. Spencer had already hit the warning button to the cabin and the emergency voice could be heard in the background telling people to return to their seats, put on their seat belts and prepare for an emergency.

Although they were carrying passengers, this was first and foremost a military aircraft. It was staffed by military personnel who acted first and thought about it afterwards. That was the essence of military training. They were ready for just such an event as this, even if they did go through their careers praying it would never happen. In this case, both men had seen action, Spencer in the Gulf War and Bosnia, and Todd in the Falklands, Bosnia, Northern Ireland and also in the Gulf.

Already the helicopter was diving, having emitted counter measures for a heat seeking and a noise seeking missile. Even as Todd started evasion tactics, deciding to go low and head for the island of Scarba, ten miles to starboard of their original track, Spencer was quickly working the threat computer to find out what was happening.

'What the hell. I don't believe it. Jesus . . .'

'What . . . got it.' Todd was looking at the same data as his co-pilot. 'It can't be. A stinger off the coast of Scotland? What the hell's happening?' It was a rhetorical question to which he expected no answer. In that, he was not disappointed. He pressed his IFF transponder which immediately alerted Machrihanish control that there was a problem. The signal on the screen of the radar which had been controlling and following their progress immediately changed and signalled an emergency. The flight controller who, only a second earlier, had noticed the violent movement of the helicopter and was about to ask the pilot what was going on had, instead, pressed his own emergency button to tell his supervisor that something was amiss.

His headset came to life and the calm measured voice of Todd was in his ears. 'This is Lima Foxtrot. We are under missile attack. I say again, we are under missile attack. Am dropping through five thousand feet now and taking all counter measures available.'

For a second the controller thought it was a hoax. This just did not happen. Not here. Never. But again, training took over. Already, he was marking in the threat, telling other controllers what was going on, requesting an immediate SAR. The search and rescue helicopter crew were in their respective messes when their bleepers went off. The two officer pilots, halfway through dinner, dropped their cutlery and ran for the doors, whilst their sergeant, who had already eaten and was looking forward to the film on Channel Four, leapt up with a curse and started running.

For all the precautions and thought which had gone into the attack, the SAR at Machrihanish had been forgotten by Habib. Even so, it would be irrelevant to the outcome.

By now, Todd and Spencer had a semblance of order and knew, more or less, what was happening.

'I have four missiles in the air.' Spencer spoke in the same voice he would have used if he'd been discussing the weather. 'All counter measures are released, noise and heat radiating at maximum effectiveness.'

Todd was grateful for the complete professionalism of the man sitting next to him. His palms were sweating but his brain was ice cool and functioning clearly. Already, he had plunged the helicopter to two thousand feet and dropping. He knew that the missiles had been launched from a ship which was clearly painted on the radar and which he knew was moving at thirty knots following their path. His mouth was dry as his eyes watched the screen in front of him.

'First missile is breaking left. It's acquired the decoy.' Spencer kept the excitement from his voice. He acted exactly as he would if this had been a simulated attack back at training. Only it isn't, his mind wanted to scream at him. By dint of will power he kept calm. 'First missile splashed.' They could see from the brief flare-up on the screen the destruction of the first missile.

The helicopter was screaming towards the water and the altimeter warning was beginning to sound. Without needing to be told, Spencer switched it off to the relief of both pilots, as one more noise abated from the cacophony still sounding in their headsets. The altimeter was reading fifty feet when Todd pulled back on the cyclic with all his strength. The aircraft immediately flared and came to a hover less than ten feet above the waves. He rammed the centre column stick hard to starboard and the helicopter heeled over and picked up speed. From the hover they started to accelerate rapidly.

'Splash two. The missile followed us straight in.'

The other two were still locked on. Luckily, the missiles had been fired at different intervals, otherwise they could never have coped. They did not realise that it was not their attackers' intention to blow them out of the sky. They were wanted alive. Or at least as many of the passengers alive as possible. The crew were an irrelevancy.

Todd had the helicopter screaming ahead at nearly two hundred and eighty knots already. The third missile was two hundred metres astern and closing fast. They were flying less than five metres above the sea which was flat calm. Even so, it was a frightening experience. With no reference points and a black night to stare at Todd was doing the impossible. This kind of flying was not in the book — any book. Nobody could go at that speed, on instruments, at that height. Except Todd.

'Missiles at thirty-five metres and five hundred meters and closing.' Spencer made himself watch the radar screen and not look out of the window. Every instinct he had was screaming at him that this was impossible. 'Christ. Losing it in the clutter. Stand by for impact.'

Todd pulled back the cyclic, turned on full power, and started to loop the loop. The helicopter was not meant to do that. However, Todd had been at the plant where it had been manufactured and remembered having a beer with the test pilot four years previously. The test pilot had done exactly this and lived to tell the tale. Todd hoped the story had been true. By now, Lima Foxtrot was standing on her tail and at the top of the arc. He stopped the backwards flip and rolled the aircraft out of it. They were at fifty metres above sea level and in danger of stalling as the red light began to flash and the two tone warning signal started.

Spencer was holding tightly to the armrests, his knuckles white. His eyes were glued to the radar. 'Missile passed underneath and splashed. Fourth missile locked onto decoy below us. We're losing it. Yes,' he yelled exultantly. 'Got it. It's blown. All four now . . . Christ, no!'

Todd had the helicopter on a straight path, picking up speed passing through one hundred and fifty knots towards the island which was now less than a mile away.

They both saw the fifth missile through the toughened perspex of the front window. Even as he began to dive, Todd knew it was too late. Bastards. After all that, were his thoughts as he still did everything he could to avert disaster. He dropped to a hover eight metres above the sea and swung the helicopter around to present the tail to the missile. If it hit the tail rotor instead of the main engine intake then they had a chance. He felt the tremor and heard the noise a millisecond before he caught the loom of the flash in the periphery of his vision. The tail rotor was blown away and the torque from the main rotors began to turn the helicopter slowly, as Todd lost control.

'Send the signal. I'll ditch on the water. Tell the passengers. As soon . . . you know the drill.' Todd shut up and concentrated on landing the helicopter on the sea. He knew that they had at least ten minutes, thanks to the new emergency flotation gear, to get everyone off and clear.

'Ladies and gentlemen. This is the co-pilot. We appreciate that you must be wondering what has been going on. We have been subjected to a missile attack. We evaded four missiles but were hit by the fifth. We are about to land on the sea.' Spencer looked at the radar screen and nudged Todd, who nodded. He had also seen the ship that they believed had fired on them, closing rapidly. 'We'll land in a few moments. There's plenty of time to get out as the floatation gear will keep us afloat for at least ten minutes, probably longer. Umm, unfortunately, the people responsible for the attack, we believe, are onboard the ship which is closing on us, right now. Stand by everybody, we're setting down now.'

There was a gentle bump and the helicopter began to rock in the swell. 'All right, start leaving by the emergency exits. Don't rush and don't panic.' He looked at Todd. 'Are you okay skipper?'

Todd nodded. 'You get out with the passengers. SAR should be airborne shortly. I'll keep reporting back as to what's going on. I'll try and procrastinate long enough so that help can get here.'

'Where from?'

Todd shrugged. 'They know what's happened. Presumably an alert has gone up which will have the cavalry galloping over the hills sooner rather than later.'

Spencer shook his head. 'There's nobody available,' he said, with honesty.

'Look, I'm going to stay here anyway,' said Todd. 'In the confusion I might not be missed. If I get a chance to get away, I'll take it. You get out through the emergency exit.' As he spoke he was busy turning the handle and pushing out the front of the windscreen. It fell away, letting in a draught of cold air. The helicopter was sitting upright and safe on the flotation gear as though they had landed at an airport. Both pilots knew this to be deceptive as it was only designed to keep them afloat long enough to get out. They could hear the yells from the passengers as each one climbed outside through one of the four emergency exits. They also heard the calm voice of Jane Felton telling them to inflate their life jackets once they were in the water and not before. Whether it was in spite of their age or because of it, all of the passengers behaved like the leaders they were. No panic, no fuss, no bother. A few could be heard complaining about the cold of the water but even that wasn't as vociferous as it could have been.

Todd was speaking over the radio. 'The passengers are getting out without any difficulty. The ship I told you about has closed to about a cable. I can see the gleam of her hull, it's white. I can't make out her name. I . . . what the hell . . .' he broke off as a machine gun opened fire. There were screams, yells and curses from the passengers who were in the water or scrambling onto life rafts which had also been launched by the cabin crew. He heard a voice shouting at the ship to stop firing.

An answering voice came back. 'If you have any weapons throw them away. Anyone caught with a weapon will be shot. Swim towards the ship now. Those of you who are not onboard this ship in three minutes will be shot. Swim away from the helicopter now.' There was a further burst of shooting and Todd could feel the bullets impacting along the fuselage. There were more shouts and curses and a lot of splashing as the VIPs floundered towards the ship. Todd heard the same voice telling them to hurry up as one minute had passed already. The shooting started again, this time a concerted firing at the helicopter. He realised that the hijackers were shooting up the flotation gear as the helicopter suddenly lurched to one side and settled closer to the water. He continued transmitting to the outside world telling them what was happening. Suddenly the cockpit erupted in a maelstrom of glass and bullets. Before he could do anything apart from realise that the cockpit was the target, he was dead. Three bullets went through his head, the nose of the helicopter dipped and sea water began to flood in. Instead of the expected ten to fifteen minutes afloat, the aircraft had lasted no more than three. Held by the safety harness, Todd was taken down into a watery grave, his blood swirling in a deep purple in the lights from the instrument panel which were quickly extinguished as water reached the batteries. Incredibly, thirty feet from the surface the helicopter stopped sinking and began to drift with the tidal stream.

Jane Felton and Billy Jones shepherded their passengers towards the ship. They were fifty yards away and could see some of the VIPs climbing the jump ladders dangling all along the side. The voice boomed again. 'Hurry up. You have one minute. If you are not here by then, we will shoot you.' The threat was repeated.

'Come on, ma'am,' Jones said to Felicity Cornwall. 'Kick harder.'

'I'm . . . I'm trying. It's just so damned cold.'

'Better cold than dead,' said Jones without feeling. He grabbed the back of her lifejacket and began to swim rapidly towards the ship, overtaking some of the others struggling through the water. He reached the side panting for breath and took hold of the ministers' hands and bent them over a rung of the ladder. 'Come on, climb,' he said harshly. She began to do so and Jones turned his attention to the next person. He couldn't see who it was but he held on to the ladder, reached out and grabbed the man's arm and pulled him into the side. 'Get up as fast as you can.'

Jones began climbing a ladder when he heard the snicker of a bolt being drawn back and let go. He looked up at the man standing behind the general purpose machine gun who had just reloaded the weapon. He saw the gun's trajectory change and point downwards. There were a dozen people still in the water, their heads lit by the loom from the searchlight the ship had aimed at the helicopter. Frantically, Jones dived from the side where he had managed to climb half way up, hit the water awkwardly because of the life jacket, and swam frantically to the nearest person. He grabbed the person by the arm and started back to the ship, four metres away. The gun opened up with a noise which was terrifying. There were screams from people in the water which quickly stopped as the bullets found their marks. Jones reached the side of the ship and began to climb the ladder, pulling the passenger behind him. The GPMG suddenly stopped. The silence was ominous, but not a true silence as he could hear raised voices, more curses, a shout and then something hitting the deck. He heard Jane say, 'Leave him alone, you brute.' Then there was a thud and a whimper. By now he had reached the deck and crawled over the side, gasping from exhaustion and fear. He could not stop shivering, the cold seeping into the marrow of his bones. The man he had helped also crawled over the side and to his surprise Jones realised it was the British Deputy Prime Minister. He raised his head as a pair of legs came into view and stopped next to the inert figure, lying gasping just a few feet away. As though in slow motion he saw one of the legs move back and kick the DPM in the side. There was an anguished grunt.

'Get up and go through the forward hatch. Move yourself.' Instead of the expected kick, Jones heard the snicker of a gun being cocked and scrambled to his feet. He stepped forward and took hold of John Williams under his arm and pulled him upright.

'Leave him. Let him get up himself.'

Jones looked into the cold-blooded and fanatical eyes of the man with the gun and said, 'No. He's an old man. He needs help.' As he spoke, the DPM nodded his thanks and helped himself by holding on to the guard rail.

Habib looked at Jones' uniform, looked him in the eyes and without warning shot him in the middle of his forehead. Jones' body was flung overboard, a look of surprise etched on his face for eternity.

Williams turned on Habib. 'You bastard, there was no need for that. I . . .' he got no further as Habib casually and contemptuously hit him across the side of the face with the gun. The foresight cut into his cheek and blood dripped down the side of his face. Williams staggered back but stayed on his feet. He then did something completely out of character. He made a fist, stepped forward and swung at Habib's face. Habib was so taken aback that he made no move to avoid the punch which landed on the side of his head. It hardly hurt but enraged Habib to the point of madness.

He grabbed Williams by the throat with his left hand and jammed the gun into his mouth. Slowly, he forced Williams to his knees. There was madness in Habib's eyes, loathing in Williams'. 'You will beg for mercy before I shoot you.'

Williams could taste blood and gun oil, but he made no sound. Having served in Korea and later in Malaya in the early sixties Williams, at the age of sixty-five, was still a brave man. If anything, he was braver than when he was younger having achieved most of what he had set out to do in life. That was something Habib could not and never would, understand.

He was about to pull the trigger when Fredericks grabbed his arm. 'This one we want alive, unless we take his body with us,' he said.

Habib shook his head as though waking up from a sleep. The light of madness faded from his eyes and he withdrew the gun. 'Get up and go forward,' he ordered.

The DPM got to his feet and with every ounce of will power walked upright and steadily away. He passed two men, middle eastern by the looks of them, both carrying machine guns, who gestured for him to follow the others. As each one climbed through the hatch combing, he or she was roughly and superficially searched. Because they had clambered from the helicopter in rather a hurry, none

158

of the ladies had handbags and few of the men had more than the clothes they stood in. A few items were taken away and thrown in a heap on the deck, but not many. The terrorists were in too much of a hurry.

The prisoners found themselves in the forward hold, among the anchor cable. It was surprisingly large, as, unknown to the prisoners, the cable locker and next two locker rooms had been opened up into one space. The place was bare, nowhere to sit except on the steel deck. Williams looked at the bedraggled figures sitting and standing. No one was talking. Shock, fear and cold had taken away their powers to think and speak. However, the enemy had made an error of judgement. Already, individuals were beginning to shake off their lethargy. You did not rise to the top of your chosen professions, especially in activities such as politics, banking and the United Nations, without being dedicated and extremely tough minded. The toughness was beginning to shine through after the trauma.

The boat heeled over and was beginning to bounce on the water as it picked up speed. Habib had rung on maximum revs in an effort to get as far away as possible before any assistance arrived on the scene.

John Williams spat some blood and spittle into a soaking wet handkerchief and said, 'Do we have any idea as to what's going on?' He looked around at the faces of those nearest to him. They responded with shakes of the head.

Williams looked across at one of the figures sitting with his back to the bulkhead. 'Ben, any thoughts?'

The Vice-President of the United States of America looked up thoughtfully and then slowly shook his head. 'I can't say I have,' he drawled. 'What I do know is that they must be some sort of crazy bastards to pull off a stunt like this. Anybody know who they are?'

There were more shakes of the heads as the spark of life after the cold and defiance after the fear, took hold. Wilma Shules, the Secretary General at the UN slowly stood up, her hand pressed against the side of the ship to give her balance. 'We need to do something. We need warm clothes, blankets, perhaps a warm drink.' By now the ship was moving at full speed and even on the calmest of water this meant a constant and rapid bouncing of the bows which was very unpleasant. A number of the bedraggled figures were beginning to feel sea-sick.

'Here's a cupboard,' said a loud Afrikaans sounding voice. Jesus Mboko was a tough, sprightly blackman, the special assistant to Nelson Mandela. At fifty-five he had had recent experience of warfare, having fought for the ANC for over thirty years. He pulled open the door, gave an exclamation of satisfaction and started pulling out rough brown blankets and throwing them behind him. Others picked them up and distributed them to those who were sitting or still lying down. One or two were bleeding, and a few were holding their heads as though they ached.

There were insufficient blankets to go round and so some sat next to each other, sharing, their combined body warmth helping to stop the shivering and reduce the chattering of teeth. John Williams had a blanket to himself which he wrapped around his shoulders while he paced back and forth the four or five paces available to him.

Suddenly he stopped and looked about him. 'Who's missing?'

They all looked from one to the other, unsure. Felicity Cornwall, the Minister for Agriculture and Fish said, tentatively, 'Where's Otto?' She was talking about Otto Grunweld, the President of the German Bundesbank and one of the most powerful bankers in the Western world.

'Dead,' said Bradley. 'I saw him shot.' He didn't elaborate about the way the German's head had suddenly vaporised in front of his eyes when the machine gun had started firing. He had only survived because he had dived down under the water and swam frantically for the side of the ship. However it had happened, he had survived.

'The flight attendant, what's his name?' asked the Deputy Prime Minister.

'Billy Jones,' said Jane Felton, looking round for him.

'He was murdered,' continued the DPM. 'Shot for helping me.' He could not disguise the anguish in his voice.

Jane gasped and put her hand over her mouth, her eyes filled with tears. Poor Billy – one of the kindest and most considerate men she had ever known.

More names were called. The realisation hit them that ten of their number were missing, including Fred Todd, the pilot.

Mboko said, 'I saw them take Ori Hirago off to one side,' he paused, as he remembered the defiance etched on the face of the director of the Bank of Sumato, one of the biggest banks in Japan. 'Somebody shot him in the head without a second thought. I saw him fall into the water.'

Out of a total of thirty-five passengers, two attendants and two pilots, twenty-nine still survived.

'Where do you think they are taking us?' asked Oliver Winter, the UN spokesman on international poverty. At sixty-six, bald and overweight he was the most nervous and scared person there. A pompous, arrogant man, he was also a bully. He owed his position at the UN to the President of the USA whose campaign Winter had heavily supported. The job at the UN was his payoff. Right then he wished he had not taken it. Like all bullies, Winter was a coward who thought of nobody but himself. It was one of the reasons he had been singularly unsuccessful at his post, unable to comprehend what was required of him.

As nobody knew, nobody answered.

'One thing is for certain,' said Bradley, also standing and shaking off the mental lethargy that had been creeping over him, 'all hell will have broken loose by now and search parties will be scouring the land.'

'Not much use, old boy,' said James Treherne, the British Ambassador to the UN, 'since we're at sea.'

There were a few smiles at the feeble attempt at wit. He and Bradley had been friends for years, having first met when he had been stationed at Fort Bragg, twenty years earlier. Then he had been a captain in the Royal Marines and on secondment as a training officer. Bradley had been one of his pupils. An unlikely friendship had began which had ripened and deepened as the years went by, in spite of the fifteen years separating them. Treherne had finally retired from the Royal Marines in the rank of Lieutenant General, just prior to the Gulf War. He was still fit, healthy and very tough.

Bradley grinned back at his old friend. 'Okay then. Scouring land and sea. The point is, what do they hope to gain? Unless they wish to kill us all, but that doesn't make sense as they could have done so already. And why kill Hirago?'

'Nothing makes sense,' said Treherne, thoughtfully.

'But since when has anything carried out by terrorists made sense?'

Ibn ben Saud nodded. 'That is true, my friend.' As the only Arab there he was more than a little concerned. There was no love lost between the fanatics of Palestine, Iran and Iraq and his own people in Saudi Arabia. He was wearing a grey business suit and looked like any other diplomat, businessman or banker. If their captors knew who he was he felt certain that they would shoot him. He had recognised Habib and knew him for who and what he was. At fifty-three, Ibn ben Saud was "Minister Without Portfolio" for his country and involved with many committees on many subjects. One of those committees was concerned with the defence of the realm of Saudi, a subject which had been blown up out of all proportion since the Gulf War. It was whilst serving on that committee that Habib had come to his notice. In spite of Habib's caution and concern not to be photographed some descriptions and photographs did exist.

Ben Saud had been certain who they were dealing with the instant he laid eyes on Habib. 'Unfortunately, I think I know who's in charge. If I'm right, this whole thing makes sense to somebody.'

'Who do you think you saw?' asked Donald Spencer quickly. He had been overawed by the company he found himself in, but as the minutes passed, he realised that they were no different from himself. They were all cold, frightened and more than a little angry.

'Habib. It was he who shot Ori.'

'Why? What was to be gained?' Felicity Cornwall asked.

Ben Saud thought for a moment before replying. He was fairly certain he knew the answer but should he disclose it to those present? He mentally tossed a coin and decided to divulge what he knew.

'Ori would have or, I should say, did recognise Habib.'

'But how would Habib know that and why kill him?'

'I believe that Habib had dealings with Mr. Hirago about two years ago. I think Habib shot him in an effort to protect his identity.'

'What do you mean dealings with him?' Bradley asked.

'You remember the terrorist attack in South Korea when the Chairman and directors of the banking and car conglomerate Hyashi were killed?'

There were a number of nods and now all eyes were on him. 'From the research I had done on Habib it appears that he was paid by a Japanese company to carry out the attack. Koreans had been about to bid for a major European company. The bid failed after the attack and the company was subsequently bought by the Japanese. My information suggested that Ori Hirago was the paymaster. It was his company which bought the European business after the events in South Korea.'

'My God,' said Jane Fenton, aghast.

'I am afraid,' said ben Saud, with a slight, cynical grimace, 'that at some levels business is done that way. It has led to a proliferation of companies supplying highly trained bodyguards, many of them ex-special forces from all over the world. The favourite being your own SAS.'

'Are you sure it's Habib?' someone asked.

'I think so, yes. I last studied his file less than a year ago. There was a rumour that he was intending to commit an atrocity against the Royal Family, although precisely what form that atrocity would take no one seemed able to tell me.' There was no need for him to say which

Royal Family as he was known to serve the rulers of Saudi Arabia with a fanatical dedication.

'That still doesn't explain who he is,' Jane said.

'I know who he is,' said the Vice-Chancellor of Germany, speaking for the first time since they had boarded the ship. Like the others he was coming back to life. His anger was being held in check by an iron will. As one of the architects for the unification of Germany and an ex-major of the German Army, Herbert Conrad at sixty was both physically and mentally tough. 'He is a psychotic killer who hides under the guise of Islam, working only for money and pleasure and not necessarily in that order. He has an assistant named Fredericks – another psychotic. However, they are both highly trained, highly intelligent and, most importantly, highly motivated.'

There were a few more nods of agreement.

'So what are they up to?' Bradley asked. He looked at his watch. 'It's now over an hour and twenty minutes since we ditched. Where are we and what can he be planning? One thing is for sure. If it is Habib, he is one smart son of a bitch and there is an objective to this. What's more important, he thinks he can get away with it, whatever it is. He's not one to sacrifice himself on the alter of Allah.'

David Golightly, Deputy Prime Minister of Israel, said, 'That's true. We have very extensive files on the man although I would never have recognised him. He works only to a well-conceived plan,' he paused. 'But I'm damned if I can see what it is this time.'

Throughout this time there were two people present who had said nothing, only listened. They were both members of the British Special Air Services, assigned as bodyguards for the occupants of the helicopter, under the guise of being Special Branch. The two American secret service guards had died in the shooting. John Stanton and Cecil McDonald were as different as chalk and cheese. The former was six feet three inches, weighed sixteen stones of solid muscle and could have been a contender for the world heavy weight boxing championship. The latter was five feet six inches, wiry, sported a long drooping moustache and would go unnoticed in a crowd of two. At thirty-three, he was acknowledged as one of the SAS's toughest sergeants. On five different occasions he had been undercover in Northern Ireland and had been responsible for the deaths of fourteen IRA terrorists and the imprisonment of another nine. By his reckoning he had failed with the nine. He would rather have counted their number with the other fourteen. Nobody made a joke of his name, Cecil. Both men were armed to the teeth.

Bradley turned to McDonald and said, 'Cecil, you've been with me on the last three visits to England. What do you make of it?'

Having spent the time listening and thinking, McDonald was ready with his answer. 'I know of Habib and I agree with all you've said. Our edge is that he will have an escape route. I don't think that will include all of his men, however many he's got with him. It will include Fredericks. We know he can't get away, as already a search will be underway. We all know that between the satellites and the types and numbers of aircraft we can get into the air there's nowhere to run.' He paused. 'There is somewhere to hide.'

'Where?' asked John Williams.

The sergeant shrugged. 'Somewhere. I don't know where.' He almost said, for Christ's sake, but managed instead to add, 'sir.' He paused and then continued. 'I

guess an island off Scotland. Far off shore or close
inshore? I don't know. I think he is holding us for a
purpose but I also think, because of what I know about
the man, that he intends that we all die.'

There were nods from some of the men and gasps
of fear from others. Jane Felton who was sharing a
blanket with Felicity Cornwall, grabbed Felicity's hands
and squeezed them tightly.

'Don't spare our feelings, will you?' said Mrs. Cornwall.

The sergeant turned his big brown eyes on the Minister
and replied. 'What would be the purpose? We need to
be ready. They,' he nodded his head at the overhead
bulkhead, 'will kid us on that if we do as we're told
we'll all live. That will be a ploy to get our co-operation.
Believe me, they intend to kill us all right.'

John Stanton had a doctorate in philosophy and could
write PhD after his name if he wished. The fact that he
looked like a thuggish boxer hid a keen and penetrating
mind. He was also a lieutenant and outranked McDonald
but had the good sense to listen to and take the advice
of his far more experienced colleague. 'I agree with
Cecil. Nothing else makes sense. We need to be aware
of what's happening and be ready for anything. That way
it's possible we may survive.'

Habib had made a number of errors when laying
his plans. The biggest of them all was to ignore the
backgrounds of his prisoners. More than half of them
had trained with one or another branch of the armed
services. They had risen high and fast because of their
ability and toughness.

'What are you carrying?' asked Bradley.

'The usual,' replied Stanton, not elaborating.

Bradley nodded. 'Fair enough.' He knew what that

meant. Both men were carrying explosives, guns, knives, and other useful items. All hidden carefully about the person and clothes so that nothing showed. Habib would not get it all his own way.

'Any ideas?' asked Wilma Shules. 'I mean, are we to fight our way out or what?' The feisty Canadian was serious even if she had never seen a shot fired in anger before today.

'No,' McDonald said more sharply than he intended. 'The object of the exercise is to live as long as possible, preferably to a ripe old age. No, ma'am,' he managed a grin to take the sting out of his words, 'we won't fight our way out. We're still alive because they want us for some reason or other. We may get a chance to do something later but for now our priority is to survive. I think they also want us alive as some sort of pawns in a blackmail attempt. Maybe they want some jailed prisoners freed. I don't know. Whatever it is, we're useful for the time being. Let's stretch out that time for as long as possible.'

The engine sound changed and the movement of the ship reduced. They were slowing down.

9

P.M. 2 May 1998. 10 Downing Street, London.

The Prime Minister was lounging in his armchair, a glass
of white wine at his elbow, looking at the television. His
wife was sitting opposite him doing a crossword puzzle,
not bothering to watch the film. Although he was staring
at the actors shooting and killing their way across the city
of New York he could not have said what the film was
about nor who the good guys and the bad guys were.
His mind was busy with the forthcoming by-election at
Windsor. Even though they had smashed the Tories at
the last election he still wanted his party to do well
at Windsor. For a few moments he dreamt of winning
the seat but then shook the idea away. That was too
fantastic, even if he was, according to the polls, one of
the most popular Prime Ministers this century. Pensively
he picked up his glass and took a sip. He was not a heavy
drinker but he enjoyed a fine wine or a decent whisky.
The Chablis he was drinking suited him; dry and very
palatable.

His concentration was so great that he did not hear the
ringing until his wife said, 'Tony, the phone.'

He looked up, startled, put down his glass and heaved
himself to his feet. At this time of night on a Saturday

it could only mean bad news. He just hoped to God it meant a disaster in some other part of the world and not at home; like another back bencher being found drunk in a gutter somewhere, or another minister leaving his wife for his secretary.

'PM,' was all he said.

'Prime Minister, this is the Air Chief Marshal.'

Suddenly, the phone was slippery in his hands. However, having been Prime Minister for a year he was used to dealing with disasters of all shapes and sizes. His voice was steady as he said, 'Dick. What's the problem?'

There being no way to soften the blow, the Air Chief Marshal came straight out with it. 'The helicopter taking the VIPs to Balmoral was shot out of the sky thirty minutes ago,' he said baldly.

'What? What did you say?' Nothing had prepared him for this news. It was unthinkable, unbelievable.

'I said . . .'

'Yes, yes, I heard you. What do you mean shot out of the sky? Is anybody dead? How did it happen? Are there any survivors?'

'PM, if you give me a chance I'll tell you. I'm on my way to you now. The Secretary of State for Defence and the Home Secretary are also on their way. I couldn't find anyone else whom we need at this point in time. Unless you can think of anybody?'

'What? No. I don't think so. We need to know what's happened before we rush into automatic.'

The Chief of Defence Staff, the highest military posting in the British Armed Forces, refrained from telling the Prime Minister that the whole point of their standing operational procedures was exactly that – no thought, no planning. That had been done years earlier and refined as circumstances dictated. SOPs were designed for automatic reaction. A very quick response until the available information dictated their follow on moves. He refrained from telling the PM just then that he had already pressed the right buttons in accordance with standing orders. The only new boy on the block, as it were, was Macnair. And whatever happened, Lockwood was determined to keep him out of the picture.

The whole idea of Macnair's unit was anathema to him. It was a useless and stupid political ploy which should never have seen the light of day. The other regular forces had always dealt with any problems which arose and dealt with them well. The British were considered amongst the finest and most professional armed forces in the world. They had no need of others interfering, especially other nationalities. For someone who had risen to the very top of his profession the Air Chief Marshal was a bigoted little Englander, the worst combination of attitudes imaginable.

'I'll be there in ten minutes, traffic permitting. Is there anything else?'

'Survivors. You didn't tell me if there were any survivors.'

At his words his wife looked up and put her newspaper to one side. What was it? A bomb? An air crash? Another disaster?

'We don't know,' came the reply.

'What do you mean, you don't know? Surely someone's got to the site by now.'

'Yes, PM, of course they have. I mean, we've found some bodies but a lot are missing. We haven't found any survivors yet, but we're looking.'

'I see. Right. I'll be in the Cabinet Room.'

He hung up and turned to his wife. Briefly he told her what had happened. 'Organise some coffee and a plate of sandwiches in case anybody wants some, please dear. Then see if you can find Anthony. He won't relish coming in, but that's too bad.' Sir Anthony Parsons was Secretary to the Cabinet and as such, the most senior civil servant in Britain, which was a misnomer in terms, as he was not particularly civil and definitely not a servant.

The PM's wife smiled. 'He won't like that.' Privately, she relished the idea of sending for the man. Since his promotion he had, in little ways, made it clear that even if the present incumbent at number ten was proud of his humble roots, he, Sir Anthony, was not proud of serving him. This was in spite of the fact that he owed his promotion to the Prime Minister – a fact which seemed to rankle with Sir Anthony.

The PM quickly donned a jacket and changed from his slippers to shoes before walking down to the Cabinet Room. He was the first to arrive and switched on the lights and turned up the heating. It was chilly in the room and he looked forward to a cup of coffee.

He heard the front door opening and closing twice in quick succession and in walked the Secretary of State for Defence and the Home Secretary. The former was a highly intelligent Scotsman who had a sound grasp of his department and an in-depth knowledge of the workings of the Ministry of Defence. He got on well with the senior officers of the army, navy and air force in spite of the fact that he was having to reduce their budget by five percent. At forty-five, slim and standing five feet ten he was good looking enough to be an asset when appearing on television. He had a stable marriage, there was no hint of scandal in his background and he was independently wealthy. He was tipped as the next leader of the Labour Party should they lose the next general election. Stuart Roberts knew that time was on his side and that one day, if he played his cards right, he would be Prime Minister.

In contrast, the Home Secretary, Charles Norheed, was a shambling, ungainly man who had reached the top of his political tree. He belonged to the left wing of the party and was a member of the "it's not the criminals fault but society's". His appointment had come as a surprise to the whole country but had been necessary for the PM, to keep a large section of his party quiet. It had worked for a few months but already the left were baying for more. It ranged from joining a single currency in Europe to increasing old age pensioners' benefits along with those for single parents. Some members of the Labour Party still thought money grew on trees! They just did not live in the real world half the time. At six feet six and twenty stone he was not an attractive figure and the party worked hard at keeping him off the television screens as much as possible. As always, he had a cigarette clutched in his left hand.

'Coffee's on its way,' the PM said by way of a greeting. 'Lockwood should be with us shortly.' Even as they spoke they heard the front door open and close and the Air Chief Marshal marched into the room followed by his "flags", Squadron Leader Paul Brice.

Lockwood and Brice had removed their hats and hung them on the coat pegs outside the room. Nearing sixty, Lockwood was old for the job and knew that he would be retiring within the year. As such, he had hoped for as quiet a time as possible to enjoy the fruits of his labours which had taken him to the very top. He believed he had reached his goal due to his ability. In reality, he had been one of the luckiest men alive and had been in the right place at the right time on many occasions. His various promotions had been looked on incredulously by his colleagues and tinged with a good deal of envy. If ever a man had been promoted out of his depth, the Air Chief Marshal was one such man. Indeed, he had been promoted several times out of his depth. He was small, slim and dapper. He did not look strong enough to carry the braid with which his uniform was covered and the stripes on his arms nearly reached his elbows. He was often ridiculed and parodied by his fellow officers who were careful to ensure that they were never caught doing so.

The coffee and sandwiches were brought in by the duty steward who laid them on the table and quietly departed. Brice poured the coffee and handed round the plates. In the company of this particular group of men, Brice knew his place.

'Right, Dick. Please be good enough to bring us up to date with what's been going on.'

Paul Brice tried to keep the scorn from his face. At thirty-three, he was tipped for the very top of the RAF. His appointment as Aide de Camp (ADC) to Lockwood, should, in the normal course of events, lead to promotion and another Whitehall job, which suited him and his wife. Unfortunately, being highly intelligent and not one to suffer fools gladly, he was having difficulty in keeping his peace, especially when asked a direct question. He was aware that in order to have a good report from the Air Chief Marshal he was required, effectively, to be a "yes" man to Lockwood which was something he found increasingly difficult to do. Like all men of limited ability, Lockwood also had limited vision which meant that he could not see the big picture and worse still, could not imagine what was beyond the horizon. Hence, the Air Chief Marshal's opposition to Macnair's new outfit. Instead of the armed forces being equipped and ready for the new century they were being held in a time warp of the eighties due to the obstinacy and stupidity of one man. Brice, being at the centre of power, was constantly amazed at how some decisions were reached.

The Air Chief Marshal cleared his throat and took out a briefing paper from the buff folder he had placed on the desk in front of him. 'We know that at 19.58 hours missiles were fired at Golf Bravo November Lima Foxtrot . . .'

'What? What's that?' asked the Home Secretary.

'Missiles were . . .'

'No. What's that Golf Fox thing,' Norheed spoke irritably.

Brice kept a straight face, only the slitting of his eyes giving away his feelings if anyone there had been astute enough to notice. As he looked at the others around the table he became aware that the Secretary of State for Defence probably had noticed his reaction. Well, that was too bad. He was becoming fed up with the whole business of watching mediocre men making poor judgements and wrong decisions.

'That's the helicopter that was shot down,' said Lockwood, resignedly, as if he too found it difficult to put up with the obtuseness of his political masters. In reality, he hid behind pedantry and bombast to hide his inadequacies. 'May I continue?'

Norheed nodded, whilst he helped himself to another sandwich, which he quickly stuffed into his mouth. Try as he might, Brice was unable to find a single redeeming feature about the man who, in political terms anyway, was one of the most important people in Parliament.

'From what we can gather, four missiles were fired from a ship off the west coast of Scotland . . .'

'Where, precisely?' interrupted Norheed again.

'For God's . . .' Lockwood cut off his rejoinder. 'Does it matter where? I'll never get this finished if you keep interrupting me.' His bluster was to hide the fact that he did not know precisely where the incident had taken place. He had not thought it was important to know.

In his soft, educated Edinburgh accent, Roberts said, 'With all due respect, Dick,' a statement that indicated that respect was the last thing on his mind, 'but the Scottish coast is long and rugged. It's very important we know precisely where this, em, not incident but atrocity, took place. After all, our response depends upon it.'

Brice let his boss stew for a few seconds before he cleared his throat to gain their attention. 'Excuse me, sir, but perhaps I may be of help?'

Roberts smiled at Brice, not surprised at the offer. 'I thought you might,' he said.

'Yes, sir. Well,' he took out an Admiralty Chart of the area from the file he was carrying and opened it over the table. He pointed at the area off Scotland with a pencil he took from his pocket. 'This is where it happened. You can see that it is a bleak and desolate area, well chosen by the terrorists.'

'How do you know that they're terrorists?' asked the Prime Minister.

Brice cut off the retort before it reached his lips. What he wanted to say was who else other than terrorists would carry out such an act, but instead managed, 'We are surmising at this stage sir, that this was an act of terrorism.' (Of course it was, he thought, you bloody fool, what do you call the shooting down of a helicopter loaded with VIPs?) He glanced at the Secretary of State for Defence who was trying hard not to smile.

'Em, yes, of course,' said the PM. 'A perfectly natural assumption. Please carry on.'

Brice was unsure whether the Prime Minister was talking to him or to the Air Chief Marshal and so leant back in his chair and looked at his boss.

'Yes . . . right . . . well . . . let me see,' flustered Lockwood. 'A search and rescue helicopter was quickly despatched to the area. From the information we have,' he looked at his notes, 'it appears that they were in the area of the, em, atrocity, within thirty-eight minutes. They used their search lights but could see very little, initially.'

'What was the weather like?' asked Roberts.

'The weather?' The Air Chief Marshal repeated.

'Yes, the weather. Surely, if it was blowing a gale they would have had an impossible task to find anything. On the other hand, if it had been flat calm, they may have found their task easier. And it will also have a bearing on how quickly we can expect some answers.'

Brice interrupted again. 'It was flat calm. There was a gentle breeze at sea level from the west and a southerly tide of two knots.'

'Thank you, Squadron Leader,' said Roberts.

Lockwood scowled and then said, 'Yes, thank you, Paul. Now, as I was saying, from the transcripts we have of the conversations which took place between the helicopter and the air traffic controller at Machrihanish, it seems that at least four missiles were fired. Obviously, one of them hit the target. After a preliminary search the pilot put down on a small island called, em,' he looked

177

through his notes again, 'called Gravellachs. Apparently, he had the idea of shutting down his engines and listening and calling, to see if there were any survivors.'

'And were there?' asked the Prime Minister.

'No,' the Air Chief Marshall shook his head slowly and sorrowfully. His hypocrisy shone through and fooled no one around the table. 'I'm afraid not. However, they did find a number of bodies.' He paused for effect. 'They had been shot. According to the report we received, machine gunned would be a more accurate description.'

'My God,' gasped the Prime Minister, 'that's terrible. Barbaric. Who would have done such a thing?'

'Terrorists?' suggested Stuart Roberts, dryly.

'Yes, thank you Stuart. I do appreciate that. What's to be done and what's happening now?' The PM directed his questions at The Air Chief Marshal.

'Well, we have already started, em, things moving. In accordance with JSOPs . . .'

'Jay sops? What are those?' asked the Home Secretary, pausing with a cup half way to his lips.

'Joint Standing Operational Procedures,' replied Lockwood. 'It . . .' he stopped speaking as the door opened and in walked Sir Anthony Parsons.

'Good evening, gentlemen,' he quickly scanned the faces and sat next to the Prime Minister. 'I gather there's some sort of flap on.' A tall, handsome and distinguished man, Parsons would have reached the top of any profession he chose. The fact that he was independently wealthy helped him to maintain his image and lifestyle. He did his job because he enjoyed it. He liked being at the centre of power, pulling the strings when necessary. Totally manipulative, highly educated and highly intelligent, he found the control he exercised over the present Cabinet extremely satisfying. Luckily for the nation he applied his intelligence on behalf of the people and luckily for democracy neither the media nor the self same people knew of his control and power. For instance, Macnair's new outfit was the brain child of the Secretary of State for Defence and had Sir Anthony's full support and backing. Without it, the whole concept would have been strangled at birth.

'Perhaps somebody would be good enough to bring me up to date?' As he spoke he helped himself to a cup of coffee which by this time was almost stone cold.

Lockwood repeated what had been said so far, giving only the highlights.

'And what does JSOPs have us do?' Parsons asked.

'We have alerted the army, navy and air force. The diving team from Faslane is already airborne and a detachment of Royal Marines is on the way from Poole. Two minesweepers which had been exercising in the Clyde have been routed to the area . . .'

Brice coughed. 'Excuse me, sir. Not minesweepers.' Didn't the cretin know the difference between a Hunt class and a minesweeper? 'Two Hunt class minehunters sir. Their search sonar is what's needed to find the helicopter.'

Lockwood glared at his subordinate. 'Yes, yes, I know that. Two Hunt class ships. We have also sent a signal to Northwood asking them if there are any other ships in the vicinity able to give assistance.' Northwood was where the Commander in Chief had his headquarters and from where the ships of the Royal Navy were controlled. At any time of the day or night the C-in-C knew precisely where his total fleet was to be found, what state of readiness they were at, and whether they could respond to an emergency such as the one which had arisen.

'And are there?' asked Parsons.

'We don't know yet. We are still waiting for a reply. It's early days yet,' said the Air Chief Marshall, shuffling his notes.

'So,' said the Home Secretary, 'we've already gone off in bloody automatic and we don't know what's actually going on.'

The Prime Minister looked at Norwood for a few seconds, controlling his dislike for the man. He was the price the PM had to pay to keep his left wing happy, a task which was becoming more difficult almost daily. Unlike his predecessor, the current incumbent at No. 10 Downing Street was, when called upon, decisive and politically fearless. He proved this over the last Iraq problem when the UK and the USA stood together in their determination to stop Saddam getting weapons of mass destruction. The tragedy of Dunblane, when sixteen small children and their teacher had been shot to death, and a further fourteen wounded, sprang to mind. Instead of banning all hand guns and rifles in private ownership, the government set up the Cullen Enquiry. Eight months after the horrific events at the primary school in Dunblane, Lord Cullen made recommendations which satisfied no one. When the Labour Party came to power they tightened up the Cullen recommendations and banned all guns. He was also a staunch supporter of Macnair and his outfit. Being a canny politician he would ensure that he reaped the political rewards in the not too distant future.

Parsons said, 'That is precisely what JSOPs and other standing operational procedures are for. The right buttons are pressed and our organisations swing automatically into action. I suggest we leave the various services to get on with their jobs whilst we consider the bigger picture.'

'What bigger picture?' asked the Home Secretary.

Parsons waited a few seconds to see if anyone else in the room was going to reply and when he realised that they weren't, took a deep sigh. 'The media, the UN, other nations. The rest of the Cabinet. Need I go on?'

Heads shook. There was no need to go on. There was a great deal to be done and little time to do it in.

'May I suggest,' said Parsons, 'that we let the military get on with their job and we'll get on with ours. Due to the international flavour of this,' he was about to say incident but decided the word was not strong enough, 'outrage, we should mobilise Macnair and his men and let them get to work. After all, they were set up to cope with international terrorism and this seems like a good opportunity to put into practice what we have been preaching.'

'I see no need for that,' said Lockwood. 'Macnair and his men are a waste of money. I told you that before. We can handle this incident without them. And besides, they haven't got up and running properly yet.'

Parsons said, 'I think now is exactly the right time to use Macnair. We can't get more of an international outrage than this and it's within our bailiwick. That means we have greatest say and control. It's a chance for Macnair to prove how, by co-operating between sovereign states, we can beat terrorism.'

Brice couldn't hold his peace any longer. 'Excuse me, gentlemen.' All eyes turned to him, making him feel uncomfortable. After all, he was not there to have any input into the proceedings, only to supply answers if the Air Chief Marshal was at a loss to do so. 'I think it's a bit premature to talk about beating terrorism. We don't know who carried out the attack, what they are trying to achieve and, most importantly, where they are now.'

'Thank you, Squadron Leader Brice,' said Sir Anthony, 'you're quite right. I made a silly statement. We need to try and track them down as quickly as possible and I think that the man with the ideas and, most significantly, the vision to do so, is Macnair. I suggest he be given operational control and allowed to get on with it.'

'I object. There's absolutely no need for that at all,' spluttered Lockwood. 'We have the men and the means to carry out this task without Macnair.'

'I disagree,' said Stuart Roberts, firmly. 'We have thrown a vast amount of resources at Macnair to tackle exactly the kind of problem we are currently facing. We need international co-operation and possible assistance and that will be easier coming through Macnair than through anyone else.'

'Rubbish,' exploded Lockwood. 'I've told you before and I'm telling you again, we don't need Macnair. Give me the resources you've given him and I can get the job done.'

'You're missing the point,' said the Secretary of State for Defence, 'then you always have,' he added with a barb. 'We need to work at this kind of outrage from an international perspective. This isn't just one isolated act. It's the latest of many. Look what has happened in France in recent months. Even the USA has been targeted within the boundaries of America and that has never happened before.'

Brice, having already spoken without getting his head chewed off said, 'I agree, sir.' Again, all eyes swivelled on him, but this time he met them without inwardly quailing. 'I recently finished the senior officer's staff college course and that was the resounding opinion of every officer there. General Macnair has the job and he should be tasked to carry out this one.'

The Air Chief Marshal was apoplectic with anger. 'That will do Brice. We won't hear another word from you.'

'Yes, sir. Only . . .'

'Only nothing. I said keep silence.'

Brice nodded his head and looked down at his briefing papers. Oh well, another promising career bites the dust, he thought.

'No, wait a moment. This is very interesting,' said Stuart Roberts. 'One of our concerns when we set up the anti-terrorist unit was how the other services would react. Now, we've all been aware what Dick here thought about it but what about the other operational officers? I would be most interested in hearing from the Squadron Leader.'

Brice looked up, startled. He saw the Prime Minister nod and heard Sir Anthony Parsons say, 'Yes, that would be most interesting and, eh, enlightening.'

Brice avoided Lockwood's eyes by staring down at his papers, doodling on a blank sheet of paper. 'Well, the consensus was that we all have enough to do as it is, without becoming side tracked into an anti-terrorist role. Apart from the SAS and MI5 we don't know enough about the problem and, worse still, we would be unlikely to get agreement to operate world wide, which is why we shall never defeat terrorism. We read and discussed General Macnair's original report and agreed with his findings. That is why, I believe, you'll find there is a great deal of co-operation between the army, navy and air force on this matter.'

'Well said,' Sir Anthony Parsons tried not to sound patronising as he meant his praise. 'That is precisely what we wanted to hear. If we announce that Macnair and his men are an international body, working under the widest remit, with full backing and co-operation from nations all over the world, we could help to establish his force. In that way, if an incident cropped up anywhere in the EU it would be Macnair and his men who would deal with it. Who knows, in time, it could even be an outrage committed anywhere in the world. We have to take this opportunity if we are to achieve the original objectives when we agreed with Macnair's plans.'

The Prime Minister made a moue and looked down at the leather note pad lying in front of him. Come on Anthony, he thought, use your much acclaimed intelligence and get me off the political hook. The Home Secretary looked sheepish, whilst only the Secretary of State for Defence looked particularly happy. It took the Secretary of the Cabinet a full two seconds before the penny dropped.

'I don't believe it. My God,' Parsons looked at the politicians in surprise tinged with disgust, an expression few people were capable of achieving.

Brice looked on with a puzzled expression on his face whilst the Air Chief Marshal looked smug.

'So what did you intend doing? Announcing soon – Look what an effort we're making!' It was at a time like this that Sir Anthony Parsons came into his own. With a private income and having reached the top, he could afford to be both honest and direct with his political masters. He had nothing more to achieve and, significantly, nothing to gain. He could be, as he had always been, true to himself. A luxury rarely granted to civil servants.

He looked at Brice who was frowning, clearly not understanding. At some stage during the meeting, the Squadron Leader had crossed the Rubicon from gopher and yes man, to equal participant. Although Brice would have been the first to admit the fact that in the present company some were more equal than others.

'Don't you see, Squadron Leader? It was all a ploy. Macnair's outfit was created as a political con. A con of the populace to have them believe the government was intent on doing something about terrorism. It was all a sham. What was to happen? Look, we've tried but now we need to disband the whole thing? What about the other governments involved? What would they have to say about . . . Don't tell me. They were in on it as well. All playing at politics instead of doing something about the problem. Why am I surprised? Talk about fiddling whilst Rome burns.' He looked at Stuart Roberts and continued, 'I'm surprised at you, Stuart. I thought you had more integrity than that.'

The Secretary of State smiled and said, 'I have. Which is why I went along with the idea in the first place. It had, has and will continue to have, my full support. This is a case of politicians being hoisted by their own petard. You see, I always expected something to happen, which would give us the chance to put Macnair and his force on the map once and for all. I didn't expect anything like this but it's ideal for our purposes. We let Macnair loose on the problem. He operates under the remit as suggested by President Clinton and he lands or falls on his own two feet. If he succeeds then he survives into the future. If he fails, well, we can always say that at least we tried. From our point of view it's a no lose situation.'

Sir Anthony had always been aware that of all the

Cabinet, Stuart Roberts was the man to watch. A Prime Minister in the making, beyond a shadow of a doubt. And if he had ever needed proof of that, he had received it this evening.

After a few moments silence Parsons said, 'It is not my place but I think it is time we made some decisions. We still have to discuss the international implications and what we are going to tell the media. In the meantime I think we should mobilise Macnair and give him free reign to find the people responsible and, hopefully, rescue any survivors.'

There was silence around the table as each man analysed his thoughts. The Secretary of State for Defence was right. It was a no lose situation if they let Macnair get on with it. If it all went belly up then what the hell. Macnair would also make a good scapegoat.

'I think we should let Macnair have his head,' said Roberts, aware that it would only take the gentlest of shoves to move matters either way.

It wasn't his place to say anything but Brice found himself nodding in agreement. 'So do I.' He then had the temerity to add, 'After all, there's nothing to lose.'

Neither the Home Secretary nor the Chief of Defence Staff said a word. They both looked at the Prime Minister who had the casting vote. He wanted Macnair to succeed but he had a tight balancing act to do. He needed his left wing as much as the right and centre of his party. He was already pushing through reforms which were anathema to a big chunk of his party, the loony left baggage he still had to carry, as represented by the Home Secretary opposite him.

'All right. Squadron Leader, phone General Macnair and tell him what's happened. Tell him he is to operate

within the rules laid down and that his primary concern
is the safe release of the prisoners.'

'Yes, sir. Is there a phone I can use or should I use
this one?'

'Use the one next door. I suspect you'll be some time.
We have other matters to discuss. I don't think you'll be
needed further. Dick?'

'What? No. I don't need you further either.' The scowl
cast in his direction made Brice think that he had very
little time left as Aide de Camp to the Air Chief Marshal.
Oh, well, it had been interesting whilst it lasted.

Brice went next door to make the call. As he did so, the
phone in the Cabinet Room rang and the Prime Minister
picked up the receiver.

'Yes, what is it?' he asked his wife.

'It's the press, Tony. They want to know what's
happened in Scotland.'

10

P.M. 2 May 1998. HMS Drake, *Plymouth.*

It was 21.45 and Nick Hunter had just sat down to a post-dinner drink in the wardroom bar. He had been busy all day getting to grips with the myriad of tasks he had to complete. Many of the others had also stayed behind to get as much done as possible. Joshua Clements from Delta Force, Pierre Flambert and Hunter had formed a friendship already and were settling themselves down to a few glasses of port when Sergeant Hughes entered. He paused in the doorway to look round and then approached Hunter.

'Sorry to bother you, sir,' he spoke softly in Hunter's ear, 'but we're needed.'

'Huh?' Hunter looked up, startled. 'What did you say?'

'The proverbial's hit the fan, sir and we're all wanted.'

Hunter put down his glass and stood up, gesturing to the others to follow him. 'What's going on, Dave?'

Hughes shrugged. 'I don't know, sir. I was just getting ready to go ashore for a few beers when I got a phone call. There's an alert on. It's not an exercise and we're trying to find as many of the team as we can.'

They were moving smartly for the door. Being a

188

Saturday, there were few other officers about but of the half dozen or so who were there, their abrupt exit could not help but be noticed.

Ten minutes later the four men had arrived at their new quarters to find another fifteen of their colleagues already there, milling around wondering what was happening. Hunter quickly realised that he was the most senior officer present and took charge.

'All right, everybody. Sit down. Let's try and find out what's going on.' He spoke loudly and everyone quickly grabbed a seat and paid attention to him. 'First of all, who started it? Does anyone know?'

The words were hardly out of his mouth when a voice behind him said, 'I did, Nick.' Macnair, the only one in uniform, walked quickly into the room.

'Sorry, sir,' said Hunter. 'I was trying to find out what was happening.'

'That's okay. Take a seat and I'll tell you.' He waited for Hunter to sit down before he began.

'Two hours ago a helicopter was shot down by missiles off the coast of Scotland. At the time it was carrying thirty-one VIPs to Balmoral. We know that some of the passengers have been shot dead and it appears that others have been taken as prisoners. Where they've been taken, by whom and for what purpose we do not as yet know. We're moving out immediately to go to the scene of the incident. Once there, we shall set up . . .'

The briefing took twenty minutes and when it finished the room erupted. Some individuals rushed to change into uniform whilst others prepared the different pallets of stores they would be taking with them. In spite of the fact that they had been in situ for less than a week, each of them knew precisely what was required.

Major Jim Carter took charge of the logistics and after a brief discussion with Macnair decided on his course of action. He telephoned RAF Lyneham in Wiltshire and was put through to the duty officer.

'Who am I speaking to?' Carter asked.

'I'm the duty officer.'

'Yes, I know that. But what's your name?'

There was a flustered pause before the hesitant voice came back, 'Em, what's the nature of your call, em, sir.' The "sir" was thrown in for good measure. The young lieutenant on the other end had no idea to whom he was speaking.

Under other circumstances Carter would have been enjoying himself. As it was, time was of the essence. 'Just answer the question before I get really mad,' replied Carter.

'Em, my name is Lieutenant Fisher.' He felt emboldened and said, 'and what's yours?'

'My name is Major Carter and I want you to listen very carefully to me Fisher, understood?'

'Em, yes, sir.'

'Good. Who is the most senior officer on the base right now?'

There was a pause. 'I suppose Captain Phillips is at home. That's, em, I suppose, technically on the base.'

'Is he in charge of the base. The CO?'

'Em, yes, sir. He's the Commanding Officer.'

'Good. What's his telephone number?'

'I don't think I can tell you that, em, sir. After all I don't know that you are who you say you are.'

Carter was normally one of the most easy going of men except when battling against stupidity. Which was really unfair as the young lieutenant had only joined the

Royal Air Force from university three months earlier and this was his first duty. He was well and truly out of his depth.

'Listen. This is an emergency and I need to speak to your CO. Either transfer me or get your CO to phone me back immediately. And I mean immediately.'

'I can transfer you, em, sir.'

'Good. After you transfer me get hold of your duty flight crew and tell them to stand by. I want a C130 here within the hour. Now get me the CO.' The last sentence was spoken in a tone that caused the young lieutenant to break out into a sweat whilst he transferred the call.

Carter heard the ringing and a young girl's voice said, 'Captain Maitland's residence, may I help you please?'

Carter could imagine the youngster at the other end of the telephone, answering the phone as she had heard the duty steward do. 'May I speak to Captain Maitland, please?'

'Certainly. May I say who's calling?'

'My name is Major James Carter.'

'I'll get him right away.' The phone was put down with a clatter and Carter could hear the voice fading into the background. 'Dad, dad, it's for you. A Major James . . .'

'Hullo. Maitland here. Who's this?'

'Sir. My name is Major Jim Carter I'm phoning you from HMS *Drake*. We need a C130 here as quickly as possible.'

'Is this some sort of joke? Because if it is I can tell you . . .'

'No, sir. It's no joke. General Macnair needs a C130 as quickly as possible. We have a flap on in Scotland and we have men and equipment to get there a.s.a.p.'

'Macnair did you say? He's the fellow in charge of this new outfit. You poached a couple of my best pilots away from me a few weeks ago.'

'That's us, sir. Look, I can't tell you what's going on, although no doubt you'll pick it up in the news soon enough. The problem is we need to go operational in Scotland and the best way of getting there is in one of your aircraft.'

'What do you want me to do?'

Carter breathed a sigh of relief. 'Sir, can you get your duty crew to fly a C130 to Plymouth?'

'I'll organise it straight away.' Maitland looked at his watch. 'I think they can be with you in say, two hours. Will that do you?'

'Perfectly. That gives me enough time to get the equipment and team to the airport.'

'What do you want us to do then? After all, I'll need to brief my crew to give them some idea as to what's expected.'

'Tell them they'll be flying to Scotland. Destination still to be determined but they can plan on Machrihanish.'

'They fly there so often the plane practically knows the way. There's one problem though.'

Hell, here it comes, thought Carter. I knew this was too good to be true. 'What's that sir?'

'Plymouth is shut until 09.00 Monday. It being Saturday today and by extension Sunday tomorrow.' Maitland dropped his bomb shell. 'It's only just occurred to me. Any ideas?'

Carter thought quickly. 'We've two options. Rout out the local police and get them to find the staff to open it or go it alone.'

'I'm sure the police will help but as it's a Saturday night

I suspect you'll have a great deal of difficulty finding the civilian staff you'll need.'

Carter thought for a few moments. 'I agree. Can your lads find the place without any difficulties if we set a runway of flares?'

Maitland gave a snort of derision. 'Naturally. My crews have been all over Africa and Bosnia to name but two places, taking in aid. Plymouth will be a dawdle to them.'

'All right,' said Carter. 'I'll get centre line flares rigged with a control light at the end of the runway.'

'Good. I'll get this end sorted out. One thing, so that I can tell my crew. Are they flying into danger?'

'We don't think so at this stage, but, to be honest, we don't know.'

'Fair enough. I'll get on to it right away.'

'I hope you don't mind but I told your duty officer to warn the crew.'

'I don't, but I doubt anything's been done. I can't see Squadron Leader Lester listening to anything young Fisher has to say, somehow.'

'Right. And thanks very much, sir.'

'Are you sure you can't tell me what's going on?'

'Positive. Sorry, sir. As I said, you'll hear about it soon enough and be able to put two and two together'

'In that case I'll probably make five. Okay. Cheerio Major.'

Carter hung up and stood in thought for a few minutes. He picked up the phone again and rang the wardroom. The wardroom hall porter answered and Carter asked to speak to the officer of the day.

'This is Jim Carter. I'm with General Macnair's outfit. To whom am I speaking?'

'I'm Lieutenant Commander Willox. You're the Pusser for the new outfit aren't you?'

It took Carter a few seconds to realise that Willox had used the naval term for the supply branch of the navy before he said, 'Yes, that's right. Major Carter. Look I need some help.'

'Fire away, old boy. If the navy can be of any assistance, then it will.'

'I need some men to go along to the transport pool and commandeer as many fifteen tonners as they can. They'll need to be able to drive the things and if there are any civilian drivers on duty they can be press ganged into service as well. Can you take care of it?'

There was a short pause. 'Yes, I can. What do you want them to do then?'

'Drive over to the East Road and our new place. Either my sergeant or I will be waiting. We'll load the trucks which will be driven to the airport.'

'Plymouth? It's closed at this time of night.'

'Yes, I know. We'll be opening it. Can you be as quick as you can as we've a lot to do.'

'Well, it's pretty unusual but okay, I'll get it done. I'll come over as well, to see if I can be of help.' With that he hung up.

Carter replaced the receiver slowly, his mind whirling. He picked up the receiver again and rang 192. 'Directory? I'd like the number for the Chief Constable please.' He listened to the reply. 'His offices, please.' He got the number and dialled.

'White Road Police Station, may I help you?'

'What's the most senior rank you have on duty tonight, please?' asked Carter.

'I'm sorry, sir. Can you tell me the purpose of your

call?' The woman constable was firm but polite.

'Yes. My name is Major James Carter. I'm phoning from HMS *Drake* and I have a serious flap on. I need help from the highest level you have to offer. Now, either I speak to the most senior officer you have or I speak to the Chief Constable. I don't mind which.'

'Yes sir. It's Chief Inspector Smithers. I'll put you straight through.'

Straight through meant a two and a half minute wait which irritated Carter but finally a gruff voice came over the phone. 'Sorry about the delay. I was, em, washing my hands. What can I do for you?'

'My name is Jim Carter. I'm a Major based at *Drake*. There's been a major incident in Scotland to which we are having to respond. Are you with me so far?'

'Certainly. It's as clear as mud. Why are you phoning me? You must know a Saturday night is the busiest night of the week for us. What with dealing with drunks, hooligans, fights and drunken drivers we have our work cut out for us.'

'I can appreciate that. However, believe me this is very important. We have an aircraft landing at Plymouth Airport in about one and a half hours time and yes, before you say it, I know the place is closed.'

'So how are you going to get an aeroplane in there?'

'We're going to set our own flight path and landing lights.'

'I don't think so. If you break in, which is what I suspect you're saying, I'll arrest you. I hope I make myself clear.'

'Look, are you kidding? Is this some sort of joke? I phoned you looking for some help. We've got a convoy of lorries taking gear and men to the airport. Once there, they'll be loaded onto a Hercules C130 and sent to Scotland for a very important mission. This isn't an exercise. It's an honest to God emergency and I'd like your help.'

'What sort of help?' The voice was no more friendly and if he had not been in such a hurry to get things done Carter might have realised it was down right hostile.

'We need an escort to get us as quickly as possible to the airport in about an hour and I'd like a couple of your men on hand when we go in to clear things with the airport authorities. I presume we'll have to cut off the odd lock or two,' he said it jocularly.

'If you do, I'll arrest you.'

'What? Is this some sort of joke?'

'It's no joke. I'm fed up to my back teeth dealing with you lot. If you go near the airport and attempt to break in then I'll arrest you.'

'Look man, this is a national emergency. If it wasn't, I wouldn't be asking for your help. We have a C130 enroute and we need access. Now are you going to help or not?'

'I told you. If you try and go onto the airport premises, I'll arrest you.'

'That's ridiculous. Look, Chief Inspector you're making a big mistake. Please believe me when I tell you that we have the backing of the highest authority in the land.'

'Military authority, that's as maybe. But I represent the civilian authority and I'm telling you, you will not be given access to the airport.'

'Why are you doing this?'

'I'm not doing anything, as you put it. You get the right permits and you can use the place. Otherwise . . .'

'Otherwise what?'

'The reason the airport is shut is because of the noise at this time of night. You need special permits to operate an airport after nine p.m. because of the noise. And as it's Sunday tomorrow, before nine a.m.'

'Look, we haven't time for all that nonsense. We need to be in and out tonight, as quickly as we can.'

'Tough. You aren't and that's final.' With that he hung up.

Carter also hung up and wondered what to do. He could see no solution so went to find Macnair. He was busy talking to some of his officers around an Admiralty chart of an area of Scotland.

'Sorry to bother you, sir, but I've got a problem.'

'Can't you solve it?' Macnair asked, intrigued. The one thing he knew about Jim Carter was that no matter how big the problem he could solve it. Usually.

'Well, no, sir. It's the local police.' He repeated the gist of the conversation he'd had with the Chief Inspector.

'Leave it to me.' Macnair took a leather bound address book from his pocket and thumbed through it. He dialled a number and after a few seconds said, 'Is that the home of the Chief Constable? Good. May I speak to him, please? Damn. When will he be back? No. Thank you. There's no message. Sorry. Yes, there is. Tell him Malcolm Macnair phoned and that I'll be in to see him on Monday, first thing. What? Nine o'clock.' He hung up. 'He's away for the weekend. Won't be back until late tomorrow night.' He thought for a few seconds and then shrugged. 'What the hell. Listen up. If we have any trouble from the local police, subdue them and carry on.'

'Subdue them, sir?' Hunter asked.

'Yes, Nick. I don't like it much but we can't have the

197

local police stopping us before we start. We'll be the laughing stock of the country if we do.'

'Yes, sir,' Hunter replied with a quick smile. 'I take it we're to exercise minimum force?'

Macnair smiled back. 'Pretty minimal.' He walked over to the coffee pot which had been switched on as soon as the flap had started. 'If anybody else wants any coffee then help yourselves. Right, where were we?'

'You were saying that they've found some bodies . . .'

'Ah, yes. Four bodies so far. There's no sign of the helicopter but there are two Hunt class minehunters on the way from the Clyde. They've also sent the diving team from Faslane.'

Hunter nodded. That made sense. 'When will they get there, sir?'

'The ships won't arrive before late tomorrow but the team from Faslane should get there sometime in the middle of the night. They'll be travelling by road. I gather they have a police escort.' The irony wasn't lost on the others.

'How will they get out to the site? It's a bit far in a Gemini with an outboard.' Hunter was referring to the rubber inflatable dinghies used by the Royal Naval clearance diving teams.

'Helicopter from Arduaine. They'll be in touch by mobile phone when they get to the area. I gather a Lieutenant Crispin Hughes is in charge. Do you know him Nick?'

'Crispin? Yes, sir. He went through my hands in ninety-three.' Hunter was referring to the time when he had been the diving training officer responsible for qualifying clearance diving officers. 'Good man. Knows his stuff.'

Macnair took a cheroot from his pocket and lit it with

a gold Dunhill lighter. 'Right, when you get there, you Nick will be SAC.' Scene of Action Commander was a big responsibility. 'Try not to ruffle too many feathers, especially of more senior officers but remember, we need as much information as we can get if we're to track down these terrorists and rescue the prisoners.'

'If they're still alive,' said Joshua Clements, pragmatically.

'If, as you so rightly put it, they're still alive. However, it doesn't make sense if they're not,' replied the General. 'Why kill some and take the others?'

'They could all be dead and are still in the helicopter,' said Pierre Flambert, pensively.

'I've thought of that. I don't see how it could be possible. The sheer numbers would have meant that at least somebody survived. No, I suspect that whoever was controlling this operation lost patience with those who were still in the water and shot them. The rest have been taken.'

'That's callous in the extreme, sir,' Hunter said, staring at the chart.

'I agree.' He broke off when he saw Isobel Sweeney enter the room. 'Isobel, what are you doing here?'

Before she could reply Jim Carter responded. 'I took the liberty of phoning her, sir. I figured that we need as much information as we can gather and she's the person who can access it.'

Macnair looked at his second in command for a few seconds before nodding and smiling. 'You're right. Sorry about this, Isobel. Help yourself to coffee.'

'Thanks, General, I will. Mind if I listen in so I can find out what's going on?' She smiled at the officers. More than one pulse picked up an extra beat or two.

Macnair turned to Carter. 'How long before you move out?'

'Fifteen minutes, no more. The duty watch have been bloody marvellous. They even brought a trolley used for carrying fork lift trucks hitched to the back of one of the lorries. That'll help when we get to the airport.'

'Good. The priority is to find the prisoners, assuming there are any. Any ideas?'

'Yes, sir,' said Isobel. 'Let me get flashed up, and I'll start pulling in all the satellite data we can get our hands on. In the meantime, I gather there was a ship involved and she has to be around there somewhere. That being the case we need an up to date pass over the area by whatever we've got up there.' She pointed upwards.

'Right, you start on that. Are the other two coming in?'

'They should be here any minute. I'll get Gareth to start on likely suspects, pulling all the files and cross-referencing them to what we know. Leo can start looking at where this ship could have appeared from. It can't have just materialised from thin air.'

'Good. I needn't tell you all that time is of the essence.'

In that, General Macnair was mistaken. Luckily, they did have time, although just then they were totally unaware of it.

'Right, Nick. You've picked your team?'

'Yes, General. Joshua, Pierre, Otto and Hiram are all coming.' The officers grouped around the table nodded. He named the rest of the team and said, 'They're helping with the equipment right now.'

The General nodded. 'Good.'

Carter walked back into the room and spoke to the General. 'That's us ready, sir. We're just waiting for the men.'

'They'll be right with you.' Macnair looked at his officers and held out his hand in turn to each of them. 'Good luck. As soon as we find out anything this end we'll let you know.'

A few minutes later they had piled into the lorries and staff cars and were en route to the airport. Although it was May, it was a moonless, clear night with, surprisingly, no hint of rain in the air.

After the altercation he'd had with the Chief Inspector, Carter had thought it wisest to keep to the speed limits and had briefed the drivers accordingly. There was going to be enough trouble once they reached the airport, without aggravating matters by having the police stop them for speeding as well.

Twenty minutes after leaving Devonport they arrived at the airport. Jim Carter was driving the front staff car with Hunter, Clements and Flambert as passengers. They had been discussing their strategy when Carter said, 'Bugger it. I'd hoped this wouldn't happen.' In front of them, across the entrance to the airport, was a police car. When it saw the convoy arriving the blue flashing lights were turned on and a figure came out in front and raised a hand.

'You know, that man is a serious fool,' said Hunter.

'Tell me about it,' replied Carter, slowing down and finally halting only a few inches from the Chief Inspector's legs. He opened the door and climbed out, quickly followed by the other three. Fully kitted, carrying weapons and small packs which they slung over their shoulders, the four looked formidable and frightening.

'I told you, you aren't allowed in,' began the Chief Inspector. He was rotund, five feet eight inches in his stocking feet and had a red, bulbous nose. He looked as if he was a man who drank too much, too often.

Carter ignored him entirely, as if he did not exist. He waved a hand and without saying a word two men ran forward, hitched a tow rope to the front of the police car and waved up the nearest lorry in the convoy of eight.

'You can't do this. Stop it. If you don't stop this minute I'll have you arrested.' The words were too fatuous to deserve a reply and so none was made.

The driver of the police car, a young constable, stood to one side, trying not to show his glee. He'd have some fun with this back in the canteen. But then, remembering what had happened a year or so ago, perhaps he wouldn't.

'You aren't going in, I'm telling you. You can't fly in or out tonight and that's final.'

'Right lads. Get that car out of the way,' Carter ordered.

The lorry revved up and dragged the car away, the back tyres locked by the handbrake. There was a faint whiff of burning rubber in the air.

Even then the Chief Inspector did not give up. 'Right, that's it. You are all under arrest.' In any other circumstance it would have been funny. As it was, it was irritating and dangerous. Carter turned to the man standing by his side, 'Sergeant, move this man.'

'Yes, sir.' He beckoned to the three men standing to one side and they closed on the hapless Chief Inspector.

'You can't do this. I'm warning you . . .'

Two of them grabbed an arm each and pulled the Chief Inspector down on the ground, none too gently. The other two grabbed a leg and they easily lifted him. They walked to the side of the road where they sat him down by the fence. Sergeant David Hughes took a pair of handcuffs from his pocket and quickly handcuffed the Chief Inspector to the fence. By now, some of the bluster was gone and the Chief Inspector contented himself with a spluttering protest.

'What about you, constable? Do you want to stop us as well?' Carter asked.

'Ahh, no, sir. If you don't mind. I'll just sit and watch things.'

'Good, you do that,' replied the Major.

'That's the gates open, sir,' Corporal Peter Walker said, throwing the major a salute.

Carter did not bother to ask him how he had accomplished it. It was time to let the team have it's head and get on with their allotted tasks, without having to explain how they achieved each one.

Major Carter waved the vehicles forward and once they had all passed through the gates he walked over to Chief Inspector Smithers.

'I'll let you go now if you just stay where you are, watch us leave and lock up afterwards.'

'I'll have your guts for garters,' Smithers said. 'You won't get away with this.'

'Look, what the hell is your problem? We've got a job to do and you're stopping us from doing it. Why?'

In response Carter received a mouthful of profanity. Standing up he shook his head sadly and walked away. The young constable sidled after him, as Smithers sat back and let his head droop tiredly to his chest, his eyes closed.

As Carter marched quickly after the lorries, already being unloaded at the hard-standing, the constable caught up with him.

'Sir, excuse me.'

Carter stopped and turned around. 'Sir, I can explain.'

Carter said nothing, just looked at the constable curiously.

'It's about Chief Inspector Smithers. What his problem is.'

Carter nodded encouragement and the constable continued. 'Well, a couple of years ago, his daughter was out on a date with a Royal Naval Sub-Lieutenant. They had been to a cocktail party and went to the Groin Exchange afterwards.'

'Groin Exchange?'

'Yes. That's what the sailing club is called. Anyway, the sub had too much to drink . . .' Here it comes, thought Carter, drunk, drove the car and killed her . . . 'and his daughter Michelle drove. Neither were paralytic, but both were over the legal limit. They were stopped by a patrol car and she was breathalysed.'

'So? Why should that make him,' he nodded his head towards the slouched figure by the fence, 'so antagonistic towards us?'

'I'm coming to that. Michelle's job depended on her having a driving licence. She lost her job, became depressed and committed suicide.'

'Because of a drink driving charge? That's ridiculous.'

'No, sir. Because her father was an inspector at the time and was in the patrol car which stopped them. The two constables who were on patrol, when they realised who she was, were prepared to let her off with a caution. Inspector Smithers insisted they do their job without giving any favours. She left a note saying she hated her father and it was all his fault. He hasn't been the same since. He seems to have developed a pathological hatred for the services. It's ludicrous, but he's been badly affected by the whole thing.'

'The poor sod,' Carter said softly. He felt in his tunic pocket for the key to the handcuffs. As he did so, the sat-link mobile phone he carried began to beep. 'Look, that's probably the plane.' Even as he spoke they could hear the loud drone of the engines as the huge C130 approached. 'We'll be gone in twenty minutes. Here's the key. Let him loose after we take off. If you can persuade him to leave matters as they are, all well and good. If not, I can tell you that there are some very big guns on our side and he won't stand a chance. I also suggest you keep quiet about tonight. It's not fair on him.'

The constable thought for a few seconds. A part of him had been looking forward to describing what had happened, but now that he had told the story he felt guilty. The Chief Inspector was more to be pitied than held up for ridicule.

'All right. I'll see what I can do. Though I don't promise anything.'

'Good enough.' Carter handed him the key, nodded goodbye, turned away and answered the phone.

It was the pilot of the C130. Even as they spoke, the flares came on and two green lights were illuminated at the end of the runway. Within minutes the huge plane was landing with a squeal of rubber and rapidly losing speed. Once stopped, the plane pivoted round and trundled towards the pile of stores like a huge prehistoric beast. It came to a halt alongside the stores and the rear door dropped down like a draw-bridge.

The co-pilot and sergeant loadmaster, the third member of the flight crew, went to supervise the loading whilst the pilot ambled over to make himself known to Carter.

'Do you know where you're going?' Carter asked after the introductions were made.

Squadron Leader Douglas Lester nodded. He was of medium height and build but sported a huge, luxurious walrus moustache as favoured by RAF pilots of the Second World War. He was a caricature of that era, a man born fifty years too late. He took nothing seriously except his flying and his moustache, which he constantly stroked.

'Machrihanish. Then back, presumably.' He was also a man of few words.

Carter nodded. 'That's right. Hopefully, there'll be helicopters ready to take us from there. I understand that units from Prestwick and Lossiemouth have been sent to ferry us and the equipment to Luing where we'll make our base.'

Lester nodded. 'That's the island south of Mull.'

'That's it. I take it you don't know what this is all about?'

'No, sir. I was told to get here, get you to Scotland and return. No questions, no pack drill, as they say.'

'I'll fill you in once we're airborne. I'll go and see how things are progressing and see you in the cockpit once we depart.' With that Carter walked away.

Hunter had left the team to get on with the loading. Most of the lorries had already begun the return journey to Devonport taking some of the duty watch who had helped hump the gear. He busied himself studying the charts he had of the area, covering the whole of the west coast of Scotland, trying to figure out where the ship could have gone. It was hopeless. He needed a great deal more information if he was to find whoever had carried out the attack and rescue any prisoners who might still be alive.

A short while later the C130 was airborne and enroute for Scotland. The airport was back to normal with no indication that anyone had been there except for the broken lock on the gates.

The constable drove away with the Chief Inspector, trying to persuade the latter to forget about what had happened. Unfortunately, his words fell on deaf ears.

Meanwhile, at Balmoral, the dinner was cancelled.

11

Midnight 2 May 1998. Off the West Coast of Scotland.

The ship came gently to a stop. The prisoners in the forward hold looked at one another, fear showing in the eyes of some of them. Others managed to mask theirs, whilst a few felt none. Two of those who were unafraid were Cecil McDonald and Ben Bradley, the Vice-President of America. The former's sheer professionalism kept the fear at bay, whilst anger did the same for the latter.

'What now?' asked Wilma Shules, wearily pushing her hair from her face. 'God, it's cold.' She voiced the feelings of all of them. What little heat there was came through the decking, heat generated in the engine room.

The handles holding the hatch closed above their heads were twisted open, and the hatch flung back. A head appeared and one word was yelled down. 'Out.'

Wearily, they got to their feet, uncertainty etched in their faces. 'I'll go first,' said John Stanton.

'No, I will,' said John Williams, pushing past and reaching the ladder. 'Don't argue. If something happens,' he whispered, 'we'll lose whatever it is you've got. Your body is too valuable to lose over the side.' He smiled, a

208

rictus of a smile, devoid of humour. 'We need to guard the guards. I love the irony of it.'

He climbed wearily up the ladder, followed by the others. Nervously, he put his head above the hatchway. Nothing happened, except that there were three armed guards gesturing him to climb out. He did so, each arm and leg aching. He shivered but looked around with interest.

It was pitch dark when he looked over the port side but when he turned to starboard he could see the sea glistening in the star lit night. He looked back again to port, intrigued at the difference in the light and walked a few steps to the side. He put his hand out to feel rough rock and looked up to see the cliff towering above them. It hung over their heads, blotting out the sky and the stars. He wondered where they were. There was a gentle wind from the west and he shivered whilst he waited for the others to climb out of the hatchway. Soon they were all standing about on the foredeck, wondering what was about to happen.

The man they now knew to be Habib appeared on the starboard bridge wing, and looked down on them. 'If you want to eat and drink you have work to do. You will take the items given to you to the top of this cliff. There you will be shown what to do. Once you are finished, I promise you a hot drink and hot food. If you do not do as you are told, or if anyone causes any sort of trouble I will have that person and one other shot.' The matter of fact statement did more to convince them than anything else. Besides which, they had already seen how utterly ruthless he was.

'Now, go down to the stern and do as you're told.'

'For God's sake man, let the women stay,' protested the Deputy Prime Minister.

By way of response Habib pulled back the bolt of his gun. 'Who spoke?'

'No one. It's all right,' said the Secretary General to the United Nations, boldly coming forward. 'We'll do our share.'

'Good. You're learning fast. Any more argument and I will shoot one of you. Man or woman, it makes no difference to me. Now go.'

They moved in single file down the starboard side of the deck, each silent and deep in thought. Some were praying for rescue, others for revenge and yet others were thinking about escape.

At the stern, the deck lights had been switched on and the prisoners could see bundles of dark sacking and a stack of shovels. Intrigued, they waited to be told what to do.

There was a noise above them, on the cliff. Suddenly, there was a shout and they all stepped back as they saw something falling towards them. It stopped a foot above the deck and proved to be a rope ladder. A few moments later, a second one appeared, hanging alongside.

'You four,' Fredericks appeared, and pointed at four of them, 'start climbing.'

'How do we know it's safe?' The man who asked was the Japanese Ambassador to the Court of St. James.

The reply was again the snicker of a gun being cocked. 'Because I can assure you, it is safer to climb than to remain. The latter means certain death, the former gives you a chance to survive.'

Jacques Beloit, the French Prime Minister, stepped forward, grabbed the rung above his head and lifted his foot to the first rung. 'I'll go first. I will call down when I have reached the top. The next one can follow me.'

'No. The next one will be right behind you,' said Fredericks.

Beloit looked at the terrorist for a few seconds. '*Monsieur*, I appreciate that you are a fool. But I also believe that you wish us to go up this rock face. If we go one at a time we may all do as you require. If this ladder breaks before we finish you will have injured prisoners and you will not accomplish whatever it is you are trying to achieve.'

Fredericks fought with his temper. Knowing the man was right did not help him one iota. He wanted to smash him in his smug French face; put a bullet through his head. However, before he did anything, Beloit turned his back and began to climb and the danger passed. At the same time, John Stanton took hold of the other ladder and also began the ascent.

It was hard going and both men saved their breath, concentrating on the task. It was over fifty feet to the top. By the time they got there, they had both taken the skin off the backs of their knuckles, which had rubbed against the rough cliff face. Stanton climbed over the edge, and lay there for a few seconds. He wasn't even breathing hard, but decided to act the part of an exhausted, out of condition prisoner. He did not want to draw attention to himself at this stage.

'Up,' the man standing over him gestured with his machine gun.

He scrambled to his feet and then bent down to help Beloit over the edge. Then he called down to send up the next two. Another terrorist materialised out of the murk with a coil of thin rope slung over his shoulder. He threw it at Stanton's feet.

'Cut this into twenty-five metre lengths.' A knife was thrown alongside the rope. Stanton carefully picked it up, not giving the terrorist any reason to do anything stupid. He quickly ran the rope through his hands, estimating the length. The smooth touch of the rope proved it to be man-made corelene, a very strong, nylon based rope favoured by divers. By the time he got to the end, he had cut off ten lengths of about twenty-five metres and left them in neat coils along the cliff edge. Six more of the prisoners had also joined him and Beliot, stamping their feet, holding their arms across their bodies, trying to keep warm.

Fredericks put his evil head over the edge and climbed up. 'Right. Drop the ends of your lines down. Those below will tie on the shovels and the sacking and you will haul them up here. Come on, get a move on.'

They did as they were told, labouring silently in the night. Stanton kept casting surreptitious glances about him, trying to work out where they were. He had already looked to the stars and worked out which direction was north. He estimated that they were on an island, about half a mile east to west and the same north to south. They were on the eastern side with a narrow peninsula wrapping itself around the bows of the ship. To the south he could make out the loom of a lighthouse and to the north there were a few twinkling lights he assumed were street lamps. To the east and west, as far as he could see there was nothing but water. He was baffled. He could not envisage where they were. The only thing of which he felt certain, was that they were still somewhere off the coast of Scotland.

Once the shovels were up, they were joined by another

ten of their number, eight of whom were handed the implements and told to go and find large boulders and stones.

'Look,' said Matthew Goodall, the Chairman of the World Bank, 'wouldn't it be easier if you told us what we're trying to do? That way we can get on and do it, get back down in the warmth and have something to eat and drink as we were promised.'

Fredericks told them what they had to do. Whilst they gathered the rocks, under the careful and watchful eyes of their guards, the others dragged up the bundles of hessian cloth. In the dark they couldn't tell, but it was a mottled grey and had been prepared specially to blend in with the colour of the surrounding rock.

Two prisoners gathered an end of the two metre wide cloth and threw the bundle back down to the ship. Once there, two others cut off the end where indicated and then used some sailmaker's thread to sew weights along the edge of the cloth. The end was then thrown over the starboard side where it hung down into the water. The weights kept the cloth taught and just under the surface of the sea, hiding the ship from prying eyes. The cloth at the top of the cliff was anchored using the small boulders and stones which the others collected.

They toiled all night, only the thought of hot food and drink keeping them going. Towards dawn, they were straying all over the island looking for suitable rocks to hold the cloth in place. It was a balance between the weight of the rocks and the strength of the prisoners which necessitated them straying out of sight of their guards. More than one thought about hiding and possibly escaping, but to where? And what would happen to the others if their guards noticed that one of their number was missing?

Stanton in particular felt it very keenly. He was on the horns of a dilemma all that long and weary night. Should he, shouldn't he? What was in the best interests of them all? Were they all to be killed anyway? And if they were, didn't he owe it to the others to try and get away, to tell their story? No matter how he rationalised it, he couldn't find it in himself to go. He was sure he could escape and survive. He had seen at least a dozen sheep hiding amongst the rocks, unused to strangers on their barren and rocky island. Food and warmth would not be a problem.

Just as dawn was breaking, they were finished. From end to end, the ship was covered by the cloth. In the half light, the prisoners could see how effective it was. It was as though the ship had been made invisible. Finally, the last of the shovels were lowered back down, the ropes were dropped to the deck and the diplomats, bankers, politicians and businessmen wearily lowered their aching bodies back to the ship. Exhaustedly, they dragged themselves across to the hold and climbed back into their prison. They were too tired to realise that the clothes they were wearing had long since dried out and that warmth, for now, was no longer a problem.

Back in the forward hold most of them sank to the floor and closed their eyes. In spite of the hardness of the deck and the little warmth they got from their blankets most of them fell into a fitful sleep. Some, however, stayed awake and huddled together in a corner.

'What do you think is happening back there?'

There were six in conference together, the two SAS guards, Cecil McDonald and John Stanton, The Saudi,

Ibn ben Saud, the Vice-President of the United States of America, Ben Bradley, the Deputy Prime Minister of Israel, David Golightly and the British Ambassador to the United Nations, James Treherne. In them burnt the sparks of anger and courage. No, it was more than just sparks. It was red hot molten lava of anger and hate. They were a force to be reckoned with which Habib had never realised. For McDonald and Stanton it was as normal as breathing, for the other four, old skills and attitudes were quickly returning.

It was Stanton who answered. 'They'll be working their butts off, that's for sure. If the special forces are given their heads, let off the leash so to speak, then we've got a chance. If the politicians have a hand in it, then God help us all.'

Bradley could not hide a grin. 'You've never spoken a truer word. If anybody's going to make a dog's dinner of it, it'll be a politician.' The silence which greeted his statement proved that the others were in accord with his assessment of the future. 'So what do we do?'

Stanton spoke. 'Has anybody any idea where we are?'

'I asked the co-pilot,' replied McDonald, 'and he reckons that we're somewhere in the Outer Hebrides. The south end, he said.'

Stanton nodded. 'That makes sense. So what do you think this is all about?'

It was David Golightly who answered. 'I've been giving it a lot of thought. I've also been remembering what I know about Habib and Fredericks. They aren't the sort to risk their lives for say, the freeing of fellow terrorists. I think they would risk their lives for money but even then, when I think back, the risks have always been minimal. You know, the more you analyse what they are, what they've done, the more you realise that there's more myth than substance. If that's the case, then they'll both be bailing out soon and leaving their colleagues,' he paused over the words, 'to hold the baby, I think you say in English.'

'So what is it they're trying to achieve?' was the plaintive question asked by Bradley.

'We don't know yet, but I've no doubt we'll find out soon enough,' replied Treherne. .

'What about the food and drink we were promised?' asked Stanton. 'Should one of us go and create a fuss and demand it?'

There was a chorus of "no" and "don't be a bloody fool". Any fuss could lead, easily, to the death of one of their number and at that point in time it was not worth risking. They were all too embarrassed to mention their need for toilet facilities during the night. Each, in his and her own way, hoped something would be done about it.

They spoke for a little while longer in a desultory fashion before they, too, turned away to sleep. Hopefully, food would come later.

During the night there had been low-voltage lights on, fixed at regular intervals along the bulkheads which had given them sufficient light to see by. Now at 10.00 a.m. the lights went out and the hum of the machinery stopped. The change woke up some of the prisoners who groaned, stretched, coughed and made sufficient fuss to wake the remainder.

'What's happening?' asked someone, with a low moan.

A little light now filtered through the half dozen portholes which lined both sides of the ship. On the port side they could see the rock face less than a metre from the ship's side, whilst on the starboard side the light was further dimmed by the cloth hanging down the ship's side. Nonetheless, they could still see reasonably well. Even as the question was asked the hatch over their heads was flung open and Fredericks appeared.

'Right, up on deck, all of you,' he ordered.

'What about some food and drink, as you promised?' asked Bradley.

'It's here, waiting for you.'

The news put heart into them all and they climbed the ladder with alacrity. Once on the deck they were made to sit in four rows, one behind the other. A large tureen of stew was placed at the feet of the front person along with a pile of plastic plates. There was no cutlery nor serving spoons.

'Help yourselves,' said Fredericks, with a grin. He was enjoying the humiliation of the high and mighty.

'What about a ladle and some spoons?' asked Wilma Shules, in the front of one of the rows.

Fredericks shook his head. 'You'll have to manage as best you can. You aren't getting any.'

Shules looked at the man with loathing and then stood up. In spite of the fact that she was only five feet five and a middle-aged woman, Fredericks stepped back and cocked his weapon. The Secretary General looked at him with contempt and then turned to the people in her row. 'Take these plates and hand them out,' she said to Golightly who sat behind her. She took one plate and then used it to ladle food onto the plates of her row, working her way along the line. The first person in each of the other rows did the same thing. When she had finished, she sat back in the front and helped herself. With as much dignity as she could muster she, like the others, used her fingers to feed herself. In spite of having to use their hands, it being

217

the first food they had eaten in over twenty hours, they ate quickly and with relish. The warm food gave them energy and hope. Within minutes they were finished and the plates were passed down the lines to be collected in the tureens. Fredericks used a small hand-held radio and muttered something into the microphone. A few moments later, two more terrorists appeared carrying large pitchers of coffee already sugared and made with condensed milk. The paper cups which accompanied the coffee were quickly passed out and the pitchers passed along the lines. No one, even those who did not take milk, or sugar, or both or who did not normally drink coffee, refused the liquid. Again, they were quickly finished and the paper cups collected.

'Now, we shall make a video,' said Fredericks with a smile.

All eyes turned on him. What was happening?

Fredericks waved at one of the terrorists who had appeared carrying the latest in Japanese video cameras, a Sansai ZX. It had a zoom lens, broadcast quality recording of voice and image, and weighed less than four kilos. The camera slowly moved along the rows of faces which looked into the lens. There was no disguising the haggard, weary looks of the prisoners after only twenty-four hours. What would they be like after a week or more?

'Now, stand up,' said Fredericks.

They did so, eyes moving between the camera and Fredericks.

The cameraman now walked along the lines, passing about a metre from each person. By his side walked a second terrorist, carrying a Russian made PSM pistol. The gun had first been manufactured in 1980 and with a simple blowback operation, had been made as slim as possible without any surface excrescences so that it was easily concealed. It fired eight 5.45mm rounds, weighed 460 grams and had been intended strictly as an issue pistol for the Soviet security forces, the KGB and the GRU. However, it had become readily available on the black market in Central Europe and the Middle East and was now the preferred handgun for terror.

The cameraman paused with the camera pointed at the face of Boris Petrov, the Russian member of the board of the World Bank. There was no warning. The second terrorist raised his gun and even as the horror of what was about to happen penetrated Petrov's consciousness, the terrorist fired. The bullet entered Petrov's forehead and exploded out of the back, throwing blood and brains in all directions. There were screams and shouts and loud curses. Above it all came the rattle of bolts being pulled back on automatic weapons and a loud shout from Habib.

'Quiet. Shut up,' more shots were fired into the air and they all fell silent. 'That's better. You two,' he pointed at two of the prisoners, 'tie those chains around his feet and throw him over the side.'

This was done in complete silence. The body was dragged to the edge of the deck and tumbled over, sliding between the sacking and the hull to land in the water and sink straight down. At fifteen metres it came to a stop on an outcrop of rock, paused for a few seconds and then slid gently through the kelp and weeds to rest on a sandy bottom a further two metres down.

'Why did you do that?' asked an outraged and choked Prime Minister of France.

'To show the recipients of our little home made video that we are serious,' replied Habib.

'Serious about what?' asked Bradley.

'Serious about our demand for one hundred million dollars ransom for your release,' came the reply.

There were gasps. 'Ridiculous,' yelled Matthew Goodall, chairman of the World Bank, and in spite of the differences in their background, a friend of the dead man. 'You know that the Western world will never strike a deal with terrorists. Never. It is the one philosophy that we are all agreed on when dealing with scum like you.'

'Scum? Scum?' repeated Habib. 'I should choose my words with care Mr. World Bank Chairman, as they could be your last. Now, get them below.'

'Wait,' said Wilma Shules. 'We need to use the bathroom. We need to use a toilet and to wash.'

Habib had been expecting someone to say something about their needs and had been looking forward to his reply. 'Give them the buckets.'

Two metal pails were put next to the hatch.

'What are these for?' she asked, aghast, knowing the reply.

'Those are your toilets. Alas, I regret to say that there is nothing else available. You will have to manage as best you can with those.'

The UN Secretary General was about to argue when she felt a pressure on her left arm and looked up into the eyes of John Williams, the British Deputy Prime Minister. He shook his head, as if to say don't argue, it's not worth it. Don't give him the satisfaction. She nodded and stepped forward, picked up a bucket, slung the handle over her shoulder and climbed down the ladder. The remainder quickly followed her into the gloom.

Once they were all below and the hatch closed, Bradley took charge.

'We know that our governments will never agree to blackmail. Not even for us.'

'Especially not for us,' said Beloit.

Bradley nodded. 'Especially not for us. That means that they will be doing their utmost to rescue us. The problem is, will they ever find us and if they do what happens then? I can't see Habib letting us go just like that.' There were nods of agreement.

Jane Felton was sitting on her blanket, leaning against the bulkhead. 'Have you noticed how quiet it is? There's no machinery running and it seems to me that it's getting colder.'

There were more nods. David Golightly said, 'It is to hide us from the satellites. If the engines or generators are kept running, the heat from them can be detected by satellite. I expect that every possible satellite currently orbiting the earth is being reprogrammed to cover this area. The cloth hanging over the ship seems very effective for hiding us from sight so the only way we could be found would be from any heat we radiated. It looks as if we shan't be radiating any for the satellites to find.

'That makes sense,' said John Williams. He turned to Donald Spencer, 'Pilot, any ideas where we are?'

'I've given it a lot of thought,' came the reply. 'Taking into account the time we spent getting here, our speed, what we could see last night. I think we're at the foot of the Outer Hebrides. One of the small islands south of South Uist. It's only a guess, mind, but I'd put my money on it.'

'So what are we to do? How does it help knowing where we are?' asked Bradley.

Nobody answered. How did it help? Maybe it was a

crumb of comfort to know they were still in UK waters, but they had been certain of that anyhow.

'We can't just sit still and do nothing,' said John Stanton. 'We can hope that rescue will come, but in the meantime, God helps those who help themselves.'

'As does Allah, my friend,' said the Saudi, with a wry smile.

'I agree,' said Bradley. 'Any suggestions?'

'I'm going to clear out that locker and turn it into a toilet,' said Jane Fenton, getting to her feet. 'I've also noticed a tap in the corner,' she walked to the back of the hold. No one else had noticed it. She turned it on and out gushed clear water. She wet her hand and tasted it. 'It's fresh. Excellent, at least we shan't die of thirst.' The discovery cheered them all up and she and Wilma Shules went to examine the locker.

'Okay, you two,' said Bradley, nodding at John Stanton and Cecil McDonald, 'what have you got?'

There was no need to elaborate. They both knew he was asking about the weapons and gear they carried. They exchanged glances, shrugged and started to unload. Both carried a specially modified Beretta 92M, a stainless steel version of the famous Beretta adopted by the US army in the late seventies. It had a shorter than normal barrel and carried only eight rounds of 9mm Parabellum bullets. The shorter barrel meant that the rifling had only four grooves and not the customary six. This in turn meant that accuracy over longer distances was sacrificed for size and weight. As the users of the guns were expected to be very close to their targets, accuracy beyond 50 metres didn't seem that important. The normal Beretta 92 weighed 850g, the specially modified version carried by the two SAS men weighed less than 500g and was the smallest weapon of its type in the world. Both men carried the guns hidden in special holsters sewn into the tops of their trousers legs. They had not been meant for easy access. When they had been captured, both of them had ditched the shoulder holsters and Colt Double Eagle Combat Commanders they would normally use, along with their identity cards declaring them to be members of Special Branch. Instead, they now had papers showing them to be members of the British Treasury and civil servants to boot.

'Any spare ammunition?' asked Bradley.

'No, sir. We've got eight rounds each, that's all,' replied McDonald. As he spoke, both men pulled off their belts, neither of which were needed for their designed purpose, and started to pull the belt apart. From one side came thin titanium and steel wire, with leather loops for holding it. It could be used on someone's throat if necessary, but, more importantly, it could also be used to saw through metal. The seams of both belts were ripped open and inside a thin band of plastic explosives was rolled out. Each belt carried two ounces of PE, enough to blow a hole in the ship's side. The buckles were quickly transformed into throwing knives.

As they worked, laying their trophies on the deck, Bradley said, 'I've only seen stuff like this in films.'

Stanton looked at him and gave a wry smile. 'That's where most of the ideas came from, sir. Hollywood dreamt them up and the secret services copied them.' He took the lace from his left shoe. The design of the shoe meant that the lace was not needed to keep it securely on his foot. Instead, it proved to be detonating cord to be used with the plastic explosive. From the heel of the same shoe he took an electronic detonator and a battery of the sort used in hearing aids. His other shoe yielded the same again. McDonald had exactly the same.

'That's it, ladies and gentlemen.'

Bradley rubbed his hands together with glee. 'Boy, I don't feel quite so naked now.'

'Hang on, sir,' said McDonald. 'This isn't much against what Habib can throw at us. In an all out battle we wouldn't last two minutes.'

'I know,' said Bradley, not losing any of his enthusiasm, 'but we ain't going into battle. We're going to look for a way out and, if the proverbial hits the fan, at least there'll be something we can do. What I mean is, they won't have it all their own way.'

Donald Spencer had not been in the gathering around the two SAS men but had been crawling all over the hold, feeling, prodding, knocking. He walked thoughtfully back to the group and asked, 'Is there a knife amongst that lot?'

'Yes, sure,' said Stanton. 'Why?'

'I've been examining this place carefully. This is what they call the fore peak, right?' he pointed to the bows. The cables for the anchors came up through holes in the deck and passed straight up through holes, known as hawseholes, in the overhead bulkhead, where they ran for a couple of metres before passing back down through further hawseholes in the deck and to the anchors. 'Now, this leads down to the chain locker and these scuppers here,' he pointed to the sides of the deck, 'lead down to the bilges. I reckon that there has to be a way of getting through this deck into the bilges. If we can, maybe we can find a way out of here without Habib and his gang knowing.'

'Then what? We've nowhere to go and nowhere to hide,' said Bradley.

'I'm not suggesting we go anywhere. What I am suggesting is that we be able to do something should the opportunity arrive. I for one don't wish to sit here like rats in a trap, waiting for Habib to call all the shots.' He sounded belligerent, and immediately looked a little sheepish.

'I agree. What do you want the knife for?' asked McDonald.

'I'm going to scrape along the deck. This ship is older than it looks. It's well preserved, I grant you that, but it's at least thirty years old. There's a lot of anti-corrosion paint on the deck and I want to scrape across it to see if I can lift one of the deck plates.'

Stanton handed him one of the small, deadly, throwing knives. 'You can try this.' The blade was two inches long and the handle the same length. In order for it to be of any use you had to aim at the throat and hit the target. McDonald could do so nine times out of ten.

'Wait,' said Oliver Thurston, the Swiss president of the Bank of Zurich. He took a red Swiss army knife from his pocket. 'This might be better.'

It had at least a dozen blades to it, some of which he showed them. 'It was a gift from my granddaughter. She always said that it would come in useful one day and made me promise to carry it with me everywhere. She's only six, so I promised.'

'Thank goodness for that,' said Spencer. 'This is much better.' He went over to the after bulkhead, at the opposite end to the bow, and knelt down. He began to scrape the knife across the deck, cutting through layer after layer of paint. Quickly, he got through to the metal and then dragged the knife from port to starboard for about a metre. He then ran a second cut, parallel to the first, half an inch away. He turned the blade over and carefully lifted one end of the strip he had cut. Once he had loosened a few inches of the paint he grabbed the end and carefully tore the strip away. It lifted neatly, leaving the bare, rusty metal showing beneath.

'How the hell did you know it would lift like that?' asked Bradley.

'I didn't, sir. I'd hoped. I had an old boat once, made of metal. The problem with old boats is that although the paint will retard rusting, it doesn't prevent it completely. After years of repainting, there isn't a proper clean surface to which the paint can bond. So, we can lift this lot, if we're careful.' Whilst he spoke, he was cutting a further strip, which also peeled away easily.

'Okay,' said Bradley, 'assuming we find a way through, what then?'

'Then,' replied Stanton, 'Cecil here, and I, will go for a recce.'

Habib was on the bridge, sitting with his feet up on the control console, trying to appear calm and relaxed. In fact, he was the reverse. If he achieved his objectives he would be wealthy beyond avarice and honoured and revered throughout his land. So far, everything had gone according to plan. He sat in the filtered half light, his world now a permanent grey, thanks to the sacking covering the ship. Fredericks appeared on the bridge.

'I've set it up. We can transmit whenever you say the word.'

Habib waited a few moments before replying. 'I think I'll have a cup of coffee and wait until six o'clock.'

He glanced at the deck clock as he spoke. It was now 15.22 hours.

'Why wait? The quicker we send the broadcast the quicker we can get things moving and the quicker we can get out of here.'

'My friend, we are exactly on schedule,' Habib rose to his feet and paced the deck. 'We should be away from here no later than Friday, as we planned. Everybody here will be dead and we shall be rich and famous. It is a heady thought.'

Fredericks shrugged. 'You know me, Aziz. I never count my chickens before they hatch.'

'What is this about chickens? We are talking about one hundred million dollars, not chickens.'

'You know what I mean. We've got a long way to go yet.'

'Maybe. Are the transponders ready?' he asked, changing the subject.

'Yes, they'll be put out tonight. Once in place, a mouse couldn't walk onto this island without us knowing about it.'

'Good. And the submersible?'

'I checked it myself. Everything is exactly as we want it to be. I've checked the batteries and the gas mix. It'll get us to the mainland, have no fear.'

'Good. Then let us have a cup of coffee and something to eat.'

'What about the prisoners?'

'What about them? They will be given no more food or drink. Where they are going they have no need of either.'

12

Midnight 2 May 1998. Machrihanish Airfield.

The SAR helicopter had actually landed on Eileach an Naoimh, a small island five miles south of the island of Mull and the furthest west from the coast of the mainland. Although it was only some half mile long and three hundred yards wide it sported a derelict chapel dating back a thousand years. Next to the chapel was a flat, open space covered in grass which supported a dozen or so sheep. After searching as best they could from the air, the pilot had decided to land and see whether they could listen for survivors. With the engines shut down the three crew members had stood on the shore line, powerful torches in hand, shouting across the water, listening for a response. They had heard and seen nothing.

After half an hour they had radioed back to Machrihanish for further instructions. They had been recalled to stand by to ferry search parties to different points on the coast. The pilot had called to the other two who were still wandering along the water's edge when he had heard a shout in reply. The co-pilot had found the body of one of the passengers. There had been three bullet holes across his chest. They had put him in a body bag and ferried him back to Machrihanish. Back at the airport they had found papers on the body which identified him as the Finance Minister of Columbia.

The Commanding Officer at Machrihanish was Wing Commander Peter Brown, finishing his time in the RAF, with only six months to go. He had hoped his posting to the outpost on the Mull of Kintyre would allow him to end his service career in peace. The day's events had ensured that this was not to be. A tall, good-looking man of fifty-five, he was divorced with two grown up sons who lived in Cambridgeshire and whom he rarely saw. The only ambition he had left was to move into the small cottage he had bought in Oban and spend his time writing political thrillers. To date, although he had thought of many plots, sub plots and love interests, he hadn't put pen to paper.

'Sir, that's Golf Bravo Hotel Delta Oscar. They are a hundred miles south and starting to descend.' The air traffic controller was referring to the Hercules C130 carrying Hunter's team.

'Good. Any sign of the helicopters from Lossie?'

'Yes, sir. They'll be here in twenty minutes.'

'Right. As with the others, get the helicopters fuelled and ready and make sure the crews are fit to fly. And before you say anything, you can tell them that we're trying to drum up more pilots but that they'll just have to keep going until we find some more qualified crew. As of 23.45 today all peace time flying rules ceased.'

'Yes, sir.' The controller kept the surprise from showing. This was unprecedented in the ten years he'd been an air traffic controller. It meant that flying hours went out of the window. Landings and take offs would be faster, fewer rules followed, and the helicopters would be kept in the air for longer periods than was normal. Maintenance would be carried out on the hoof, so to speak.

Forty minutes later, the Hercules landed, taxied to the side of the airport and began to unload. Hunter went to find Wing Commander Brown whilst Carter and the remainder of the team sorted through their equipment.

Hunter and Brown met up in the control tower.

'Sir, I've been appointed SAC,' said Hunter, without preamble.

Brown nodded. 'Yes, I know. I'm surprised. I would have expected a full blown Admiral at least with all that's been going on.'

Hunter smiled cynically. 'No, sir. This is too delicate and political for an Admiral to get his hands dirty. I'm afraid that it's a very lowly Lieutenant Commander who'll carry the can. In this case, me.'

'Well, I can't say I envy you. Tell me what you want and if it's in my power I'll get it for you.' Brown smiled. 'And if it's not, I know a man who knows a man, etc.'

'Thanks, sir, that's very good of you. Perhaps you can brief me as to what's been happening so far.'

'First things first. What about feeding your lads?'

'We brought our own. We're fully self contained and I expect something's being sorted even as we speak.'

'Fair enough. What about you? Would you like a coffee?'

'Yes. Thank you, sir.'

A leading aircraftwoman appeared with a tray of mugs and a pot of coffee. 'Sandwiches will be along shortly,' she said and left the tower to return to the kitchen. Every member of the small staff at Machrihanish was up and working.

'Is there any sign of the helicopter that was shot down?'

'No, nothing, I'm afraid. We've found one body so far.

The rest could still be inside the fuselage but from what the pilot radioed in, I doubt that.'

'What's your opinion?'

The Wing Commander frowned, and then shook his head. 'Actually, it would take more than a single missile to blow one of those beauties apart or to cause it to sink so quickly that most if not all the passengers were unable to escape. And anyway, the pilot reports that they were evacuating. So I think they got out.'

'We know that at least one got out,' Hunter pointed out reasonably.

'So what's happened to the rest?'

'Good question,' Hunter replied. 'We can only surmise that they've been taken by whoever carried out the attack.' He stood at the window, surveying the floodlit airfield, deep in thought. 'Do you know the helicopter they were flying in?'

'Yes, pretty well. I never qualified in her myself but I know a lot about the type.'

'Tell me all you can. For instance, after ditching what would happen?'

Hunter listened avidly. He was thinking about the helicopter not as a flying machine but as a sunken object. He wrung the last details he could from the Wing Commander until he was satisfied. Finally he said, 'Can I hear the tapes of your last contact with the helicopter?'

'It's all ready. I've had a copy made so you can listen as often as you like. You may pick up something useful. I've listened twice and can tell you with certainty that the pilot managed to avoid four missiles before being hit by a fifth. It was quite a feat of flying, I can tell you. You also hear the pilot telling us that they have started to evacuate the helicopter. Then nothing.'

Hunter nodded and slipped the cassette into a portable player handed him by the Wing Commander. Although the time lapse was over an hour from when the helicopter was first under Machrihanish control until it was shot down, the conversation on the tape lasted only six minutes. The whole period was condensed into less than a dozen transmissions.

Listening to it told Hunter nothing more than he already knew, although it did convince him that most, if not all, the passengers had evacuated the helicopter. He gazed thoughtfully to the north. So where are you? he asked himself. And more importantly, are you still alive?

He turned from the window and said, 'Have you a secure line I can use?'

Wing Commander Brown gestured to the phone. 'That's about as secure as you can get. Ministry of Defence network via Faslane.'

'Thanks.' He picked up the handset and dialled. After a few rings he was through to the dockyard at Devonport and asked for General Macnair. 'Sir, it's Hunter.' He gave a brief situation report and said, 'Can you get Isobel to do something for me?'

'Isobel? Certainly. What do you want her to do?'

'Well, there's no sign of the downed helicopter. It's flat calm, no wind and according to the tide tables, we're half way between neap and spring tides. From what I've been told they've carried out as thorough a search as possible under the circumstances.'

'So what's your point?'

'My point is that we won't know where to start in the morning. The helicopter can be anywhere. Looking at the tidal stream, there are speeds up to four knots in some places. Now, from what I can gather, once in the water, the helo could lie just under the surface and go with the tide. Diving won't find it because by daybreak she could be as many as fifty or even a hundred miles from where she ditched.'

'Point taken, my boy. So what do you suggest?'

'See if Isobel can find detailed computerised information on the tides in this area. If she can, get her to program into her computer the characteristics of the helicopter. Ask her if she can run the program to give us an idea of where the helicopter could be. I could sit with a pair of compasses and a ruler and do the same but I doubt I'd be anywhere as accurate as she could be.'

'I'll arrange it. Any idea where she could go for the information?'

'Yes, I've been thinking about that too. Tell her to phone the Marine Biology Department at Glasgow University. I think there's a part of the department which has spent the last few years looking at the tides and the weather to see how they affect fish migration around the Western Isles.'

'How do you know that?'

'Let's say I had, em, biblical knowledge of one of the students a few years back.'

Macnair chuckled. 'Biblical knowledge, eh? That's a very old way of putting it.' He became serious again. 'Anything else you think you may need?'

'Who are the COs of the two Hunt class on their way?'

'Wait a moment, and I'll find out.' The General referred to a pile of signals he had received during the previous four hours. 'HMS *Brecon* is Lieutenant Commander M. Schofield and HMS *Chepstow* is Commander D. Blockhurst.'

233

Hunter's heart sank. 'General, Mike Schofield will be as good as gold. David Blockhurst will give me problems.'

'Problems? How?'

'Apart from the fact that he doesn't like me he will definitely put difficulties in my way if I'm SAC and not him.'

Macnair thought for a moment. He was fully aware of the kind of difficulties which could be caused by an unco-operative senior officer. The biggest problem with all the armed forces in so called peace time was that there were few opportunities for an officer to shine, to be noticed and hence, hopefully, promoted. Whether it was the army, navy or air force the senior middle ranks were the worst, from major or lieutenant commander up to brigadier or captain RN. 'Okay, leave it to me. I'll make it clear which side his bread is buttered on.'

'Thank you.' He did not add that he did not think it would help much.

After he had rung off Hunter turned to Wing Commander Brown, who had been listening in the background.

'Sir, I need to get my team to the scene.'

'Now?' Brown looked at his watch. It was 00.45.

Hunter nodded. He didn't explain that as a new outfit none of them had worked together and so none of them knew how they would each behave in a combat situation. At least by having them camped out together, working over their equipment, checking things continuously, some sort of rapport could be built up. It was little enough, but it was all he could do at present. Until they were in action, they would never know how they worked together. As he stood at the window Hunter was certain of one thing:

running around Scotland like headless chickens would not find the ship and the prisoners. So what would?

He left the control tower to find Jim Carter. After discussing matters with him, they agreed that it would be better if the team went to where the incident had happened. At least they could help the diving team from Faslane look for wreckage and any bodies swept up on the shore. Carter was to remain at Machrihanish. The team would be under the command of Joshua Clements, the American from Delta Force and Hunter was going to be air lifted to HMS *Chepstow*, the Hunt class minehunter under the command of Commander David Blockhurst; a prospect Hunter did not relish.

The Sea King helicopter was hovering over the stern of the ship by 04.10. HM Ships *Chepstow* and *Brecon* were sailing at best speed just off the south west corner of the Mull of Kintyre. *Chepstow* was in the lead, with *Brecon* two miles astern. In order to facilitate the transfer of the passenger from the helicopter to the ship, the ship had turned onto a heading of due west to get the optimum wind across the deck from the right sector. The pilot lined up the helicopter, gauged accurately the necessary speed to keep the hover as steady as humanly possible and signalled that it was now clear to lower the winch. Hunter nodded his thanks and slipped over the combing into the buffeting down draft. Quickly, he was lowered down. Before his feet landed on the deck an earthing pole was raised to touch the wire on which he dangled, so that the static electricity which builds up in a helicopter in flight and can be fatal if not earthed, would be discharged. He landed on the deck, unhooked the carrying strop from the winch wire and waved to the pilot. Hunter shucked off the strop, hung it back on the wire and ducked quickly out of the way. The helicopter was already turning away as the wire was being winched in. Within seconds the clatter of the helicopter was receding into the distance, back to Machrihanish.

Having served for two years on HMS *Chepstow* as the first lieutenant, Hunter was fully conversant with every intimate detail of the ship. He gave his bag to one of the ratings of the deck crew and made his way to the bridge. As he did so, he heard the pipe 'Secure from flying stations. Morning watchmen close up. Call the hands will be at the normal time of zero crack sparrow fart.' Hunter smiled. That was the naval vernacular for early.

On the bridge there was a welcoming committee of the Captain, Commander Blockhurst and his First Lieutenant, Lieutenant Martin White. As was usual, Blockhurst and White were both qualified diving and mine disposal specialists, like Hunter. As was typical in an elite and small specialisation such as MCD (Mine Clearance Diving), they all knew, or knew of, each other.

Blockhurst had been seven years ahead of Hunter at Dartmouth, and had been a first shot commander. It was rumoured that he was going places, perhaps all the way to the top, something which had never been achieved by other officers in the same specialisation, ever. The MCD branch of the Royal Navy had always been made up of misfits and loners, individuals who loved the navy but hated the bullshit. Blockhurst had proven to be the exception to the rule.

'Hullo, Nick. Welcome aboard.' At least, thought Hunter, he was going to be civil.

'Hullo, sir.' They shook hands and Hunter was introduced to White. This was White's first appointment since qualifying as an MCD officer and he had been in the job for nearly two years. Blockhurst had only recently taken command.

'Care to tell me what's going on, Nick?'

'Yes, sir. Perhaps we could go down to your cabin?'

'Right. Martin, I believe you have the watch.' He knew full well his First Lieutenant had the watch. As was common on most small ships of the Royal Navy, the second in command had the morning watch from 04.00 to 08.00. It was his task to get the ship working by 08.00 before he went for his breakfast.

Hunter followed Blockhurst down to his cabin. For a small ship it was relatively spacious. The cabin had a bunk, a desk and chair and a small sitting area with two easy chairs and a low table.

'So what's going on?' Blockhurst asked after they had sat down.

'Have you heard anything, sir?'

'Only that a helicopter had crashed and we were to proceed to the scene to look for it and any survivors. Oh, and that you were to be the SAC.' Blockhurst stood six feet in his socks and was as skinny as a bean pole. He had long tapering fingers which he pressed together, his elbows resting on the arms of his chair. As he spoke, his eyes slitted, the effort to hold his temper threatening to be too much for him.

'And I take it you feel you should have the job?'

'Naturally. I am the senior officer present. I have sent a signal querying the order and pointing out a few of the pertinent facts to the situation.'

Hunter had wondered how he was to solve the dilemma of getting co-operation from somebody who probably saw himself as an adversary in the present situation and now that he was face to face with the man, the answer came to him.

'Sir, it's a poisoned chalice. Believe me, you don't want the job.'

In spite of himself Blockhurst was intrigued and couldn't help asking, 'Why ever not?'

'Because the helicopter was shot down by terrorists. It was carrying a load of VIPs to Balmoral. Some people have been killed but it is obvious that many more have been taken as prisoners. For what purpose we can only surmise at present. My task is to find them, get the prisoners released unharmed and not leave anybody behind to stand trial. If you get my meaning.'

'Good God. You can't be serious.' Blockhurst was thinking furiously. He did not like Hunter, it was true. Not because of the man himself but because of his casual attitude to the navy. Hunter was an MCD officer of the old school. A superb diver and a real expert in the field of explosives, Hunter did not fit well into the general navy. If Hunter made commander he would be lucky, very lucky. Whilst he, on the other hand, had realised a long time ago that with the down-scaling of the armed forces, and the Royal Navy in particular, small ships would play an increasingly important part. Specialising in diving and mine disposal, he had been assured of command. This was the second time he had been the commanding officer of a Hunt class minehunter but this time he was the most senior officer afloat in the minewarfare squadron. He commanded the whole squadron when at sea. If he played his cards right he could get a staff job next, followed by command of a frigate. Hunter was right, it was a poisoned chalice. By giving maximum help he would be seen to be doing his bit. If it all went wrong, Hunter would be to blame. If he succeeded, the help received from the squadron would be noted. Success seemed unlikely at that moment.

'So what do you want to do? Go to the area off Mull and begin hunting?'

Hunter was pleased at the ease with which Blockhurst had agreed to help, but on the other hand, knowing him as he did, he was not particularly surprised. Blockhurst could always be relied upon to do one thing – whatever was right for Blockhurst.

'That's the idea, sir. However, in the meantime I've asked one of my people to get as much data as possible on the tides and currents around the Mull at this time of year and to try and compute where the helicopter could be by now. Hopefully, we'll have an answer by mid-morning.' Hunter stood, unable to stifle a yawn. 'In the meantime, I'd appreciate it if I could get my head down for a few hours.'

'Right, of course. The Jimmy's arranged a bunk for you somewhere. Ask him. Goodnight, Nick.'

Hunter bade good night and left the cabin. He took the steps to the bridge and found the first lieutenant with an open nautical almanac working out the time of sunrise. 'What are you doing, Martin? The satnav will give you that information to the second. You don't need to use the books anymore.'

'I know, sir. It's just that Commander Blockhurst likes to see the workings out and the time entered in the log.'

Hunter made no comment but his look said enough. 'Where am I sleeping, Number One?'

The First Lieutenant of a Royal Naval vessel was known as The Jimmy, Number One or sometimes, by his name. The last was not very often.

'I've put you in the old midshipman's grot, sir. It's empty at present.'

'Excellent, thank you. Goodnight.'

'Goodnight, sir. Oh, you'll find your case there already.'

Hunter nodded his thanks and went below. The midshipman's grot was a spacious cabin with four bunks in it. Usually, there would be at least two midshipmen onboard and visitors would be expected to share. In this case he considered himself lucky to have the place to himself. It seemed to Hunter that hardly had he crawled between the sheets, when he heard the pipe, naval jargon for an announcement, over the ship's broadcast system.

First came the trill of the bosun's call followed by the adenoidal announcement, 'Wakey, wakey, rise and shine, you've had your kip now I want mine. Breakfast will commence serving in fifteen minutes.'

Hunter looked at his watch, 06.30. He thought about going back to sleep; he had not got to bed much more than an hour and a half ago but then thought better of it. He had a lot to do.

After a shave and a shower he felt almost human again and made his way down one deck to the wardroom. Two other officers were already at breakfast and introductions were made quickly. Mark Harris, a young lieutenant, was the Navigating Officer, and Peter Henderson, a sub lieutenant, was the Correspondence Officer. The lieutenant's job was self explanatory, whilst the sub dealt with all official correspondence to and from the ship. It was a tedious and often thankless task. However, in times of peace a ship was known by it's correspondence, or so the saying went.

'What's going on, sir?' asked the navigating officer.

Hunter told them briefly, whilst he waited for the

steward to bring him eggs, bacon, and toast. He had already helped himself to orange juice and coffee. 'No doubt the Captain will be briefing everybody shortly. Who's the coxswain onboard?'

The coxswain of a minehunter was not only in charge of all the ratings onboard, answerable to the first lieutenant for the running of the ship, something like a regimental sergeant major, but he was also a diving and mine disposal specialist and in the same branch of the navy as Hunter.

'It's Liz Taylor, sir,' said the correspondence officer.

'Liz? Excellent, he and I go back a long way.' Sometime, long ago, the then Able Seaman Albert Taylor had been given the nickname of Liz, in honour of the famous actress and the name had stuck. Now a Fleet Chief Petty Officer, Liz Taylor was a legend in the diving branch. As he often said himself, "been there, done that and lost the tee-shirt that proved it." He was one of the men Hunter had recommended to Macnair as a recruit.

Hunter finished his breakfast and went up to the bridge. There he found three busy people, the officer of the watch who was the first lieutenant, the helmsman and the bosun's mate. Because the ship was on automatic pilot, both able seamen were busy cleaning the bridge, polishing what few brass objects there still were in a modern navy and generally tidying away.

'Where are we, Number One?'

'That's Gigha Island, sir,' replied the first lieutenant. He was sitting in the captain's chair on the starboard side of the bridge, scanning the sea through a pair of binoculars.

Hunter went over to the chart, checked the ship's position and used a pair of dividers to estimate the distance and hence the time of arrival at their destination.

They would be at the incident area by noon at the latest. He picked up a pair of binoculars and scanned the horizon. Being a Sunday there was nothing to see. No other ships, no fishing boats, just a calm, grey sea to the south west, the island of Islay to the west and Gigha Island to the east. He looked at the water ahead, scanning the surface, looking for any unusual pattern in the sea. Luck had been known to play a part when it came to searching for submerged objects and luck was something they had not had too much of so far. Seeing nothing he went back to the chart table and lifted down a copy of the nautical almanac and tide tables. For the next twenty minutes he made his calculations.

The basic problem he had was that, although the tide tables gave the strength and direction of the tide on the surface at any point in time, they did not give the sub-surface picture and, of course, he could not make the tide calculations at intervals of say, less than an hour. Painstakingly, he marked the chart from the time of the incident, through the night. He then double-checked his work and stood looking down at his results. He went across to the bridge intercom which connected him directly to the captain's cabin and called down. He decided to make it official.

'Captain sir, this is SAC on the bridge.' By using his designation as Scene of Action Commander he hope that Blockhurst would remember their conversation in the middle of the night and do as he was told. Although the telling would be in the form of a request.

'Captain.'

'Sir, I've been making a few calculations and I think we should go to Hunting Stations shortly and head up through the Sound of Islay. I can show you my reasoning whenever it's convenient to you.'

There was a short silence. 'It's seven thirty now. Will zero eight hundred do for Hunting Stations?'

'Yes, sir, if I can slow down and head for the Sound.'

'Right, do that. Oh, and don't forget your ship astern.'

'No sir, I won't,' replied Hunter. If all Blockhurst wanted to do was get the last word in then that was okay with him. Anything, as long as they got the job done.

'You heard that, Number One. If you didn't know, I'm in overall command. Send to *Brecon* reduce speed to five knots and change course as required to maintain station. Tasking signal to follow.'

The officer of the watch used the VHF on the bridge whilst Hunter began to compose a tasking signal for both ships. The signal was written and sent as though he was a third party, divorced from either ship, instructing both captains to carry out a particular task. Complex as an idea, the Royal Navy had spent hundreds of years refining a system which broke the idea down into a series of simple but lengthy instructions. The signal was from task group 50.1 to task units 50.1.1 and 50.1.2, effectively HMS *Chepstow* and HMS *Brecon*. A call sign was designated for the task group commander, Hunter, and the task was allocated: minehunting. The signal took twenty minutes to devise and, once he had finished, Hunter sent for the petty officer in charge of communications and signals. He handed him the pad and was about to call Blockhurst again when he appeared on the bridge.

The First Lieutenant vacated the Captain's chair and made his customary morning report. 'Thank you, Number One. Well, Nick, what do you intend to do?'

With that question, the ball was deposited firmly in Hunter's court. 'Worse case scenario as far as I can work out is that the helicopter has drifted as far as the northern end of the Sound of Islay, or is somewhere between Colonsay and Islay. I've looked at the tidal atlas, double-checked the tide tables and erred on the side of spring rather than neap tides.' This meant he had made his calculations based on a bigger rise and fall of the tide and hence faster currents for the area. There was no way, based on the information available to him, that the helicopter could have drifted further than a point at least ten miles to the north. Even so, he was going to start hunting within a few minutes, just in case. Everyone had heard of sod's law, which said that if anything could go wrong, it would. At sea, it was dos's law. Sod's law backwards – much more likely to go wrong, and with evil consequences as well.

At that moment, a leading seaman from the communications department appeared and handed the signal log to the captain. He read Hunter's signal and said to the first lieutenant, 'Hunting Stations at zero eight hundred. We start from,' he heaved himself out of his chair and crossed to the chart, 'here, just off Brosdale Island and go through the Sound. Line abreast, five cables apart, SOA to be seven knots. Send to *Brecon* . . .' Hunter heard no more as he made his way down to his cabin. He needed to think in peace for a few moments. Having tasked the ships nothing more was needed from him. Two of the most expert minehunting crews in the world could manage without him.

Minehunting was a simple enough concept. By moving slowly through the water a specially designed sonar could look at the seabed and paint a picture of everything down there which was solid. Hence rocks would show, as would man-made objects such as mines. This was particularly effective when looking for ground mines but worked equally well with a moored mine floating a few metres below the surface but anchored to the seabed. The crews were highly trained at finding and identifying whatever the sonar picked up. A good team could tell a rock from an empty coke can. Seven knots for their speed of advance was fast if they were looking for a mine because the faster the ships went the greater the degradation of the picture on the sonar screens. However, a mine was, at most, two or three metres long by a metre in diameter. A helicopter was a hundred times bigger and when it showed on the screen it would blast a bright strobe light which could not be missed. So instead of the usual speed of three or four knots, Hunter was happy to progress at the faster speed. Even so, there was a great deal of sea to cover. The sonar, on wide beam, could cover an area of about a thousand yards wide, depending on the depth of water and the angle of the beam to the vertical. Five cables or half a mile apart would cover the whole width of the Sound of Islay in one pass. If the helicopter had not come this way, the problem would be greatly increased in the more open water north of the island.

Part of his tasking signal was to instruct lookouts on both ships to scour the shores looking for the downed helicopter. It was always possible that it had been washed up somewhere. The worst potential situation was that it was in the shallows, neither one thing nor the other; undetectable by the sonar and impossible to see by the lookouts. For that there was a third string to his bow. He had tasked the diving teams to go close inshore and search from their inflatable boats. No diving, just a surface scan. The water was so calm and clear, they ought to be able to see a helicopter if it was just under the surface.

As he sat thinking through what he should do next, he heard the pipe. 'Hands to minehunting stations. Hands to minehunting stations. Close up blue watch in the ops room. Away divers. Coxswain to the bridge.'

Throughout the ship, in a scene repeated onboard the *Brecon*, there was what would appear to a civilian's eyes to be chaos. Having been warned the previous night what was going to happen, the men were primed, ready to go to work. This was what they trained for and this was what they were damned good at. If there was a helicopter down there, they would find it. Provided they looked in the right place.

What had he left undone? As far as he could tell, nothing, but there was no doubt about it, he was not happy. Even if they found the helicopter, what would it prove, that some people were dead and some still lived? It would not help them to find the terrorists or anybody who was still alive. The problem was, it was the only place to start, until they had more information.

Hunter left the cabin and made his way back to the bridge. He wanted to talk to FCPO Taylor to see if he had any ideas. When they met, there was a warm exchange of handshakes and Hunter was invited down to the coxswain's cabin to discuss whether anything further could be done.

Fleet Chief Petty Officer Taylor was indeed a legend. During the Falklands war he had defused three bombs which had been dropped by Argentinian aircraft onto three different ships. Although each vessel had received a direct hit, a perverse irony and luck attended the attacks. None of the priming mechanisms in the bombs had been set correctly! Fortunate, indeed, for the destruction of the three ships might well have altered the course of the war. Using a set of manuals and a lot of luck, Petty Officer Taylor as he was then, with Lieutenant Paul Schofield, had defused the bombs. Unfortunately for Schofield the fourth bomb he had tried to defuse had exploded, earning him a posthumous George Cross. Taylor had lived to collect his, along with a bar. As Chief Petty Officer Taylor he had been the coxswain of HMS *Chepstow* when Hunter had been the First Lieutenant and so they knew each other well. Apart from a mutual respect for each other's professionalism, there was also a mutual liking, which was a good thing with a small, highly specialised team operating in one of the most dangerous professions in the world.

Taylor sent for a couple of cups of coffee and sat opposite his ex-boss, a grin showing through his now greying beard. At five feet four, he was a bantam of a man, as hard as nails and a truly expert diver. He was of the opinion, rightly, that diving was the means of transport to the job. Once there, you still had to know what you were doing.

'You heard from the Captain what's going on?'

The coxswain nodded. 'Yes. He briefed me and said he'd be briefing the ship's company once they had shaken down into minehunting stations. It's a pretty bad state of affairs, isn't it?'

Hunter nodded. 'Yes, Liz, it is. You don't have any ideas do you?'

'Not at the moment, Nick, but I'll give it some thought. I've got to go and talk to the lads and tell them what I want them to do. After that, if you want, we can go and look at a few charts. After all, the bastards have to be somewhere.'

13

General Malcolm Macnair was pacing around the room. It was now just after 10.00 and Isobel had finally managed to contact somebody at the university. They did indeed have a comprehensive profile of the waters around the western coast of Scotland, at all depths. The information was considered to be valuable but could be purchased. Macnair had then spoken with the bursar of the university and explained the situation. She had promised to sort something out, the result of which was a telephone call to Isobel. For the last few minutes the information held in the computer at Glasgow University had been down-loading into Isobel's computer. The transmission ceased and Macnair said, somewhat impatiently, 'Have you got it all?'

'Just a moment, please sir, whilst I check,' Isobel said sweetly, when what she really wanted to do was to shout at him to leave her alone to get on with it.'

Macnair sensed her mood and said, 'Sorry. I'm going to get a coffee, do you want one?'

She nodded. The only way she could consume more coffee than she did was to have it supplied intravenously. Her fingers flew across the keyboard.

It was then that Hiram B. Walsh arrived. The United States Lieutenant Colonel, who was operationally second in command, strode into the room.

'Hiram, you're back,' Macnair said, stating the obvious.

'What's going on?'

Macnair told him to take a seat whilst he was brought up to speed with events. Afterwards, Walsh said, 'Jeesus . . . What do you want me to do? Take over from Nick?'

Macnair shook his head. 'We need more information about the helicopter and I think we need that from the manufacturers. Can you get onto them now and ask them for more information about the flotation gear. What happens if its shot up and so on? I suspect they've got plenty of computerised situations showing what could happen if a rotor fell off or a bomb exploded.'

Walsh nodded. 'Sure. There'll be hundreds, if not thousands. And it'll all be top secret. They won't release the information to us unless . . . unless I get a really big gun to fire for us. And I know just the man.'

He picked up the telephone and direct dialled Washington.

'Slade,' was the abrupt reply after only one ring, in spite of the fact that it was the middle of the night.

General Slade was Hiram B. Walsh's uncle, about three times removed on his grandpappy's side, as he explained it to Macnair later. The result of the call was that twenty minutes later Isobel was in E-mail contact with the helicopter manufacturers being given all the data she needed.

She nodded her thanks when the General put a mug of coffee by her side but she did not stop what she was doing. After a few moments she sat back, picked up her mug and simultaneously pressed the return key.

'All we can do now, General, is wait.'

'How long will it take?'

'I don't know. Not long, I shouldn't think. Scanning the detail we received from the university shows me that they've done an incredible job amassing so much information. Without computers it would be virtually useless, but with them, we can get an amazingly accurate picture as to what is going on in the seas around Scotland. Ah, here we go.'

Macnair and Walsh stood behind her chair and looked avidly at the results of her work.

On the screen appeared a detailed chart of the area in which they assumed the helicopter had ditched and the exact time. Superimposed onto the picture appeared the helicopter, landed on the water. As they watched, it slowly sank and at the same time drifted down the screen.

'Can't we speed this up?' asked Macnair, impatiently.

'What? Oh, sorry. Yes, of course. This is actually the computed speed of the event. Let me increase it by a factor of one hundred and see where it leads us.'

They watched the helicopter sink. A message block appeared in the top left corner of the screen showing its depth below the surface, the depth of the water to the seabed and the speed at which it was travelling. In the top left hand corner was displayed the time as it related to the events unfolding on the screen. The helicopter floated along the coast of Jura as far as a point about a mile off Rubh A Mhail, the north eastern corner of the island. There, a strange thing happened. The computer paused and the time stopped on the display. After a few seconds two helicopters appeared, one moving towards the Sound of Jura and the other more to the west and the sea between Jura and Colonsay.

'What the hell?' Macnair paused with his mug half way to his lips. 'What's going on?'

Even as he asked the question, above each helicopter image appeared a figure in percentages. The image drifting towards the Sound showed 39%, and the one heading to the west showed 61%. Isobel interpreted the display for him. 'This image here,' she traced it with her finger tip, 'has a thirty-nine percent chance of being correct. This one here, has a sixty-one percent chance of being right. That's because at the point where the second image appeared the water diverges.'

Macnair thought about it for a few seconds and asked, 'What if we put the helicopter ditching a hundred yards to the west or east, what happens then?'

Isobel smiled. 'I've thought of that. If we run this to eleven o'clock and see where it could be, I'll re-run the program with the helicopter at different crash points. Say, covering a mile across. The position north or south shouldn't matter that much, except it will be that much further along or back up the track. We can then make an educated guess as to where we think the helicopter is.'

After a few more seconds, the computer time showed 11.00 hours and Isobel marked the position where both helicopters were expected. She restarted the program and moved the ditching position by a hundred yards. She increased the speed by a further factor of five and sat back to watch what happened. She repeated the process a total of ten times. The results were amazing. In every case, the image of the helicopter doubled at about the same point and moved off in similar directions to the first track shown. The probability that the helicopter went through the Sound varied from 36% to 41% whilst the probability that it went the other way ranged from 64% to 59%.

'Fascinating,' said Macnair, looking at the screen. 'According to the computer we can expect to find the helicopter here at eleven hundred hours.' He touched the screen. 'Do you have the latitude and longitude for it?'

Isobel pressed a few buttons and the latitude and longitude appeared next to the helicopter.

Macnair picked up his satellite link phone and pressed a speed dial button. 'Nick? Where are you?'

'Hullo, General. I'm on the bridge at present.'

'Nick, I'll make allowances for your lack of sleep last night. I couldn't care less if you're taking a shower. Whereabouts is the ship right now?'

'Sorry, sir. Just passing Port Askaig. That's halfway through the Sound.'

'Okay. Now listen. Isobel programmed the computer with the data we got from the university and some help from the bods at Bath. She reckons the helicopter should be around a position two miles north of Nave Island at eleven hundred hours.' It was odd that when referring to time and the twenty-four hour clock, the army always added hours whilst the navy never did.

'If I continue at this speed I'm sure I can eliminate the Sound as a likely place for the helicopter to be found. If I then task the ships to follow the track you have we should be around the site nearer to fourteen hundred. Ask her where that will be and then ask her if she can send me a copy of the tracks she's created. I'll copy them into the ship's navigation computer and run down the track.'

'Agreed. Have you received a sitrep from Carter or from Machrihanish?'

'Yes, sir. It's as much as we expected.'

'Right, keep me in the picture.' He rang off. 'Can you send your information to Nick, Isobel?'

She nodded. It only took a few moments to send what she had to HMS *Chepstow*. There, the information was loaded into the navigation computer and the track displayed on the plotting table in the operations room. Nick stood and studied it for a few moments before going to find the coxswain.

It was Liz who reminded him about dos's law.

The General telephoned Downing Street and asked to speak to Sir Anthony Parsons who quickly took the call.

'Hullo, Tony. I thought I'd bring you up to date with the situation so you can tell the PM.'

'Thanks, Malcolm. I appreciate it. Any news?'

'Nothing positive. The minehunters have been tasked, but they'll be at least three or more hours searching the area.'

'Anything found around the crash site?'

'Yes, so far we've recovered six bodies. All have been shot, I'm told by machine gun, except for one. A body in uniform has a single bullet hole in the forehead. I gather it was one of the flight attendants. Forensics are busy analysing all the ammunition.'

'Any idea who the others are yet?'

'Yes. There's a list on its way. It should be with you shortly. The diving team from Faslane arrived in the middle of the night and have been seconded to my lot. They are carrying out intensive underwater searches in an area from one mile north of Gravellachs to one mile south and one mile west.'

'That's a big area to cover with divers.'

'Agreed. We're using our two-man sledges as well as

a towed diver search. We should cover the area in about another hour or so before we move the box south.' A towed diver search was where the diver was connected to the inflatable by a light line. He sat on the end of the line, just above the seabed and held on to a handle above his head. He was towed at about three knots through the water, able to scc all round him. It was in this way that, so far, two of the bodies had been found. The others had been washed up on the shore line, all in very divergent spots. This meant there was no way anyone could predict where more bodies would turn up, assuming there were more to be found. All they could do was to continue with the search patterns already established. Hundreds of police and army personnel had been drafted in and were arriving literally by the bus load. Jim Carter had taken over the logistical task of feeding the searchers and was now busy thinking about what to do when night fell. There was no question that the search would continue using torches, but what about resting and sleeping? Macnair did not want a further death or injury caused by a tired searcher falling off a cliff.

'What's happening about the media? I gather from one of my lot that a camera crew has arrived on the scene.'

'So we understand. There's a news briefing being called for three o'clock.'

'That's a bit late, isn't it?'

'Probably, but we can't do it any sooner. We've had the Dickens of a job contacting the various governments and telling them what's happened. You can imagine what it's been like tracking down government officials and politicians on a weekend.'

'I take it the stance is that we don't, under any circumstances, do a deal with terrorists?'

'Correct. We are also demanding the release of any hostages and that those who perpetrated this ghastly crime should give themselves up to the authorities immediately.'

Macnair snorted. 'That's a bloody laugh. This is one careful and clever operation. Have we any idea yet as to who's behind it and why?'

'Nothing has come this way so far. If I hear anything I'll let you know. Look, I'm sure you don't need me to spell it out but there's a lot riding on this. If you can come up with the solution and you know what that is, then your future is assured. We'll be able to force the concept of an international anti-terrorist group down the throats of the politicians. If you fail, then you won't last more than a couple of months while you're all disbanded and sent back to your own countries.'

'I know that,' said Macnair. 'I don't need reminding. But if that were to happen then I don't need to remind you terrorism will be the winner and decent law abiding citizens world wide, the losers.'

'I know, Malcolm. That's why I fought for you in Cabinet along with the Secretary of Defence.' He lowered his voice. 'There are some here who are too cloth eared to listen and even if they do hear, they're too self serving to see the big picture. All I'm saying is, you've got to succeed.'

'Okay, thanks. I do appreciate what you're saying. Anything else?'

'There's something coming in now. Let me call you back if it's important.' Parsons broke the connection and Macnair replaced his receiver, thoughtfully.

'Isobel, now we've given that information to Hunter, I want us to start something else. Get on to GCHQ and have them down-load every bit of information from every satellite that's passed over Scotland since yesterday afternoon.'

'Will do, General. What am I to do then?'

'Can you ask your computer to identify any ships travelling up the west coast? Then get to work isolating each one until we are as sure as we can be which ship did this. Then home in on the vessel and get as much of her signature as you can, acoustic, magnetic and, most importantly, heat.'

'I doubt if I can get any of the first two but I should get something on the third. Why?' Isobel stood, stretched and walked across the room to refill her mug.

'If we can get the satellites searching this quadrant here,' Macnair swept his hand across the north west of Scotland, 'we might be able to find the ship from her heat profile if nothing else. If we can also get a photograph from the satellites couldn't you try and get the computer to match her shape? Do you see what I mean?'

'I don't think . . . yes. I think I see.' The penny dropped. 'We use the latest satellite pictures of the area and superimpose a picture of the ship, assuming we can get one. If the ship's picture can fit an outline somewhere on the coast then it could be what we're looking for.'

'That's it. Do you think it can be done?'

'Easily. But wouldn't it be far quicker to look for a heat signature similar to the ship's?'

'I've thought about that. One problem is that there will be millions of sources of heat all over the west of Scotland, from centrally heated houses to factories and other ships and boats.'

'Yes, I know. But what if I program into the computer

257

to scrub all heat sources not right on the coast? Then, take a satellite picture from, say, a week ago and tell the computer to ignore any matched heat sources? What's left will surely be the ship.'

'It's worth a try. Let me talk to GCHQ and find out who you should contact.'

Macnair telephoned GCHQ and was soon talking to Clive Paterson. 'Mr. Paterson, you don't know me but my name is Malcolm Macnair, General Malcolm Macnair. I wondered if you could help me?'

'That was quick.'

'What was?' Macnair asked in confusion.

'I've just been speaking with Sir Anthony Parsons and he told me to expect a call from you. I've just hung up in fact.'

'Ah, well, I haven't spoken to Tony. I'm phoning for reasons of my own. What did Tony want me to ring you about?'

'We obviously heard about last night about ten minutes after if happened. One of my operatives here, named Sarah Fleeting, has been working on something for quite a while. She thinks she knows who did it.'

'What?' Macnair said, startled. 'How can she possibly know?'

'I told you, she's been working on something for some-time now. A few days ago she predicted that something like this would happen but she and her counterpart in the CIA, thought it was most likely to happen at the World Cup.'

'What would happen?'

'They didn't know. If they had, then we would have warned somebody. Sarah is an expert at putting together information from all sorts of wonderful and weird places and making sense of it. She has been tracking a terrorist named Aziz Habib for years now.'

'Habib? She thinks he's behind it?'

'You know him?'

'Not personally,' the General replied, with a certain amount of irony, 'but I've heard about him.'

'Well, according to Sarah, this has all the earmarks of Habib. Furthermore, she was of the opinion a week ago that something was going to happen. Hell, she predicted it but to be honest had no way of knowing it would be this. It doesn't make a lot of sense. What's Habib up to?'

'We don't know. The reason I called you was because I'm after some information regarding satellite pictures over the western coast of Scotland.' He explained what he wanted and why.

'I see no problem in supplying you with the information but I have to warn you that interpreting a satellite picture is not an easy matter. It takes years of training to be able to do it properly.'

Macnair didn't hesitate. 'Who's the best you've got?'

'Sarah,' replied Paterson and then regretted it immediately.

'Send her along as well. We can use her for the duration of this emergency.'

'Wait a moment,' Paterson protested. 'If she leaves here we'll be short handed and we'll lose one of our best operatives. No, I'm sorry, you can't have her but you can have all the information she's got.'

Macnair appeared to give in. 'All right, that'll have to do I suppose. Is Sarah there now? She is? Good. If I pass her over to Isobel Sweeney they can discuss with each other what they need to do and what information would be of most use to us. Thank you very much for your co-operation.'

As soon as he replaced the receiver the phone rang. It was Parsons. 'I've had some interesting news from GCHQ. They think it's a terrorist named Aziz Habib.'

The General interrupted Parsons and told him about the conversation he had already had with Paterson. He then explained about Sarah.

Ten minutes after his conversation with Parsons ended the phone went again. This time it was Paterson. After cursing Macnair he told him that Sarah would be at Devonport sometime on Monday morning.

'No, I'll have her here today. There's a helicopter on it's way to pick her up. As soon as she finishes talking to Isobel and they've done their thing with the computers, send Sarah home to pack a case. Tell her to pack enough to last at least a week. By the time she gets back to GCHQ the helicopter should be there. She can be here by eighteen hundred hours at the latest.'

'Wait a moment, Macnair. She's been on duty since eight o'clock this morning and is due to finish at four. She might have made other plans.'

'Look, Paterson, tell her I'm sorry. This is about as big an emergency as we get in peacetime and I need her here and the sooner the better. By all means ask her but I expect her to be aboard that helicopter when it returns.' He hung up without saying goodbye. Blasted civil servants!

Isobel had also finished speaking to Sarah and was busy down-loading the vast amount of information she was looking for. Sarah had given her a few ideas about how to accomplish what she wanted to do but it was daunting, to say the least. She was now out of her depth, up to her neck and paddling furiously in an attempt not to sink. She was also too bright not to admit it.

'I'm sorry, General, but I need some help. Even with Leo and Gareth I can't manage this. I need expert help.'

Macnair smiled at her. 'Isobel, you've just gone up ten points in my estimation and let me tell you, you were about as high as you could get as it was. The girl you were talking to just now, Sarah, she'll be with us in a few hours.'

'She will? That's strange. She didn't mention it.'

Macnair's grin widened. 'That was because she didn't know.'

The General left Isobel, Leo and Gareth to get on with it. He had other things to do, not least to find the remainder of his team, and get them to work. Some had drifted back over the weekend, others had phoned in when news of the incident began to break. Macnair wanted his specialists all over the west coast of Scotland, looking, prying and most importantly, taking charge. He had cleared it with the Cabinet Office, which effectively meant Sir Anthony and Stuart Roberts, the Secretary of State for Defence, and the necessary orders had been passed out. Leave it to Macnair and his men. Help in every possible way; but pass the responsibility to them. That order had been filtered through the military and civilian emergency services. They were one step from declaring a national emergency in Scotland which would have mobilised tens of thousands of people, from army, navy and air force reservists to special constables and part-time firemen. It was a measure of how matters stood that this course of action had been discussed and finally dismissed, although not lightly. It was still possible, if a lot more manpower was needed in a hurry.

In the meantime, all leave for the armed forces and police had been cancelled. Plans were being drawn up to search every nook and cranny of the western coast of Scotland whilst at the same time orders were being sent that if anything untoward was spotted, no action was to be taken without Macnair's authorisation. There were collective sighs going up all over Britain at the thought that responsibility for this one was to be someone else's. A few bothered to look at a map and for the first time realised how long and difficult the west coast of Scotland was.

The General phoned Hunter just before five o'clock that afternoon. 'Anything, Nick?'

'No, sir,' the frustration obvious in Hunter's voice. 'After we finished the Sound we followed the tracks Isobel sent but there's been nothing. We've taken layer readings and I have to say that conditions are as near perfect as we can hope.' Layer readings meant searching and checking where there were layers of water at different temperatures. At that time of the year, in that location, there were none. The water was well and truly mixed, uniformly, from seabed to surface. The difference in temperature from top to bottom was less than three degrees centigrade.

'There's no possibility that Isobel's made a mistake is there?'

'There's always a possibility, Nick. What did your own calculations tell you?'

'They gave me a similar picture to the one she came up with but not with the same degree of accuracy because I had only surface tides and currents to work with. There has to be some reason for us not finding . . .' he trailed off.

'Nick, are you still there?'

'What? Sorry, sir. I've just had a thought. Isobel's calculations were based on the helicopter finding a neutral buoyancy depth and floating. We missed something. What if the helicopter has been machine gunned and her buoyancy affected? She wouldn't have found a depth to float at but would have bounced along the seabed. Hell, it could have jammed somewhere. Look, ask Isobel to get back onto Bath and discuss this with the boffins. Then re-run the program and see what she comes up with. Oh, and ask the university to give us as much seabed information as they have for the area – if they know if there are any rocky outcrops, or deep gullies, for instance.'

'Right. I'll get onto it right away. You should know that so far they've found nine bodies scattered around the seabed and the shore.'

'Nine? That leaves thirty unaccounted for.'

'Correct. If you don't find the helicopter by daybreak tomorrow I want you to rejoin the team at Luing. Jim has set up a first-class base with everything you need. Work it from there and see if you can figure out where the hell the bastards have gone.'

Macnair broke the connection and told Isobel what he wanted.

'I have the details on the seabed already,' she said, taking a sip of freshly brewed coffee. 'I needed them for the other calculations. Let me contact America again and see what I can do, rather than Bath.'

She spent sometime "speaking" to the manufacturers before being sent a revised program. According to the information she now had, the whole profile of the helicopter's movements would change. Having done it so often earlier that day, it only took minutes to re-run the combined programs to get an entirely different result. Again, using the same splash points as before, she plotted the different courses that could have resulted. In each case, the helicopter was shown to drift for between three and four nautical miles before hitting the seabed. Then, it scraped along the bottom, very slowly, bouncing a little from time to time, her buoyancy nothing like the previous assumptions. At seventeen hundred the helicopter was shown to be three miles due west of Corpach Bay, off the Island of Jura. The minehunters were currently looking in an area over twenty miles to the south west.

Macnair contacted Hunter immediately with the information.

He had finished his conversation when his phone rang again. 'Malcolm? It's Parsons. We now know what it's all about.'

'We do? How?' Macnair held the phone to his ear and walked over to the coffee machine. He had been on the go since six o'clock the previous morning and fatigue was setting in.

'At five o'clock this evening we received a satellite broadcast from the ship. It showed the prisoners standing on the deck. We're currently identifying as many as we can.' He paused. 'The film also showed one man being shot.' Parsons fought to keep his voice level. It was one thing to see violence in a film, knowing it was make believe; it was quite another to see a man have his brains shot out.

'Who and why?'

'Boris Petrov, the Russian member of the board to the World Bank. The why is easy. It was done as an example. To prove they mean what they say.'

'And what do they say?'

'They want one hundred million dollars deposited in a Lebanese Bank before Friday the fourth of May. If not, they will start shooting a hostage every hour. They said that it would take twenty-eight hours. Obviously meaning they have twenty-eight more hostages.'

Macnair said, 'Tony, this doesn't make sense. Everybody in the world knows we don't deal with terrorists under any circumstances. So what are they trying to achieve? Apart from the money, have they asked for anything else?'

'Nothing. We're equally foxed this end. The broadcast they made has been picked up by millions of homes all over the world. The phones here have gone non-stop since it happened. To be honest, apart from stating the party line of the Western governments, that we don't deal with terrorists, we are in a quandary.'

'The people held by the terrorists are amongst the most influential in the world, many coming from families who are incredibly wealthy. What will you do if they decide that they want to pay?'

'We haven't discussed that possibility as yet. I thought about it as soon as we received the broadcast and to be frank, I don't know what to advise. Collectively, the people we're talking about have more influence than HMG, world wide. Our only advantage at this moment is that we control matters because the incident occurred on British soil. But even that's a doubtful control.'

He was right about Her Majesty's Government having little control. Although for the last seventeen years, under a Conservative Government, the UK had been tough on terrorism, it was being continuously undermined by organisations such as the Court of Human Rights in the

Hague. That was one of the reasons why Macnair and his unit had been established in the first place. If the families of the hostages wanted to pay up there was little they could do about it. Except find the hostages before the deadline was reached.

'What are you going to do now?' asked Macnair.

'Stall for time. That's all we can do. There's a lot riding on this and by extension, on you. We can't be seen to give in and at the same time we can't just let these people die. Hell, members of our own Cabinet are amongst them.'

'Any chance of having a recording of the tape sent here?'

'Yes. I'll speak to the controller of Westward Television at Plymouth. I'm sure he can send round a tape. It should be with you in an hour. Is there anything else?'

'Not at present. We still haven't found the helicopter but now we've received the tape it's not that urgent. We know how many are still alive so our task is to find them.'

'Wait a moment. I've just been handed a paper.' There was a pause. 'All the hostages shown on the tape have been identified. I gather we've also identified the nine bodies found off Scotland so that leaves who?'

'The pilot.'

'Yes, of course, the pilot. Presumably he's still with the helicopter.'

'Presumably. Sorry, I need to go. Someone's just come in whom I need to talk to.'

They said their "goodbyes" and hung up. Macnair walked across to introduce himself to Sarah Fleeting who had just arrived carrying a suitcase and a bulging briefcase. He introduced her to Isobel, Leo and Gareth.

'So what have you got for us, Sarah?' he asked, after giving her a cup of coffee.

'I've brought my complete file on Habib and what I've learnt over the past six weeks or so. I've also got some ideas I'd like to share with Isobel about what we can do with the satellites.'

'Fine. Share them with me as well.'

Sarah sat at a computer console and got to work, her fingers flying across the keys. A picture appeared and she explained. 'In those files you have statements and information gathered from all over the place – from America and Turkey and also from assets we have on the ground in the Middle East. Since first thing this morning when I found out what happened, I've been convinced the man behind it all is Aziz Habib and his right-hand man, Derek Fredericks. By sifting through everything we have, I think they came to Britain on board this ship.' She showed a close up of a ship steaming across the Bay of Biscay, taken from an orbiting satellite. It was fuzzy and would not have led to an identification but at least it was something to go on. She then described the ship's movements and finally showed it passing south of the Mull of Kintyre.

'Once I knew what I was looking for it was relatively easy to track. I ran the satellite pictures from a dozen different sources and told them to ignore everything except that ship. I then ran them together so that I could overlap each one, ensuring a continuous picture from Sardinia to the Mull. I have managed to identify her as the MV *Nymph*. Lloyds of London operates every day of the year and it was not difficult to get details about her. They're in this folder.' She handed it to Macnair who quickly read the information.

'Next, because of certain factors, I lost the *Nymph* off the coast of Jura. However, if you give me a few moments I think I can get a look at this area,' she pointed at the screen, 'once I've called up a few of my friends in space.'

'Friends in space?' asked Leo.

'The satellites. I've been checking and last night there were at least three which passed over this location, one spy satellite, one weather satellite and a communications satellite.'

'What use is a communications satellite?' asked Macnair, willing to display his ignorance to satisfy his interest.

'Apart from sending and receiving millions of television and telephone messages it also happens to carry a camera for the CIA. I happen to know that because I've worked closely with the boys and girls at Langley for the last few years. If the camera was running it may have picked up something. Now,' she pressed more buttons, 'let's see what we have.'

The first picture appeared showing a small dot on a sea of black. She did something with the keyboard and it magnified to show a ship moving very slowly south of an island. It took only a few seconds to identify the island as Mull. Sarah stopped the picture and again went to work on the keyboard. After a few seconds she said, 'Yes, no doubt about it. It's the ship I've been tracking from Sardinia.' She switched back to the satellite picture. They saw the ship move slowly across the screen, travelling west to east. Next, incredibly, they saw a missile launch from the ship. Sarah zoomed the picture out and there, on the screen, in the top left hand corner, was the helicopter. As they watched they saw the helicopter suddenly move very violently and then the picture faded.

'What the hell! What's happened?' Macnair asked, shaken by what he had been watching.

'Relax, General, we're changing satellite pictures, that's all.' Even as she spoke the picture changed. The same happened a few minutes later but not before they saw the heroic efforts made to avoid the missiles and the fifth missile fired from the island. They watched as the helicopter landed on the water and the ship closed in. They could not see what was happening but they did see the MV *Nymph* head off west, picking up speed rapidly, before the picture faded completely.

'Good God,' Macnair spoke for all of them. They were stunned both by what they had seen and the technology which had provided it.

'Can you see where that blasted ship went?' the General asked, hopefully.

'I've checked every satellite in orbit,' Sarah replied, her hands twitching, desperate for a cigarette, 'but nothing went that way for another two hours. I've left instructions at GCHQ to ask every satellite that comes within reach if it has pictures of the world between fifty-five to fifty-seven degrees north and five to seven degrees west. So far there's been nothing, but,' she looked at her watch, 'during the next four hours there'll be at least four possible recordings. After that there'll be none. That'll be every satellite interrogated.'

'And if there's nothing?' asked Isobel, getting up to make fresh coffee.

'Then we resort to plan Beta,' replied Sarah, unable to hide her sense of mischief even in these trying circumstances.

Curiously enough, it was General Macnair who fell for it. 'What's that?'

'I don't know, I haven't got one. I was hoping you guys might have a few ideas.'

14

By taking it in turns they had stripped bare an area of two metres running the full width of the hold. The strips of paint had been rolled into a ball and thrown out of a porthole. They hid the bare patch under a blanket, on which two of the prisoners would sit should the hatch above them be opened. Now that the sun had set, and without even the radiated warmth from the engine room, it was quickly becoming cold. In spite of the fact that it was officially springtime, warm, mild weather came late to that part of Scotland.

Apart from everything else, the buckets had been used, and now there was a smell permeating the air which they all tried to ignore. Some managed it, more or less, whilst others like the fastidious Felicity Cornwall, British Agricultural Minister, found it unbearable.

They had not only cleared the deck plating but had also managed to pick clean the areas around the bolts which held the plates in place. The screwdriver blade on the Swiss army knife had not been up to the task of undoing the bolts and had twisted out of shape without moving one.

The co-pilot, the American Vice-President, the German

271

Vice-Chancellor and the French Prime Minister sat looking at the bare plates and cursing the bolts.

'Any ideas?' asked Beloit.

'We need something a lot stronger and with a great deal more leverage,' said Bradley, stating the obvious.

'We've searched this place from top to bottom,' pointed out Conrad, in his guttural, German accent, 'and found nothing.'

Cecil McDonald walked over to them, 'Here's something.' He held out the handle he had taken off one of the buckets.

Spencer took the handle from him and fitted it into the slot in the head of the bolt. 'It fits well enough,' he announced. He took a firm grip, using both hands, and twisted. He felt something turn slightly.

'Stop,' said McDonald. 'You're only succeeding in bending the handle. It's not strong enough.'

Disappointed, Spencer sat back and the five of them stared at the bolts, hating them. 'If we could heat them up somehow, really hot, then perhaps we could shift them.'

McDonald smiled. 'That's a possibility.' He took a piece of plastic explosive from his pocket and kneaded it over the bolt.

'You aren't going to blow that are you?' asked Bradley. 'Someone might hear. It's too dangerous.'

McDonald shook his head. 'No. But I am going to light it. Has anyone got a lighter? A match won't do.'

He was handed a gas lighter. He flipped open the lid, struck a light and adjusted the flame so that it was almost like an oxy-acetylene torch. He put the lighter on the deck with the flame aimed into the plastic explosive. After only a few seconds the PE caught light and burnt with a great deal of heat and little smoke. It took nearly two minutes to burn away and as the fire died down Spencer re-inserted the handle into the bolt and turned. After a few seconds he felt it turn. At first he was fearful that it was the handle twisting again, but then realised it was the bolt turning. Quickly he unthreaded it and scooped it away to a corner where it was left to cool down. They repeated the process with a second bolt. Herbert Conrad inserted the blade of the Swiss army knife between two of the metal plates and gently pushed down on the handle, trying to lever up the deck plate. He didn't dare push too hard for fear of breaking the blade. He rocked it back and forth until the plate lifted a little. He moved the knife to the other side and did the same again and after a few moments the plate lifted clear. Eager hands took hold and pulled it away. The plate was nine inches wide by three feet long and in the centre of their prison running from port to starboard.

McDonald put his head down into the hole to have a look. All he could see was darkness. He put his hand down into the bilge and found it to be surprisingly dry, only an inch or two of water in the bottom. He reached around as far as he could but found nothing forward or aft, though he felt keel ribs to port and starboard.

'We need to remove another one or two of these plates,' said Bradley, 'if anyone's going to crawl down there.'

'If we remove another one, I'll get through,' said McDonald. 'The only trouble is, I'm loath to waste more plastic. You never know when we might need it to go bang.'

The others nodded. Spencer tried turning another of the bolts but to no avail. Now that one of the plates had been removed it was possible for Spencer to work the bucket handle under one edge and try and move the plate. He pushed the handle back and forth straining until it was in danger of bending. The plate lifted a fraction. Three of the others kneeled along the edge and took a grip on the plate and pulled and pushed for all they were worth. The plate was loosened slightly.

McDonald stopped them and took out the thin cutting wire which he threaded behind the bolt. He took hold of both ends and awkwardly pulled the wire back and forth. It slipped through to the bolt and he began to saw. It took almost ten minutes to cut through the half-inch-thick bolt. The other side was much easier and soon they had lifted a second plate.

By now it was almost pitch dark in the hold. They were all exhausted, physically and mentally, in spite of the fact that they had only been in captivity for barely twenty-four hours. However, they also felt a real satisfaction at having done so much. They replaced the plates and settled down as best they could for the night.

The following morning they had housekeeping problems. The two buckets they had used in the makeshift latrine were full to overflowing and the stench was worse.

In the locker where they had found the blankets and which was now being used as the head – the naval term for latrine – was a short piece of plastic pipe. One of the men used the saw blade on the Swiss knife and mid way along the length of the pipe cut half way though it. He then sliced down the length of the pipe and removed the section he had cut. Whilst James Treherne held the pipe out of one of the portholes, Matthew Goodall carefully emptied one of the buckets into its end. The effluent collected in the end of the pipe and when it was tilted a little further poured out through the porthole. The second bucket was emptied in the same way and then thoroughly washed. It was an extremely distasteful job and not one which sat easily with the men and women in the hold but as the Prime Minister of France said, 'As a politician I've seen, smelt and touched worse,' which raised a wry laugh from the others.

They sat round waiting for one of their captors to appear with breakfast and discussed what options, if any, were open to them. By ten o'clock they were in a militant mood and Herbert Conrad climbed the ladder and knocked on the hatch. After what seemed an age the handles were thrown back and Conrad beat a hasty retreat back down. The hatch was thrown open.

'We want some food and drink,' shouted up the German Vice-Chancellor at the face that appeared above them.

For a reply, the terrorist pointed his pistol into the hold and fired. He did not aim at anybody and he said nothing. The fact that the bullet missed even after it ricocheted off the deck, into the bulkhead and ended up a spent force in the bow, was total luck. The hatch was slammed shut and locked.

There was a stunned silence amongst the prisoners, each of them aware at how close they had been to another death or serious injury.

It was the American Vice-President who said, 'I guess that's their way of telling us there's no breakfast.'

There was a collected expulsion of air, as if they had all been holding their breath since the shot was fired.

'It makes sense,' said McDonald. 'If we aren't fed, or given anything to drink we weaken and become more compliant, which suits any guard not just these guys. I suspect they won't be opening that hatch again.'

The experienced ex-soldiers amongst them nodded. It made perfect sense to them and followed precisely what they had been taught, oh, so many years ago.

Stanton had already pulled up the two plates and had his head in the bilges, trying to see what was down there. He lay for a few seconds, until his eyes became accustomed to the greater gloom. Slowly, he began to make out certain things. From the deck level to the bottom of the hull was a gap of nearly a metre. The cross members of the ribbing were twenty centimetres thick and about the same in width. The bilge he was looking into ran about a third of the length of the ship before ending in a solid bulkhead.

He sat up. 'It's a piece of cake to get through but we'll have to remove some more plates to get out again.'

That was only to be expected. The question was, when should they begin?

'This is too important an opportunity to mess it up by being careless or in too much of a hurry,' Wilma Shules opined. 'We daren't get caught. The consequences are far too grave to consider.' They all knew what she meant. There was no doubt that Habib and his men would shoot a few of them as an example.

McDonald had already stripped down to his underpants. 'I'll go down and feel my way around and see if I can hear or see anything. Close the hole behind me. I'll knock when I want to come back out.'

'How long will you be?' asked Bradley.

His reply surprised them. 'All day, naturally. I want to sit and listen and get a feel for what's along there. There might be cabins or stores or even the engine room. I need to know if people are moving around and where. Then tonight we'll tackle lifting a plate or two and getting through.'

He climbed down, ducked beneath the deck and crawled along the bilge. As he went further aft, the bilge flattened out and deepened slightly. He could tell that was happening because the water in the bottom went from about two inches deep and six inches wide to closer to a foot deep and two feet wide. At first he tried to keep his hands, knees and legs dry but soon gave it up. Within a few minutes he had reached the bulkhead and as far as he could go. Along the way he had noticed pipes, some electric cable and a powerful bilge pump.

He sat for sometime in the almost dark and listened. He could hear his fellow prisoners moving around, the sound magnified by the hollow of the bilge. He mentally tuned out the sound of them and concentrated on the deck above him. He heard nothing. He sat there for nearly seven hours. During that time he continued to hear nothing and was becoming hopeful that was because the area above him was empty of their captors. He was about to crawl back to the forward hold when there was a clang over his head, the sound of something being dragged along the deck and then a further silence. Damn, damn, damn. What the hell was that and, more importantly, why had the noise been made? He could see no light above him, not even a glow along the seam of the deck plate. Was that because he was under a storeroom where there was no light to be switched on? It wasn't very likely that there'd be a store room with no electric light. Perhaps something had been dumped in there and so no light had been necessary? Perhaps it was sleeping quarters and no light was turned on so if there was another occupant he wouldn't be disturbed. But then the noise would have woken anyone else. He strained to listen for more sounds but was rewarded with complete silence.

Perhaps there was a carpet on the floor or some sort of tiles. Perhaps it was a bathroom with a special sealant on the deck. His mind whirled with possibilities until he finally gave up. He settled down to wait where he was for a while longer.

When he finally looked at his watch and decided to return to the forward hold he had been sitting in the bilges for nearly ten hours. He was freezing, cramped, hungry and thirsty. Being a member of one of the toughest, elite regiments in the world, his personal comfort was of little consequence to him. He could go on for many more days yet. He needed to get back to the others to collect the penknife. It was time to start on the next set of deck plates.

Back in the hold he quickly dressed and helped himself to a drink of water, briefing the others as he did so.

'I think we should wait until midnight, by which time most of them might be asleep. I'll go back down and start cutting around the edges of a plate and see if I can move one.'

'I've been thinking,' said John Williams. 'It's impossible to know what you're going to find or even if it's possible to get through once a plate is removed. After all, you could be under anything and remember, space on any ship is at a premium. So the chances of there being something over your head and, therefore, impassable, are very high.'

McDonald nodded. The thought had already occurred to him but there was no choice.

'Don't go along to the other end. Go immediately to the other side of this bulkhead here,' he tapped the metal wall.

'Why? What's the point here or there?'

'I know something about ships and usually the engine room is midships, living quarters aft. The chances are that on the other side of this,' he tapped again, gently, 'is a store room or at least a space which is seldom used. Like the battery room.'

McDonald nodded. 'I suppose that makes some sort of sense. All right, I'll do as you suggest.'

In fact, it was Stanton who went into the bilge just before midnight and felt around the plating immediately on the other side of the bulkhead. The plate seams were quickly located and the knife slipped through easily. He cut around the plate, pushing the blade in as far as possible. Nothing impeded it. Once he had cut all the way round he pushed against the plate to see if it would move even a fraction. It was solid. He felt round the nut into which the bolt was screwed and scraped away the rust. Next, he worked the cutting wire into a corner of the nut and began sawing back and forth. It was awkward, cramped and tiring but he kept at it. Suddenly, the wire slid through and the nut dropped into the water in the bilge.

He used the awl on the side of the penknife, a clever blade used for making holes in wood before putting in a screw, and pushed against the bolt. It didn't move so he thumped it with the palm of his hand. The bolt flew out and landed on the deck above with a clatter. Stanton froze, beads of sweat dampening his brow. He strained his ears to listen but could only hear the muted shuffling and noises associated with nearly thirty people sitting in an empty hold trying to stay quiet.

After a few minutes he started on the other bolt and, ignoring his aching muscles, sawed frantically. A short while later the second bolt was cut and he was able to move the deck plate with a little pressure. He pushed it open and put his hand through, feeling around. On the forward side was the bulkhead, but in the other three directions he could feel nothing. He systematically felt around the deck until he found the bolt and lifted it into the bilge. He didn't want anyone else finding it lying on the deck. He used the handle from the bucket to extend his reach and found there was something to port and starboard but nothing aft.

It was the middle of the night when he climbed stiffly out of the bilge and back to the others. Because he had been working so near to them he had been able to whisper what he had found and now it was time to decide what to do next. It did not take long. Donald Spencer climbed down and started work on the next bolt. By the time he had sawn off the nut he was exhausted, not having the strength or the stamina of the two SAS men. He changed places with Ben Bradley who insisted on doing his share. Perhaps not all politicians were so bad after all, thought Spencer.

It took Bradley the best part of half an hour to cut through the bolt but he would not quit or change places. By the time he was finished, there was a definite lightening of the gloom of their prison. Another dawn was breaking.

He climbed back into the hold and this time McDonald and Stanton went down together. They lifted the second plate and climbed up into the Stygian darkness. Feeling around, it took them only a few seconds to realise that they were in some sort of locker room with shelves stacked with tins and other items. They found the door and tried to push it open. It was firmly locked and neither could feel a way to open it. They took a few items from the shelves and climbed back into the bilge, carefully replacing the two plates behind them. Although they had heard nothing the day before, it was always possible that the locker room would be used by one of the terrorists.

They each passed up the few tins they were carrying and then scrambled back into the hold.

'Look at this,' said an excited Jane Felton. She held one of the tins up to the porthole and squinted at the labelling. 'These are peaches.' She spoke with awe in her voice, as though she held the elixir of life in her hands.

'And this is a tin of Soya beans,' added Ben Bradley.

The other two tins consisted of peas and cold custard. If the tins were opened and the contents shared out they would each have a tablespoon of food to eat.

Everybody was now crowding round, wanting to touch the tins. To make sure for themselves that they were real.

'We can get more,' said Felicity Cornwall. 'Find something we can make a proper meal with.'

'No, we can't,' said Stanton emphatically.

There was an indrawing of breath, a collective anger, aimed at him. Voices of protest were raised until the French Prime Minister silenced them with a word of warning.

'Stop it. Listen to this man. You are behaving as though you haven't eaten for a week not just for a couple of days. Now, I am sure there is a good reason why Mr. Stanton said what he did.'

'Thank you. We must remember our objective. It is to escape alive not to feed ourselves. What if we remove more cans and it's noticed? What then? It won't take Habib long to find out what's happened and then what? He's shown how utterly ruthless he is. Do you think he won't shoot a few of us as an example?'

There were a few sheepish shrugs and nods of the head. 'If we're to survive then we need to remember at all times our objective.'

'Now, we'll open these tins and mix all the food together. Soya beans are disgusting if they're not cooked but are full of protein. The custard is full of carbohydrates and the peaches and peas are also good for us. So we mix the lot, mash it together, and eat it.'

Nobody argued. After opening the cans with the pen-knife, Stanton got Jane Felton and the UN Secretary General to wash their hands and then to carefully mix the food, mashing it together. It would have been easiest to empty the tins into one of the buckets but, mindful of the use they were put to, nobody could stomach that idea. By the time they had finished each tin contained a solid, revolting-looking mess, which was shared out equally. As expected, they each had a tablespoonful of food which tasted surprisingly good, considering the circumstances. The predominant flavour was custard, which was just as well. One or two of the prisoners gagged as they tried to swallow but for the remainder, the food was taken eagerly.

Little though it was, it helped. A small amount of energy was released; it seemed that little bit less cold, and optimism, of a sort, returned. At least there was a possibility of escape although they had a long way to go to reach safety.

By mutual, unspoken consent, in spite of the fact that the hold was full of people who, in one guise or another, were leaders, they turned to Stanton and McDonald when the American Vice-President asked, 'So what do we do now?'

Stanton looked at his watch. 'It's ten thirty. It's now Tuesday. If we try to escape the chances are we'll be caught and punished. I think we need to know more about the ship and the people who are holding us. I know we've discussed it and from our combined recollections we've guessed that there are ten or so of them. Where are they onboard? What are they doing? How do they intend to get away? How long do they intend keeping us here? What are our own people doing? If you think long and hard enough we could find a hundred questions we need the answers to before we do anything.'

There was agreement. The mood of optimism prevalent only a few minutes earlier shrivelled as quickly as it had blossomed.

'So what I propose is that we keep quiet and just stay here. Cecil and I will go back into the store room and see if we can't help ourselves to some more gear without leaving any traces that we've been there. The trouble is, it's as black as Hades in there and we don't want to disturb the place too much in case it's noticed.'

'What about getting through the door?' asked Ibn ben Saud.

'We'll do that one way or another,' replied McDonald enigmatically. 'Tonight, I'll go on a recce. See what I can find out; get a better idea what we're up against.'

'Won't that be too dangerous?' the German Vice-Chancellor asked. 'The last thing we want is for you to be captured.'

'He won't be,' replied Stanton. 'When he puts his mind to it Cecil here is like the invisible man. Believe me, he won't get caught.'

With those words of praise singing in his ears McDonald settled down to get some sleep. It was going to be a long night.

*   *   *

283

Habib paced the bridge. So far everything had gone according to plan. Three days at the most and they would be away. They would leave behind carnage, confusion and a lot of dead men and women but it would be worth it. It would prove once and for all that nobody in the West was safe. He would have his money and his pay masters would have . . . nothing, Habib thought contemptuously. He had sold them the idea like a man selling a second-hand car. More than a year earlier he had sown the concept in the minds of the leaders in Tehran. Knowing how they thought and operated it was necessary to drip feed them with ideas; to stoke up their already pathological hatred of all things Western. No, the hatred extended further than that. It was to all things non-Moslem.

His idea had been simple enough. Cause mayhem not only in the West but throughout the world. Prove that there was no hiding place from the long arm of the true believers. In the meantime, by using their hard currencies to take options in certain types of investments and certain currencies, they could make a fortune. Iran was trading internationally again, after many years of being excluded, and the price of oil was as stable and strong as they could wish. They could move billions. It was often the case with the Imams that their insular outlook on life, their single-minded dedication to their religion, left them totally unable to see beyond their narrow confines. The world literally passed them by. However, they did have enough sense to hire people who knew what they were doing. Even so, Iran was sinking slowly but surely into a medieval state whilst the remainder of the world strode forward eagerly to embrace the future and the next century. Hence their need for hard currencies and profits. Hence the plans that had been made.

Habib was not expecting the ransom demand to be paid, but he had to go through the motions. He wanted the West to be sucked into his trap. Not for the sake of his paymasters. Indeed, it was not even a part of the deal. He was doing it for himself. He was going to go down in history as the greatest terrorist the world had ever seen. Not only would he kill over thirty of their businessmen, politicians and bankers but he would also kill a great many of their special forces. The trap had been baited, it only needed a little sweetening to make it irresistible.

His men were ready to die. The fools!

15

P.M. 4 May 1998. Cabinet Room, 10 Downing Street.

'We are agreed that no ransom is to be paid?' The Prime Minister asked for the third time that day.

'No, PM. We are not agreed.' The irritation was beginning to show in Sir Anthony Parsons' voice. He controlled his temper and sublimated his annoyance beneath a veneer of polite speech. 'We have agreement from all the political leaders of the countries involved. However, the families and some of the organisations are prepared to pay. So far, we have received pledges in excess of one hundred and fifty million dollars and, what's more, we have actually been given twenty million by the Saudis. They want Ibn ben Saud back. Or at least his elderly parents do.'

The Prime Minister shook his head in despair. 'Won't these people ever learn? If we give in, then the demands will never cease. The nature of terrorism means that they will come back for more and more. We have to make a stand otherwise all is lost.'

'Well, I wouldn't quite say all,' said the Foreign Secretary, quietly. He was a contemplative, highly intelligent and highly educated man. After a short time in the

286

City where he had found it ludicrously easy to make money, he had entered politics for the challenge. Eight years after becoming an MP he was in one of the top government jobs. At forty he was a relative youngster, going prematurely bald, a fact which caused him a great deal of anguish. The cartoonists of the press had a field day playing on the fact.

'What did you say?'

'Prime Minister, I said not all is lost. Look at it from the point of view of the families. They want their loved ones back. Let somebody else make the stand and be sacrificed. As long as it isn't them. It's human nature.'

'But we must present a united front.' The Home Secretary leaned forward, hitting the table with his forefinger, highlighting each word.

'Yes, we know that,' replied Stuart Roberts. 'But it will have to be a political front. We cannot prevent a deal being done by others. It's not possible. The press can make as much of that as they will but at the end of the day it cannot be stopped. We can condemn the action of dealing with terrorism, we can threaten and bluster for all we're worth and it's not worth diddly squat, as our American cousins say. All we can do is work flat out for a military solution to the problem. Even then, we could have problems if we fail.'

'We must not fail.' The Prime Minister looked up sharply, appearing more wan than usual.

'There are no guarantees,' said Roberts, twiddling a pencil in his left hand, his right reaching for his cup of coffee. 'We still don't know where they are being held and even if we find out, we shall still have to carry out the rescue.'

'I understood that Macnair and his lot are working on something.'

Parsons replied. 'I spoke to General Macnair a short while ago and he says that they do have some ideas. However, he also added that he would tell us as soon as he had anything concrete to go on.'

With that they had to be content.

'Prime Minister, we really need to work on what we are going to say to the press this afternoon,' said Charles Norheed. 'If Macnair can deliver then all well and good. We have a deadline of Friday to come up with the money before they start shooting the hostages.'

'If they start shooting them,' the PM said.

'After what we saw on the video there can be little doubt,' Parsons stated baldly.

The others around the table nodded.

'All right. What can I say at the press conference to make us sound at least reasonably confident?' asked the Prime Minister.

There was a silence as each of them thought of a suitable reply. Finally, Roberts spoke. 'Concentrate as much as you can on the political agreement. World-wide political agreement, I might add. Also tell them about finding the helicopter and that we are concentrating our efforts to find the terrorists along the Mull of Kintyre.'

'I thought we were . . .' began the Home Secretary.

'Yes, yes,' said Roberts testily. 'Of course we aren't looking along the Mull. Let the world think we are. Our efforts are further north and west but don't tell the press, for God's sake. We want as much secrecy as possible. That way, Macnair might have a chance of accomplishing something.'

'What do I say if I am asked about the attitude of the families of the hostages?' asked the PM.

'Prevaricate. Say something like, there's ongoing discussion with the families but don't mention that some are ready to do a deal.'

'What if they already know?' asked Parsons.

'Then shrug and move to the next question.'

'When do I announce the names of the dead bodies we've recovered?'

'At the very beginning,' said Roberts. 'Give the press so much information about those killed that they have enough to make the headlines with it tomorrow. We're preparing background eulogies right now. Make them all out to be bloody heroes and keep press attention diverted for the next few days.'

'I gather that the pilot was a hero, from what I've been shown,' said Parsons.

'Yes, he was. Wax lyrical about his flying skills and how he escaped four of the missiles but was hit by the fifth,' said Norheed. 'Christ, man, you've got enough information to give to the press for half a dozen press conferences without giving away any secrets.'

Yes, thought the Prime Minister, but it's me who'll be out there taking a roasting, not you. Why the hell had he ever wanted this job in the first place, he wondered for the hundredth time since the crisis began?

'We are now certain that the instigator is Habib,' said Parsons, handing around a brief summary of what was known about the man. 'Although he proclaims himself to be a freedom fighter, whatever that is, and a true believer, we are certain that he operates solely for money. We've been putting together what we know about this operation and to be perfectly frank we can't make sense of it.'

'What do you mean, you can't make sense of it?' asked Norheed. 'I thought it made perfect sense. He wants a hundred million dollars.'

Parsons looked at the Home Secretary for a few seconds whilst he gathered his thoughts. 'It's not as simple as that. Habib does not enter into anything lightly. He has been a shadowy figure for years in the world of terrorism but little has been known about him. Thanks to some amazing work done by two of Macnair's computer people we now know a great deal more. We have had co-operation from security services the world over and thanks to our friends in Turkey we even have a photograph.' He handed out a grainy, poorly focused black and white, six-by-eight still of Aziz Habib taken about ten years earlier.

'If he walked through the door right now I still wouldn't recognise him,' said Roberts.

'Agreed,' said Parsons. 'However, we have been given information on a dozen other operations that Habib has been involved in and when analysed together we find some interesting facts.'

'Such as?' The PM asked, intrigued.

'Habib has made a name for himself with the fundamentalists as being against the West. He has blown up aeroplanes, let off bombs at the Olympics and the Commonwealth Games, and even hijacked a liner – all in the name of the true faith.'

'Habib is a fanatic?' Norheed asked.

'No, but those who pay him are.'

'Iran?' asked the PM.

Parsons nodded. 'Mainly. But he has also carried out work for Saddam and the Libyans. We believe, though we can't prove it, that Libya paid Habib to down the PanAm airliner over Lockerbie. His motive is pure greed and, to a lesser extent, power and prestige.'

'It seems the world would be a much better and safer place if he wasn't in it,' Roberts said.

Parsons nodded. 'A lot of people would agree with you. It's incredible that it's only since Macnair got to work with his team that we've been able to put this dossier together. Habib has been operating all over the globe which may account for the fact that Western security services have never arrived at the complete picture. It's frightening really. This is terrorism at its worst. We need to put a stop to him once and for all and this seems to be the ideal opportunity.'

'Provided we find him first.'

Parsons smiled at the Prime Minister. 'Oh, we'll find him all right. Maybe not this time. But one day. We now have so much to go on that Mr. Habib will find the world a small place in which to try and hide.'

'Never mind one day,' said the PM, annoyed. 'I want him stopped this time.' He sounded like a petulant child, not an endearing characteristic for the leader of a country.

There was a rap on the door and the Prime Minister's Personal Private Secretary entered the room. His job was to keep the Prime Minister informed and to ensure that any decisions made were implemented by the civil service. He took his place at the table and placed half a dozen thin buff folders in front of him.

'Good afternoon, gentlemen. These are copies of the eulogies for the people who were killed.' He handed them around.

They each opened their folders and quickly scanned the papers. There was a separate sheet for each of the dead men starting with the pilot, Fred Todd.

The index of names showed:

Otto Grunweld, President of the German Bundesbank.

Abdul Atikan, Egyptian industrialist.

Thomas Sato, Japanese industrialist and United Nations Ambassador.

Antonio Carrusso, Brazilian banker and World Bank Director.

Steven Holiday, Australian media magnate and multi-billionaire.

Richard Hussman, Swedish industrialist and multi-millionaire.

If any of the men had been alive to read what was written about them they would have had difficulty in recognising themselves. The way in which they had died meant that they had achieved a certain martyrdom, a heroic status which was untrue. The statements said a lot about their good works, their commitment to the future of mankind and its betterment. Nothing was said about their ruthlessness and single-minded dedication to their own, personal causes. All were now family men, leaving behind loving wives, children, grandchildren. Nothing was said about the mistresses, the wife-beating and, in one case, the suspected paedophilia.

The only statement where the facts were accurate and needed no embellishment was regarding Wing Commander Todd. A real hero and family man, he would be sorely missed by all who had known him.

After skimming through each paper, there were one or two raised eyebrows and even one chuckle from Charles Norheed when he read about Steven Holiday. If ever a man deserved to get shot it was Holiday. He had destroyed more lives with his newspapers than Habib had with his guns and bombs. True, only a few of his victims had died, mainly by their own hand, but the destruction of lives was just as complete.

Just before four o'clock the Prime Minister went into the press briefing room which was packed with reporters. Owing to lack of space only three television cameras were allowed in, the BBC, ITV and CNN. The transmissions by each would be live and relayed world wide. The remainder were newspaper reporters from around the world. Over eighty news organisations were represented. Each reporter had been told they would be allowed one question and no follow-ups. They had not liked it and none of them intended to follow the instruction. The Prime Minister was on the podium for nearly three minutes before the room quietened and he was able to begin.

General Macnair stood with Walsh and watched the broadcast. The General was praying that the Prime Minister did not give away any operational information. So far only the eulogies had been distributed.

'Prime Minister,' a hand was raised in the front row.

'Yes, Bill?' The PM smiled at Bill Smith, the political correspondent for the *Daily Mirror*.

'Is it true that we are doing a secret deal with the terrorists to buy the freedom of the captives?'

'No, certainly not. I have said time and time again, this government will never deal with terrorists.'

'Then why has a spokesman for the Japanese government said that they are in contact with the terrorists and are negotiating the release of the hostages?'

It was not true, but exaggeration never hurt a good story.

The Prime Minister gripped each side of the lectern, hard, his knuckles showing white. 'I don't believe that is the case. I spoke to Mr. Nagasaki only this morning and I can assure you that he assured me that he and his government stand behind our decision never to negotiate with terrorists. I mean, naturally we are negotiating with them, but we will never give in to their demands. If we did . . .' he was off with the party line which gave him a few minutes of sounding tough without committing his government to anything.

The next half an hour passed in a similar vein and the Prime Minister was about to end the session when a journalist in the back row caught his eye. 'Yes, Charles?' He spoke to a correspondent for the *Sunday Times*' Insight team.

'Prime Minister, is it true that there is now a new and highly secret anti-terrorist organisation in being, whose role is to tackle terrorism?'

'I'm not sure what you mean. We have special branch, MI5, MI6, military intelligence. What more do you want?'

'No,' the single question rule had been ignored since the beginning, 'I mean a military operational unit under command of General Macnair whose task it is to shoot first and ask questions afterwards.'

For a few moments the PM did not know whether to deny or admit their existence. Then he realised that this was the ideal opportunity to make political capital. After all, there had been no intention of keeping Macnair's force a secret forever.

'It is true that following the anti-terrorism conference held in France and chaired by President Clinton a decision was taken to create an elite force for dealing with terrorists wherever they might try and operate.'

'And does that force now exist?'

'Yes, it does.'

'And are they ordered to shoot to kill first and ask questions afterwards?'

'No comment.' Which was about the worst thing he could have said.

'What about human rights?'

'Whose? Do you mean those of the victims of the outrages perpetrated by the terrorists? The maimed and killed men, women and children who just wish to live a life of peace and safety? Is that whose human rights you mean?'

'No. I mean the rights of the terrorists to be tried for their crimes and brought to justice using minimum force.'

There was complete silence in the room. Not even the rustling of a paper, a cough or a snide aside to a colleague. He knew that the men and women he faced were amongst the most cynical in the world. They had seen everything, heard everything and had tried most things. They wrote and reported on just about every subject under the sun; albeit with a conclusion that reflected the views of their editors and, by extension, their proprietors, but at the end of the day they held a deep and passionate loathing for terrorists like any other sane person.

The Prime Minister then did one of the cleverest things he had ever done in his life. He said nothing. He stood and looked at the reporter who had asked the question. The cameras rolled and after a few seconds, when it became apparent that he was not going to respond, there was a stirring amongst the others. Someone turned on the questioner and told him to shut up. And then it started. There was abuse as well as vitriol from all across the room. The PM let it continue for a few more minutes and then he called them to order.

Once they had settled down again he looked at the reporter who was trying not to catch the PM's eye, finding a great deal to interest him in his shoe laces all of a sudden. 'I think that answers your question. Thank you ladies and gentlemen,' and with that he quickly left the room.

Macnair had been rooted to the spot. When it was over he wandered across to get another cup of coffee, deep in thought. Was there any real harm in their existence being common knowledge? It had been inevitable that it would have come out sooner, rather than later. He just would have preferred it if he could have had a victory to announce as well. Like the safe freedom of the hostages and the death of Habib and his men.

The helicopter had been found within two cables or four hundred yards of the computerised position after the new parameters had been input. The only occupant had been Todd, still secured in the pilot's seat. The black box had been recovered and was already being analysed, although nothing new was expected.

Hunter had returned to the island where his team was bivouacked and was now waiting to be tasked. All over the West of Scotland questions were being asked. Photographs of the ship were being distributed by the cart load, as every bay, inlet and loch was searched. It was a mammoth task, but there seemed that little else could be done.

Macnair went over to the computers and watched Sarah and Isobel at work. They and the other two, Leo and Gareth, were miracle workers as far as he was concerned. They had worked virtually non-stop, each taking it in turns to get a few hours' rest. In order to facilitate matters, Macnair had camp beds made up in two of the small offices so that they and he could get some sleep when the need arose. Sarah had used her incredible network of contacts in other countries to amass the information which resulted in the file about Habib. Macnair had sent only a précis to the Cabinet Office as so much of it was speculation and hearsay. None the less, it made fascinating reading. The problem was that there was no sense to this operation. Something was missing but he was damned if he could see what it was.

Whilst Sarah had been putting together the report, Isobel had been busy with the satellite pictures. The MV *Nymph* had been tracked out to a point eight nautical miles west of the island of Tiree. She had been moving at nearly twenty-five knots, without lights, heading almost due north. Due to lack of satellite coverage the picture ended there. World-wide co-operation with almost every organisation which had a satellite in space had resulted in there now being twenty-four hour coverage over the whole of Scotland and for hundreds of miles out into the Atlantic and south to Ireland. There was no sign of the ship. Every possible direction and speed the ship could have travelled in was computed and pictured. It was not to be found anywhere. That could only mean one thing. It was hidden somewhere along the Scottish coast.

Having first thought that it might be possible to get the heat signature of the ship and compare it to the tens of thousands of heat sources detected by the satellite, Macnair was disappointed to learn that the satellite could not tell one heat source from the next. It could only detect the heat, without being able to tell whether it was from a fire or a nuclear engine. Human help was needed.

Working all through Monday night and well into Tuesday afternoon, Isobel and Sarah had created a chart of the area which showed all heat sources at the time of the incident. They could see the ship clearly, which appeared as a red dot on the screen. There were over ten thousand dots in total. Because of the size of the engines and the heat emanating from the ship they were able to tell the computer to ignore all sources of heat showing less than a certain number of therms. The picture cleared to less than a thousand dots. They then took the same picture from the night before and again from the week before that. They compared pictures and told the computer to scrub all heat sources which were common to all three. They were left with four dots, all ships, two were fishing vessels, one was a coaster carrying coal north and one was the *Nymph*. It had worked.

Now that they knew it would work they updated the time frame. They took a recent picture of the Outer Hebrides and one for each twenty-four hours of the previous three days. They used the same thermal energy strength as before and told the computer to scrub all heat sources which appeared in each picture. All sources were wiped out.

Disappointed, they tried the same technique all over the coast and islands. Each time the dots were totally scrubbed.

By midnight on Tuesday all four of the operators were tired, irritated and getting on each other's nerves. Macnair had rested for a couple of hours but had been woken by their bickering. He recognised the problem and ordered them to pack up and get some rest. They had achieved miracles and once they got going again, with fresh minds and rested bodies, they would find the solution. Nobody argued. The two women went to their camp beds as did the two men. Within moments they were asleep leaving General Macnair to stare at the screens of the western islands and Scotland.

Although he claimed to be a Luddite when it came to computers, it was not true. Modern technology was a vital part of the military's capabilities and Macnair had been in the forefront of handling computers and their associated kit. He was not in the same league as the four he had sent to get some rest, but he was no slouch either. Now that the programs had been created, Macnair was able to compare the photographs of the heat sources for himself. He got the same results as they had. Finally, in exasperation, he closed the computers down at about three o'clock and went to his bed.

All of them were back at their consoles by eight o'clock. They were refreshed, raring to go and handing round bacon rolls when Macnair joined them.

'I spent hours last night comparing pictures,' he announced, helping himself to a roll. 'All the dots kept wiping out. So what are we missing? Are we totally in the wrong area? Could the ship have reached somewhere we haven't thought of?'

Sarah shook her head, her mouth full of bacon and bread. She swallowed, took a sip of coffee and then spoke. 'It's impossible, General. Unless that ship can do fifty knots then it has to be somewhere on the pictures we've taken.'

'But where?' asked Leo, helping himself to another roll into which he squirted a generous helping of tomato sauce.

'What if we are doing this all wrong? Forget about heat signatures for the moment. Suppose we get an up to date picture of this whole area and superimpose last week's picture. We tell the computer to compare the two and, wherever there is a difference, we put the profile we have of the ship on and see if that makes the difference.'

It took them half the morning to get ready. Finally, they superimposed the previous week's picture with one less than an hour old. At first, they thought there was something wrong with the programming because almost none of the coast lines coincided. In their excitement, they all forgot one simple fact. It was Macnair who realised the problem.

'We need to pick a time when the height of the tide is exactly the same or about as exact as we can get it.'

'Damn,' said Isobel with feeling. 'We've wasted half the morning.'

Macnair's satellite phone warbled. 'Nick? What's happening your end?'

'Not much, sir. I've spent hours pouring over charts and satellite pictures of the whole area. I've run time, speed and course calculations until I'm blue in the face and I've done a lot of thinking. If I was Habib, I would be in the Outer Hebrides somewhere. The southern end. It's deserted, there are a great many small and medium uninhabited islands and if he decides to make a run for it he's right on the doorstep of the Atlantic.'

'So what do you propose?'

'I'm moving from here to Barra. Tonight. I'll fly in slow and easy, without making too much noise. Once we're there, I'll set up search parties to start down at Barra Head which is the southern most tip of the southern most island called Berneray.'

'Okay, Nick. That's as good a use of your time as hanging about where you are.' The General told him what they had been doing about the heat sources and the débâcle with the profiling of the coastline.

After saying their goodbyes Macnair sat with his feet on the desk, reading again the file he had on Habib. He was still missing something but for the life of him he couldn't see what.

His phone went again. 'General, it's Hunter. I've been thinking about what you've been doing. Suppose Habib had thought of the same thing? What would he have done once he got to wherever he was going? He'd shut down his engines and let the ship cool down.'

'Yes, I suppose that makes sense,' Macnair agreed. 'But so what?'

'Try something entirely different. Tell Isobel to reduce the thermal signature to the minimum possible that is still detectable. Get her to magnify the readings as much as she can and keep eliminating the comparative heat sources.'

'I get you,' said the General. 'If the ship is cooling down we might get a trace.'

'Precisely. It's got to be worth a try.'

'Leave it to me, Nick. I'll call you if we find anything.'

Isobel and Sarah worked all afternoon reversing the program. Now, instead of looking for a heat source of a certain strength they began to eliminate those sources which were detectable at a lower and lower thermal energy reading. They used the first picture they had available after they lost the ship, in the assumption that the MV *Nymph* was already hidden with her engines and generators shut down. The time lapse from when the ship was last seen to the new picture was nearly ten hours. Was it too long a delay?

'Right, that's all images scrubbed at that magnification.' They stared at the screen. Nothing. Isobel now magnified the heat sensor reading by one hundred, the maximum they could take it to. Hundreds of dots appeared on the screen. It took them a little while to realise that they were now finding everything from a motorcycle engine to a light bulb. Again, by comparing the picture with one a week old they were able to eliminate most of the heat spots on the screen. They stared at the resultant four dots.

Using the zoom control on the computer they could home in on each spot. The first three were obviously land locked and probably a small vehicle of some kind, like a lawn mower.

The fourth gave rise to mounting excitement.

'General,' Sarah called, unable to keep the glee from her voice, 'I think we've found something.'

Macnair was there in three strides, looking over her shoulder. 'Where?' he barked.

Isobel pointed. 'Look at this. You can see a faint spot just here,' her pencil touched the screen. 'It doesn't appear on a picture taken the day before and, look, it does show on a picture taken less than two hours ago.'

Macnair looked carefully at the screen and then at a chart lying beside it. The island of Pabbay in the Outer Hebrides. 'Got you,' he said, reaching for his phone.

Currencies and blue chip stocks across the world began to shudder and tremble. As the enormity of the outrage was realised, the effects began to mushroom. Vast sums of equity values were wiped out as shares were devalued along with the currencies of America, Japan, Britain and other European countries. Fear swept through the institutions as endemic as it was irrational. As positions were taken the Iranians gleefully watched their profits mounting. It was better than they had hoped. At the last valuation, they were set to clear seven billion dollars of profits, after all costs.

Knowing what the outcome of the hostage crisis was to be, the Iranians made a fundamental mistake. They stayed in the markets with open positions instead of taking their profits. After all, they rationalised, if this happened in a hostage situation when the rescue of the VIPs was a possibility, what would be the results if the outcome was the death of all the hostages?

16

Hunter and his team had already began to strike camp when his phone rang. 'Hunter,' he listened to the General.

'Roger, sir,' he acknowledged the information given to him. 'I need to study the charts and as soon as I know what I'm doing I'll phone and brief you.'

'Listen up, lads,' he shouted. 'Stop what you're doing and gather round. The fifteen officers and men walked across to Hunter who was seated out of the wind, in the lee created by the highest of the chapel walls still standing. 'That was the General.' He opened out a chart and pointed. 'He reckons that this man Habib and his followers are here, tucked alongside this island. They found a slight heat source which has now faded completely but, and this is the clincher – they've run two profiles of this area, using satellite pictures taken at the same state of the tide. You can see how this cliff bends round to this point called Rosinish, well, there's a distortion of the cliff. It seems to have grown in size roughly corresponding to the size of the ship.'

'Can't they see anything with the satellites?' Major Carter asked.

'They've looked. The rock is grey all along this bit of coast line. Different shades at different angles. The conclusion the General has come to is that they have camouflaged the ship somehow.'

'So what are we going to do?'

'We continue to Barra only we'll go the scenic route. The helicopters will fly north before crossing to North Uist and dropping back down here.' He ran his finger south. 'We'll stay low all the way to Vatersay, here. That's five miles away and we shouldn't be seen. We'll unload and use the attackers to bring us to this point.' His finger rested on Sandray. 'From there it's chariots. Any questions?'

There were none. After only a few days of running up the equipment together, searching and diving in the area, they were already coalescing into a formidable team.

'Right, let's go.' Hunter phoned Macnair and told him about his intentions.

The men returned to their tasks. Their equipment had already been repackaged into carrier bags which were easily handled by two men. Even so, there was a mountain of gear. The helicopters were called up and the first landed at dusk. Jim Carter left on the first one with six of the team and as much equipment as they could squeeze on board. He would start setting up camp at Vatersay where they would have their satnav, satcomms and radio links. Because of the long detour to the north, west and south, the journey took nearly two hours and it was after 22.00 when they arrived at their destination. Two more helicopters followed at fifteen minute intervals. Hunter was in the last, eager to get started yet aware that great care was needed.

By the time he had landed, Hunter had a plan of

sorts mapped out. The nature of their operations was such that flexibility was the key word. Each man in the team had been selected because he could think and act for himself, as well as be relied upon in the toughest of circumstances.

Carter had already set up the tents and connected the two diesel generators. Small and silent, each was capable of pushing out twenty kilowatts of power without tripping. That was enough to boil ten electric kettles each, which was more than sufficient for their requirements.

They went about their assigned tasks sorting the equipment which was the latest and state of the art, supplied from all around the world. They had the best of everything. The attacker was an inflatable boat which, when blown up, could carry four men with ease. It was a metre wide and four metres long. The bows and sides were self sealing buoyancy tanks each one no longer than a third of a metre and a third of a metre in diameter. It would take a lot of holes to sink an attacker. The rear transom was reinforced keflar, the same material used in their body armour. The outboard was completely silent when running and ran not on petrol but from a special gas mix carried in a flexible container which ran the length of the keel. After the boats were inflated, the gas was added using a special hand pump. Once full, not only was the bottom made more rigid but there was added buoyancy as well. Fully laden, the boats were capable of speeds of twenty knots.

Strapped to each of the attackers were the underwater sledges. Although they looked something like the two-man chariots made famous in the Second World War, there was no technical similarity apart from the fact that these, like their predecessors, were torpedo shaped.

Made from reinforced plastics, they carried two divers, one sitting behind the other. Each diver carried his own self-contained breathing apparatus, which recycled the gas, scrubbed the carbon dioxide exhaled and then mixed oxygen and helium in the right quantities for the depth. As helium is a much lighter gas than nitrogen, the helium dissolves in and out of the blood stream more quickly and more easily. This means that the chances of getting the bends are vastly reduced. In fact, the system had been computed to ensure that the divers would run out of gas before they could stay long and deep enough to be affected by the bends. Even so, there was enough gas to allow a diver to operate at fifty metres for an hour without having to make any stops when resurfacing. If they had been using ordinary air, after five minutes at fifty metres they would have been running into long decompression times.

Each diver could plug into the sledge and use the gas carried there, hence saving his own. The new lithium batteries which were contained in the torpedo shaped body gave sufficient power to drive submerged for twenty miles at five knots. They wore throat mikes and had receivers sewn into their neoprene hoods which were good for transmitting underwater up to thirty miles, and, unlike previous similar gear, did not have to be line of sight. Hence, they could each speak to Jim Carter back at base. The same equipment was used on land which meant that each man was in contact with everybody else at all times.

The sledges contained a full armoury of explosives, weapons and, fixed to the front, a type of spear gun. These carried exploding heads and were good for eight shots each.

Their diving goggles had been modified so that once on-shore the goggles became light intensifiers which allowed the men to see in the dark. Unlike previous goggles, these were not bulky with elongated lenses. A simple switch on the side powered-up the tiny battery which in turn drove the chip that modified the soft lens. Pitch black was turned to day, although the scenery had a light blue tinge to it. Furthermore, a sudden bright light did not blind the wearer as the chip could react so fast the light was immediately filtered.

All weapons had built in silencers. A rifle shot could not be heard at five paces, a pistol at three.

The equipment was checked and loaded. Each man knew what was required of him and they worked in virtually complete silence.

'Is that everything finished?' Hunter asked. 'Good. Jim, I'm going to talk to the General. I want a last hot meal and drink served before we leave.'

'It'll be ready in ten minutes, Nick.'

Hunter thanked him and went into the largest of the tents, which held their communications gear. Within seconds he was talking to Macnair.

'We're ready to move out, sir. It's now zero three ten and I want to leave in twenty minutes for Sandray.'

'Roger that, Nick. When do you intend attacking?'

'The deadline is Friday before they start to shoot the hostages so I'll need to move in tomorrow night.'

'I have to tell you that there's a great deal of pressure being brought to buy off Habib. Private deals are being made even as we speak. I understand that there has been direct contact with Habib and a promise that the money will be wired wherever he says if he just walks away.'

'What's been Habib's response to that?'

'We don't know or perhaps more to the point no one is telling. Something about all this doesn't make sense.'

'General, I'll let you do the strategic thinking and I'll work on the tactics. I take it the world and his mother knows what's happening?' Hunter asked dryly.

'Certainly not,' Macnair was affronted. 'I've told our masters that we hope for a break-through in the next forty-eight hours and that if necessary they would have to stall and negotiate for an extension after Friday. The last thing we need is a loud-mouthed politician blabbing to the press that we know where the hostages are being held.'

'One thing which will act in our favour is if the ransom is paid. It could buy us time, if we need it. Naturally, the ideal result is no money paid, hostages safe and Habib and his men dead. The first is irrelevant if Habib isn't around to collect.'

'It's an idea. Let me think about it.'

'Roger, sir. If Habib is where we think he is then he's not going anywhere.'

'I take your point. Good luck, my boy. I'll speak to you later.'

Hunter left the tent, grabbed a plate of enriched stew and a cup of coffee. He briefly told the men about the conversation he'd had with the General and a short while later they departed.

There were twelve of them on the raid and four plus Carter back at the base. At Vatersay Bay they launched the attackers. Each man picked up a corner and carried it into the water. Carter and his four men manhandled the two underwater sledges alongside two of the boats and strapped them on. A hearty shove and each attacker floated free. The engines were started and like shadows they faded into the night.

With their LIGs on – light intensive goggles – the night turned to day. The throat mikes and ear phones worked well, and communications back to base were loud and clear. They travelled out of Vatersay Bay and then south towards Sandray. The fine weather that had been enjoyed for the previous few days was passing. An occluded front was gathering and sweeping towards Scotland. With it would come wind and rain. Already the sea was beginning to pick up and white caps were sweeping in from the Atlantic. Once in the Sound of Sandray, a mile-wide stretch of open water, the boats began to rock slightly, though not uncomfortably. The attackers were seaworthy in sea states up to six or seven and wind strengths of seven or eight on the Beaufort Scale.

The men wore camouflaged uniforms, light body armour and carried enough assorted weaponry to take on a regiment. Strapped around their necks like a halter and secured at their waists were thin, very effective life vests. If anyone fell into the sea, a hydrostatic pressure switch operated and the life vest inflated automatically. Capable of supporting three hundred pounds when fully inflated the vests had, on exercises in the past, saved more than one life.

In less than half an hour they had landed on the eastern side of Sandray, dragged their equipment ashore and set up camp. Unlike the camp they had left, there were no tents and there would be no cooking. Above high water, they dug deep trenches and used an upturned attacker as the roof. Within less than an hour of landing, all equipment was hidden and the men were under shelter, getting some sleep.

Hunter, Joshua Clements, the American Delta Force Captain, and the French Lieutenant, Pierre Flambert, went out on patrol. They spread across the southern edge of Sandray, dug themselves in and waited for the dawn which was not long in coming. They were now within three miles of the enemy.

At midnight, Stanton and McDonald crawled into the bilges and up into the locker. It was time to make a further reconnaissance of the ship. McDonald had already flitted like a ghost throughout the vessel on the previous night. He had been in cabins which contained sleeping men, had looked in on the bridge to see Habib and one other deep in conversation, and had watched as three guards patrolled the upper deck. He had found the moon pool and had located the weapons and explosives hidden there. He had been tempted to help himself to a gun or two but had thought better of it. They weren't ready yet, and it was too risky if someone noticed a gun missing.

The lock was held in place by four screws which, as on the previous occasion, took less than three minutes to remove. Whilst undoing the screws McDonald vowed to himself that he would buy a Swiss army knife at the first opportunity.

Carefully, they lifted away the lock and pushed open the door. Both men carried their guns and knives. If they were caught, they would not go quietly to their deaths.

It was pitch dark as they felt their way along what they knew was a short corridor with two doors on either side leading to further lockers.

The previous night, McDonald had returned laden with

food and soft drinks for the hostages. By rearranging the goods on the shelves he had effectively left things appearing the way they had been. The most joyous greeting was when he held out a roll of toilet paper and some soap.

The water tight door at the end of the corridor was opened by pushing up a heavy handle. As this led into the section of the ship which was occupied by the terrorists, the lifting of the handle took nearly ten minutes – millimetre by millimetre. When it opened, the door swung towards them slowly, making a high squeaking sound that was heart-stopping.

Stanton took up a position behind the door. If McDonald was discovered he would be his back-up. Neither man acknowledged that he would probably be too late.

In bare feet, the SAS sergeant flitted along the corridor, stopping frequently to listen. In a situation like this, it was his ears, nose then eyes in that order that would warn him of danger. Stanton stayed behind the door, covering the corridor and sleeping quarters.

Unlike the previous occasion when he had searched the ship, tonight he had an objective. After discussing the situation with the other hostages they had decided that they would stand a better chance of survival if they were armed. Tonight, McDonald was going to raid the armoury.

It took over twenty minutes to make his way to the moon pool area. Once safely inside, he carefully closed the watertight hatch and switched on the light. He went straight to the locker which he knew contained the guns and explosives. It came as a shock to find the locker empty and for a few moments he thought he was looking in the wrong place. Convinced he wasn't, he sat back on his haunches to ponder his next move.

What the hell had happened to all those explosives and weapons? He began to search the whole area, looking in the other lockers and searching amongst the diving gear – all to no avail.

He leant against the underwater chariot and surveyed the hold. It took him a few moments to realise that the bolts holding down the deck plating had been removed and that there was a series of holes along the deck. Intrigued, he stepped forward, bent down and hooked an index finger into one of the holes. He lifted the plate clear and stared down into the bilges. For a few seconds he saw nothing then he noticed a wire coming out of the water. He reached down, put his hand into the bilge, and froze in shock. He had found the explosives. Gingerly, he felt along the packets. As he moved along the hold he replaced the last plate he had lifted so that at any point in time only one needed to be replaced if he heard anybody approaching.

Each block of plastic had a detonator running from it. As he worked his way along McDonald ran his hands along the detonating cord which, as each strand was added, became thicker. By the time he got to the end, it was as thick as his wrist. The cords had been carefully secured around four further detonators and led to an electronic firing device. After careful examination he decided that it was a remote control device to be fired once their captors had escaped.

Perhaps they had already left and the bomb he was standing over was about to explode? Beads of sweat sprung to his brow.

He heard a noise from outside, metal knocking metal.

Quickly, he replaced the deck plate and retreated across the hold. In one corner was a large wicker basket which contained diving suits, neoprene vests, fins and other pieces of diving paraphernalia. He opened the lid, burrowed underneath and closed the lid behind him. He wasn't a moment too soon. The door opened and in came two men.

'That's strange,' said Habib, 'the light is on.'

'Some fool has left it on, Aziz,' replied Fredericks. 'Come on, let's check out the chariot and get it ready to launch.'

McDonald listened to their movements, his gun cocked, in case he was discovered. He was sure when the others spoke of Habib they had used the name Aziz. If this was Habib should he climb out and shoot him now? What about the bomb? Could it be set off by a remote control carried by one of the two men? If it could, was it possible to shoot both before one of them detonated the explosives? Christ, he was in a quandary. Would Stanton come in or was he, as agreed, staying as back-up, ready to move if needed?

'We will start the generators and engines in the morning,' said Habib. 'It is time that we let the British know where we are.'

McDonald tensed. That didn't make any sense at all.

'Do you still expect them to arrive tomorrow?' asked Fredericks.

'No, my friend. By the time they are organised and their cowardly politicians have decided they should attack I would expect them to be here on Saturday morning or, more likely, Saturday night, Sunday morning. What is most likely to happen is that they will begin to negotiate for more time. It has been a boon to us that we have been offered the money from the families and friends of our,' he chuckled, 'guests. It is a pity that we will not be able to accept such generosity.'

Habib and Fredericks were busy checking the submersible, making sure, yet again, that it would launch and work without any difficulties.

'I have ensured the transponders work,' said Fredericks. 'If anyone sets foot on the island not only shall we know it but we shall know where. The picture back to the receiver is very good.' They had placed over two dozen transponders around and across the island. These were twelve-inch-long, half-inch-diameter rods which created an invisible beam from one to the next. If the beam was broken, a signal was received which showed precisely where it happened. They would be able to stand on the bridge and watch the British blunder across the island and into their trap.

'We shall kill as many of them as possible. That is why we shall wait until the last moment to detonate the bomb.'

'It will be a great moment in history,' said Fredericks, half believing it.

As the two men left the hold, switching off the light behind them, McDonald heard Habib. 'Friday morning, we shall give the British an incentive to come to the rescue of the prisoners.'

McDonald stayed where he was for a further fifteen minutes before venturing out, in case one of them returned. It also gave him time to think.

A trap? Was that what this was all about? But why? McDonald's difficulty, as had been shown so often in the past, was that he was applying the logic of a Westerner where no logic existed. Which was why he and the majority of the world would never understand their enemy.

He retraced his tracks and soon afterwards he and Stanton were back in the hold with the others. McDonald told them what he had learned.

'You're telling us that we are sitting on a floating bomb?' asked Felicity Cornwall, hysteria rising in her voice. 'My God. We have to get away. Do something.' She grabbed McDonald by the arm. 'Help us. Oh, my God.' Panic was in her eyes, fear in her voice.

'Be quiet, my dear,' said the steely tones of Wilma Shules. 'We are in no danger for a day or two yet. We know what they are planning and we know when. We have the ability to come and go practically as we please. So all is not lost. What do you think was meant by an incentive to come to our rescue?' She addressed them all, aware of the answer.

'They mean to start shooting us,' Stanton said, matter of factly.

'That means we need to do something before it happens,' said Herbert Conrad. 'We are agreed that we shall not sit still and watch them shoot any more of us, yes?'

'Yes,' said Bradley. 'Sergeant, Lieutenant, what do you suggest?'

The two SAS men told them. They approved.

Hunter spoke softly into the throat mike. 'Can you see anything?'

Two negatives were the replies. It was midday and a steady rain was sweeping across from the Atlantic, hindering visibility, leaving the island an opaque blur.

They stayed where they were until dusk was falling. Due to the rain and the clouds it grew dark earlier and by 19.00 the three men were crawling away from their lookout points back to the others. Nothing of any significance had been seen.

'Right,' said Hunter, 'we leave in four hours. Slow and easy. We listen, look and then close in.'

Into his ear piece came the voice of Jim Carter. 'Nick, I've just had a long and interesting conversation with the General. It appears that the ship is radiating heat and that the thermal reading from the source is building up relatively quickly.'

'Hell. Does that mean they are about to leave?'

'We don't know. That was the initial thought. A moving target would be far more difficult to attack. Perhaps they are planning some sort of escape. Who can tell?'

'How long has this been going on for?'

'The heat build up? About two hours. Which of course is what is nonsensical about it. Diesel engines don't require to warm up for more than a few minutes before a ship can get underway.'

'Perhaps they were waiting for cover of darkness.'

'So why start up when they did? They obviously knew about our detection techniques otherwise they wouldn't have switched everything off in the first place.'

'So what conclusions have you or the General come to?'

'Me? Well I'm just a simple supply officer and the General can't think of a reason.'

'Jim, whatever you are, it isn't simple. And if the General can't think of any reason I can't either. There is one obvious possibility but it doesn't make sense.'

'What's that?'

'They want us to know where they are.'

On that sobering but inconclusive thought they ceased speaking to each other. The others had also heard the conversation but had nothing to offer by way of an explanation.

At midnight Hunter, with Sergeant David Hughes of the SAS behind him, launched his sledge. Lieutenant Sam McReady of the Royal Marines Special Boats Service had command of the other, with Jan Badonovitch of the Russian Spetsnaz behind him.

The remainder of the team set out to paddle their attackers across the Sound of Pabbay. Silence and secrecy were the watchwords that night.

Onboard the MV *Nymph*, the prisoners made their own preparations. The attacking force was to consist of the two SAS men, Bradley, Jesus Mboko, David Golightly, Ibn ben Saud and Donald Spencer.

'Now remember what I told you,' said Stanton. 'The plastic I've put around the hatch cover can be detonated by pulling this safety clip out. I've wired it to safety fuse which will last about three or four seconds. When it reaches the detonating cord the PE will explode. It doesn't appear to be much but believe me, it will blow the hatch combing to smithereens and if there's anybody caught in the blast he'll be cut in half.'

James Treherne nodded. He had been trusted to set off the trap should it be needed. He had also been trusted with one of the revolvers.

'If you hear any shooting, the rest of you start crawling into the bilges. That way, should anybody shoot through the hatch you'll be relatively safe.'

'What about the bomb?' Felicity Cornwall asked, fearfully.

'I hope to have it defused long before the shooting starts,' McDonald replied. 'Right, let's go.'

There were whispers of good luck and Stanton led the men through the bilges and into the locker. They went in their bare feet, wearing only trousers and shirts. Two of them were hardened, fit and expert at what they were about to do. The co-pilot was young, fit and had never been in so much as a fist fight in his life. The remainder were middle-aged men who had been exposed to violence and had trained in warfare of one sort of another. No longer as tough in body, they were certainly tough in spirit. The idea of giving no quarter came easily to all four of them – an Arab, a Jew, a black South African atheist and a white American Protestant.

They stood for what seemed an age in the passageway, whilst the watertight door was slowly opened. Once open, McDonald and Spencer made their way to the moon pool. It was imperative that the bomb be dismantled as soon as possible. The others went to find a gun or two.

Habib was seated on the bridge, his feet in their usual place on the console. That evening he had distributed a special drug to his men which would keep them wide awake and fully alert for the next forty-eight hours. After that it would not matter. For himself and Fredericks he had further pills, which were sufficient to keep them going for a week. After that they would need a great deal of rest and recuperation, but he was planning on that anyway.

The pills made him jumpy, edgy. The act of sitting nonchalantly in the chair took will power. After a few moments he gave it up, slipped to his feet and paced from one side of the bridge to the other. The cloth hanging over the ship was irritating him as he badly wanted to look out of the window. Finally, unable to resist it any longer, he went out on to the bridge wing and tore open the cloth, letting it drop to the sea below. That was better. He could now look out to sea, and feel the wind on his face. After all, he rationalised, he wanted to be found so there was no longer any need to hide.

What he did not want the British to understand or guess was why he wished to be found. Damn those pills. He would have to get the cloth replaced before daybreak. He could hear the slow and quiet movement of his men about the ship, patrolling, ready. Six of his men were dug in on the island, and four were wandering the upper deck of the ship. Fredericks was below making a fresh cup of coffee and he, Habib, was on the bridge in command of the greatest terrorist act of its kind in history. Perhaps not in numbers but certainly in the quality of the targets.

A number of things happened at once, though Habib was oblivious to them. It was, in fact, the beginning of his nightmare.

McDonald and Spencer reached the moon pool and got quickly to work. McDonald pulled up the end plate and carefully pulled out the first of the detonators. He slipped the detonator off the detonating cord and dropped it through the open moon pool into the sea. Spencer began from the other end once he was shown what to do. It was time consuming work. A primed detonator is highly dangerous and if knocked or dropped can explode. Should one go off and by turn set off one bar of the plastic explosive, then it would be curtains for them all. The sympathetic detonation which would occur would blow the ship and everybody on board into little pieces.

The only consolation would be that nobody would ever know what happened to them.

There were eight blocks of plastic weighing half a kilogram under each plate. They were laid side by side and in continuous contact, forming a long bridge which stretched the length of the bilge. McDonald had decided to do it this way rather than cut the connections from the main detonators in case it was booby trapped. He could plant simple bombs of this nature but had no skill when it came to anything sophisticated. Any booby trap would be around the electrical end which was why each detonator had to be individually removed and ditched. Progress was slow. It was not until he was half way through that McDonald castigated himself for a fool.

'What did you say?'

'I'm a bloody idiot,' was the whispered reply. McDonald went to the plate next to the main detonators and removed it. He took out the first two detonators, slid them from the detonating cord and threw them away. Next he lifted out the first two blocks of PE and dropped those into the water.

'If this end is booby trapped and we do something which accidentally sets it off this end, the explosion cannot jump this space. So I'll work my way back, removing the detonators and lifting out every third or fourth block. You do the same. Every gap we create reduces the chances of a sympathetic explosion. Understand?'

Spencer nodded. Great, the whole ship would not go up, just them.

Stanton was in the corridor that held the cabins. He had been into four so far, ready to kill anyone he found there.

Much to his surprise the cabins were empty. It took only moments to check them all.

'It appears that they are all up and about,' he whispered to the others.

'Take a cabin each,' replied Ibn ben Saud, 'and see if you can find a weapon of some sort. I know these people, they are careless. They may have left something behind. But quietly, I beg you.'

They dispersed to search each cabin. Mboko was kneeling at the drawers under the bunk when his door opened. For a moment he thought it was one of the others but then realised it was a terrorist. It was a toss up as to who was the most surprised. The terrorist had his rifle slung across his shoulder and tried to swing it clear. It caught on the door with a clatter as Mboko sprang from the deck, launched himself the few feet that separated them, and hit the terrorist with his fist a smashing blow to the throat. The man gargled and his knees buckled but he did not go down. Before either could do anything more, a hand grabbed the terrorist across the mouth, pulled his head back and another hand rammed a knife into the exposed throat. There was a gentle gurgle as he died and Stanton lowered the body to the deck.

'Are you okay?'

'Yes, thank you. You came just in time. What shall we do with him?'

'Stuff him in this cupboard out of the way. But before we do, relieve him of all his weapons.' Apart from the rifle, an automatic Heckler and Koch HK33E, they found a pistol and a commando knife.

'Have any of you used one of these before?' Stanton waved the rifle before him.

'Yes, I have,' said Mboko. 'It was very popular in

322

the jungle, especially the sniper version.' He took the weapon and deftly checked the magazine, put a round up the spout and set the safety catch. He grinned at Stanton.

'Yep, you know it all right. What about this?' He held up an Austrian Glock 20, in production from 1990 only. It was one of the best automatic pistols made.

'I don't know that particular model, Lieutenant,' said Bradley, 'but I have handled guns like it in my time.' He took the pistol and examined it carefully. 'No safety, but a second pressure switch on the trigger.' It took him a few seconds to figure out how to work the magazine but then he had the gun cocked and ready to fire.

In their search they had found some spare ammunition, and two divers' knives but no more guns. Even so they felt much safer. The odds were beginning to move to a more equitable distribution.

The Arab and the Israeli were given the divers' knives before they started to move further into the bowels of the ship.

'Stop,' Hunter said through his throat mike. 'Stop. Everybody. Attackers do you copy?'

Each of the three attackers acknowledged the order. They were less than fifty yards from the beach and just inside a lee. The second sledge came to a hover alongside him.

'Jim, do you copy?'

'Loud and clear, Nick. What's wrong?'

'It's a trap. That's what's wrong. We're going into a trap. Can you patch me through to the General?'

'I'll try, Nick.' The words which travelled through the water had an echo and a slur to them which meant a lot of pauses between phrases and sentences. After a few minutes a new voice was heard by them all.

'Nick, it's Macnair. Do you copy, over?'

'Loud and clear, General. Sir, it's a trap. The report you sent me about Habib and his previous operations all indicate a willingness to kill.' He paused every few words. 'The engines have been started to tell us where he is. He's expecting us. Not tonight maybe, but soon. He'll start killing hostages tomorrow whether he gets the money or not. He doesn't care about the money. He's well financed already. This whole operation has been to create chaos with the maximum loss of life. Hence the earlier deaths.' He paused again, waiting for some response. When none was forthcoming he said, 'General, did you copy that?'

'Affirmative. Sorry. I was thinking. I believe that your analysis of the situation is correct. What do you want to do? Withdraw?'

'Negative, General. I say again, negative. If we go in tonight we might catch him by surprise. But it means we have to be extra careful. If it's a trap then there will be surprises we can do without.'

'Such as?'

'Such as men on the island not on the ship. Also, if I was him, I'd have the ship wired like a bomb. Detonation probably by remote control. What else could he do?' Hunter asked, broadcasting to his team.

'Transponders, boss,' came the reply.

'Damn.'

'They're clever and very difficult to detect.'

Hunter now recognised the voice as the Scottish sergeant from the Royal Engineers, Don Masters. 'Don, you said difficult. How difficult?'

'Well, boss, it's necessary to spot the transponder sticking in the ground somewhere. If we can find one without tripping an alarm, then we can usually find the others.'

'How so?' Hunter asked.

'Because they are line of sight connected. Find one, lie low and look in all directions for the next.'

'What do you do then?'

Masters told him.

Habib was on the bridge wing, staring out to sea. His imagination was working overtime. Everywhere he looked he could see a canoe or a small boat being paddled towards the ship. Then the wave would break and turn back into the sea again. He went into the chart room at the back of the bridge to stare at the screen of the island which showed the position of the transponders. The island itself was a tracing, superimposed on the dots which marked the position of each transponder. Faint lines showed on the screen, criss-crossing the map. A rabbit couldn't walk across the island without an alarm being sounded.

Satisfied, he went over to stand by the bridge chair, worried without knowing why but putting it down to the side effects of the pills he had taken.

Fredericks reappeared on the bridge and reported that all was quiet around the ship. He went across to the radio and called up the men who were scattered around the island. Each reported that there was nothing to see.

Habib looked at his watch. Thirteen minutes past three. When should he start the executions? He would leave it until midday. The marvels of technology, he thought. We can film a death, transmit it to a passing satellite in a condensed format that takes a second and tell the satellite to broadcast it then or later. Untraceable, up-to-the-minute pictures. That will get a reaction from the phlegmatic British, he thought.

McDonald and Spencer had finally completed the removal of the detonators. It was too big a job and would take too long to remove all the blocks of plastic explosives, so they contented themselves with ditching every third or fourth into the sea. Their job finished, they made their way back to the forward hold and the other hostages. It was McDonald's task to protect them as best he could should their captors try and kill them, particularly once they learned that the explosives had been rendered inoperative.

McDonald crawled into the bilges to find that most of his fellow prisoners had managed to climb in and hide, taking up all the available space. In the hold itself sat in splendid isolation, James Treherne, British Ambassador to the United Nations.

'What's happening?' asked McDonald. 'Have you heard anything?'

'Not a sound. Did you dismantle the bomb?'

'Yes. You get down with the others. If they do open the hatch and start shooting then you should be safe down there. Not even a hand grenade will penetrate those metal plates.'

'What about you? Something should be happening by now. Habib will have to react soon. If you hide with us, if they do shoot or throw grenades, you'll have a better chance of survival as well. Hell, this would be a death trap, just sitting here.'

McDonald could not disagree. 'I need to be able to set off the trap if one of Habib's men appear,' he argued.

'Can't you lengthen the detonating cord so you could operate it from in the bilges?'

McDonald looked at him askance. 'I'm a first-rate, unadulterated fool,' he said. He went quickly to the opening to the bilge and said, in a loud whisper, to the ambassador, 'Sir, you stay here. All we need is a length of about twenty feet of cord and there are hundreds of feet in the moon pool.'

McDonald once more made his way quickly and silently to where they had dismantled the bomb. It took him only seconds to retrieve a suitable length of detonating cord and return. He replaced the short length of cord with the longer piece and followed the ambassador into the bilge. He could set off the explosives without showing himself.

Hunter pushed forward the handles and twisted the throttles towards himself. The two-man sledge moved from the hover into a gentle dive and picked up speed. He set the automatic controls to a depth of ten metres and a speed of four knots and headed towards the ship.

The nose of the sledge contained a sonar transducer which emitted a wedge shaped beam with an angle of forty-five degrees left to right and up and down. The echo that returned was translated into a picture on a small screen in the panel in front of him. It was like looking at a radar screen. Now that they were lined up less than a hundred yards from the ship's side the rough cliff face of rock was easily discernible from the smooth metal of the vessel. He aimed the nose of his craft at the bows of the ship. He had ordered the other sledge with McReady and Badonovitch to the stern.

It was exhilarating gliding silently through the water. The sea was pitch black but as they moved they disturbed tiny microplasms of plankton which glowed an eerie green, giving a false sense of speed.

'Slow down,' Hunter ordered over the throat mike. 'Hover underneath the stern whilst I check with the attackers.'

'Josh, what're your positions? Over.'

Joshua Clements was having the time of his life. This was what he had trained for ever since leaving college in Colorado. He had missed the Gulf War by less than a week and had regretted it ever since. He was a true patriot, willing and eager to serve his country. For him, it was the Stars and Stripes for ever – right or wrong. However, for all his gung-ho attitude, he was no fool. He intended to come out of this alive, with all the men under his command, which was why he was taking it "nice and slowly".

'Nick, we are on a small beach with a sand bank rising about two metres. If there are transponders, they'll be set in the higher ground for line of sight coverage. We have pulled the attackers ashore and Don is about to go up and take a look. Over.'

'Roger that. We'll stay in the hover next to the ship until you're ready to move,' replied Hunter. 'We still have plenty of time.'

Don Masters crawled very slowly up the steep sides of the sand bank. Like the others he could hear and speak to all his team mates, using his throat mike and ear piece. His light intensifying goggles showed the world about him in a faint blue tinge but as clear as if it was noon on a bright summer's day. At the edge of the bank he carefully used his hands to drag sand away, creating a hollow to crawl into. Once he had done that, from a pocket in the thigh of his right trouser leg, he removed a powerful periscope to scan about him. Hardly more than a pencil thick, it was impossible to distinguish from the long strands of tufted grass growing in clumps along the edge of the sand bank.

He took his time. First, he identified a local high point and concentrated on searching it. Fifty metres from where he lay was a small hummock. If he had been laying transponders that was exactly where he would have put one. In the wind, the grass and small bushes waved and rustled. The rain came in squalls, making it difficult to see clearly, but between showers he was practically able to count the blades of grass. It took less than ten minutes to find the first one.

'I have a transponder in sight.' It was sticking a few inches above the soil, solid and unbending in the wind. He changed the magnification from times fifty to times two hundred and fifty and felt he could reach out and touch the device. He examined the area to the left and within three minutes found the next one. Once the first was found, finding the remainder was relatively easy, as they had to be within line of sight of each other.

'How far to the first one?' asked Clements.

Masters turned a small serrated button on the side of the scope and moved the cross-hairs in his sights until they touched the image of the transponder. He read the distance from a scale at the top left of his vision. 'Fifty-three metres.'

'There are none nearer than that?'

'No, sir. That's the closest. I'll go ahead and you all follow straight behind me.' Masters crawled away on his belly. He made no sound as he wormed his way across the bleak, open landscape, pausing frequently to listen and sniff the air. He was half way across when he said, 'Stop.' He lifted the periscope again and spent a few minutes searching the land. Directly into the wind he saw something move. It took him a few minutes to be certain. 'I've one target dead ahead, three hundred metres.' The terrorist was smoking a cigarette. Even at that distance, Masters had caught the faintest whiff of tobacco smoke, more imagined that substantial, but enough to warn him.

Peter Weir was an Olympic standard rifle shot. A corporal in the paratroopers, his marksmanship was astounding. He crawled up next to Masters to have a look. He used his sniper scope to look at the target.

'I see him, clearly. Nobody else in the picture. Do you want me to take him out?'

Clements and the rest of the team stayed back and down. The fewer heads looking the less likelihood of being discovered.

'Nick, we are now in position. We are ready to begin, over.'

'Roger that, Josh. It's a go. Good luck. Out.'

'Shoot him,' said Clements.

Weir took sight. He was using a McMillan M87R, with a specially built in silencer. It had a glass fibre stock and a hinged butt and carried ten rounds of .50 ammunition. Less than ten kilograms in weight, it was the ideal rifle for these conditions. He settled the butt into his shoulder and took aim. The rifle gave a faint cough, hardly moving in his hands, and the terrorist died.

Masters had ascertained that there was no one else in sight and crawled rapidly to the transducer. He carefully and slowly raised the transducer which had the effect of not breaking the beam, but angled it up a degree or two.

He unscrewed the base and four batteries dropped out. As it was now no longer in the network, the other transducers ignored it and continued to operate as though it had never existed. No alarm sounded on the ship. Although they were a clever and almost foolproof piece of technology, this was their Achilles heel.

Master's continued to search the island for as far as he could see. After only minutes he had identified a further four transducers. He pointed them out. At this point, knowing what to do and look for, the team split into four groups of two and went their separate ways. Each heading for the next transducer and a possible terrorist.

Stanton and the others had reached the aft deck. They had found nobody asleep in the cabins or wandering around in the ship. It meant that their captors were out on deck, on the bridge or on the land. The lights were out in the saloon, as they had been throughout the rest of the ship. The five men slowly traversed the room, stepping around the furniture, as quiet as ghosts.

Stanton stopped at the door and looked through the glassed port hole in the middle. The others had spread out and were looking through the reinforced glass which made up the rear bulkhead.

'I see nothing,' said ben Saud, softly.

'Wait, patience,' replied Stanton. 'Somebody is there or will appear soon.'

'How can you possibly know that?' Bradley asked, wanting to get a move on – to end it.

'The deck space is too big not to be patrolled. Someone will appear. Now, no more talking. I'm going out there. Cover the other two doors.' He pointed to the door they had entered by and a door which led outside and along the port side. 'I'm going to wait until one of them comes along. We need to improve the odds before we go to war.'

With that he opened the door and, keeping low, stepped out onto the deck. He moved very slowly, careful not to bump into anything. The sacking turned the darkness of night into an even deeper, more claustrophobic gloom. He paused frequently to listen and to smell. There was a clink and the sound of footsteps coming down the starboard side. The terrorists felt safe for the moment and though they were alert, they did not see the need to be careful.

Stanton did the completely unexpected. He realised that there was only one way for the man to come and so he squatted down in his path, a knife in his hand. He ducked his head to hide any faint gleam his face might throw up and froze. The footsteps came nearer, directly towards him. He saw a foot at the periphery of his vision, stood up suddenly and, even as the man came to a startled halt, drove the knife through his throat and up to his brain. He held the body there, on the end of the knife, whilst he listened for any further footsteps. All was silent.

He lowered the body to the deck and wiped the knife clean on the terrorist's coat. He then picked up the body, slung it over one shoulder, retrieved the dead man's gun and returned to the saloon.

He dumped the body behind one of the sofas before turning his attention to the gun he had picked up.

David Golightly recognised it immediately. 'Mine, I think,' he said. 'It's an Israeli Uzi and I know it like the back of my hand.' Probably one of the most famous submachine guns in the world, it was also made under licence in Belgium and Germany. The magazine held forty rounds. It was a formidable weapon.

'Right, let's go,' said Stanton. 'Mr. Bradley, you and I will take the next deck while you three search this one. Don't forget to look in the life boats. One searches and two keep watch.'

With that they split up. Stanton and Bradley returned to the after deck and the steps leading up to the next deck. They crept upwards, guns cocked, eyes and ears straining. Stanton went to port and Bradley to starboard. Stanton neither saw nor heard the man, crouched down tying up his shoe lace. Bradley was three metres away when his peripheral vision caught sight of the figure rising from the deck, behind Stanton. Bradley shot him, twice, the sound tearing apart the night and destroying any need for more stealth.

Habib was thinking about the fame and fortune which would soon be his. He paced the bridge, now wishing it was all over. Having started the engines and the generators to give away their position to the British he began to wonder if that was enough. Should hc also rip away the sacking so that their satellites could see him as well? The British were stupid enough to need all the help they could get to find him.

He picked up the radio transmitter, about to call each of his men on the island, to get a report. Then he realised that Fredericks had done so less than fifteen minutes earlier and thought better of it. He did not want them to know how nervous he was becoming. Fredericks stood on the bridge wing, looking out across the sea, through the hole Habib had torn in the cover. He enjoyed the wind and the squalls of rain, a legacy of a Yorkshire upbringing coupled with spending too long in hot, arid countries.

Habib went into the chart room and took a look at

the route he and Fredericks intended to take when they escaped. Four hours underwater was not that hard to do. He looked at the picture of the transponders, puzzled by what he saw. Surely the shape was wrong? Startled, he realised that a third of the transponders were now no longer showing and even as he stared, another beam disappeared. Damn it, why were they malfunctioning? Even as the thought took root he heard the two shots, deafeningly loud in the early morning gloom.

Hunter had stopped the sledge by the bows. They surfaced slowly, hardly causing a ripple. The deck loomed five metres above their heads, out of reach. From a pocket on the sledge he took eight electro-magnets and handed four to Hughes. Nothing was said, there was no need. They strapped a magnet to each knee and fitted one into each palm. They connected the left knee magnet with a flexible wire to the left hand magnet and did the same with the right side. By pressing the button on the side of each hand held magnet a powerful current was released to the hand and knee simultaneously. Quickly, Hunter began to climb. Like a limpet he crawled up the sheer side of the ship, left then right, moving a few inches at a time. It was easy to achieve but needed concentration. If he let go both buttons at the same time, he would drop back into the water.

He reached the deck and raised his head above the breakwater. A man sat on a hatch a few metres away, his back to him. He was in a quandary. If he continued, he would make a noise, of that there was no doubt. Yet he could not stay there forever. The two gun shots made his mind up for him.

As the man before him jumped to his feet with a loud exclamation, looking aft, unslinging his gun, Hunter slipped over the side. The noise he made went unheard. It was the ripping open of the Velcro fastening across his holster which alerted the guard. As he spun round, Hunter had his gun out and was aiming. The first snap shot took the terrorist in the right arm, knocking his gun away, the second created a third eye in the middle of his forehead, stifling the yell which had begun with the first shot. The silenced weapon made the sound of a muted cough, barely audible three feet away.

On the island they had shot two more terrorists as they crawled across the land, making use of every piece of cover available. Ten of the transponders had been deactivated and they were now nearly half way across.

They each knew the whereabouts of the others in the team. They knew that Hunter was climbing the ship's side and that McReady and Badonovitch were on the aft deck.

So far they had not been discovered. Bill Davidson, another SAS sergeant, was in a gully, silently passing a low, decrepit stone wall when he heard the sound of water. It took a second, but he realised it was coming from the other side of the wall and was the sound of a man urinating.

He eased forward, up to the wall. Carefully, he raised his head to look. The terrorist stood facing him, in a hollow, his head level with the top of the wall. The man was looking down, shaking himself, prior to rezipping his trousers.

Davidson coughed. The terrorist looked up in alarm, to stare into the eyes of the SAS sergeant. It was the last thing he saw as Davidson shot him twice. The first bullet hit him in the right eye and the second in the heart. Davidson reported in.

At that point they heard the sound of the two shots coming from the ship. Unsilenced weapons meant that somebody had been spotted and the terrorists were firing, or so they thought.

It took two minutes of cross-checking to discover that no shots had been fired at any of them. So what on earth was happening?

McReady and Badonovitch slipped quickly across the deck and into the saloon. They saw nobody. It was their task to search the ship, to kill anyone in their way and to find and protect the prisoners.

They were a few minutes ahead of Hunter, as it had been an easier job to climb over the stern without having to use the magnets.

They flitted through the interior, finding nothing. The cabins were empty, as was the engine room.

They were about to enter the part of the hold which held the moon pool when the shots were fired. They thought that Hunter and Hughes had been discovered and were about to return to the upper deck to help when Hunter's voice came through their ear pieces.

'Sam? Are you all right?'

'Affirmative, Nick. What's happened?'

'No idea. I've taken out one raghead. Who were those shots fired at?'

'Not us. And the others are nowhere near here yet. Perhaps one of them was shooting at ghosts.'

'Or shadows. Yes . . .'

The sound of a machine gun cut him off. Hunter and Hughes rushed to the bulkhead leading to the bridge and cowered there, wondering what was going on.

* * *

Habib shouted, 'They're here. The British have arrived already.' He ran back onto the bridge, grabbing his machine gun and cocking it.

Fredericks was crouched on the bridge wing, looking aft towards the sound of the shot. It was why he neither noticed nor saw the man on the foredeck being shot by Hunter. Neither did Habib, who was alongside his friend, trying to see aft.

'Abdul, Khan, anybody, can you hear me?' Habib shouted.

'Yes Aziz. It is I, Khan. Abdul has been . . .'

It was then that the machine gun opened up. David Golightly, Deputy Prime Minister of Israel and a veteran of the Seven Days War, blasted the area the voice was coming from. Golightly was crouched behind a small locker, fixed to the deck underneath the life boats, which contained lifejackets for use by the crew and passengers. Khan had been leaning against the davit, three metres away and all but invisible. When he replied to Habib he had straightened up and shown himself. The Uzi shredded Khan's left shoulder and heart. He was dead before he hit the deck.

Ibn ben Saud was within sight of the bridge wing and dimly saw the two men crouched there. He started firing his revolver at them, missing in the dark as both men dived for the deck.

Hunter and Hughes had found a door in the side of the ship and were cautiously opening it. They still had no idea what was going on as no bullets had been aimed at them and they knew that McReady and Badonovitch were between decks.

They were in a short passageway which traversed the width of the ship. There were two cabins on either side

337

which were palatial and obviously used by the owner and special guests. In this case Habib and Fredericks.

A staircase opened up on their left. They climbed it quickly but carefully. They heard more firing.

Ben Bradley and Mboko were on the starboard side, covering each other, moving forward. They saw one of their captors when he suddenly began shooting at them from behind the lifeboat davit on their side of the ship. The man was too eager, too frightened. The shots went wild. Both Bradley and Mboko ducked down and returned fire. Their bullets struck around the terrorist, too close for comfort. He tried to dart away when Mboko shot him through the thigh, sending him flying but out of sight around the front of the bridge.

The pain helped Ismail Sullieman to conquer his fear. A deathly silence now hung over the ship. Then Habib called out in Arabic. 'My men. Answer me. Khan, Sullieman, Abdul . . .' there was a fusillade of shots aimed at the bridge. Stanton had worked his way into a position to be able to fire at Habib and Fredericks.

Both men no longer cared what was happening. With one accord they darted into the bridge and down the stairway. Quickly but carefully they headed for the moon pool. It was time to leave. They would let their bomb solve the problem.

Sullieman was incensed. The pain and rage he felt filled his heart. What had happened? What had gone wrong? He no longer cared. With a curse he limped to the hatch leading to the hold that held the prisoners. Not being privy to Habib's plans, he intended to kill as many of them as possible. Great would be his reward in heaven. He threw open the hatch and leant in. Into the pitch dark he began to shoot, hosing down the hold with his machine gun.

*   *   *

McDonald and the others had heard the firing. There was nothing they could do but wait with a rapidly waning patience and a growing fear. As always, fear of the unknown was the worse fear.

One thing was certain, McDonald was determined to kill as many of their captors as possible. It was now a fight to the bitter end, one way or another. From the firing of the first two shots to the throwing open of the hatch was a time lapse of less than seven minutes. Even as Sullieman began to shoot, the bullets ricocheting harmlessly across the empty hold, McDonald pulled the igniter. The detonating cord fired and instantly ran its length. The detonator exploded, setting off the plastic explosives. The charge was shaped to fire inwards which it did, cutting Sullieman's arms and head off. The explosion reverberated around the ship, stopping everybody in their tracks.

It took Hunter only seconds to establish that none of his men had been hurt. Thanks to the night vision goggles, when Stanton came into sight, crawling on his stomach, Hughes was able to put a hand on Hunter's arm and call out. 'John, it's David Hughes. Don't shoot.'

Stanton froze, then a big grin spread across his face. 'I never thought I'd live to see the day when I'd welcome your dulcet Welsh tones, Taff. Where the hell did you come from?'

'In a minute. Is there anybody else with you?'

'Yes, there are five of us.'

'Listen up,' Hunter spoke into his throat mike. 'There are five friendlies out and about. I say again, five. Be careful, we don't want any accidents.'

He then raised his voice. 'This is the British Army.

Throw down your weapons and come out with your hands in the air.'

'Boy, am I glad to hear you,' came back an American voice. Bradley and Mboko popped up from a stairwell on the starboard side. Ibn ben Saud and Golightly appeared from behind a locker.

'What was that explosion on the bow?' Hunter asked.

Habib and Fredericks slammed shut the door to the moon pool, pulled tight the locking arm across the door and rapidly fixed it locked with specially constructed chains. It would take a powerful explosion or cutting tools to get through the door, neither of which they ruled out.

It took only minutes to change into their diving suits and prepare the submersible for launch. Habib spared one minute to make a satellite-linked phone call. It was fully encrypted and was an instruction that put into effect ready-made deals liquidating all of his assets into cash. He had decided to take his profit now, just in case. As soon as the submersible was in the water Habib started the engine and prepared to dive.

'Wait, my friend. I want to check that our little surprise is still ready and waiting.'

By now, they could hear shouts of relief and happiness coming from their former prisoners. Habib rushed across the hold and checked the main firing detonators and their connections. He was satisfied. Unknown to him McDonald had left the firing sequence so that the bomb appeared to be intact. He could still win, albeit he might not kill as many of the enemy as he would like.

He flooded the buoyancy tanks and they gently sank into the sea. As they did so they heard a loud thump, reminiscent of a controlled explosive charge being fired.

Once clear of the hull, at a depth of four metres, he engaged the variable pitch propellers and the little craft moved slowly ahead, picking up speed.

Hunter had established the situation and reacted accordingly. He sent Sam McReady and Jan Badonovitch on to the island, to prevent any terrorists reaching the ship and to establish a safe area close by. The bomb in the hold might have been disabled but it was possible other devices had been secreted about the ship. Time was of the essence.

The released captives were escorted out of the bilges and into the relative comfort of the saloon. Unfortunately, Felicity Cornwall, the Minister for Agriculture, went into the hold, saw the two arms and head of Ismail Sullieman and promptly had hysterics. It was Wilma Shules, the United Nations Secretary General, who slapped her face to stop her wailing. The woman began sobbing and had to be helped to the saloon. Hunter's order of priorities was to ensure the safety of the VIPs and then wipe out Habib and his men. It was his only excuse for what subsequently happened.

'Boss, this is Sam. It's clear up here for about a hundred yards. I can see three uglies wondering what's going on. They've heard the shooting and are yelling to each other. They keep looking this way and I think one is using a radio.'

'We need to get everybody off just in case there's a bomb we know nothing about. Is it safe to do so?'

'No problem. There's a wall fifty metres from the ship they can hide behind. Got to go Boss. One of the ragheads is coming this way.'

Sam McReady and Badonovitch settled down on either side of a path, hidden by boulders. The man was bent forward, moving quickly towards the ship, oblivious of danger.

It wasn't fair but there again it wasn't a game or exercise. The terrorist had passed the two hidden men when they both shot him in the back. Two shots each meant he was dead before he hit the ground. McReady reported the result to the others.

With the ship evacuated, Hunter turned to Stanton. 'Is Habib amongst the men killed on the ship?'

'No. I think there's another one missing as well. A European. I don't know his name.'

'We think it's a man called Fredericks. Any ideas where they might be? One thing is for certain, Habib isn't going to blow himself up.'

'Christ, yes. The centre hold. There's a submersible which they can launch from inside. That must be how he planned to get away.'

'Hell. Taff, follow me. John, you and Cecil cover your backs in case Habib comes this way.'

Ben Bradley hoisted his gun. 'We can take care of ourselves,' he said with a smile. 'Why don't you go and do what you need to? We can look after things here.'

One thing was certain, you did not argue with the Vice-President of the United States of America. Hunter nodded and darted quickly back to the ship. It took only minutes to establish that the door to the centre hold was locked tight.

Hunter removed the plastic explosives from the bag he carried and quickly rolled it into a half-inch thick, metre length. He pressed it around the door, creating a circle. Next, he and Sergeant Hughes ran their fingers around the explosive, squeezing it into a triangular shape, helping to direct the blast into the door. Two detonators were inserted with a one-minute fuse.

They quickly hid from the blast which, when it happened, blew a neat, round hole in the middle of the door.

It took seconds to establish that the hold was empty. They rushed to the moon pool and looked into the water. Bubbles, caused by the cavitation of the submersible's propellers broke on the surface.

17

It was still dark, although there was a lightening of the sky to the east. As far as they could tell, two terrorists were still alive. Both of them were in a hollow near the centre of the island. Nervously, they peered around them, shouting in Arabic, desperate for an answer. There were no replies. Nothing but the wind which was picking up, and the occasional flurry of rain. Deepening clouds to the west bore the threat of a rain storm which would be with them soon.

McReady and Badonovitch closed in on the two men from one side, whilst the remainder of the team approached from the other three. They halted less than two hundred metres from their target. The terrorists were clear in their sights, unable to see their enemies, who blended in so well with the surrounding land.

It was effectively a turkey shoot when Clements gave the order to open fire. Neither of the men saw or heard a thing. A hail of death fell, each man receiving more than a dozen bullets. The silence was unbroken apart from the sound of gulls taking to the air now that dawn was breaking. They had breakfast to catch.

*   *   *

Hunter realised it was the submersible with Habib onboard, escaping. Without a pause he said, 'Taff, follow me. We need the sledge.'

He dived into the water and swam strongly down and out of the ship. Hughes was right beside him. They reached the bow and climbed aboard the sledge. Whilst Hunter started the engine and carried out the minimum of checks, Hughes told the others what they were up to.

They stayed on the surface, heading in the direction they guessed Habib to have taken. They could get up to ten knots on the surface which dropped to six maximum once under the water.

'Bubbles, Boss. Green three zero.' This meant thirty degrees to starboard, and after a few seconds Hunter saw them too. Unfortunately, they carried no grenades or other bombs. They each had pistols, which were of no use in the present circumstances, but they had the spears carried in the bow of the sledge. Virtually on top of the bubbles, Hunter dived the sledge just as the sun broke over the horizon and a new day began.

At a depth of eight metres they saw what could have been a shark, a short distance ahead. In the strengthening light they made out the sleek lines and knew it was Habib and Fredericks. In diving, Hunter had dropped behind and now tried to close the gap. The submersible was suddenly no longer where it was supposed to be. It had vanished.

Habib had estimated that they were a mile from the ship. He blew the tanks, shifted the planes to full rise and popped to the surface. That was when Hunter lost him.

Once on the surface he reached down into a side bag and removed the remote control transmitter. He and Fredericks looked gleefully at the ship, unaware that it was now deserted. He pressed the button. Nothing happened. He did it again, and again and again. He was incandescent with rage. He cursed, screamed and kept trying. Finally, Fredericks reached over his shoulder, removed the small box, and threw it into the sea.

'Stop it, Aziz. It's over. The bomb didn't go off. Now we have to get away from here as fast as possible. Head east. We've a long way to go if we're to escape.'

'The British . . . the British. Where did they come from so fast? It isn't possible. They should never have got here until tomorrow. I had it all planned. They will pay for this. I will blow ten, twenty, aeroplanes from the sky. I will teach them to thwart me.'

By now the sea was picking up to a state four or five, with waves seven or eight feet high. It was uncomfortable astride the submersible and sea sickness threatened. As they dived beneath the surface, less than a hundred yards away Hunter and Hughes appeared, trying to pick up their trail. It was impossible. They had been lucky earlier on, aided by the angle of the sun and the waves. Now, the sea was so cluttered and chaotic, there was nothing to find.

They made ever increasing circles, searching desperately for Habib, but to no avail. Less than an hour later, they dived to the relative calm beneath the waves and returned to the island.

Earlier, Major Carter had radioed for helicopters, and half a dozen Sea Kings were already on their way – ETA, forty-five minutes.

After checking that there were no unexpected surprises left on the ship, the VIPs returned to the relative comfort and warmth of the saloon. Clements had already collected the bodies of the terrorists and dropped them unceremoniously into the hold that had been the former captives' prison.

When told what had happened to the Russian banker, he had also arranged for a diver to recover the body. It was now wrapped in a piece of tarpaulin, on the island, alongside the ship, ready to be airlifted off.

There wasn't much chatter. The aftermath of the danger and the adrenaline rush which had sustained them, left them drained.

Soon it was time to leave the ship to meet the helicopters. After many expressions of thanks and good will they trooped ashore to begin their journey back to civilisation via Machrihanish.

In the meantime, Hunter had made his report to Macnair. Already, a huge manhunt was being organised. After discussing the various possibilities with the General, and getting detailed information about the submersible from McDonald and Stanton, Hunter had drawn the conclusion that Habib would head directly east for the Scottish mainland. It was also his opinion that an escape route had been planned and was now being implemented. Finding Habib was not going to be easy.

They collected their equipment and returned to the base on Sandray. There Carter gave them a hot meal while they waited for another helicopter to return and pick them up. Losing Habib was a blow but could not be helped. The whole operation was a success. The captives had been released unharmed and most of the terrorists were dead. Still, Hunter was dissatisfied.

He poured over a chart of the area whilst the remainder of the team struck camp. He was still working out times and distances when the first helicopter arrived to take them back to Machrihanish.

Aboard the helicopter he continued thinking. If he was Habib, where would he go? What would be his best escape route? The shortest distance to the mainland. Why? Battery power, speed under the water, range of the submersible. Would that be safe? Yes, because the ship and all its occupants would have been blown to kingdom come. So there would have been nobody looking, or more to the point, nobody caring. Escape would have been easy. And now? And now Habib had to stick with his plan. There was no other.

'Pilot, can you hear me?'

'Affirmative.'

'Can you patch me through to General Macnair?'

'Stand by.'

Two minutes later he was talking to the General. 'Sir, it's the only thing which makes sense. Habib will head straight for the mainland and that means transport to get away in. If you look at a map of the area his only chance is to get ashore between Ardnamurchan and Mallaig. For a lot of reasons I can eliminate various points along the coast which leaves me Loch nan Uamh, Loch Ailort and Loch Sunart. I want to land the team at the points I've suggested.'

'I see no reason why not. All right Nick, it's still your operation on the ground. The rescue was text book stuff but we only got the foot soldiers. We want Habib and we want him badly. What we don't want is him coming back for more. It might not be so easy next time.'

He split his team into four. Hunter landed at Glenuig and, on a rock overlooking the Sound of Arisaig, settled down to wait for Habib. By his calculations, it would take Habib at least another three, if not four hours to appear.

They waited until dusk. It was a long and frustrating day with no sight of their enemy.

Hunter had been right to a certain extent. He had made only one small error. Habib had gone to the Isle of Skye. To his own estate fronting onto Loch Harport.

They were forced to ditch the submersible in deep water a mile from shore when the batteries ran flat. It then took them an hour, swimming on the surface, to reach Talisker Bay.

They had taken their time once they had turned east after leaving the ship, keeping their speed down to three knots. It had taken them most of the day to get to Skye, by which time they were numb with cold, hungry and thirsty. But it meant that they did not approach the coast until dusk was falling and they were indistinguishable from the waves and rocks dotting the shore line. They landed on a sandy beach and crawled ashore, almost too exhausted to stand. After a few minutes' rest Fredericks grabbed Habib under his arm and pulled him to his feet.

'Come on, Aziz. We can't stay here. There's a car waiting for us at the distillery.' He was referring to the Talisker distillery, famous for its Talisker single malt whisky.

'Just give me a few minutes to collect my strength. My legs are like rubber.' After a short while, he rolled over and pushed himself to his knees and then, with Fredericks' help, to his feet. Like old men, they helped each other along the track, careful not to be seen nor to make too much noise.

It was fully dark when they got to the white building of the distillery. As usual there were flood lights on, lighting up the whole area. However, a short distance away they found a Range Rover waiting for them, the keys left on the front nearside tyre. Quickly they stripped out of their diving suits and climbed into the clothes which had been left for them. On the back seat was a cardboard case containing a dozen Talisker malt whiskies, eight, twelve and twenty years old. In a special box was the piece de resistance: a fifty-year-old Talisker, single malt, which cost more than all the other bottles put together. If they were stopped, their trip to the distillery was the reason why they were on that road at that time. Nobody did stop them and within half an hour they were at the estate. The Laird of Arnaval was home.

Earlier that day orders had gone out recalling the money which had been wired initially to a bank in the Cayman Islands and then on to Istanbul. From there, it would have gone to Monaco where it would have been dispersed to ten different banks throughout the world. Habib had almost received one hundred million dollars in ransom money, but thanks to the rescue of the prisoners it was already being recalled by the families and governments who had paid. The announcement of the rescue had already stabilised the financial markets around the world. Fickle as they were, the markets had returned to the positions they had been in prior to the incident starting. The Iranians had been too greedy and had not closed out their positions. Not only did they not make a profit but the reversal was so sudden and extreme that they were now hitting losses. Frantically the Iranians instructed their brokers and bankers to get out of their positions. By the time they did the Iranians had gone from a paper profit of nearly ten billion pounds sterling to losses of five hundred million. Habib would not be receiving the one hundred million dollars due to him from the Iranians.

The Prime Minister had announced to the world that the hostages had been freed and that the operation had been a resounding success. He took the opportunity to further declare that the multi-national force he had been instrumental in setting up was a success and it was the intention of Her Majesty's Government to ensure its continuation. Funding and manning would be requested from member states in the near future. Unfortunately, he also took the opportunity of announcing the name of the man who was now recognised as the most wanted terrorist in the world, Aziz Habib. The second most wanted was Derek Fredericks, his long-time colleague and aide.

The General was beside himself with rage. 'I wanted to keep it quiet. To give us time to track Habib down before he knew we were on to him. Why,' he asked rhetorically, 'do politicians have such big mouths?'

'You've got it wrong, General,' said Sarah Fleeting, mischievously. 'It's because they've got big mouths that they're politicians.'

Macnair smiled in spite of himself, 'True, very true.' His temper was back under control and he was thinking furiously. 'Have we any further information about him?'

'I've contacted everyone I know,' said Sarah. 'Believe me, all the stops have been pulled out. The co-operation we've received has been wonderful. Every scrap of fact and fiction, and there's a lot more of the latter, has come in.'

'Is it of any use?'

'If you mean does it tell us where he is in Scotland

then I'm afraid the answer is no. I've unearthed some information about his financial situation but nothing that's of much use. I've traced three dummy companies in Bermuda and two in Gibraltar. They consist of nothing but cash and investments and not a great deal of that either.'

'When you say not a great deal, how much do you mean?' Macnair was pouring himself yet another cup of coffee, vowing to reduce his caffeine intake once this operation was finally over. He waved it at Sarah who nodded. If he drank as much coffee as she did he'd have the shakes.

'About a million in each.'

'A million? In each?' Macnair almost choked. It sounded like a lot of money to him. But then, like the majority of career officers, he knew little about money and cared even less, as long as he had enough for his modest needs. Being a widower with two grown up children left him more than adequately provided for. 'Dollars?' After all, if it was Polish Zloties it wouldn't be worth a damn.

'Pounds sterling,' was the reply, which somehow did not surprise him that much.

'Do you remember I mentioned a Turkish security officer named Zim Albatha? He sent me what I can only describe as an enigmatic message?'

He nodded. 'Something about a package that's on it's way?'

'Yes. Zim and I have been in contact on various issues over the years. He's been very helpful, especially if you consider that Turkey is a pro-Western, reasonably democratic country which probably has a better chance of understanding the Middle East than we do.'

'Seeing as how Islam is the religion of ninety-eight

percent of the population and they have their own Kurdish problem it's hardly surprising.'

'Precisely. Well, Zim had a sister . . .'

'Had?'

'General, I'd tell this story a lot quicker if you let me get on with it,' Sarah said without rancour.

'Point taken. Please proceed,' he replied graciously.

'Zim's sister was an air hostess onboard Sabena flight 101.'

'I remember it well,' said Macnair.

'Zim helped to investigate the atrocity and according to him it was carried out by a young terrorist named Habib. It was the first time that the name showed up. According to Zim, he did it for a fat fee from Saddam.'

Macnair settled himself at his desk, his coffee forgotten, getting cold in his hand.

'Since then, Zim has been keeping everything he could find about Habib. A lot of what I have on Habib has come from him and, of course, I send him everything I get from other sources.'

'So what's this mysterious package you were on about?'

'I've no idea. I got the call this morning. Zim just said that a package was on its way and would be here about lunch time. Which it nearly is. I do know that he doesn't trust telephones, E-mail or any other message sending format including the post.'

'So how have you two kept in touch?' Isobel asked, absorbed by the story.

'Zim has his own code which he uses. I know it sounds melodramatic but that's the way he is.'

'His own code? That would take a code cracker with

a computer about three minutes to break,' said Macnair, scornfully.

'You'd have to know what language it was in first,' Sarah replied with a smile.

'What language it was in? It would have to be English or Turkish and I don't suppose you speak Turkish,' said Macnair, 'so I guess English.'

Isobel's smile had a hint of superiority about it. 'How clever,' she exclaimed. 'A code and a foreign language. I take it you use everything except Mandarin?'

Sarah nodded. 'Even Latin,' she replied.

'How in the world can you do that . . . Don't tell me . . . Computers.'

'Correct, General. I get the information in Zim's code and after inputting it, knowing the language it's in, the computer deciphers and translates all in one.'

'It seems a bit far fetched . . . a bit footery, as they say in Scotland, to be worth the bother.'

'There's no doubt that Zim is a bit paranoid but there have been at least two attempts on his life to my certain knowledge in the past six years. He believes the Iraquis have been behind both, but he's not sure.'

'Interesting. I look forward to receiving the package. Now, I had better begin to compose my report to Downing Street. The modern military is run on paperwork which is its biggest failing.'

Less than twenty minutes later his phone rang.

'General Macnair, please.'

'Speaking.'

'Sir, this is the main gate. I have a Turkish gentleman here by the name of Mr. Albatha who says he wants to see you.'

'What? Right. Excellent. I'll be along right away.' He

hung up and reached for his beret. 'Well, well, well. That's a turn up for the books. Or should I say Sarah, you're package has turned up?'

Sarah looked up from her computer.

'Yes, in the form of Mr. Zim Albatha himself.'

With that surprise announcement he left the room, jumped into his car and drove to the main gate to greet the unexpected arrival.

Macnair and Albatha instinctively liked each other. After shaking hands, Macnair signed the visitors book at the gate and drove back with his guest. Albatha still moved stiffly, a legacy of the gun wound he'd received at the hands of Habib, but he was healing fast.

In spite of the length of time that they had been corresponding Sarah and Albatha had never met, though they felt they had known one another for years, so it was a strange but friendly meeting.

Macnair got straight down to business. 'What have you got that's so important you travel all this way?'

'I should explain that I am on sick leave,' his English was precise, but spoken with a thick accent. 'So I have come here to, how do you say? Recuperate. However, I really came to bring you this.' He opened a large envelope he had been gripping in his hand and took out a ledger. 'In here are exact copies of everything that I have put together about Habib over the years. I mean,' he corrected himself, 'everything to do with his finances. It has always been my belief that money leaves a trail from its source to its end user. It is the tracking, the following of the money trail that is difficult. I have never managed to follow this trail to its end because it is so muddied; so difficult to follow. It occurred to me when I was lying in the hospital that perhaps it was time

355

for me to show this to Sarah and her wonderful computer to see what they could make of it.'

He handed her the loose-leafed ledger. 'It is in my code and in Turkish,' he explained.

Sarah nodded and set up her computer scanner. She worked quickly and very soon the pages were being scanned into the machine. When she had finished, she gave it certain instructions and within seconds the information appeared on the screen in English. After running through every page, satisfied that it was all there, she printed out a copy of the document. It was fifty pages thick and crammed with information. As Albatha said, some of it useful, a lot of it useless, but hopefully, in it, the lead they were looking for.

By the time they finished for the night they still had not found what they were after. There were dummy corporations, dummy bank accounts, real accounts with significant sums of money in them and companies which actually existed. Habib could have been a wealthy and legitimate businessman if he had wanted. He owned a fruit canning factory in Cyprus, a shoe manufacturer in Thailand and a vineyard in South Africa. He had interests, albeit significant minority interests, in goldmines, a diamond mine, a South Korean micro-chip manufacturer and an Argentinian ranch. They had found out that much and were not even half way through all that Albatha had collected. Isobel had cross-referenced the information using data held on world-wide stock markets and companies and had estimated that they had found around forty million dollars' worth of Habib's assets. Albatha had known about them all except the ranch. The computer had tracked that down through six dummy corporations.

They would continue the following morning. At 21.00 Macnair insisted on calling a halt and taking them out for a meal and a drink. They deserved it after what they had achieved during the past week.

Hunter called off the stakeouts at midnight. Wherever he was, Habib was not coming ashore on that stretch of Scotland. He had kept in touch with Macnair who had been able to confirm that the satellites had picked up no ships or even small boats in the area.

Habib had gone to ground well and truly. Dispirited, they crawled into their sleeping bags and got some rest. Dawn found Hunter already up and looking at his charts. He remeasured the distances and recalculated the range that Habib could have travelled. The only place possible was the Isle of Skye. Mentally paraphrasing Sherlock Holmes, he murmured to himself, 'When all factors have been eliminated then the improbable becomes possible.'

After an early breakfast Hunter telephoned Jim Carter, getting him out of his bed at Machrihanish. Two hours later, two helicopters appeared, each with a civilian coloured Land Rover slung under it.

Their equipment had been sorted out and most of it was sent back in the helicopters. Some weapons and diving gear were kept. A short while later Hunter drove away with Joshua Clements and Sam McReady in one vehicle and David Hughes, Jan Badonovitch and Pierre Flambert in the other. The remainder of the team he sent back to the airbase. He had no plan other than to drive to Skye and act the part of visitors on a fishing and shooting trip. He intended to search the island in an attempt to find Habib. He knew there was little chance of doing so but with a little luck he might find something.

It was a long detour to get to Skye. There being no coast road, they drove to Fort William and then north to Spean Bridge. From there they followed alongside Loch Lochy as far as Invergarry before turning north west. They were now on the A87 which led them directly to what had been the ferry crossing of Kyle of Lochalsh. Now there was a bridge to Skye, a controversial and expensive crossing, hated by the local inhabitants.

During the drive the three men had discussed the merits of heading for Skye but in the absence of anything else could think of no reason why they should not. Perhaps Habib had never come this way in the first place. Perhaps he had gone out to sea and been picked up in spite of what the satellites told them. There were so many "what ifs", that they kept going round in circles.

Hunter's satellite phone rang, 'Hunter.'

'Nick, we've got him,' said Macnair.

'How?'

'We've been digging into his financial affairs which, I can tell you, have more blind alleys and dead ends than Hampton Court Maze. An offshore company bought an estate on Skye about three years ago. We've traced that company, through various holding companies, back to Habib. There's no doubt it's his and, I'd put my money on it, that's where he's gone to earth.'

'I would too. It's the most reasonable explanation of where he could be. Have you got any details?'

'Not yet. We cracked this about twenty minutes ago and we've been double checking, just to make sure. I've been onto the police in Edinburgh. Someone is going round now to see if there are any plans or information held in the Land Registry Office. There should be something, especially as the place changed hands only a few years ago. Hopefully, even a map.'

'That makes sense, General. What about some of our lot on the island, sealing exits, the bridge, the ferry.'

'I'm sorting a few things out now. We'll get a heavy team in mufti,' he used the old-fashioned Indian army word for plain clothes or out of uniform, 'and have them around Lochalsh and scattered across the island.'

'I should think he's got a way out. A boat hidden away somewhere. Or the submersible ready to go again if he needs it. A fox in its lair has more than one exit and I would expect him to do the same.'

'I concur. So we'll tread softly, very softly. I want this man stopped. The more I've learnt about him the more I'm sure that if we don't get him he'll create further havoc and cause a lot of unnecessary deaths and suffering. This is a seriously evil man.'

'Right, sir. I think it would be prudent if we get rid of the Rovers and hire something more suitable for the fishing, hunting types we so obviously are. I'll see the local police. How much should I tell them?'

'Nothing. Don't speak to them. We can't be sure who they'll speak to and inadvertently blab something. Habib will have spread a great deal of largesse over the island I should think, just in case.'

'You're right.' Hunter thought for a moment. 'I'm going to turn round and go back to Fort William. I'll hire cars there. I noticed there's also a tourist information centre on the front. We'll go there and book accommodation on Skye. I'll make up some story if I need to.'

'By the time you've done all that, I should be in a position to fax you more details about the estate. How are you for gear?'

'No problem. I think the best description is "armed to the teeth". We've got some PE but not a lot. I take it any teams you send up will be on the phone?'

'Affirmative. Thank God for satellite communications. It's about as secure as you can get.'

With that he broke the connection.

By the time Hunter and his team had returned to Fort William, finished their preparations and were finally approaching Skye, it was early evening. This time they drove Range Rovers, were dressed as they thought city slickers in the country would dress, and had arranged rooms at an hotel, less than a mile from where Habib had his estate.

The hotel was a fine, old-fashioned country mansion, out in the wilds. Whilst standing at the reception desk, filling in the registration card Hunter realised that he was being addressed. 'I thought it was you, Lieutenant Commander Hunter.'

He turned to face a very attractive female, smiling at him. He wasn't feigning the perplexed look he gave her.

'You don't remember me, do you, Lieutenant Commander? Doreen Jessop. You saved my daughter's life at Poole. *The Overdraft.*'

Then he placed her. 'You're husband's name is Arthur,' he managed.

'Yes, but luckily he isn't here.' She tucked her arm possessively into his. 'Let's go to the bar.'

18

The bar was old, scarred and long. There were over a hundred bottles of whiskies lined up on the shelves, and keg fizzy beer on the pumps. The wines on offer left much to be desired but those who really wanted a bottle could order one. This was whisky country, and fine whisky country at that.

Spoilt for choice, Hunter picked a local, peaty tasting Laphroaig, whilst Doreen had a Grouse with lemonade. When he had his drink, Hunter carefully added a few drops of water to the malt.

'Isn't that sacrilege? To add water to a fine whisky?'

He grinned. 'Nope. It brings out the flavour. Just a smidgen of water releases the trapped bouquet.'

They settled in big easy chairs in front of a roaring log fire. 'Where did you hear that from? According to Arthur a malt whisky should only be drunk with one thing.'

'What's that?' Hunter fell for it.

'Another malt.'

They both laughed, at ease in each other's company.

'Speaking of Arthur, where is he?'

'Not here,' Doreen smiled impishly back at him in a manner which made his heart race a little faster.

'Self evidently. But I didn't ask where he wasn't,' he smiled, to take any sting out of his words, 'but where he is.'

'London. We came here to get away; arrived two days ago but he's been called back. The story of my life,' she said, with a certain degree of bitterness. 'Anyway, that doesn't explain how you know about whisky.'

Hunter grinned. 'In ten years in the navy, I've been on at least half a dozen distillery runs.'

'Distillery runs?'

'Sure. Everywhere the Royal Navy goes we get to go on goodwill visits. If there's a brewery or distillery in say, fifty miles, we get to visit. As a junior officer, I was inevitably detailed to go with the lads to keep an eye on them. So I picked up a lot, mainly about drinking the stuff, I must admit. I'll tell you a true story, shall I?'

She nodded and smiled over the rim of her glass, making and holding eye contact.

'This wasn't a distillery run but a trip to a brewery in Liverpool. When we got there, the person who knew all about the process and could show us around was off ill. Instead, a young secretary was detailed to accompany us and tell us all about the process. I kid you not.' Hunter grinned at the recollection. 'After about three minutes, it became obvious that she knew absolutely nothing about the process of making beer. Do you know what happened?'

Doreen shook her head, intrigued.

'One of our older able seamen, by the name of Hunter, my namesake, began to correct her, whenever she made a mistake. Anyway, after a few minutes he ended up conducting the tour and telling us all about it. It was hilarious. When we got to the hospitality bar at the end we were well feted with beer as a result. But anyway, it means I know how to drink whisky.' He raised his glass in a salute to her.

She raised hers back. At that moment they both knew what the result would be for the night. There was no hurry, they would take their time to get to know each other.

Hunter stretched his long legs out in front of the fire and forgot for a while why he was there. It was easy to do so in her company. They each asked questions of the other's lives, more than a little interested. Hunter asked her at what age she had been married. What was the age of her daughter? A few minutes later he asked her how long had she been married before Lucy was born.

Doreen smiled at him, having asked her own questions as well. 'That makes me three years older than you.'

Hunter started to laugh so hard that he had to put down his glass in case he spilt some of the fine, old drink. 'Was I that obvious?' he managed at length.

'Was I?'

'Yes.' Which resulted in more, nonsensical laughter.

'So what really brings you here and why have you been abandoned?'

'Well, after what happened at Poole I was all for leaving the bastard. Unfortunately, he persuaded me to come away with him. He brought the boat up to Troon in Ayrshire and I flew to Glasgow to meet him. That was eight days ago. We came on here, he got a phone call and here I am. He said he'd be back in two or three days and suggested I wait for him to return. That was yesterday. I had a phone call an hour ago and he said he'd be away a bit longer than planned but to expect him by Wednesday.'

'Em, a daft question I know, but why is he needed

on a Saturday? After all, I thought he was a solicitor or something.'

'Well remembered. Correct, he does solicit for a living.'

'I've heard it before,' Hunter said. 'The only difference between him and a prostitute is that a solicitor isn't as honest.'

'Well, in this case it's true. He was needed by his girl friend who happens to be fifteen years younger and pregnant.'

Hunter kept a straight face. 'Are you sure?'

'Am I sure of what?' There was more than a trace of bitterness in Doreen's voice. 'The girl friend I've known about for months – the last in a long line. The pregnancy is new. I overheard him on the telephone.' Suddenly, she chuckled, 'I was as mad as hell at first but not now. Look at the outcome.'

Hunter raised an eyebrow, somehow keeping the smile off his face. 'Is there an outcome?'

He left her room as dawn was breaking, aware that he had work to do. What he really wanted was to stay with her, send out for the Sunday papers and have a long, languid breakfast in bed. Unfortunately, it was not to be.

In the dining room, he had settled down with a glass of orange juice and was waiting to be served a full cooked breakfast when the others in the team wandered in. There was the usual ribald commentary which quickly died away when there was no response.

'When you've finished breakfast,' said Hunter, 'I'll tell you what's going on.'

A Scottish cooked breakfast consisted of bacon, fried eggs, mushrooms, a slice of black pudding, a thick slice of sausage and a potato scone which is cooked in fat. Although he was hungry, Hunter could not help reflecting on the mortality of the Scots due to coronary heart failure. However, he'd had a busy night and had worked up an appetite.

After the meal they congregated in his room. They knew where to go and information about Habib's estate was coming in all the time. Teams of police all over the country were rousting law abiding and peaceful citizens from their beds to get the information they wanted.

After buying the property Habib had begun to turn it into a fortress. In order to do so, he had to use different agencies with different skills. Unfortunately for Habib, when he bought the place, he had used a solicitor to carry out the conveyancing who had, inadvertently, named a certain architect's practice in a letter which was found in the title deeds.

The architect proved to be a reserve officer in the territorial army. He was more than willing to help in every way, including supplying to the police as much as he had in his records and as much as he could remember. Which was a lot. That had already enabled the police to find an electronics specialist who had worked on the estate and was very enlightening. All this activity had taken place during the night, as hundreds of men and women worked to combat Habib. Unbeknownst to him, Habib had achieved the almost impossible; he had made the British establishment angry!

'Okay, this is a plan of the estate.' Hunter laid out the faxed papers on his bed while the others crowded around. He ran a pencil around the perimeter. 'It extends to over thirty thousand acres and is mainly forest, hills and this old quarry. There are deer, sheep and highland cattle. This old distillery, here,' he pointed, 'is abandoned but is being restored. The locals think he's a cross between Santa Claus and Jesus Christ for all the good he's done in this area. The General said that he encountered real opposition when he asked questions about Habib.'

'I hope nothing gets back to Habib to alert him,' said McReady.

Hunter grinned. 'Interesting you should say that because I said exactly the same thing.'

'And?' asked Clements.

'And the General had a superintendent of police lifted and taken south to help with their enquiries. Nothing sinister. Just to stop him communicating inadvertently or deliberately with Habib. Interesting power that, don't you think?'

They nodded, impressed in spite of themselves.

'There's one thing I don't get,' said Clements, stroking his chin pensively.

'Only one, Josh?' kidded McReady. 'And what's that?'

'If we know he's there, why don't we knock on the door and arrest him?'

'Actually, there are a host of reasons. The first is, we don't know he is there, officially. If he is, he's keeping a very low profile. Secondly, say we did knock on the door and arrest him, then what? What proof do we have that this man did what we know he did?'

'Witnesses. The prisoners saw his face. After all, as he'd intended killing them, why should he have kept himself hidden from them?'

Hunter shrugged. 'Somebody who looked like him? His staff and a few locals in his pocket swear he was on the estate the whole time? What then? A half-decent barrister would make mincemeat of the prosecution. And anyway, you're forgetting something.'

'What's that, Nick?' asked Pierre Flambert.

'There's not going to be a trial.'

The team about him nodded.

Hunter continued. 'In that way, there's little expense, no messing around with juries and wasting time, no appeals to the Court of Justice in the Hague because we know what that means. Then no more hijacks and other terrorists demanding Habib's release. Nope,' he shook his head. 'All in all, we take him out and hopefully it's finished.'

All morning, information came in on the satellite fax and telephone. The detail was astonishing and all about the property and surrounding grounds. Habib had used eight different agencies to build protection around the estate.

Josh Clements summed it up. 'Christ, Fort Knox would be easier to get into.'

'Any thoughts?' asked Hunter.

McReady said, 'Boss, if we went up to this point here,' he indicated on the Ordnance Survey map of the area, 'we could set up a parabola listening device. The new digital one can be beamed at a hundred locations simultaneously so we can cover all the windows on this side.'

Hunter nodded. 'Makes sense. Especially as the kitchen, lounge and dining room are on that side of the house. We might learn something of use. Remember though, the most important thing is not to be seen.'

'All well and good,' said Clements with his laconic, Texan drawl, 'but that doesn't get us any nearer the place.'

Hunter picked up a pencil and pointed at the map.

367

'According to all the information we've received, the defences in place are as follows. There's a high wire fence, not electrified but with a highly sophisticated sensing arrangement. If anyone touches it, not only does the alarm go off here, in the guardroom,' he pointed to a substantial building about fifty yards from the main house, which had once been stables for a dozen horses, 'but also they can pin-point the location and automatically the cameras zoom in on the spot. Cameras are every thirty yards and there are eight around the house itself.' Again, he pointed to each one on the house. 'On this side of the fence there are trembler sensors buried throughout the grounds with no way of knowing where. Anybody walking through will be found immediately. The glass in the windows is about the best money can buy. No bullet and precious few other things will penetrate it, so a sniper shot is no good. All windows and doors are alarmed, and according to this,' he picked up a sheet of paper and waved it, 'possibly wired with a lethal dose of electricity as well. That's supposition by the contractor who put in the burglar alarm but I would guess it's true.' The others nodded their agreement.

'What's left?' asked McReady.

'What's left is the coast.' Hunter pulled out a large scale Admiralty chart and laid it out. 'Again, from the information we've got, there are similar sensors all over here, but not on the short strip of beach. However, there are transponders all along here and possibly criss-crossing inland as well.'

'What about a frontal attack?' asked Flambert.

'It would be suicidal. I suspect he's got the place protected well enough to keep an army at bay,' said Hunter.

368

'For what purpose?' Flambert asked. 'It doesn't make sense. Suppose what you say is true. He'd be killed or taken for sure, because nobody can hold out forever. Then what? He'd be in prison until he rotted.'

'Pierre,' said Hunter, 'if you were a woman and were a lot more beautiful I could kiss you. Think about it. You're right. So what is all this about?'

'All what?' asked McReady, perplexed.

'All this,' Hunter waved his hand at the maps, charts and information. 'To give him time. Habib isn't the suicidal, martyr type. He needs time to escape. Ergo, he has a way out.'

'Makes sense,' said Clements. 'How, where and what?'

Hunter shrugged. 'We need more information. In the meantime, let's take a very, very careful look around.'

'You know, looking at the map, I would have thought the only safe way in and out for Habib was by sea,' said McReady.

'What about a tunnel?' asked Hunter.

'To where Boss? Even if he got a few hundred yards he'd still have to escape the island. My bet is he can get to the sea and probably use his submersible to get away. If he's as canny as he's made out to be then a seaplane picks him up and he's away. That's what I'd do.'

'It makes sense. But there doesn't appear to be anywhere for him to escape from undetected. Look at this coastline. There's nothing, no river, no caves marked.'

'That doesn't mean to say that there are none,' replied Clements.

'What about a helicopter?' asked McReady.

'No good,' said Hunter. 'It wouldn't get a hundred feet before it was shot down. No, the way out has to be subterranean or subsea, but in which direction and

369

what does he do afterwards? Thinking about it I suspect that Sam's right. It's to seaward and then a plane or fast boat. I suspect he's making the necessary arrangements even now. So we don't have a lot of time to get him.'

'There is a possible way in,' said Flambert, thoughtfully.

'Let's hear it, Pierre,' said Clements.

'Para-sail onto this flat roof here,' he pointed. 'We need to take a closer look at the cameras and where they're pointing. If this area is not covered then I could land there easily.'

'Without detection?' asked Hunter, sceptically.

Flambert shrugged. 'Probably. We have a new type of chute. The aerosail senses when a landing is about to be made and an ingenious row of small canisters sewn into the fabric lets helium into the sail, almost like a flat balloon. It's like an airbrake and stops you dead about three centimetres off the ground, or in this case the roof. You then land more gently than a feather.'

'Have you used it?' asked Hunter.

'Sure, lots of times. It works really well. It was developed by us a few years ago although we haven't used it on an operation yet.'

'Let me tell the General and see if he can get us a couple. Just in case.'

Hunter phoned Macnair, told him of their thoughts so far and requested the aerosails from the French. Macnair promised to get onto it and would call him back only if he had a problem. If not, they would be on the island within twelve hours.

'Okay, let's go for a walk. Keep things low key and quiet. I understand that there are at least half a dozen of Habib's own men on the estate and there are probably

other workers too. We need to know as much as we can.'
While he was speaking, Hunter was putting the maps and
papers away.

Habib was in the room he called the library. Three of
the walls were covered with books, one wall of which
was nothing but hard-core pornography and blue-movie
videos. The room itself was large, over ten metres wide
and fifteen metres long. It was the height of two men and
so big that even with central heating it was difficult to
keep warm in the winter. A huge roaring fire dominated
the centre of one wall, whilst opposite was a row of
windows stretching from waist height to the ceiling.
He was standing at one of the windows, looking out,
pondering his next move.

Everything was in place. The plane was ready to pick
them up, the submersible's batteries were fully charged.
The problem was, did he need to go? There had been a
great deal of fuss in the news about the event and the
rescue and the fact that their names were known was
a blow but not disastrous. He had achieved one of his
objectives. He was now the most famous terrorist ever.
He had also begun to reinvest his cash. His profits were
in the order of hundreds of millions of pounds. He still
had to contact Iran to find out where his money was, but
that could wait.

How could the British possibly know that the eminent
and rich Italian gentleman who owned the estate was
him, Habib; that he was a freedom fighter for all the
oppressed peoples of the world? He grinned, wolfishly.
He'd be believing his own press next. After that fiasco
he now needed a major success. Fame needed to be
fuelled. He needed to apply his planning and resources

to an immediate, world numbing atrocity. He owed the West something spectacular. He'd show them. Ten, no twenty aircraft to be blown out of the skies at the same time – the ultimate crime. He would work it so that they would all blow up at or as near the same moment as possible. Hundreds of thousands, maybe millions, would be put off air travel for life. Chaos and financial problems would abound. Airlines would be bankrupted. Now, that appealed to his warped sense of humour.

Already messages had been sent, certain arrangements had been made. All that was needed was his presence in Cyprus to set the whole thing going. When should he go? That was the dilemma. If he waited a week before he left, the hue and cry may have died down. Not that he could not travel in and out of any country without alerting Customs and Immigration, it was just more expensive that way and although he spent lavishly, he hated what he considered to be waste.

As he stood there, his plans crystallised into certainties. He'd leave in one week's time. He would take out the twenty aircraft. He would get his one hundred million from Iran. He would retire.

Fredericks came in carrying coffee for them both. 'Well, Aziz, what have you decided?'

Habib turned with a smile on his face. 'I'll tell you, my friend.'

When he had finished Fredericks smiled and said, 'Excellent. That will make a lot of people take notice. Let's add some stupid request to the event afterwards.'

Habib grinned, sipped his coffee and thought for a few moments. 'How about the release of . . . of all Irish freedom fighters. Or . . . or we send another twenty planes to hell.'

Habib was up and pacing, unable to contain his glee. 'That'll cause the British serious problems. Were the explosions as a result of a request by the IRA? We announce responsibility for the events but blame the IRA as the paymasters. By Allah, think of the complete and utter chaos in Britain and Ireland. That will pay them back even further for interfering in my operation. Twenty-eight more deaths would have saved the lives of thousands as well as the trauma of the backlash against the IRA. Wonderful.' He rubbed his hands together, barely able to conceal his mounting excitement. 'I thought originally that we would stay here a week; instead we will leave on Friday. Excellent.'

The digital parabelum aerial picked up Habib's words loud and clear. It was relayed immediately to Hunter sitting in a parked Range Rover over three miles away. Though appalled at what he was hearing, Hunter was also elated. Got you, you evil bastard, he thought.

Hunter had a long and detailed conversation with Macnair. At the end of it, he made his way slowly back to the hotel. His mind was racing, his options limited.

He sat in his room eating a cheese sandwich and washing it down with a cup of coffee. Already the island was flooding with both special forces and Macnair's men. In twos and threes they were infiltrating the whole area. There would be no escape this time. Only Hunter knew better. As he read all that Macnair had faxed him about Habib and Fredericks, Hunter became convinced that the two men were not sitting in a trap; they were too canny, as the Scots said. There would be a way out, of that he was certain.

Sam McReady and Pierre Flambert joined him in the middle of the afternoon.

'I don't like it,' said Hunter. 'Habib will never allow himself to be caught like a rat in a trap. Ergo, he's got a way out. The problem is where and how?'

'Well, Boss,' said McReady, 'it's not in the air. It can't be. Anything flying can be shot down. Likewise, anything on the ground from a racing car to a bus can be stopped.'

Hunter nodded. 'My thinking exactly. Which means an underwater escape route. We've examined every chart and bit of information there is about the area and there is no way, from where he's holed up, that he can get to the sea and escape by sub. It's impossible.'

McReady nodded. 'Sure, because there's something missing.'

'What?'

'Boss, if I knew what it was, it wouldn't be missing, now would it?' he grinned.

'You're right. So, paraphrasing Sherlock Holmes again, when you've eliminated all other avenues, whatever is left, no matter how impossible, is the answer.'

'I don't think,' said McReady, pouring himself another coffee and wandering over to the window to look out at the stark countryside, 'that he quite said that but I know what you mean. So what's left?'

'He has a way of getting to the sea which we don't know about.' Hunter pulled open the Admiralty chart and the Ordnance Survey map of the area and compared them.' He tensed. He took a pair of dividers and measured distances. He looked at the chart again and sat back, a puzzled frown on his face which slowly cleared. 'I know how he can do it,' he announced.

Flambert and McReady looked at him with interest. 'It's simple. At least, I know how, but I don't know where.' He picked up a paperback book about the history of the island and turned to the chapter about the estate which Habib now owned. 'It says here that in 1847 a distillery was opened to produce a malt whisky which was sold to the blending barons of Glasgow. They used the peaty flavour to enhance a poor grain whisky made in Fife. It made a few people very wealthy, amongst them, the local estate owner named the Laird of Arnaval.'

'So?'

'So, Sam, look at this.' He showed them the book. 'You can see from this map that the house is here, the hills are here, and here's the distillery,' he pointed. 'The distance to the distillery from the house, in a straight line, is less than five hundred metres. But listen to what it says here.' Hunter read from the book. 'The distillery took advantage of the natural fast running and deep burn which entered the northern end of the valley, ran for half a mile and then disappeared into the ground. The site of the distillery was established at the spot where the burn disappeared. However, in order to gain access from the house, it was necessary for the Laird to take a long detour of over five miles on rough terrain, which did not suit him. Instead, soon after the distillery was in operation, he caused to be built a tunnel, which connected from the cellars of the house with a private room in the distillery. It was said at the time that coal miners from Ayrshire were brought in to do the work for a guinea a week and all the whisky they could drink. Unfortunately, after a number of accidents and deaths, the whisky allowance was stopped. After the death of the Laird, the cost of ensuring the tunnel was safe became prohibitive and it was bricked up and abandoned.

It has become lost in the annals of time.' Hunter looked up. 'I'll bet anything you like that Habib has found the tunnel and made it his escape route.'

'I wouldn't take the bet, Nick,' said Flambert. 'But what does he do then? He cannot hide in a tunnel forever.'

'No, but he could get into the burn and escape down to the sea.'

'What is a burn?' asked the Frenchman.

'A stream.' Seeing the perplexed look on Flambert's face he added, 'A small river. It's vital in the production of whisky. A stream of pure water which, around here, passes through peat to give the water and the whisky its great, local flavour. What if Habib's able to get to the burn and follow it to the sea?'

McReady nodded, a smile on his face. 'It makes sense to me, Boss. Mind you,' he looked at the map, measuring distances with his eyes, 'it's a good mile from the distillery to the coast. It would be a hell of a journey.'

Hunter stood up to stretch and pace the room. 'I didn't say it was easy, only that it was possible. The only problem is, we don't want to tip our hand to Habib as he could easily have the old distillery bugged and watched.' A plan was forming in Hunter's mind even as he spoke. He stopped at the window and stared out, not seeing the scenery, absorbed in his thoughts.

'Okay, I have it. Pierre, get on to Jim and arrange to have the sledges brought up here – nice and quiet. Tell him to use civilian trucks with one of our lads driving. Also tell him that I want one of the new bathyscopes as soon as possible. That's needed urgently. In the meantime, I'm going to see a lady about a boat ride.'

He left the room to look for Doreen, whom he found sitting in the large, comfortable lounge, reading a novel. She looked up when he entered.

'Nick, what a pleasant surprise. I thought you would be up to your thighs in water at this time casting your rod or whatever it is you do.'

Hunter had told her that he and the others were there to do some salmon fishing, enjoying the peace and quiet of Skye.

'I have been,' he lied, with a disarming smile, 'but after three fruitless hours I've given up for the day. Actually, I've come to ask you a favour.'

She looked at her watch and sighed. 'I suppose you can use my body, even if it is only the middle of the afternoon. Only,' she paused and looked at him, a twinkle in her eyes, a smile on her face, 'I insist on a bottle of champagne. The house bottle will do.' She reached out and took his hand.

Hunter smiled back. 'It's not that. I've actually come to ask if I can borrow *The Overdraft* for a few hours tomorrow. I want to take a look around the coast. Just for a few hours,' he added hastily, as she withdrew her hand.

'I'm not sure about that.' She had turned serious and then said, 'What the . . . You can on two conditions . . . No, three.'

'What are they?'

'You tell me what's going on, I go with you, and I get the use of your body.'

The room they were in was large, well lit by French windows reaching almost to the ceiling, with a big roaring log fire in front of which they were sitting. Around the room there were a dozen pastel covered easy chairs, each with an occasional table alongside.

Two walls were lined with books, some old classics and some modern paperbacks. On one wall, glassy-eyed, stuffed heads of deer stared down on them and Hunter stared back, collecting his thoughts.

'It's no good squirming like that, my lad. It's obvious you aren't here for the fishing, so you must be up to something.'

'Like what?' he asked, playing for time.

'Like I don't know what, but something. If you tell me, I promise not to tell anyone and you can have the boat.'

'What makes you think I'm up to something?'

Doreen sighed, exasperatedly. 'Of course something's up. Don't you think I haven't noticed what's going on?'

'What do you mean?'

'Nick, the island is crawling with small groups of men. I've seen them. You know some of the others who are here although you pretend not to. But you can't help passing a glance, making a gesture. It wouldn't be normal if you could. Forget the rubbish you read in novels and see in films. In real life it's not like that.'

Hunter was taken aback by her astuteness but decided to continue denying it. 'I don't know that you're talking about. I guess the island is pretty popular at this time of year for salmon fishing. Weather's improving and the midges aren't out yet.'

Doreen shook her head. 'Nick, I have never seen so many young, fit and . . . and so totally aware men in my life. It's uncanny. They miss nothing. They're alert, drink little and talk in whispers. It's not normal. Fishermen are usually middle aged, running to seed, drink too much and boast too loudly.'

Hunter had found Doreen to be an intelligent, amusing and entertaining companion. To that he could now add highly observant as well. But could he trust her to keep quiet? That was the sixty-four thousand dollar question.

'Doreen, do you know what the Official Secrets Act is?'

'Of course I do. I signed it when I joined the Inland Revenue back in 1982.'

'The Inland Revenue?'

'Certainly. All members of the Revenue sign the damn thing. Believe it or not it's the same form as used by all of government. It's part of the secret society we live in. Why?'

'That makes it easier, I suppose. What I'm about to tell you comes under the Act.'

'Oh, goody,' Doreen squirmed happily in her chair, shucked off her shoes and tucked her legs into the chair as only a woman can. 'I love secrets.'

Hunter told her an abridged version of the events that had led him to being on Skye. He kept his voice low, continually looking around the room in case anybody entered without them noticing.

'So this man you're after is here on Skye?'

'Yes. There's no doubt.'

'What are you going to do? Arrest him?'

Hunter did not reply, only looked at her for a few seconds.

'Oh . . . Oh, I see.' Doreen put her hand to her mouth for a moment, realising the implications of the silence. 'Yes, that makes sense. No costly trial, no hostages to future terrorism. I must say, I do approve.'

'You do?' Hunter was surprised.

'Of course. This man is a mad dog and should be put down. Don't look so surprised, Nick. Believe me, women are more deadly than men in things like this. I can't stand

Lord Longford and the rest of the bleeding hearts. They have caused more damage to Western society under the heading of civil liberties and prisoners' rights than any other single thing that I can think of. What about victims' rights? What about the rights of the rest of society which are infringed for the sake of the minority? Did you know that since the death penalty was abolished convicted murderers have been let out of prison and forty-four of them have murdered again?' She was off on her hobby horse, which Nick was happy to ride along with. This was a side of Doreen he hadn't seen and he enjoyed the intelligent debate, although there was little argument.

An hour later Hunter ordered tea and scones to be served before he left the hotel. Dusk was falling, a brisk wind was blowing and there was a hint of rain in the air. Once out of sight of the building and into the trees, he took his headset from his pocket and put it on. The circuits were silent. He announced he was on the air and asked for reports. All was quiet so far. Men had been seen wandering with aimless purpose near the house, obviously guards and obviously not Scottish or even British. Hunter was aware that when Habib had bought the estate the locals had thought that there would be jobs created, helping to run the neglected property, but Habib had brought in his own labour. Little was known about them and they seldom, if ever, appeared locally, except when crossing to leave Skye. It had been put about that there were plans to reopen the distillery but in the three years Habib had been there nothing had come of it. The locals had learned quickly to ignore the comings and goings of Habib and his men, respecting their privacy as only a Highlander could.

Around the perimeter of the estate, men settled down to

keep watch. Cleverly hidden, well armed and in constant contact with each other, they were prepared for anything which Habib might try. A deadly force was poised at Habib, ready to strike.

By the time the Iranians could close off all their accounts they had lost nearly two billion dollars. Within two hours the Ayatollahs had passed out their orders. The cull had started. Responsibility for what happened was shifted from person to person. Each time another victim was summarily accused, found guilty and beheaded. By the time the madness ended ninety-eight people would die. Only three of them would know what it was all about. Habib's death warrant had also been signed.

19

'The Prime Minister would like to have an answer,' said Norheed, the Home Secretary, taking a biscuit from the plate in front of him and putting the whole of it into his mouth.

Macnair looked at him for a few seconds, marshalling his thoughts. How far could he trust these men? From what he knew about politicians, not too far at all. They were always trying to score political points. He did not want to risk any of them talking to friends, enemies or, worst of all, the media, before Hunter and his team had finished. If anything was said in the House of Commons, under Parliamentary privilege, before they got Habib, then they could lose him for a long time. And what he was planning to do in revenge for his failed attack brought a cold sweat to Macnair's brow.

'I've told you all I can at present,' he replied carefully, fingering his empty cup in front of him. 'We have Habib holed up in a remote corner of the Highlands. We are sure that he has a bolt hole and until we find it we don't wish to make a move.'

'How can you be sure?' asked the Prime Minister, leaning back in his chair, the onset of a headache nagging

382

at his temples. 'I mean, how can you be sure that he has a bolt hole?'

'We can't be sure, but from what we now know of the man it seems highly likely.'

Norwood was scornful. 'Highly likely?' he spoke, spraying crumbs of shortbread onto the table in front of him. He ignored them. 'Is that all you can say? That it's highly likely? Well, General, let me tell you that isn't enough, not by a long chalk. We are under a great deal of international pressure to get Habib and all we can do at present is deny we even know where he is. We have egg on our faces and we want results. Now.'

Macnair listened to the bluster of the fat man sitting opposite him. Being a soldier he found it difficult to deal with the devious, duplicitous nature of politicians. So he thought before he made his reply, carefully choosing his words.

'Home Secretary, I have an excellent officer on the ground at the scene. We have Habib contained, he's not going anywhere. If we rush in and he escapes we'll have a lot more egg on our faces, as you put it, than if we do it my way. Now, if you would care to take responsibility for the operation then I am sure we can arrange that. Provided it's suitably documented, of course, and I shall order my men to do whatever you say.'

Macnair had picked on a politician's Achilles' heel. Responsibility in writing. Undeniable at the enquiry. Political suicide. The Home Secretary wasn't ready to commit such an act personally.

'I don't think that will be necessary,' came the stuffy reply. 'I am sure the officer knows what he is doing.'

'So do I. Thank you, Home Secretary.' Macnair kept

a straight face with difficulty. You pompous twit, he thought.

'What are they doing next?' asked the Prime Minister.

'If you mean the team on Skye, they are looking for the underground stream which they believe is Habib's escape route. If they don't find it by Thursday they are going in anyway.'

'We must hope that they find it,' said the Secretary of State for Defence. 'I take it that we shall keep a complete news blackout on proceedings?'

'God, yes,' said the General with vehemence. 'One whiff of anything and Habib will be away like a puff of smoke. We cannot afford to cock it up at this stage.'

'I agree,' said the PM, helping himself to a cup of cold coffee. 'However, we need to say something to our allies, so that we can keep them quiet. Make them think we are on top of the problem.'

'With all due respect, Prime Minister, say nothing. Not a word. Let them think we've cocked up. It'll only be for a few days and then you can make the announcement that he's dead,' said Macnair.

'Are you absolutely positive that you'll get him?'

'Prime Minister, there are no absolute positives. I'm as sure as I can be that he won't escape this time. But you have to remember that he's a slippery customer. He will have covered all his bases to the best of his considerable ability, which is why I want to find his escape route.'

'Yes, yes, so you keep saying,' the PM was becoming testy. 'But you have no idea of the pressure we are under to get a result. I suggest that you send your men in no later than tomorrow night – effectively a day earlier than planned.'

'I must protest, Prime Minister. Leave me to make the

operational decisions and you make the political ones. That way we'll achieve our objectives.'

'When I suggest something I expect it to be carried out, General Macnair. Do I make myself clear?'

Macnair knew there was no use in further argument. He did the only thing he could. He gave in gracefully and left shortly afterwards.

He gave vent to his feelings once he was in his car and heading back to Brize Norton where a helicopter would take him on to Plymouth. His thoughts about politicians in general and the Cabinet in particular were unprintable.

Macnair switched on his satlink telephone and dialled. 'Nick? I've just left the Cabinet Office. I'm afraid that you have to go in tomorrow whether or not you've found Habib's escape route.'

'Why, General? That doesn't make sense. We know that Habib's going nowhere before Friday. We have at least an extra day to find his hidden exit.'

'I know, Nick. I argued until I was blue in the face but I've been told it's politics and that's final. Just do your best. Do you have everything ready?'

'Affirmative. All the gear has been delivered and checked out. We're already looking. As regards to the attack, we intend dropping from twenty thousand feet onto the roof using the C130. We can't be heard from that height.'

'I agree there, my boy. Well, you know what you're doing so I'll leave it to you. In the meantime I intend trying to break into one or two of Habib's bank accounts and find out more about his finances.'

'Can you do that?' Hunter couldn't keep the surprise from his voice.

'Not me, Nick, but Sarah can. Thank goodness she's honest, that's all I can say.'

On that happier note he broke the connection.

Hunter was onboard *The Overdraft* with Doreen. He was fishing idly off the stern of the boat while she was tweaking the autopilot from time to time, keeping their heading safe as they hugged the shore of the island. The boat was barely making headway as they moved through the Soay Sound.

Luckily, it was a rare, fine spring day, there was barely any breeze and few clouds in the sky. Although it was just past 15.30, it was still warm and both of them wore tee-shirts and shorts. Hunter hoped that if they were noticed, they would be taken for what they appeared to be, a couple out enjoying the fine weather and the fishing.

Over the stern ran the bathyscope. It automatically followed the contours of the seabed at a height of one metre. It was cylindrical, less than six centimetres long and two centimetres in diameter. On the deck it was connected to a small screen which read out the parts per millilitre of salt in the water. Having studied the maps and charts of the area, Hunter had come to the conclusion that the burn which fed the old distillery reached the sea somewhere along a three mile stretch of coast. Wherever the fresh water mixed with the sea, the salt content would reduce significantly. This had been shown to be the case each time they had passed a stream or small loch. Nothing found so far fitted what he was looking for, but he was not disheartened. They were coming up to the section of coastline he considered to be the most favourable.

The Overdraft was less then five metres off the cliff which towered above them. The depth of water was over fifteen metres with little sign of any further shelving and a gentle swell made the transiting of the area quite pleasant. In rough weather this would be a dangerous and uncomfortable place to be.

The sea was a translucent green, with clumps of seaweed and algae floating intermittently past the bow. According to the chart there were no rocks that could constitute a hazard, but Doreen was extra vigilant, just in case. Hunter's rod twitched and the line started to run out. He let the fish go for a few metres and then put on the brake. The tip of the rod bent, twitched up and down as the fish stopped in surprise and then bent over at ninety degrees as the fish tried to escape. Hunter had no finesse when it came to fishing and started to reel the catch in. He gave no thought to the breaking strain of the line or the power of the fish. Suddenly, the line went slack, the rod straightened and then bent again as the fish took a run. It was checked for a moment, the line broke and whatever was on the end was away. Even as the fish was escaping, Hunter's attention was caught with the drop in salinity figures showing on the screen by his side.

'Doreen, slow down and come round, will you please? I had something then.'

'What?' she asked.

The saline figures had crept back up to normal already. 'I'm not sure. Let's just do it again.'

She quickly reversed course and transited the same area. The readout changed at the same spot. Hunter raised the bathyscope slowly, noting the changes. The water gradually became more saline until, near the surface, it was the same as the surrounding sea. Somewhere, near the base of the cliff, fresh water was pouring into the

Sound. From where he stood, there was no evidence from whence it came.

'Let's drop the anchor and have a drink or something,' he said loudly, though there was nobody within earshot to hear him.

'Or something,' Doreen grinned lasciviously back at him.

Due to their proximity to the cliff, Hunter let go the starboard anchor, used the engines to swing away from the cliff and then let go the port anchor. He then adjusted the anchor cables until they were both equal in length. The boat was now moored, with a very small swinging arc which stopped her going anywhere near the cliff face.

Doreen had gone below and put the kettle on. She sat on the settee, waiting in anticipation for Hunter to join her. She felt like a teenager again, wonderingly exploring sex. There had been only two other men before she had married, she had been faithful throughout her marriage and after seventeen years she found this an adventure.

Hunter was already stripping off his tee-shirt when he entered the saloon. He saw her reclining and grinned at her. 'Not now, Josephine,' he paraphrased Napoleon, 'I've work to do.'

'Work?' Doreen was perplexed.

'Yes. I'm going to use the diving gear we put on board this morning and have a quick shufty down at the cliff. I need to see if there's a way in and out big enough to take a two-man submersible.'

'What about me?' she was a little put out.

Hunter looked at her in some surprise. 'What about you? I mean, I don't want to be rude, but this is important.'

She was about to make a petulant remark when she

realised how childish she was being. He was right. Work first and play later. 'Sorry,' she quickly stood up, all thought of sex banished, ready to help. 'What can I do?'

'Cut a three metre or so length of that blue rope you have in the aft locker. I'll get changed and get this over with as quickly as possible.'

Ten minutes later Hunter stepped off the stern platform with hardly a ripple. The water gave him an initial shock; it was very cold so early in the season. As his body warmed up the neoprene he became more comfortable. The first thing he did was to wrap the length of blue rope around the two propellers, jamming them. If anybody found Doreen she was to claim that she was alone with the engines out of action and that she was sending for help. Next, he turned head down and finned towards the bottom. The water was crystal clear and details of the seabed were easily distinguished. There was a jumble of boulders which had collected there over the millennia, eroded from the cliff by the sea. Long fronds of seaweed swayed enticingly in the gentle swell of the water, sea anemones and star fish added to the colour. Even after hundreds, if not thousands of dives, Hunter still found diving an exciting and invigorating occupation.

He was two thirds of the way down when he saw a shadowed patch in the cliff. He swam cautiously forward, the last thing he wanted was to encounter a conger eel, especially as they had been known to grow to a significant size in this part of the world.

At ten metres, according to his depth gauge, the cliff suddenly went back into a deep recess. He switched on the torch he was carrying and shone it along the face. It was at least five metres to the cliff and he cautiously swam inside. The distance between the seabed and the rock above him was, he estimated, a further five metres and as he swam in, the natural light dimmed. Halfway along he felt a pressure on his back and looked up. There was a huge gaping hole through which he could feel the flow of water. He finned upwards but as he neared the hole he realised that the pressure of the water was pushing him out. He exerted himself again, doing the equivalent of an underwater sprint. His outstretched hands touched the rock, failed to get a grip and he was swept back down. Panting, he rested for a few moments, quickly regaining his breath.

More brains, Hunter, less brawn, he said to himself. He judged himself to be in the middle of the hole and pulled the inflation tab on his lifejacket. It immediately filled and he again finned furiously towards the hole. The additional buoyancy helped and he kept going. As he went higher, the weight of the water lessened and it became easier. He was suddenly aware that he was ascending more quickly than the air bubbles he was exhaling and was in danger of losing control. He tried to vent the life jacket but could not keep up with the increase in volume in the jacket as the pressure decreased. If there was solid rock above his head, at the speed he was going, it would knock him out if not kill him. He grabbed the knife strapped to his right leg, withdrew it and slashed the jacket. The air burst out and his mad ascent stopped. He looked upwards; the cliff was a metre from his head. His depth gauge needle was just off the zero line. He was almost at sea level.

He was able to swim forward, the current not too strong. After a distance which he estimated to be about a hundred metres he was able to surface. He shone the torch about him. He was in a huge cavern, stretching hundreds of metres ahead and soaring twenty metres above his head. The surface of the water swirled and eddied as it sank into the hole behind and beneath him.

Hunter finned slowly forward, trying to penetrate the gloom. He shivered. The water was several degrees cooler than it had been in the sea. After swimming for a few minutes he realised there was a ledge running at water level around the edge of the cavern and swam to it. He shucked his dive bottles and weight belt, tugged off his fins and clambered onto the ledge. He shone the torch in front of him, heard a squeal, and shuddered as over a dozen water rats ran in front of him before they leapt into the water. In the torch light he saw their grey heads gleaming then, as one, they left the surface and vanished. Normally, he was far from squeamish, but there was something about rats he hated.

A few minutes later he reached the end of the cavern. The ledge opened out into an area at least ten metres wide and ten metres deep. Secured at one end was the submersible. He looked at his watch. He had been away from the boat for over forty minutes and Doreen would be wondering where he was. He quickly looked around the area, identifying various pieces of equipment and stores. He considered putting the submersible out of action but then thought better of it. He was not ready yet to tip his hand to Habib. Satisfied, he made his way back to where he had left his diving equipment, strapped the bottles and belt back on and re-entered the water.

He shivered as the cold hit him anew. He swam back to the sink hole, slipped beneath the surface and went with the flow. When he was above the hole he paused to run the torch over the rock above and around him. Satisfied with what he saw, he flipped over and swam gently towards the bottom. Very quickly the weight of the water took hold of him and pushed him down towards the seabed at a rate of knots. Halfway down, he flipped over and began to fin for the surface, hard. He continued down but now at a more controlled speed. Even so, when he hit the seabed he had to bend his legs to absorb the impact before he swam away from the cliff face towards the light.

He looked up to see two hulls floating above his head. He unclipped a small apple float from his waist and tied the end of the line to a suitable rock, letting the float go free. The line quickly unravelled and the float shot to the surface where it bobbed in the gentle swell.

He was about to follow it up when he paused to think through his strategy. How long had the other boat been there? Who were they? Were they the Ungodly?

Out of the corner of his eye he saw something move and realised it was a lobster scuttling across the sand. In a flash he swam down on it, grabbed it across its back and started for the surface. The lobster arched its back, its claws curled back as it tried to get a grip of his hand. It must have been about eight pounds, a tasty morsel which was now snapping its tail in fury, trying to break loose. A few metres beneath the hull of the boat he slipped his weight belt and let it drop to the seabed.

When he reached the surface, he held the lobster above his head and spat out his mouth piece. 'Hey, Doreen, look at this. Supper,' he yelled happily. His eyes took in the scene, which appeared peaceful.

A head appeared above him as he climbed onto the platform on the stern of *The Overdraft*. He had already undone the straps holding his bottles in place and quickly slipped them off. He kept hold of the lobster, climbed quickly to his feet and stood grinning inanely at the stranger before him. He pretended bewilderment as he looked from the face to the gun pointed at him.

'What? What?' Hunter took a step through the swing gate, absorbing the scene before him.

There was the man holding the gun less than half a metre from him, a second man sitting on the transom of the inflatable boat, holding it close to *The Overdraft* and from the sound of it, a third person below.

Hunter did not stop for any further thought. By their complexions they were obviously Habib's men and the fact that they had guns did not bode well for Hunter's and Doreen's futures.

'Look.' Hunter shoved the lobster within inches of the face before him. Instinctively, the man looked at the lobster and bent his head back. Hunter shoved the gun hand away to one side, pulled his knife and rammed it into the exposed throat. The dead man gurgled and fell over the stern taking the gun with him, leaving Hunter holding the knife.

The other man in the boat cursed, let go of *The Overdraft* and lunged for a weapon lying in the bow of the boat. Hunter stepped onto the gunwale and leapt at the back of the man, landing with both feet. The man was caught with his knees on the transom seat and his hands grabbing the gun. Hunter drove his feet down and heard the spine snap, the man making a fearful shriek.

He grabbed the Uzi, slipped the firing catch off and climbed back onto *The Overdraft*. The scream made the third man rush out from the forward cabin. Hunter shot him in the forehead, stepped over the body and carefully made his way into the boat. There could be a fourth man below.

Instead he found Doreen, sitting deathly pale on the deck, her mouth taped, her hands tied in front of her. Her eyes flooded with relief when she saw Hunter, and two big tear drops rolled down her cheeks.

He knelt by her side, undid her hands and gently peeled the tape away. 'It's okay, Doreen. It's okay. Hush now. You'll be all right.'

'What . . . what happened to those men?'

'They won't bother you again. Just sit there for a few seconds while I tidy up.'

Hunter stood up, went back on deck and jumped down into the inflatable. The man with the broken back had somehow turned himself over and was lying against the side of the inflatable.

He glared at Hunter, spat and said, 'I will tell you nothing.'

Hunter looked at him in genuine puzzlement. 'What do I want to know?'

'You want to know what we are doing here. I will tell you nothing. We came to steal from you. I will tell your police that. Nothing more.'

Hunter's smile was not a pretty sight. He shook his head, and pointed the Uzi at the man. 'There will be no police, no trial, no help,' he spoke quietly. 'I know why you came. You're one of Habib's men.' The man's jaw dropped open in shock. 'Habib carried out an attack against this country. He will die in about,' he made a pantomime of looking at his watch, 'about seven hours from now. I know about the submersible and he isn't getting out that way. So what else do I want to know?'

The man moved his mouth wordlessly, shocked beyond imagination. Hunter put a single bullet between the man's eyes, putting him out of his mental and physical agony.

Quickly, he grabbed the dead body on *The Overdraft* and threw it into the inflatable, untied the painter holding the two boats together and pushed towards the third body. He pulled it onboard and tied the three bodies to the boat. Next, he slashed every compartment of the four-metre boat and slipped into the water to swim back to *The Overdraft*. He paused on the deck to see the bodies and boat slip beneath the water, taken down by the weight of the large outboard engine.

'Are you okay?' he asked Doreen who was now sitting in a chair, using a tissue to dab her eyes.

'Yes, thanks. Just a bit shaken, that's all.'

Hunter knelt next to her and took hold of her hands. 'You've been incredibly brave. Just hang on in there. We'll get back to the hotel shortly. You take a long, hot bath, drink a lot of brandy and go to bed.'

'Is that the best advice you can give to a girl who's been tied up, threatened and who expected to die?' she shivered.

'It's the best I can do for now,' was the reply. 'I've got a lot to do tonight. But I'll give you all the comfort you want and need when this is over.'

'When will that be?'

'Like I said, tonight. With these three gone we don't have any choice anyway. Habib will be suspicious when they don't turn up, besides which, I've been ordered in no later than tomorrow night.'

Doreen nodded, blew her nose and climbed unsteadily to her feet. 'Right then, let's get this show on the road.'

He took hold of her and held her trembling body in his. 'You're incredible, do you know that? It's fine to be scared, you know. True courage is when you keep going in spite of your fear.'

'In that case I'm the bravest person in the world as, right now, I'm scared out of my wits.'

They quickly recovered both anchors and headed back to the jetty near the hotel where the boat was berthed. A short while later Doreen was having her bath and Hunter was holding a briefing.

20

Midnight 13 May 1998. Isle of Skye.

Habib was pacing the large room. 'I tell you my friend, I do not like it. The others should have been back long ago. We have heard nothing from them since we sent them to look at that boat near the cliff.'

Fredericks took a drink of his whisky. He felt the same as Habib. The three men should have been back long before now. The boat they knew to be back at the hotel, along with the woman who owned it. The man who had been with her had left Skye shortly after six o'clock with another man. Where they were going, neither Habib nor Fredericks knew. Being helpless was not a feeling that Fredericks enjoyed and to assuage his worry he was drinking too much.

'There could be any number of explanations,' he said lamely, as he had done so a dozen times that evening.

Habib snarled at him. 'So you keep telling me but none make any sense. I sense the British are up to something. They are a devious, cowardly race of people who cannot be trusted at anything.'

Fredericks let the slur on his race pass him by. There was no arguing with Habib when he was in this mood.

'Is everything ready if we need to go?'

'Yes, Habib,' he bit off the retort that he had said so more than once already that evening. 'We have the remainder of the men alert and on guard. If anything happens we shall have plenty of time to get away.'

Habib nodded. He knew that, he just wanted the reassurance. This waiting and uncertainty was new for him. In the past he had always been in control. Now he felt that control had slipped from his fingers, that unseen forces were massing against him. He shook himself and took a grip on his feelings.

'I think we should warn Smith that we might need him tomorrow at Loch Boisdale.'

'Are you sure?' Fredericks was relieved. He also had a bad feeling about the night.

'Yes, I'm sure. Do it now.'

Fredericks stood up and walked to the telephone. Their escape route was simple. Submersible to Loch Boisdale on South Uist to be met by a seaplane. From there to Eire and on to Spain. The seaplane had landed at least a dozen times at South Uist during the previous two years and so would not come as any surprise. The excuse for being there was that it was collecting sea samples for the university. Which university and what the samples were used for was never expanded upon.

He was replacing the receiver, having passed on the order, when they heard the shooting.

Earlier, Hunter and Pierre Flambert had driven like maniacs off the island and down past Loch Duich. In the foothills leading to Glenshiel they waited for a helicopter to pick them up. The wait was less than five minutes before they heard the familiar thwacking sound of the rotor blades thrashing the air. Soon they were airborne and heading south as fast as possible.

By 22.00 they had landed at Machrihanish, changed to a C130 and were once again in the air, heading north, back to the Isle of Skye.

Don Masters and Bill Davidson were in a copse of trees overlooking Habib's house. They had set up a mini-dish which was tuned to a passing satellite. That in turn sent a signal to a receiver carried by Hunter and Flambert. The dish carried a ground based laser which was centred on the flat-roofed conservatory. Satisfied that all was in order, they moved stealthily though the trees and towards the perimeter fence surrounding the house.

There, they settled down to wait. Their targets already in their sights.

Hours earlier, Captain Joshua Clements and Sergeant Sam McReady had approached the cliff in their inflatable. McReady held the direction finder which was homed in on the apple float. Within minutes he saw the dayglo orange float and took hold of it, the boat drifting to a halt. The nylon thread it was attached to was incredibly strong and there was no danger of it breaking. However, just in case, they also dropped an anchor into the water to help hold the inflatable steady.

Both men were already dressed in diving gear and had been fully briefed by Hunter. Clements slid silently into the water, adjusted his goggles and mouth piece and gave the thumbs up sign to McReady.

McReady handed Clements the end of a length of nylon rope and quietly left the surface. He finned rapidly to the bottom, following the line from the apple float and soon found himself in the recess in the cliff. He tied off the end of the rope, gave a series of five sharp tugs on the rope which meant "I have found, started or completed work," depending on the situation, and waited.

McReady lowered a small pallet into the water, tied by a loop of nylon to the rope running to the seabed and hauled the rope tight. The pallet sank quickly, and landed with a thud next to Clements. This operation was repeated three times, whilst the fourth was lowered more gently to the bottom.

Clements now had over one hundred pounds of plastic explosives and associated equipment at his feet. A few moments later McReady joined him. Hunter had warned Clements what to expect when swimming up through the waterfall, but even so it still came as a surprise. He only just managed to slash his life jacket in time and raise his hands above his head to prevent a serious impact on the rock. As it was he gave both his hands a pounding as he came to a stop.

Again, he gave the five sharp tugs, known in the Royal Navy as "bells", and McReady inflated the lifting bag tied to the first pallet and pushed it up against the water. They only used their voice communications when it was necessary and for a simple operation like this, old-fashioned line signals were more than sufficient. The pallet hung there for a few seconds and then slowly began to rise. In spite of the water pushing it back, the bag continued upwards, helped by Clements who was reeling in a line attached to the pallet. After a few minutes, the pallet began to accelerate but this time, unlike a life jacket, the vent holes in the lifting bag could cope with the air expansion and the pallet did not rise out of control. Once on the surface, Clements undid the rope he had used as an up haul, tied a small weight to it and sent it back to McReady. The operation was repeated until all four pallets were floating alongside Clements, pinioned to the roof of the cave by the bags.

Thanks to their underwater communications gear, Josh Clements was able to warn McReady about the ride up and so he appeared alongside the other man in a more controlled manner without hurting his hands or head.

They both now lit the lamps which were attached to their headsets, illuminating the way forward whilst leaving them with their hands free. Clements deflated one of the lifting bags until the pallet it supported was neutrally buoyant and swam with it up the tunnel. Once at the end, he clambered onto the ledge, took a powerful torch off the clip on his belt and shone it around the chamber. There were a myriad of satisfying cracks lacing the rock face above his head. He began to unpack the plastic and work it into the cracks.

McReady at the other end of the tunnel faced the outer wall of the overhang and did the same thing. It was slow, laborious work, as there could be no chance of a misfire. When they had finished, nearly an hour later, both men were satisfied.

They ran their detonating cord from a dozen firing points and connected it to an electric igniter. Then they set about honeycombing the tunnel with fine fishing line, anchoring the line into cracks in the tunnel wall using marlin spikes. The line was then tied off on the igniter switch. That was the last thing they did. Any object moving into the invisible lines criss-crossing the tunnel would set off two explosions, ten seconds apart. The first would seal the exit, the second would seal the way back.

Satisfied they had done a good job, both men went with the water flow and dropped back to the seabed. They had extinguished their lights and approached the surface well away from the inflatable. They both had guns ready, specially sealed to be carried underwater, but for use in the open air. All was quiet, no other boat was in the vicinity. They swam back to the inflatable, started the electric motor and quietly left the scene.

The night was silent, a half moon hung in the sky, there were few clouds and no wind. A light frost was in the air but after their exertions neither man was feeling the cold. The sound of gun fire, though expected, was still shocking as it ripped the silence asunder.

Sergeant Jimmy Smith of the Paratroop Regiment and Jan Badonovitch made an unlikely team. In the short while they had been working together a special relationship had built up that was uncanny. Each knew instinctively what the other wanted or required and acted accordingly. That night, as they approached the wire fence surrounding the immediate house and grounds, they were in tune with each other and ready for any eventuality.

They were aware that dogs were roaming the grounds; specially trained to be utterly silent, they were vicious killers, a cross breed of German Shepherd and Russian Wolfhound. Semi-starved, the pack of six dogs had complete freedom once the house was shut up for the night. In the morning, they returned to their kennels when tempted by food.

Badonovitch threw handfuls of poisoned meat over the fence and gave a low whistle. Even the knowledge that the pack was there did not prepare either man for the heart stopping, sudden appearance of the silent dogs.

Suspiciously, they sniffed the meat. The poison was contained in capsules imbedded in the meat and so there was no unexpected smell. First one and then another of the dogs snatched at the meat, terrified that the food would be taken from them before they had a chance to eat it. Four of the dogs gulped the food and swallowed the capsules without breaking them. Two of the others bit into the capsules and were killed instantly, without a murmur.

It would take time for the meat to be ingested and the capsule to dissolve and that was time they did not have. The dogs sensed the presence of the two men and stood at the wire, looking at them, hackles raised, silent.

Badonovitch aimed his gun at the nearest head and fired into the brain, as did Smith. Their guns emitted a cough that could not be heard at ten paces. The other two dogs stood there, unmoving, unaware of their fate. They too were quickly despatched in the same manner.

The attack on the house was not going to be a subtle, quiet approach but neither was it to be full-scale, open warfare. Hunter had been given *carte blanche* as to the *modus operandi* but within certain guidelines. Devastating, but silent fire was the order of the day.

There was no doubt that the fence was wired for alarm systems and the grounds covered by at least six surveillance cameras. Their night vision goggles made the scene before them as clear as day and they were ready to commence the attack. They also had their targets in sight.

Peter Weir, the Scots Corporal, another SAS member, and his long time partner and friend Sergeant David Hughes, previously of the Welsh Guards but now also a member of the famous Hereford regiment, were at the front of the house. They had used all their trade craft to reach the fence without discovery. It was said with some truth, that a member of the Special Air Services could make an American Apache seem like an arthritic old woman in a wheelchair when it came to moving silently and undetected. Being the front of the house, they had established that the area had the most protection, as if Habib had expected any attack to be a frontal assault. One thing they had not spotted earlier was that there were two small pill boxes about half a metre high standing at either corner of the house. Weir identified them immediately he saw them and, against orders, spoke softly into his throat mike.

'Pill boxes left and right.'

The remainder of the teams heard the message and stiffened. Pill boxes held sensor operated machine guns which would open up when a target presented itself. The dogs were able to roam without hindrance because the sensors had been set not to respond to the relative lightness and small imprints of a paw. A fifteen stone man and his foot marks was an entirely different matter.

More care was now taken by the others. The ground was examined metre by metre until they had found what they were looking for. They identified eight pill boxes in total. If they had made a move without spotting them, it would have been certain death.

The last team consisted of the German Lieutenant Oscar Graff and the Italian Captain Hugo Parrotti. Both men were highly experienced in anti-terrorism work though this was the first time that the German had ever worked outside his native country. Only recently had the German

Constitution been changed allowing the German armed
forces to operate away from Germany. Graff was one of
the first men to do so. Although German forces were on
their way to Bosnia in a peace keeping role his would
be the first gun fired in anger by a German in a foreign
country since the end of the Second World War.

'Bingo, thank you, my friend,' said the Italian into his
throat mike. They had identified the pill boxes.

'Listen up,' the voice in their ears told them. They
recognised Hunter and instinctively all eight men looked
up into the heavens. It took a few seconds to notice the
way the stars came and went as the two aerofoil wings
dropped towards the roof. 'Landing in fifteen seconds.'

Hunter and Flambert had jumped from the Hercules at
twenty thousand feet. They wore specially heated clothing
with an all encompassing hood. To have done otherwise
would have killed them from cold within minutes. They
tumbled through the air for a few thousand feet, in radio
contact with each other, both very much in control. Then
they had opened out their arms and legs and stabilised
their flight as they both plummeted towards the ground.
They could see for miles across the country, towns,
villages and streets lit up as far as the orange glow of
Glasgow nearly a hundred miles south.

They both checked that they were receiving the signal
from the dish set up on Skye and then settled down to
enjoy the ride. At four thousand feet Flambert's aerofoil
opened and two seconds later so did Hunter's. The latter
was now riding fifty metres behind Flambert.

The signals they were receiving were automatically
translated into instructions to the foils and they were
unerringly steered towards the flat roof.

From the reports he had received over their personal transmitters Hunter was aware that the teams were poised, ready. It was only necessary to flush Habib out and send him into the trap.

Hunter looked down, the view of his world changing from panoramic to tunnel vision of the house. The night glasses had a range of less than a mile and he now switched them on. Immediately the world about him lit up like daylight suddenly erupting and he could see everything in fine detail. Flambert's foil was turning into what gentle wind there was and automatically flaring to let him touch down on the roof. Hunter saw the pill boxes open up and the machine guns cut Flambert almost in half. Flambert was dead before his brain registered what had happened. He made no noise, no transmission. Hunter would land two seconds behind him.

He was twenty feet above the flat roof and about seven or eight above the pitched roof of the main house. He hit the sudden release button on his chest and dropped from the foil's harness. His feet hit the slates and he began to slide down the roof towards his death. His momentum was rapid and there was no purchase for him to grab to stop him tumbling down beside the still body of Flambert. He whipped out the knife he had strapped to his right leg and smashed it as hard as he could into the slates. The knife sliced through, shattering them. He was still sliding down, both hands gripping the knife, his momentum had eased but the knife kept cutting. Desperately, his legs hanging over the three-feet drop to the flat roof, he turned the knife in his hands and the blade brought him to a dead stop. The strain on his hands and arm muscles was enormous but he managed to pull himself up, tuck his feet into the drainage pipes running around the roof and ease himself up. The guns had ceased but now there was a different noise. It was breaking glass, followed by the raucous chatter of machine guns firing.

When the guns opened up on the roof none of the teams waited to see what was happening. Their original instruction was to wait for Hunter's signal or until something went wrong. They figured the latter, and it was time to go.

Each man fired an explosive bullet from his rifle which took out all eight of the pill boxes. Next, using the same method, the surveillance cameras were dealt with. Next, previously laid explosives erupted all along the fence, taking down nearly all of the metal stanchions which held it up. They collapsed inwards leaving a clear field to cross.

However, none of the teams had a death wish. They fired a volley into the windows, one using the explosive bullets and the other using ordinary steel capped ammunition. Although the windows were bullet proof they could not withstand such an onslaught and they erupted inwards sending sheets of glass flying into the rooms, shredding the curtains and slashing furniture.

Habib was already running from the room with Fredericks at his heels. In the wide corridor they were safe as it did not connect with an outside wall or window. This was the centre of the house. Above was the landing which led to half a dozen bedrooms and two bathrooms. From one tottered a blood stained figure who hit the banister and fell over, landing in an unmoving heap. He had been cut to pieces by the flying glass.

They could hear their men returning the fire. One man at each side of the house. They knew that they only had seconds in which to escape, before the British streamed into the house. There was a loud explosion to one side and firing from the front of the house ceased. Habib tore open the door to the cellar and rushed down the steps. Fredericks closed the door behind him and threw across three heavy dead bolts and a metal bar.

They continued their headlong flight, leaving the remainder of their men to fend for themselves. Habib threw a switch which lit up the long and musty tunnel to the old distillery. They ran along it, throwing up clouds of dust around their feet. At the end of the tunnel they tore open a hermetically sealed cupboard and quickly dressed in their diving suits.

When they were ready Habib found the breath to say, 'They will pay for this, I swear. The British will pay with a blood bath.'

Fredericks nodded. Adrenaline and fear had washed the alcohol from his blood stream leaving him stone cold sober. Both men undid the ropes holding the submersible in place, pushed off from the side and started the machine. Habib eased it slowly away towards the exit tunnel and freedom, only ten minutes after the shooting had started.

Hunter climbed across the roof until he was next to one of the pill boxes. He slid down behind it, placed a small explosive charge and climbed back onto the roof. Five seconds later the box was blown to smithereens. He scrambled across the roof to the other side and did the same to the second one. Next he jumped onto the roof and rushed over to Flambert. There was nothing to be done for him. Only the rubber insulation suit stopped the body from breaking in two.

Hunter quickly divested himself of the restricting suit and moved to the attic window which had been their target. The firing was still heavy, although it seemed to him that it was only on three sides of the house. He kicked in the window and climbed cautiously through. He carefully worked his way across the attic, stepping from crossbeam to crossbeam. At the far end he knelt beside a trap door. He inserted his knife in the corner and lifted carefully. He was looking down onto the landing, in the corridor which Habib and Fredericks had fled only minutes before.

He threw back the door and dropped feet first, his gun ready. He darted along the landing to one of the doors from which he could hear the sound of shooting. The door was slightly ajar, and lying flat on the floor he swung it the rest of the way open. Bullets were flying through one of the windows and smacking into the wall. Underneath the window lay one of Habib's men. For a moment Hunter thought he was dead and then he saw him turn his face towards the door.

Hunter shot him twice in the head. He realised which side of the house he was on and said into his throat mike, 'Okay Jimmy, stop firing before you hit me.' The flying bullets stopped immediately.

Smith and Badonovitch now moved forward quickly but carefully, each covering the other until they reached the wall of the house. They took a surreptitious look inside and then gave the all clear for their side.

Weir and Hughes had also reached the front door which they promptly blew out with a lump of plastic explosive. They both waited for the dust to settle before attempting ingress. One casualty was enough and neither man was keen to meet his maker just yet.

'Boss, we're at the door. Ready to go in.'

'Stay where you are,' said Hunter. 'I'm behind a door about thirty feet from you and I can see a raghead hiding.'

Hunter had descended the stairs quickly and carefully and made his way towards what he guessed was the front of the house. He had opened a door and stopped to survey the scene when the front door was blown in. He was looking into a substantial hall, bigger than most ordinary houses. There was a sweeping staircase and three doors leading away to other rooms. The man to whom he was referring was kneeling with his back to him, at the foot of the stairs, waiting to shoot whoever came through the front door.

The door where Hunter stood creaked and the man turned his head. The last thing he saw on earth was the figure of Hunter, dressed in camouflage greens, wearing his night vision goggles and looking like an apparition from hell. Hunter's first shot smashed the man's arm and swept his gun away, the second hit his other shoulder and the third went through the bridge of his nose and out of the back, taking a chunk of brain with it.

All firing had stopped as the teams moved into the house. They confirmed five dead and two missing. Hunter threw open the doors in the corridor at the back of the house but, at the third one, found it locked.

He took PE from a pouch and squeezed it all around the edge of the door then set two detonators from one timer and stepped away. Three seconds and the door was blasted open.

The teams moved on, working quickly but carefully. They checked for hidden booby traps but found nothing. Hunter checked the lapse time since Flambert had been killed. Eight minutes. In the tunnel they could see the recent foot marks in the dust and, with Hunter leading, they ran silently towards their goal. At the end, where the tunnel opened onto the underwater lake, they paused.

'I'll look,' he said into his throat mike. On his knees, he put an eye around the end of the wall and was in time to see the heads on the submersible sink beneath the water. He stood up and called the others after him. He stood there smiling, his hands on his hips, waiting.

It was more a rumble than an explosion. The water swirled, an artificial wave swept back towards them but petered out before it reached them and then the overhead rocks at the far end collapsed, sealing the way back.

Water rats darted here and there for a few seconds, in a panic but unable to decide what was threatening them. After a few moments they stopped their aimless running, looked at the figures standing by the tunnel and quickly disappeared.

Habib and Fredericks did not see Hunter and his men arrive. They were concentrating on their escape. In spite of their hurry, they had been careful to ensure that everything was in full working order. They still had a long way to go and the British would be after them, of that there was little doubt.

Habib switched on the forward light on the submersible so that he could see where he was going. Once clear, he would switch it off to preserve the battery power for the journey ahead. He looked at the gauges, air okay, depth right, the drop through the water fall would be coming up in about two minutes.

He looked ahead, his eyes accustomed to the light. He received an impression of criss-crossed lines in front of him but before his brain registered and understood what he was looking at the submersible ploughed into them. It was hardly checked in its forward momentum as the lines pulled the switch. The forward explosives detonated, there was a shock through the water and the roof ahead of them caved in. Although the submersible bucked and kicked, both men survived without serious damage. They had settled on the bottom to collect their thoughts when the second explosion occurred. This time they were much closer and were flung from the sub, tumbling through the water, both men had enough sense remaining to grip their mouthpieces tightly between their teeth.

Habib was hyperventilating and knew that if he did not get control of his breathing he was in trouble. Fredericks, the more experienced diver, had already managed to calm himself down enough to swim forward towards the exit. It took a few minutes of frantic searching to realise that there was no way out.

He swam back to the submersible to find Habib sitting there, holding onto the handle bars, as if there was somewhere to go. Fredericks swam up to him and looked him in the eyes from a few inches and shook his head. Next, he swam back the way they had come. Again, it took only seconds to realise there was no way back. They were trapped in a watery grave until their air ran out. Panic swelled up and threatened to overpower him. He fought it back, making himself calm down and start searching for a way out again. This time he took it more slowly.

While Fredericks was searching, Habib sat frozen, sitting on the submersible, in an almost catatonic state. Fear had him gripped by the throat and threatened to overspill in vomit. The search allowed Fredericks to get control of himself, the waves of panic rising and subsiding, but after twenty minutes he knew there was no exit.

He sat on the seabed for a few seconds and raved against his countrymen in particular and life in general, which had left him to a fate like this. Then, without stopping to analyse what he was doing he ripped the face mask and mouthpiece away and breathed in the water deeply. In his mind was a brilliant white light which quickly faded to a darkness that would last him for eternity.

Habib was panting again, hyperventilating to an extent that caused his vision to narrow like looking down a long black tunnel with a faint light at the end. His heart was pounding and, if he could, he would have opened his mouth and screamed. But his brain was locked on to the idea that he had to keep his teeth clamped shut and the mouthpiece firmly held between his teeth. For an hour he sat there, until at last his mind began to function again. It was like coming out of a drugged sleep, he was shivering, freezing cold, his immobility adding to the heat lost from his body.

He looked around him as reality, unfortunately for him, gained ascendancy in his mind. He climbed stiffly off the submersible and swam to the wall of rock in front of him. He found the same as Fredericks. He then swam back, paying no attention to Fredericks' body staring grotesquely down, trapped against the overhead rock.

He searched for a way back but found none. As the horror of his situation took hold, Habib became more and more frantic. Darting back and forth, swimming madly and aimlessly, he tore at the rock, succeeding only in ripping out finger nails which went unnoticed in the cold water.

Finally, he sank down besides the submersible, in the light, taking what little comfort he could from it, afraid of the dark; afraid of the demons he knew were waiting for him when he crossed to the other side. He had always been on the edge of insanity and now he tipped over into it. Before his air ran out he was a gibbering wreck, pleading to Allah for help one second, cursing him the next. Now that Fredericks was dead there was sufficient air carried by the submersible to last fifteen hours. It would take Habib that long to die – finally, sucking on the mouthpiece as the air finished.

21

Hunter and his team dived at both ends of the tunnel to ensure that there had been no escape by Habib and Fredericks. Satisfied, they sat in the grounds of the house and waited for the helicopters to come to take them away. Their job was over. Somebody else had to clean up the mess – in the jargon, to sanitise the area. Although they had used weapons that were silenced, Habib and his men had made a lot of noise. Already questions were being asked and none of them wanted to be around when answers were needed. Hunter had reported the outcome of the attack and the news of the one casualty who was now lying next to them in a body bag. None of them had been together long enough to become well acquainted, but danger and a reliance for your life on the other man, nonetheless, made lasting friendships. They would miss Pierre.

The helicopters arrived around midday. By then, the equipment was stripped and packed and those who were leaving the island by road were on their way. Only the attack team was left. Hunter saw them off and, now in civilian clothes, made his way back to the hotel. He had a goodbye to make.

She was sitting in the lounge, aimlessly turning the

pages of a magazine, unable to concentrate. She looked up when Hunter walked through the door.

'Nick, you're back?' Her smile was brittle around the edges but there was relief in her voice.

He nodded. 'Just like the proverbial penny. It's all over. I've sent the others on their way. I'm still here to tidy up the loose ends.'

'Oh? Am I a loose end?'

'No, of course not,' Hunter knelt besides her seat and took her hand in his. 'I mean settle the bills, check the rooms, make sure we've left nothing behind. We can't have the hotelier threatening HMG with a lawsuit for non-payment of room bills, now can we?'

'I suppose not. What will you do then?'

'Well, that really depends on you. I told the General how you'd helped and that I thought we owed you something. He said that if I was thinking in terms of money then I was to forget it. He couldn't authorise payment to a civilian for services voluntarily rendered.'

'I'm glad. I wasn't in it for the payment. I wanted to help.'

'I know that. So I wangled three days leave from him instead. I said that the least I could do was help you to take the boat to Fort William. Which reminds me. What about your husband?'

'I had a telephone call from him about an hour ago. He was just leaving his office to catch the shuttle to Glasgow. He intends hiring a car and driving up. Should get here this evening.'

'Ah, I see.' Hunter stood up, withdrawing his hand.

'He told me he was sorry and that it had all been a silly mistake and could I forgive him.'

'And could you?'

She smiled up at Hunter. 'I said that of course I forgave him and that he was to hurry as quickly as he could.'

She enjoyed the look on Hunter's face but then decided to put him out of his misery. 'Only I won't be here. I was hoping you'd get here, because I'm leaving. When he arrives I will be long gone, taking *The Overdraft* with me. If you fancy a bracing sea cruise then I hope you'll come as well.'

He smiled and nodded. 'Just give me fifteen minutes to clear things up and we can go.'

Hunter saw the hotel receptionist, who was surprised when he settled the bills of the others in the team, unaware that they had even known each other. He quickly made sure that the rooms were empty of personal gear and any stray pieces of military equipment and rejoined Doreen down at the boat.

The Overdraft had been refuelled by tanker, stocked with food and her water tanks filled. The bar was replenished and a bottle of champagne sat in an ice bucket.

By the middle of the afternoon they were fifteen miles south, enjoying the continuing warm weather. That was when Hunter's satlink phone rang.

'Hunter.'

'Nick, I'm sorry but I need you,' said Macnair. 'Isobel is on her way by helicopter. I want you and her to take Habib's place apart.'

'What for?'

'Habib had a great deal of money. We tracked some of it down but according to Isobel there has to be more. I want you and her to find it. She knows what she's looking for. I want everything he had.'

'Is this to add to your pension, sir?' Hunter asked, knowing full well the answer.

'I wouldn't know what to do with it if I had it, Nick. No, I want access to funds which are unaccountable. To use when and how I see fit. For bribery and corruption when I need it. You, Jim and Isobel will be the only three people to know anything about it. If I fall under the proverbial red bus you three will carry on until a successor is appointed. Think of the latitude it will give us if we have access to the sort of money I think Habib had.'

'What are we looking for, sir?'

'Computers, floppies, bank and investment information. That's why I've sent Isobel.'

'When's she arriving?'

'In about three hours. I want you to get stuck in right away.'

'What about the sanitation squads? They'll be in the way.'

'No they won't. They've finished already. There's nothing to find there now except broken glass and pock-marked walls. I've had the police cordon off the area to keep the press away as well as any inquisitive sightseers. You can go in as I've warned them that you'll be arriving.'

Hunter looked at Doreen, his face a picture of indecision. He sighed and finally said, 'Roger that, sir. I'll be at Habib's, waiting for her.'

They said their goodbyes and Hunter switched off the phone. He looked at Doreen and shrugged. 'You heard.'

She began turning the boat around and managed a sad smile. 'Duty calls, I take it.'

'Afraid so. You know, had I been James Bond I would have pretended that I couldn't hear and we would have sailed off into the sunset.'

'Unfortunately, you're not and we can't. What I can

do is put the boat on autopilot for the next hour while you and I drink a bottle or two of champagne together.'

The autopilot was on for nearly two hours and it was with a great deal of regret that Hunter said farewell to Doreen who decided to wait for her husband after all.

Hunter was there when Isobel's helicopter landed on the lawn. They went inside the house and started a cursory look around each room, looking for something as obvious as a computer or a safe. After three hours they had found nothing and were both sitting in the library.

'Any ideas?' asked Isobel.

Hunter shook his head. 'Nope,' was his despondent answer. 'Looks like it's been for nothing.'

Isobel shook her head. 'I don't believe it. I've spent days putting together all I could find on Habib. He needed instant access to a lot of money. We know how that's done.'

'I don't,' said Hunter. 'I thought instant access was a low interest paying account with a building society.'

Isobel shook her head sadly. 'You poor, poor naval officer. Habib will have millions stashed in off-shore banks all over the world. He'll have been able to contact the account direct, feed in certain information and transfer money all over the world. He'll have been able to buy and sell shares on any stock market world wide and he won't have needed to talk to anybody. It would all have been done by computer and satellite communications.'

Hunter smiled. 'I know. I was just kidding.' He stood up and wandered around the room looking at the books. He ran a finger along some of them and commented, 'He should have changed his housekeeper. This place needs a dusting. You know, if it had been me I would have kept the information near to me. He probably took it with him so it's buried under a few tons of rock in a watery grave.'

'Not necessarily. Think about it. He could never be sure he'd have time to collect what he needed before making an escape. It makes more sense to hold all the information in a number of places so that he had access whenever he needed it. No, I bet it's here somewhere.' So saying she looked around the room and suddenly stood up. 'What did you say about this place needing dusting?'

'Just that; look at it.' Hunter waved his hand around but then looked to where Isobel was pointing. In the middle of a wall of books a square section looked less dusty than the rest. Hunter stepped across, grabbed hold of the books and started pulling them from their shelves.

'Well, well, well. What have we here?' He had exposed a wall-mounted safe, a metre square. 'Well done, Isobel.'

'How are we going to open it?'

'Easy as PE,' was the reply.

Hunter took a wad of plastic explosive from a pocket and shaped it like a Toblerone chocolate bar. He then kneaded it onto the safe along the hinges. He quickly inserted a detonator and small electric timer and calmly walked Isobel out of the room. A few seconds later a loud bang was heard and they returned to the safe. The door was hanging off its hinges, supported by the lock. A hefty pull on the door and it came away exposing the contents.

Inside they found bundles of money in different currencies, bearer bonds each with a face value of one hundred thousand dollars and looking through them Hunter estimated there were at least two million dollars' worth, and two computer disks.

Isobel took the discs and loaded the first one into her laptop computer. The first question was for the password. Hunter was looking over her shoulder. 'That's torn it,' he said. 'What do we do now?'

Isobel gave him the sort of look you get from a mother when her favourite son is being particularly obtuse and said, 'This is what we expected. All the data is on this piece of plastic. All we do is go round the password. Watch.' She typed in a number of instructions, the computer thought about it for a full second and then the file opened before their eyes. Isobel's fingers flew across the keyboard. 'As I thought, we've got everything.' She took out the disk and inserted the next one. This one contained details of Habib's investments on various stock markets. After ten minutes, during which time Hunter enjoyed himself counting the money he had found, she looked up.

'I estimate that Habib had about four hundred and fifty million dollars.'

'What?' Hunter was shocked. 'There's also nearly four million pounds Sterling here, I reckon. Hell, terrorism really pays.'

'Not if you're dead,' said Isobel dryly.

Hunter grinned. 'True. Can I buy you dinner?' He waved a bundle of notes in his hand.

'Later. I need to phone the General to see what he wants me to do.'

She took her sat-phone and rang Macnair. She explained what she had found.

Macnair said, 'Well done, to both of you. As we've already discussed, I want the lot in an off-shore bank account under our control. Can you do it and how long will it take?'

Isobel pondered her reply for a few seconds. 'It'll take me about six or eight hours and I've already got the account established, just in case we were successful.'

'Good for you, Isobel. Get cracking and give me the details later.'

They broke the connection and Isobel turned to Hunter. 'I'll get started. Do you think you could find me something to eat? I'm starving.'

'Sure. I'll leave you to it.' He wandered away to the kitchen and started preparing a meal. He returned half an hour later with omelettes, bread and a bottle of red wine.

'How's it going?' he asked. Isobel was sitting at the table watching her computer screen which was linked to her sat-phone.

'Great. So far I've shifted about a hundred million. That's been the easy stuff. I need to conjure up some sales orders for a load of shares which will take me a while but it's easy enough.'

'Can you stop to eat?'

'Sure. The computer runs itself now.' She pushed the screen away from her and took the food offered. 'Say, this is good.'

'Thanks. I specialise in omelettes,' replied Hunter, pouring them each a glass of wine. 'What are we going to do with the cash?' He nodded at the bundles lying on the table.

Isobel looked at him. 'Nobody would ever know if we just split it and took it with us.'

Hunter nodded. 'I was thinking exactly that when I was cooking. Financial freedom is a powerful inducement but,' he shrugged, 'I'd know and somehow I can't do it.'

Isobel nodded, relief flooding her face. 'That's exactly what I thought. We'll give it to the General. Let him decide.' The computer bleeped at her and she quickly moved seats to get at the screen again. She typed in further instructions, watched it for a few seconds and moved back to her plate.

'We've now moved over two hundred million,' she looked at her watch. 'It'll be a long night.'

At four o'clock in the morning she announced that she was finished. She had sold hundreds of different shares from over two dozen stock markets, liquidated hundreds of millions in various currencies and dozens of accounts and moved the lot to one bank account in the Cayman Islands. 'I was wrong,' she added, 'but not by much. We now have four hundred and eighty-five million, nine hundred and seventy-six thousand, four hundred and thirty-three dollars and sixteen cents.'

'Jesus H. Christ,' was Hunter's reply having been roused from a doze in front of the fire.

'I'll phone the General with the news.' He picked up the telephone and made the call.

'That's it, sir,' said Hunter, 'except for the cash and bearer bonds we found here. Four million pounds' worth, take or leave a few thousand.'

'Good. The cash will be the foundation of our widows and orphans fund.'

'What?'

'You know as well as I do that if one of our men die their families aren't exactly left financially secure. And what about one of our lads' parents if he has no widow or orphan to leave his pension to? Nope. We'll give a million pounds to our people, whenever it's needed.'

'Good idea, sir,' said Hunter. 'We can make a start.'

'Yes, I know. I'll see you tomorrow.'

They broke the connection and Hunter told Isobel what

423

Macnair had said. She looked wistfully at the money, 'I know what I said, but . . .'

Hunter picked up a single bearer bond with a face value of a hundred thousand dollars and handed it to her, 'Go on, take it. I'll never tell.'

Isobel held it in her hand for a few seconds and then, regretfully, replaced it on the pile. 'I can't,' she said.

Hunter smiled and shrugged his shoulders. 'Aren't we pathetic?'

'No, just honest. Which is just as well, I suppose.'

Hunter smiled enigmatically. What he saw no reason to tell her was that although he lived within his means as defined by his salary as a naval officer, he was, by any consideration, wealthy. The wealth was inherited and came from his mother's side of the family. He would not inherit the Earldom of his Great Uncle David, his first cousin would do that, but he would inherit a fine house in Scotland along with enough capital to run it when the time came. If he decided to leave the Royal Navy there was also a job waiting for him in "the family firm", which was really a misnomer. The family firm covered many activities, from banking to real estate to manufacturing companies. He could choose whichever one he wished, whenever he wanted. The strength of the Griffiths family continued to come from within. They were like the musketeers, "one for all and all for one" – Hunter often thought that should have been their family motto, instead of "The Family, First and Foremost".

A few hours later they heard a thwacking noise and went out to meet the helicopter. They were en route back to base within ten minutes. Unknown to Hunter another incident had already occurred and he was wanted by Macnair, urgently.

A Million Tears

*A mighty epic – the first of four books chronicling
the lives of the Griffiths family.*

This is a tale of love and hate, murder and suicide, poverty
and wealth – the story of a family whose devotion to each
other helps them to succeed where others fail.

*Dai's world was confined to the close-knit South Wales
mining community where the most exciting event in his 10
years of life was a trip to the market town of Pontypridd.
But he has his atlas and he has his dreams . . .*

'A Million Tears' is the realisation of those dreams.
From the hardship and poverty of Wales in 1890 to the
optimism and wealth of America, the Griffiths family
strive for success. Follow Evan, the head of the family,
as he fights his way from coal-miner to businessman to
politician. Dai, whose search for adventure takes him to
the exotic corruption of the West Indies, and Sion, who
has to grow up fast to survive the brutality of the west.
There's Uncle James who will stop at nothing to save
the family and finally Meg, the rock of the family, the
constant in all their lives.

This is a compelling story of adventure and love, tragedy
and survival. A wonderful story by a master storyteller.

ISBN 1-902483-00-6

A Million Tears II
The Tears of War and Peace

*The second of the four books chronicling the lives
of the Griffiths family.*

It is 1911 and David Griffiths is back in Wales, bored and
lonely. He travels to London at the behest of their family
friend, John Buchanan, to start a new business in banking.
There he gets caught up in the suffragette movement and falls
in love with Emily. Against the backdrop of women's fight
for votes and the looming First World War, the Griffiths build
a vast, sprawling company encompassing banking, aircraft
manufacturing, farming and whisky distilling.

The enmity of a German family follows them tragically
throughout this period, leading to murder and revenge. At the
end of the war, thanks to a change in the Constitution, Evan is
invited to run for President of the United States. The family rally
round for the most important battle of Evan's life.

With the Brown-shirts running rampage across Germany,
David and Sion are soon involved in a battle for survival.

*Sir David Griffiths is a colossus of a figure, striding across
the world and through the century, a man of integrity and
bravery, passion and dedication. Determined to win, nothing
comes before the family.*

The story is as compelling as ever. Historical fact woven into
the fictional characters makes a breathtaking tale of adventure
you will not want to put down.

A Million Tears II will be published in the summer of 1999
by Good Read Publishing Ltd.

ISBN 1-902483-03-0